The shining splendor of our Zebra Lovegram logo on the cover of this book reflects the glittering excellence of the story inside. Look for the Zebra Lovegram whenever you buy a historical romance. It's a trademark that guarantees the very best in quality and reading entertainment.

A TENDER YEARNING

"What do you want of me?" Jessica finally whispered. She could feel his light breath on her cheek. His nearness was intoxicating.

"I don't know, Jess." Adam traced the line of her jaw with the tip of his finger. "I tell myself I want nothing from you or anyone else, but"— he drew in his breath—"there's a bond between us. You feel it, don't you?"

"I feel it," she said softly.

Adam smiled, cupping her chin. Slowly, he lowered his mouth to hers. "No good could come of it."

"We shouldn't," she heard herself respond as she wove her fingers through his sleek, shining hair. "I mustn't . . ." But as the words slipped from her mouth she was already pulling him to her.

S̶ his gentle, exploring kiss hesitantly, but as th̶ within her, she clung to him. . . .

THE BEST IN HISTORICAL ROMANCES

TIME-KEPT PROMISES   (2422, $3.95)
by Constance O'Day Flannery
Sean O'Mara froze when he saw his wife Christina standing before him. She had vanished and the news had been written about
in all of the papers—he had even been charged with her murder!
But now he had living proof of his innocence, and Sean was not
about to let her get away. No matter that the woman was claiming
to be someone named Kristine; she still caused his blood to boil.

PASSION'S PRISONER   (2573, $3.95)
by Casey Stewart
When Cassandra Lansing put on men's clothing and entered the
Rawlings saloon she didn't expect to lose anything—in fact she
was sure that she would win back her prized horse Rapscallion
that her grandfather lost in a card game. She almost got a smug
satisfaction at the thought of fooling the gamblers into believing
that she was a man. But once she caught a glimpse of the virile
Josh Rawlings, Cassandra wanted to be the woman in his embrace!

ANGEL HEART   (2426, $3.95)
by Victoria Thompson
Ever since Angelica's father died, Harlan Snyder had been an-
gling to get his hands on her ranch, the Diamond R. And now,
just when she had an important government contract to fulfill,
she couldn't find a single cowhand to hire—all because of Snyder's threats. It was only a matter of time before the legendary
gunfighter Kid Collins turned up on her doorstep, badly
wounded. Angelica assessed his firmly muscled physique and
stared into his startling blue eyes. Beneath all that blood and dirt
he was the handsomest man she had ever seen, and the one person who could help beat Snyder at his own game.

*Available wherever paperbacks are sold, or order direct from the
Publisher. Send cover price plus 50¢ per copy for mailing and
handling to Zebra Books, Dept. 3313, 475 Park Avenue South,
New York, N.Y. 10016. Residents of New York, New Jersey and
Pennsylvania must include sales tax. DO NOT SEND CASH.*

LOVE'S SWEET BOUNTY

COLLEEN FAULKNER

ZEBRA BOOKS
KENSINGTON PUBLISHING CORP.

To my grandparents, Judy and Les,
who after fifty years of marriage
still ride the carousel.

. . . With a special thanks to Aunt P.

ZEBRA BOOKS

are published by

Kensington Publishing Corp.
475 Park Avenue South
New York, NY 10016

Copyright © 1991 by Colleen Faulkner

All rights reserved. No part of this book may be reproduced in any form or by any means without the prior written consent of the Publisher, excepting brief quotes used in reviews.

First printing: February, 1991

Printed in the United States of America

Chapter One

Ogden, Utah
August 1881

The steam locomotive gave a whine and then a whistle and the passenger car Jessica Landon had just boarded lurched forward. Her fifteen-year-old brother kneeled on the seat beside her and hung out the window, waving.

She tugged on the tail of his plaid cotton shirt. "Sit down, Mark. Who are you waving at? We don't know a blessed soul in Ogden, Utah."

The tow-headed young man plopped down on the dusty seat beside his sister. "Not waving at anyone in particular, just waving 'cause everyone else is." He nibbled on his fingernail. "Where is Ogden, Utah, anyway?"

She slapped his dungareed knee. "You should have been studying your geography lessons instead of slipping away to shoot coon."

"Studying lessons is girl-stuff." He lifted his

5

hands, aiming and firing with an imaginary rifle. "I'll take care of the man's work—shootin' Indians and such. You think you could get me a Winchester rifle when we reach Washington? Every man needs a Winchester."

Jessica sighed, shaking her head as she glanced out the window. She knew leaving Tennessee was the best thing she and Mark could have done. Jacob Dorchester had left her no other choice. But she hadn't realized how hard the trip would be. She wiped her perspiration-dotted forehead with her red bandanna and then tied it around her neck. She hadn't known how hot and dry the West would be in July or how slow the trains would move . . . how unorganized the entire railway system was. The trains never ran on schedule. It was taking her twice as long as she'd anticipated to get to Washington territory.

Jessica leaned forward to touch the bundle of apple tree saplings lying on the seat facing her. The damp newspaper felt good beneath her fingertips, even if it did stain them black. These trees, the two horses in the cattle car behind them, and the small carpetbag that lay at her feet, were all she and Mark had left of her parents and their farm in Tennessee.

A little red-cheeked girl with long, blond pigtails peeked over the back of the seat in front of Jessica and smiled. Jessica smiled back. This wasn't a time for sadness or regrets; it was a time of rejoicing. She and Mark had escaped Jacob's clutches and soon they would be in Washington buying their own piece of land . . . starting that apple orchard.

Jessica waved at the child with her index finger.

6

"Hello, there. My name's Jessica. What's yours?"

The girl of five or six screwed up her mouth in obvious indecision. When she spoke it was in a loud whisper. "My ma says I ain't to talk to people on the train. There's lots of baddies that eat little girls, you know." She studied Jessica through a veil of blond-fringed lashes. "I'm Emily. Emily Memily's what my pa calls me. You don't eat little girls, do you?"

Jessica laughed, tucking a lock of her damp sable-colored hair behind her ear. "It's too hot to eat little girls, don't you think?"

Emily broke into a grin, showing a hole where her front tooth had once been. "We're going to Seattle. My pa's a gunsmith. He's gonna make rifles for my Uncle Elsmere."

Jessica caught one of the little girl's yellow blond braids and gave it a playful tug. "That's my brother Mark. We're going to Washington territory, too."

Emily poked her finger through a tear in the sparsely upholstered seat. "Is your pa going to make guns for Uncle Elsmere, too?"

"No." Jessica stared out at the passing scenery as the train chugged north. The land was desolate, dry, and void of trees. "My papa's dead; my mama too." She met the child's inquisitive gaze. "My brother and I, we're on our own."

Emily's mother turned around in the seat. "Excuse my girl," she apologized. "She can't mind her own knitting. Emily, sit down and let the passengers be."

"It's all right." Jessica gave Emily a wink. "I could use the company. I'm Jessica Landon and this is my brother Mark." She indicated with a wave of her hand. Mark was busy drawing pictures of cavalry

7

soldiers with his finger on the dusty train window.

Emily's mother gave a nod. She wore an immense faded blue poke bonnet that shielded her face. "Please to meet you, Miss Landon. I'm Kat Wiedenhoeft. My husband sittin' in front of us is Billy."

"I got a sister Holly Dolly and a baby brother," Emily piped in. "We call him Pauly Wally."

Jessica looked up at Kat. "Emily says you're headed for Seattle. We are too."

Kat nodded. "My brother Elsmere says it's beautiful there. Green, you can't see anything but green. We've been seven years in Texas trying our hand at cattle. I'd be happy if I never sets eyes on mesquite and chaparral again!"

Jessica laughed with her. "We're from Tennessee. Mark and I are going to buy land for an apple orchard and for raising horses."

Kat glanced over the back of the seat at the apple saplings. "I brought a rosebush with me. It was my mama's and hers before that."

Jessica sat back on the seat, falling into easy conversation with her newfound friends. "The train's crowded. I didn't expect to see so many people traveling."

"There's some families movin' like us. Others"— Kat indicated with a nod of her chin—"are businessmen."

Jessica glanced over at the man in the dark suit seated across the aisle from her. His bowler hat was pulled down over his eyebrows. Clasped between his knees was a leather money bag. Jessica lowered her voice to a whisper. "A bit hot, wouldn't you think, in that starched shirt?"

8

Kat lifted her infant son on her shoulder and began to pat the sleeping child. "Railroad business most likely. My Billy says they make 'em all wear a coat, a hundred and ten in the shade or not."

"You think there's money in that fancy case?" Jessica mused aloud. Her own blue and gold carpetbag lay on the floor between her and Mark. Every cent made from the sale of her father's farm was in that bag. "He's sure got a death grip on it."

"Let's hope it is money, railroad money." Kat passed her sleeping son into Emily's arms and the little girl sat down, disappearing from Jessica's sight.

"Why?"

Kat wiped her perspiration-soaked face with the corner of her apron. "Because then they've got a lawman aboard. My Billy says the Union Pacific's got the best detectives in the West working their passenger trains. We won't see no holdups as long as they got a lawman aboard."

Just then the rear door of the car slid open. Kat and Jessica both looked up at the same time. Jessica drew in her breath. For an instant she feared the train was under Indian attack!

The man who had entered the car, and now walked calmly down the aisle glancing from one passenger to the other, had hair the color of a polished crow's wing. His skin was a shade of burnished copper Jessica had never seen before. He was a tall imposing man with broad shoulders, dressed in a pair of leather breeches and a faded blue cotton shirt. His shoulder-length hair was pulled back in a knot of feathers and brightly colored beads. Down his back trailed a shabby black wool hat. On each hip he wore black-handled pistols that Jessica recognized immediately as premium Bisley Colts.

"Wow!" Mark breathed. "Get a look at him! You think he's gonna rob the train?" Mark swung his imaginary rifle onto his shoulder and beaded in on the stranger. "I could take him at ten paces if I had that Winchester."

The Indian passed their seat and for an instant he met and held Jessica's green-eyed gaze. His eyes were as black as the pits of hell, with fire and brimstone raging just beyond the pupils. Jessica moistened her upper lip. The spell was broken and the red man moved on.

"Da-gone, Jess!" Mark leaned over his sister, trying to catch another glimpse of the mysterious man before he exited the front of the car. "That was a real Injun! You think he was one of the ones that killed poor old General Custer at Little Bighorn?"

Jessica exhaled with exasperation. She wiped her damp hands on her soft suede traveling skirt. "Of course not, Mark. Use your head. Now sit down and stop gawking!" She waited until Mark had taken his seat. "Those were Sioux Indians, from the Dakotas. The government's got them under control. They don't let them off their reservations!"

Kat pulled off her poke bonnet, fanning her sunburned face with it. "Pshew! I don't know what he was, but he was the best-lookin' man I think I ever set eyes on." She glanced over her shoulder. "'Cept of course my Billy," she amended.

Her Billy, a spindly five and a half feet tall, with a sparse pate of blond hair, grinned and returned to his whittling.

Jessica dared a smile. "He was something, wasn't he. I never saw skin that color." She looked up at the door the redman had just disappeared through as if she could somehow conjure him up again. "It was like fresh turned soil, baked red by the sun."

"Jess," Mark breathed, taking Jessica's arm. "I think we're gonna get held up."

Jessica frowned. "That's enough, Mark. You'll be frightening people." But as the words fell from her mouth the grip Mark held on her bare arm made her look up and out the window.

"Dear God!" Jessica gasped as the train brakeman threw on the brakes and the train wheels screamed on the track.

Kat gave a high-pitched cry, reaching for her nearest daughter.

Jessica watched, mute with horror, as four masked men on horseback raced by the train window, a dust cloud in their wake. "Do as you're told," she managed, clutching Mark's hand. "No one will get hurt as long as we sit tight and don't cause any trouble." She slid her carpetbag under the seat with the toe of her riding boot. "Just think of that apple orchard we're going to have, Mark. We'll get through this, you and I—together."

Fearless, Mark craned his neck as the rear door of their passenger car slammed open. Jessica pulled him down as he bobbed up out of his seat. Passengers were beginning to scream.

Kat sobbed quietly in the seat just ahead. "I knew we should have stayed in Texas, I knew it, Billy."

"Please, Mark," Jessica begged, holding him down with the pressure of her hand on his leg. "For

11

once, do as I say."

Two men wearing red bandannas around their faces came down the aisle. "All right, folks, empty your pockets. Ladies, get them rings off your fingers!" the blond masked man instructed, waving a flour sack in one hand. Both robbers carried loaded rifles.

Jessica sat ramrod straight in her seat. Mark's hand clasped tightly in hers. "Pray," she whispered. "Pray for the bastards' souls!"

"Da-gone! Look! That passenger's one of them!"

Jessica looked up to where Mark pointed. A man who'd boarded the train just in front of them at Ogden and had been sitting a few seats ahead was out of his seat. Jessica had remembered his red shirt, though she didn't recall seeing his face. Across his nose and mouth he now wore a black bandanna.

"Do as they said and nobody gets hurt," the thin man in black mask ordered shakily, brandishing a Smith & Wesson pistol.

Behind her, Jessica could hear the bandits moving forward. Metal clinked as jewelry and coins were deposited into the flour sack.

"I can't get it off," a woman moaned from behind Jessica. "I can't get the ring off."

Jessica glanced over her shoulder to see a middle-aged woman tugging desperately at a ruby ring on her index finger.

Her little husband sat beside her twisting his hands in anguish. "She can't get it off," he explained to one of the bandits. Sweat dripped down his hollow cheeks.

"What's goin' on here?" the black-masked man

demanded, passing by Jessica's seat. It had suddenly become obvious that he was the leader.

"She says she can't get the rock off'en her finger," the blond-haired bandit explained.

The black-masked man glanced at the sobbing woman. "Then cut her finger off," he answered with a nervous shrug.

The woman gave a high-pitched shriek and fell back against the upholstered seat. Her husband tugged desperately at her finger.

Jessica leaned over to whisper to Mark. "Sit tight!" She yanked her carpetbag from the safe haven under Kat's seat and dug into it, coming up with a tin of salve.

Kat grabbed for Jessica. "Don't do it! Don't call attention to yourself!"

"I'll get it off," Jessica volunteered, coming out of her seat. She fell to her knees in the aisle and took the woman's hand. "I'll just grease it up a little."

"It won't come off," the woman sobbed hysterically. "My hands swell in the heat. They always have!"

"Sure it'll come off," Jessica assured her. "All you need is a little goose grease to loosen it up!" With trembling hands she worked the thick jelled salve over the woman's red, swollen finger.

"Hurry it up!" the outlaw's leader ordered. "We ain't got all day, boys!"

"Just a minute," Jessica cried. "I've almost got it!" She gripped the slippery ring and twisted. To her relief it popped off into her hand. "I've got it!" She thrust her hand in the air and the dark-haired bandit snatched it from her.

13

"Thank you! God Bless you!" the woman cried, still sobbing.

The two bandits pushed by and Jessica was shoved back, separating her from Mark.

"Hey! You can't take that!" Mark hollered, bouncing up out of his seat.

The blond bandit straightened up, Jessica's carpetbag in his hand.

"Mark! Sit down!" Jessica warned. An ominous shiver snaked up her spine. She was suddenly so frightened that she barely recognized her own voice.

"You can't have that!" Mark shouted belligerently, snatching the carpetbag out of the bandit's hand. "That's my sister's!"

Tears slid down Jessica's cheeks. She tried to reach Mark but the black-masked man caught her by the bandanna around her neck and shoved her out of his way. She hit one of the seats and her straw bonnet flew off her head, her dark brown hair falling over her shoulders.

"What's goin' on up here? I thought I told you two to hurry it up!" The leader waved his pistol, looking to the front and then to the rear of the railway car. "We got to get off this train, boys. That damned redskin Sern's aboard!"

"The k . . . kid's givin' us a hard time," the blond bandit stammered.

The leader grasped Mark by a fistful of his blond hair. "You giving my boys a hard time, kid?"

"Take the bag! Don't touch my brother," Jessica shouted. "He's just a boy. You can have the bag! It's got money in it! A lot of money! Just please don't hurt him!"

In a split second the bandit reached for the carpetbag and Mark gave a shout of angry protest, shoving him off balance. Jessica dove for her brother, but the brown-haired bandit swung his fist catching her in the mouth and knocking her down. The black-masked bandit's pistol belched smoke; the sound filled Jessica's head as if it was an afterthought. She saw her brother reel backward under the impact of the shot through a veil of tears.

"No!" she heard herself scream. She climbed over the seat, shoving passengers aside. Men and women screamed as they dove for cover.

Sobbing, Jessica reached Mark. He was sprawled out, half on the seat, half on the floor. His eyes were closed as if he was sleeping, but a puddle of crimson blood stained his faded shirt and the fabric of the seat. "Oh, God, no," Jessica moaned as her tears fell on her young brother's cheek. She stroked his unmarred face with the back of her hand. "Don't leave me. You're all I have left, Mark. I'll buy you that Winchester, I swear I will." Her lower lip trembled.

Mark was dead. She knew he was dead. There was a great, gaping bloody hole in his chest.

In a rage Jessica flew up out of the seat hurling herself at the black-masked bandit. "You killed him!" she raged. "You killed my brother!" She slammed into the startled man, pummeling him with her fists.

The blond bandit caught her by the waist and started to drag her off his boss.

"Get her off!" the leader shouted. "Get this crazy bitch off me!"

"I can't!" the blond bandit cried.

Jessica struggled to rip the carpetbag from the leader's hand. "You're not going to take my brother and my money, too!"

Suddenly the front door of the car swung open.

"Lay down your guns!" bellowed a deep, resonant voice.

The masked bandit gripped Jessica, hauling her to her feet. "Put it down, Sern," he shouted in a trembling voice.

Jessica looked up to see the Indian standing in the doorway, both pistols raised. "I said lay down your guns!" Adam Sern ordered.

The black-masked leader broke into nervous, high-pitched laughter as he raised his pistol, pressing the barrel into Jessica's temple. He held her in his iron grip, her back pressed to his chest. Jessica's entire body shuddered with fear.

"You blind or stupid or both, Sern?" the leader called. "There's one of you and five of us."

"Six, you mean, boss." The man in the bowler hat with the leather money bag came up out of his seat and backed his way down the aisle.

"I don't care how many of you there are, you're who I want," Adam told the leader. "You're the one I take out first." He took a step forward, his dark eyes narrowing dangerously. "Let the woman go."

"In a pig's eye!" the outlaw chided. "You drop *your* fancy-ass pistols or I put a lead ball through this pretty young gal's head."

The passengers grew quiet as they pressed their bodies to the floor of the train in anticipation of more gunfire.

Jessica could hear the outlaw's pocket watch

ticking. "Don't," she whispered. "Don't!" Her green-eyed gaze met the redskinned lawman's. "Don't give up your weapon for my sake. He killed my brother!"

"Shut up!" The masked man gave her a shake.

Jessica could feel the bandit trembling. He was afraid of the Indian; she could hear it in his voice. They could all hear it. "Shoot him and I'll take my chances getting out of the way," she shouted.

The outlaw pulled back the hammer of his pistol. His two partners and the man with the leather money bag were behind him, backing their way out of the passenger car. Jessica could hear the other two accomplices outside the train already mounted on restless horses.

Jessica squeezed her eyes closed. *I know I'm going to die,* she thought. *But if I live, as God is my witness, I'm going to track this man down and make him pay for Mark's death.* Bitter tears ran down her pale cheeks. *This man will die by my hand.*

"I'm not joshing with you! If those fancy pistols aren't on the floor by the time I count to three, I kill her. How's that going to look on your shining record, Sern?" the leader of the bandits badgered. "Two deaths on your hands?"

"Don't!" Jessica cried.

"One . . ."

Adam slowly lowered his Colts, all the while his gaze fixed on the bandit's.

"Two . . ."

Adam dropped his first pistol and kicked it with a snakeskin boot.

"Please," Jessica begged. "Shoot! I don't mind

dying. Be a man!''

"Three!"

Jessica's lids fell in anticipation of the shot, but instead of pistol fire she heard the Indian's weapon hit the floor and slide forward.

Her eyes flew open. "Coward!"

The black-masked leader tipped back his head in laughter. "Honorable, Sern," he commended. "But stupid."

Jessica felt the bandit's hold loosen as he raised his Smith & Wesson pistol to fire on the redskinned lawman. "Noooo!" she screamed as she heaved her weight backward knocking the outlaw off balance. The pistol fired and she heard the Indian pitch backward as she and the bandit fell to the floor. Struggling to free herself, she scratched the outlaw's face with her fingernails, managing to dislodge his black bandanna. For an instant, she saw his face before she escaped his grasp.

The leader of the bandits scrambled to his feet, replacing his mask. "Let's go!" he cried with alarm, snatching up Jessica's carpetbag. "Get off the train!"

Jessica spun around in time to see the outlaw taking the money bag from his accomplice in the bowler hat. "Not you, Stevenson!"

"But boss! You can't do this. You promised this was the last time I'd have to be a courier for the railroad. You said I could join your boys."

"I lied." The outlaw shrugged, lifting his pistol. "These good folks know your face and you know me."

To Jessica's horror, the outlaw fired on his own unarmed man. The bile rose in her throat and she

18

turned away. Suddenly none of this seemed real. The dead courier fell in the aisle. Passengers screamed as the bandits lifted their pistols and shot into the air as they made their escape.

For a long minute Jessica leaned over the back of a seat listening to the sounds of the pounding hoofbeats as the murdering outlaws rode off. They had killed Mark and taken everything she owned! No one could do this to her and get away with it! Not after what she'd been through in Tennessee with Jacob Dorchester!

Slowly Jessica lifted her head, wiping her bloody mouth with the back of her hand. At her feet lay the Indian lawman. Her gaze fell to his crown of inky hair. The gunshot wound was superficial; a bullet had grazed his right temple. He was already beginning to come to.

"You were supposed to protect us," she told the unconscious man in a bitter whisper. "You should have saved my brother."

One of his Bisley pistols lay in the aisle. Its handle was inlaid with shiny black stone. *Onyx*, she thought. She picked it up, shifting it from hand to hand. The sound of the frenzied passengers faded in the background. "It was your duty," she whispered, half-crazed with grief. "These men can't do this and get away with it."

Stepping over the prone lawman, she walked through the front door of the car and leaped to the ground. The bright noonday sun pierced her eyes as she made her way down the track to where the cattle cars were. With a slow deliberateness she lifted the iron bar and swung open the door. Tucking the lawman's prized pistol into the waistband of her leather riding skirt she pulled herself up onto the floor of the car. From a storage box in the corner she retrieved a bridle and saddle. Locating one of the two Appaloosas she and Mark had brought with them, she mechanically saddled up as she'd done a thousand times before.

A moment later Jessica was astride. She gave a click between her teeth and the mare whinnied. Sinking her heels into Hera's flanks, they sailed out of the cattle car hitting the hard, dry ground with a bump. Wheeling around Jessica flew past the passenger cars and headed north in pursuit of the outlaw and his gang.

Chapter Two

Adam Sern struggled against the depths of unconsciousness. Even though breathing came easily, he felt as if he was below the surface of a body of water. He could hear the train passengers talking in hushed voices. A woman sobbed. He felt the hard flat floor of the train car beneath him . . . but he couldn't will his limbs to move.

I've been shot, he thought.

Memories of the train robbery flashed through his head. Goddamn the Union Pacific Railroad and their ninny-headed executives! They hadn't trusted him. They'd honestly thought he was the man informing the Black Bandit of the railway payroll deliveries. They'd lied to him, telling him the payroll would be on the following day's train. He hadn't been prepared. By the time he'd reached the dead engineer and run through the cars to where the Black Bandit was, it was too late. The boy was already dead. . . .

Slowly, Adam lifted his hand to his temple and felt

the sticky blood oozing from his wound.

"He's comin' to," someone murmured.

Adam lifted his eyelids and tried to focus. He struggled to sit up. A blinding pain seared his head.

Billy grasped the lawman's arm and helped him to sit upright. "You all right? Danged lucky I'd say you were. We thought you was dead for certain."

Adam cradled his head in his hands. "They're gone . . . which way?"

"North."

Kat offered Adam an uncorked flask of whiskey. "Here you go, drink. It'll put the wind back in your pipes."

Adam shook his head. "Water if you can find it. And something to staunch the bleeding." He applied pressure to his temple with his fingertips. Blood trickled down his cheek. He was damned lucky. The bullet had only grazed his head instead of hitting him square between the eyes as the Black Bandit had intended. Thank God the outlaw was a poor marksman. His men usually did his shooting for him.

Adam slammed his balled fist on the floor in frustration. He couldn't believe that murderer had slipped through his fingers again. "Goddamn it!" He glanced up at Kat who was still leaning over him. "Pardon, ma'am."

Kat gave a dry chuckle. "I've heard worse, said worse on occasion." Someone handed her a cup of water and she brought it to his lips.

Adam accepted the tin cup and sipped from it. The warm water slid down his parched throat. "You said they went north?"

"That's right." Billy pulled off his hat to scratch his head. "The funny thing is, that girl went with 'em."

Adam looked up. "What? What girl?" Somehow he knew. An image of a slight woman with haunting green eyes flashed through his head. He'd only seen her for a moment, yet those eyes, that face, was seared in his memory.

"Hush your mouth, Billy," Kat chided, beginning to bind Adam's head wound with a strip of white linen. "She wasn't *with* 'em!"

"I said, what girl?" Adam repeated sharply.

"She was sitting behind us. She said her name was Jessica Landon. The dead boy was Mark. She was talking to my wife just before them outlaws held us up."

Kat glared at her husband. "They killed her brother! She couldn't be one of them!"

"How do you know, Kat? You talked to her for half an hour. How do you know that kid was really her brother? The courier was with 'em. He's deader than a doornail. Maybe the girl was in cahoots with them, too."

Kat shook her head, turning her attention back to her patient. "I'm telling you, lawman, Jessica wasn't with those murdering thieves. She was a nice girl. She and her brother were headed for Washington territory like us. She was going to plant an apple orchard."

"Did they have a horse for her?" Adam questioned Billy.

"I don't know. She left after them. We didn't see her mount. She ran off the train, disappeared for a minute or two, and then suddenly she was ridin' by like her tail was on fire."

Adam nodded, deep in thought. Nothing would surprise him about this Black Bandit. Adam had been trying to catch him for months. He was sly as a grandfather fox.

"Um"—Billy offered Adam the pistol he'd retrieved off the floor—"here's your gun. Real nice."

Adam took back his pistol. The weight of it felt good in his hand. "There should be another."

Billy bit down on his lower lip. "She took it."

"The girl?"

Billy nodded. "For a minute I was afraid she was going to shoot you there on the floor."

Adam wiped his mouth with the back of his hand. "You think you can take a horse from the cattle car and ride along the tracks to the next stop?" Slowly he got to his feet.

"I reckon I can." Billy straightened proudly.

"You get to Loco and tell them what happened. They'll send another engineer out and someone to check over the engine before they start her up again." Adam glanced at Kat as he ran his hand over the neat bandage she'd wrapped around his head. "Thank you, ma'am. I appreciate it."

"That ought to stop the bleedin'." She wiped her hands on her apron. "But you need to see a doctor just the same. You don't want an infection spreading. We had a horse that died with a scratch on its ear. The infection went straight to its brain."

"Next day or so, I'll have it looked at." Adam slid his pistol into its holster. He felt unbalanced without the other.

"Next day or so? What are you talkin' about? They ought to have this train moving by tonight, hadn't they?"

Adam pulled his leather hat up off his back and pushed it onto his head, covering the bandage. "I'm not riding in with you. I have to go after them."

"And leave us here alone?" a passenger cried.

"You'll be safe enough. You've certainly got no fear of robbery and the Indians are peaceful around here."

"Peaceful with their own kind," the man grumbled.

Adam shot him an icy glare and the man backed off. "Anyone got a canteen?" Adam asked quietly.

A knapsack was offered by one of the passengers. Another brought forward a battered tin canteen filled with water. Adam thanked both donors and swung the leather straps over his shoulder. "Come on, then." He signaled Billy with a wave of his bronze hand. "Let's get two horses from the cattle transport. We'll return them to their proper owner later. The railroad can reimburse the owners for their trouble."

In the cattle car Billy saddled the nearest horse, but Adam took his time, checking out first one and then another. He chose a spotted Appaloosa stallion from the rear of the car. The animal had the finest lines he'd ever seen. Whoever owned the magnificent beast knew his horse-breeding. Speaking softly to gain the skittish horse's confidence, he saddled him up.

Outside the cattle car, Adam and Billy mounted. Adam offered his hand. "I'm Adam Sern. They'll know my name in Loco." He looked away. "I'm sorry for what happened back there on the train."

25

Billy accepted his hand and pumped it. "Billy Wiedenhoeft. Pleased to meet you, Mr. Sern. But it weren't your fault. These trains is always gettin' robbed."

"My job was to protect that boy."

"I'm tellin' you, the way I see it, it couldn't be helped. The boy spooked the one in the black mask and his gun went off. I don't even know if he shot him on purpose. If you'd been there you couldn't have done anything. None of us could."

Adam withdrew his grasp from Billy's. "Can you take care of the boy's body? I'll try to get back to Loco, but it just depends on which way the bandits go."

"I'll take care of him and any belongings that were theirs."

Adam nodded, brushed the brim of his hat in salute, and rode off.

The bandits' trail was easy enough to follow—five men on horseback, followed by a lighter rider, ten minutes behind them. The green-eyed girl . . .

Adam rode hard. He was a good three-quarters of an hour behind them. The hot sun beat on his neck. The pounding of the Appaloosa's hooves on the dry, cracked earth reverberated through his body filling him with a strange exhilaration. Out here, alone in the open spaces, he felt whole. Here there were no accusing eyes, no bitter prejudices. It was only out here that it didn't matter that he was a half-breed.

Adam's mother had been a teacher, an Ojibwa maiden. His father had been a Philadelphia physician who had traveled north into Canada to doctor among the native Americans. He had made a six-month journey and stayed fourteen years. A smile crossed Adam's solemn face. There had been nothing but happiness and laughter in his mother's village. The Ojibwa had no prejudices. It made no matter that he was half white. Adam's father was adopted into the tribe and Adam was a child of the *People*.

Adam's smile fell.

But then the measle epidemic had come when he was twelve, spread by a load of moth-eaten blankets brought by a well-meaning missionary. Adam's beautiful mother had died in his father's arms. Heartbroken, his father had cared for those villagers, still struggling against the dreaded disease until he, too, fell sick and died. Adam had remained untouched. When word reached his grandparents in Philadelphia, they sent for him and a new life began. Adam shed the clothes of an Ojibwa boy and became a man. He was educated in the finest boy's school in Philadelphia, and then sent to Harvard University to pursue a career in law.

Adam sunk his heels into the Appaloosa's hindquarters. Years had passed and still these memories were painful. The bandits' trail turned east toward Brigham City. Crossing a small dry streambed, Adam rode on.

It wasn't right. He had graduated at the top of his class, yet he had never been treated as an equal. His grandfather's money had bought him an education, but never acceptance. The older he became and the more serious the Indian uprisings in the West became, the more Adam was shunned.

Then Adam's grandfather had died and Adam had not been permitted to take the bar exam. He was found unacceptable due to his "mixed racial heritage." The words echoed in his head. He had been so angry he'd left Philadelphia for the cool forests of his birthplace. But there, among the Ojibwa, he had not found his peace either. He had been too long in the white man's society. He missed libraries, newspapers, contact with the outside world.

So, now here he was, working for the Union Pacific Railroad, mostly on the Central Short Line, guarding their passengers and valuables. He gave a groan. He wasn't guarding them too damned well, was he?

Adam slowed the Appaloosa to a walk, giving him a breather. He was gaining on them. The woman, Jessica, as she called herself, was slowing down. It was obvious by her tracks that she was beginning to have a difficult time keeping up with the others. Adam wondered why they hadn't waited for her, though the Black Bandit certainly wasn't known for his kindness. He seemed to have little loyalty among his men. New men joined his gang frequently as older ones were either killed or just disappeared and were presumed dead.

Adam took a sip from his water can, patting the stallion's neck. He could see from the tracks that the woman had separated from the rest of the bandits and was continuing north. The outlaws were headed northwest. The question was, who did he follow? It took only a moment to decide and then he was riding at breakneck speed again. Jessica Landon . . . he'd catch up with her and find out where the bandits were headed. He'd arrest her, take her back to Loco, notify the railroad of what was happening, and

28

gather provisions. Then he'd track the Black Bandit and bring him to justice.

Jessica slid off Hera's back, resting against her for support. "God, it's hot out here," she murmured. Dropping the horse's reins, she walked a few feet, covering her brow with her hand to ward off the glare of the sun.

She gave an exasperated sigh. "So which way did they go, Hera? The land was flat and seemingly godforsaken. I know I was just behind them, but now I'm confused. These don't look like the same tracks I was following."

The mare nickered in reply.

Jessica turned back. "Little help you are." She dropped her hands to her hips. "They can't be too far from here, but which way?" She was near to tears. After all that had happened back in Tennessee—Papa's death, Jacob—things were supposed to be going right now. Moving west was a new start. Mark had been certain they would find success in Washington.

The thought of Mark and his broken body made Jessica stiffen with anger. Her anger, her desire for revenge, was all she had left. If she thought about her brother now, she'd crumble.

"Well," Jessica said aloud. "I guess we'd best backtrack. We've got to find water, too." She was beginning to realize that it had been foolish to run off half-cocked without water or provisions. Out in this heat a man could die in a day.

Suddenly she heard the sound of hoofbeats. Glancing over her shoulder, she saw a horse and rider appearing out of nowhere, racing toward her. She hurled herself into the saddle. "Hah!" She sank her heels into Hera's flanks, whipping the reins. Dust flew as the mare dug her hooves into the brittle earth and leaped forward rearing on her hind legs. Jessica leaned over, threading her trembling fingers through the Appaloosa's mane as the animal galloped away. She didn't know who was pursuing her . . . one of the bandits maybe.

Adam urged his stallion faster as the green-eyed woman took off, headed due north. Her mount nearly matched his in speed, but slowly he was gaining on her.

The hoofbeats behind Jessica grew louder. Looking over her shoulder she recognized the redskinned railroad detective . . . and he was riding *her* stallion!

"Give up!" Adam shouted. "Dismount!"

Frightened, Jessica laid her crop on Hera's neck. "Come on, girl. Come on!" The hot, dry wind whipped at Jessica's hair.

"I said dismount, before you're hurt!" Adam was so close that he could see her bright red cheeks . . . those green eyes.

"You let them get away!" Jessica shouted into the wind. The horses were neck and neck.

Adam tried to reach for her and her hand whipped out, snapping him across the wrist with her short, stiff riding crop. He cursed beneath his breath and reached again, this time catching her around the waist.

Jessica screamed as she was torn from Hera's back.

Adam had meant to drop her into his lap, but she struggled so hard that she unseated him. Suddenly they were both tumbling. They hit the ground hard, limbs wrapped around limbs.

Jessica shoved herself up on her elbows, her legs tangled in the half-breed's. "What are you doing chasing me?" she demanded, giving him a kick as she freed her leg.

Adam grabbed her by the collar of her soiled blouse. "Oh, no you don't. You're not getting away!"

She slapped at his hand, twisting free.

"Stupid Indian!" she shouted, leaping up. "Those men just killed my brother! They took my carpetbag with all the money I had in the world!" A tear slipped down her dirty cheek and she dashed it away with the back of her hand. "They took my mama's picture."

Adam came to his feet, eyeing her steadily. She didn't sound like she was with the Black Bandit. She sounded lost, confused, on the verge of hysteria. He yanked his hat up off the ground and banged it on his knee. "So what, might I ask, are you doing out here in the middle of nowhere riding like the devil himself was after you?"

Jessica wiped her nose with her sleeve. "Chasing the outlaws."

Adam couldn't help himself. He burst into dry, angry laughter. "But they went that way." He pointed west.

She refused to meet his gaze. Her hands fell to her hips. "If you're so sure which way they went, why aren't you chasing them? That is your job, isn't it?"

He cringed inwardly. She knew how to cut right to the quick. "My job is to follow *all* suspects."

Jessica looked up. She touched her chest. "Me? Now it's my turn to laugh. I told you they killed my brother." She kicked at the ground, stirring up a cloud of white dust in his face. "*You* were supposed to be guarding the train. *You* were supposed to be protecting my brother."

"I'm sorry."

She looked away, exhaling slowly. She hadn't expected the half-breed to admit to his failure. "So now that you know I'm not one of the outlaws, do you think maybe you ought to get back on my horse and ride after them?" She laced her voice with sarcasm to cover the pain.

"Your horse?" For some reason he wasn't surprised.

She stared out over the desert. Both Hera and Zeus had come to a halt in a patch of grass a hundred yards away. "They're a pair. My brother and I meant to raise horses . . . and grow apples."

Adam stared at the magnificent beasts for a moment. "Adam," he said finally. "Adam Sern."

"What?"

"My name's Adam Sern."

"Well, Adam Sern, are you going to take my horse and go after the outlaws or are you going to point me in their direction and let me go after them myself?"

He snatched his onyx-handled pistol from the band of her riding skirt. "Neither. I'm going to catch those horses and see you safely back to Loco."

"So that's it?" she demanded incredulously. "They just go free?"

He frowned. "Of course not. But I need provisions if I'm going to track them."

"And what happens, *if* you catch them?"

"They'll stand trial, naturally."

Jessica flounced off toward the horses before Adam had finished his sentence. *Trial, my eye,* she thought. *I'm going to track that murderer and kill him myself!*

Chapter Three

Jessica and Adam rode into Loco as dusk settled on the small Utah town. Like many other towns that dotted the West, it had sprung up as a direct result of the railroad. There was a train depot, a telegraph office, a bank that also served as the post office, a Baptist church, two general stores, three saloons, and a whorehouse situated a discreet distance from the church.

Jessica looked up at the sun-bleached false fronts of the rickety frame buildings as she and Adam came down the main street. A dog barked in the distance. The tinny sound of piano music wafted through the warm night air. Laughter and lamplight spilled through a saloon door. An occasional pedestrian hurried down the plank sidewalk. Jessica wrinkled her nose. The town smelled of dust and cow dung.

Adam rode Zeus to the door of the second saloon they came to and swung out of his saddle.

A faded wooden sign hung in silence overhead, undisturbed by the slight breeze. THE RED MOON

SALOON, the hand-painted letters read. A DECENT
ESTABLISHMENT FOR FOOD, DRINK, AND LODG-
ING.

Jessica glanced doubtfully at the swinging lou-
vered doors. "This the best place to stay?"

"The only place," Adam answered. "I'll get a room
for you."

Jessica dismounted. "No money . . . remember?"
She was hot and tired. All she wanted was a cool bath
and a soft bed. She didn't want to think, she just
wanted to sleep.

"The railroad will pay for it. You can catch
another train out in a day or so. I'll make the
arrangements."

She gave a laugh that was sarcastic and accusing.
"I'd be a fool to depend on you, wouldn't I, Mr.
Sern?" She patted Hera's silky neck as the mare drank
from a water trough beneath the hitching post.

Adam twisted the Appaloosa's reins around his
hand. He felt responsible for Jessica's situation, but
she made it damned hard for him to be gracious.
"Suit yourself." He shrugged, tying the stallion
securely to the post. "Thank you for the loan of the
horse. I've never ridden one so fine."

Jessica watched Adam Sern as he strode through
the doors of the saloon and disappeared inside. If she
ever saw that redskinned lawman again, it would be
too soon. She hated him as violently as she hated the
man who had killed her brother. It was *his* fault! It
was Adam's! She gripped the rough wood of the
hitching post. He should have been there to protect
Mark! He should have been able to save him!

With a sigh, Jessica walked up the two steps to the

saloon and went in. Approaching the bar, she waited for a tall man in wire-rimmed spectacles to finish serving Adam a beer.

"Yes, miss, can I help you?" He wiped his thin hands on a damp apron he wore around his waist.

"I need a room, but I haven't any money. I was aboard the train when it was robbed. They took everything I had."

The bartender shook his head. "You're lucky you didn't lose your life. It's a wonder you weren't all killed! That Black Bandit, he's a bad one. Never any tellin' what he might do."

She nodded as her eyes strayed to Adam seated at a table near the staircase. "Do you have a room, and can I pay for it later?"

He came around the oak bar. "No need to worry, miss. Mister Sern's taken care of it. Food, too. The railroad is good about reimbursing me for my trouble. Best customer I got."

Jessica was tempted to turn and walk out the door. She wanted no help from Adam Sern. He was as guilty of her brother's murder as the outlaw who'd pulled the trigger. But she knew she couldn't let her pride get the best of her. She needed some food and a good night's sleep if she was going to come up with a plan on how to catch the outlaw.

She looked up at the bartender who was twirling one end of his waxed mustache. "All right, thank you." She managed a grim smile.

Jessica followed him past Adam's table and up the stairs. He opened a room for her at the far end of the hall.

"It's small but it's clean, miss."

She nodded, stepping into the cubicle. There was a narrow cot against one wall opposite a chair and a table with a washbowl and pitcher. A small window dominated the outside wall. "This'll be fine." She turned back to him. "Could I possibly get a bath?" Subconsciously she smoothed her dusty skirt.

The bartender grimaced. "Sorry, miss, but the only bathhouse in town is closed. I ordered a tub, a big brass one, but it ain't come yet."

She nodded. "Some hot water then?"

"I'll send it right up, and there'll be stew and bread for you waitin' downstairs."

Jessica stretched out on the worn but clean patchwork quilt that covered the cot as the bartender left the room, closing the door behind him. She squeezed her eyes shut, resting her head on the feather pillow.

The first thing she had to do was see to Mark's body. She rubbed her teary eyes. She couldn't think about her brother, not now. What good were tears anyway? Revenge was what she wanted . . . blood.

Jessica sniffed. Once Mark had a decent burial, then she'd deal with the Black Bandit. She'd have to figure out a way to get some money to buy provisions. She'd start collecting information about the outlaw and his men. Surely the townspeople would know something. She wouldn't go off after the outlaws half-cocked this time; she'd have a plan.

A knock sounded at the door and Jessica opened her eyes, staring at the punched-tin ceiling. "Yes?"

"Hot water, miss," came a young girl's voice.

"Come in."

Jessica watched as a pretty, freckle-faced redhead

filled the bowl on the washstand with water. The child nodded her head and backed out of the door, closing it again.

Jessica washed her face and neck, then her arms with a gritty bar of lye soap left on the washstand. Rinsing off with cool water from the pitcher, she dried herself with a cotton towel the girl had brought. A small cracked mirror on the wall caught Jessica's eyes and she peered into it. Her heart-shaped face was pale, her brown hair a tangled mess. Running her fingers through the thick mass, she tied it back with a stray strand of hair. At least she looked fit to be seen in a public dining room now.

Before Jessica had made it down the staircase she spotted Adam Sern. He was seated at the same table, staring up at her with those heathen black eyes of his. She brushed past him, refusing to give him so much as an acknowledgment.

She took a seat on the far side of the room, near the window. A few patrons glanced up at her, but then returned to their talk and drink. Four men, a few tables over, concentrated on a game of poker. The same red-haired girl that had brought Jessica the water appeared with a plate of stew and a mug of amber liquid.

The girl blushed slightly as she laid down the plate and mug. "I brought you cider 'stead of beer, but Mr. Moore says you're welcome to the beer."

Jessica glanced up.

"All paid for," the redhead went on, faster than before. "Courtesy of the railroad. Mr. Sern, he took care of it."

Jessica spread her napkin on her lap and lifted her

fork. "You know Mr. Sern, do you?"

"Reckon I do. He's the one who got me this job." She lowered her voice. "My ma worked over to Miss Lill's, but she died and I didn't have no where to go. Never knew my pappy."

"So Mr. Sern helped you out . . ." Jessica took a bite of the stew. It was hot and spicy.

"Mmm hmmm. He got Mr. Moore to hire me and give me a room in the attic." She smiled proudly. "I go to school in the winter."

Jessica's gaze involuntarily went to Adam. To her horror he was staring straight back at her. She turned away, taking a bite of biscuit. "I loved school when I was your age. My papa used to drive me in his rig on rainy days."

"Well, guess I'd best get back to the dishes, but if'n you need any more stew or bread, just give me a holler. My name's Pauline."

"Thank you, Pauline. This is more than I can possibly eat."

Nodding, the girl scurried off.

With her stomach comfortably full and her thirst quenched, Jessica found it easier to think logically, pushing her emotions aside. She needed money for Mark's funeral and to buy provisions, but she didn't have time to find a job and work for it. Every day that passed could be putting more distance between her and the outlaws. No, the obvious answer, the only answer, was to sell one of the horses. She glanced up at the bartender who was drying a stack of clean glasses. "Mr. Moore."

He came around the bar, a glass and towel in hand. "Miss Landon, what can I do for you? More stew?"

"No." She pushed aside her plate, lowering her voice. "I've had plenty, thank you. What I want to know is, is there somewhere in town where I could sell one of my horses?"

He adjusted his spectacles. "Horses like those Appaloosas? Not likely. The livery stable is owned by Walt Morris and he's as cheap as a two-bit whor"—the bartender reddened—"excuse me, miss. No, Walt don't look for good horses, just live ones—or barely."

"One of the townspeople, maybe?" She asked hopefully. "I could give them a good deal. I need money to bury my brother who was killed in the train robbery."

"Miss, each one of those horses you got out there, at a bargain, is worth more than most folks in Loco make in a year."

Jessica studied his thin face. "There isn't *anyone?*"

The bartender scratched his chin. "Come to think of it, there is."

She broke into a smile. "Who?"

He gave a nod of his head. "Mr. Sern, of course. They say he's a rich man—money in the East."

Her face fell. Not him . . . "You're certain there's no one else?"

The bartender went on polishing his glass. "No, I'm telling you, if you want to sell a piece of horseflesh like that, Adam Sern's your man."

She watched Mr. Moore walk back behind the bar. She didn't want to speak to that half-breed, much less bargain with him. Just looking at his tall, muscular frame, made her uncomfortable. She sighed. But what else was she going to do? And he had noticed

41

Zeus' superior breeding.

Taking the last gulp of cider, Jessica rose out of her seat and walked toward Adam's table. He watched her as she came toward him. When she reached his side he stood and pulled out the other chair. She accepted it.

Adam sat down again and leaned across the small wooden table. "What can I do for you, Miss Landon?" His voice was low and provocative.

She found herself lost in the depth of his ebony eyes. She hated Adam Sern, but there was something about him that intrigued her, that drew her toward him. "I—" She looked up at the green glass chandelier, trying to rally her thoughts. She returned her gaze to his. "I need money, so I was wondering if you'd be interested in purchasing that horse of mine," she blurted out.

Adam sat back in his chair and crossed his arms over his chest. He regarded her through hooded eyelids. There was something about this Jessica that frightened him; he could feel it deep in the pit of his stomach. It wasn't like the fear a man had when he heard the rattle of a snake's tail, or saw the flash of gunfire. It was worse. There was something about her emerald green eyes, the curve of her rosy lips, the set of determination in her chin that made Adam think he needed to get as far away from her as possible—as soon as possible. He'd buy both of her horses at an exorbitant price if that was what it took to get her on a train and out of his life.

"So?" She leaned toward him, pressing her elbows on the scarred tabletop. "Zeus is in prime form, sired more foals than I can count. And he can run until you drop dead. His line of Appaloosas have been in my father's family since before the war." When Adam made no comment, she opened her mouth to speak again, but he held up a broad palm.

"You don't have to sell me on the stallion's finer points, they're obvious." He paused. "I'll take them both."

Jessica shook her head. "Hera's not for sale."

"I'll pay you well. Enough to get a start on buying some land in Washington territory for that apple farm of yours."

"I said, Mr. Sern, the mare's not for sale." She leaned back in her chair. It was her turn to regard *him*. She needed Hera if she was going to track the Black Bandit. Besides, the mare was all she had left of her papa and Mark.

Adam's dark eyes narrowed. "You *do* intend on getting on that train for Washington, don't you?"

"After I see to my brother's body." She gazed at him with feigned innocence. "Where else would I go, Mr. Sern?"

There was something about her tone of voice that concerned Adam, but he couldn't put his finger on it. "Name your price."

She lowered her voice to a whisper.

Adam chuckled at her reply. "You strike a hard bargain, madam."

"I understand you can afford it."

"People in this town have loose jaws—nothing better to do but flap them."

"So do we have a deal?"

He offered his hand and she accepted it, giving it a shake. An odd, hot tingle rose up her arm as she withdrew from his grasp. She wiped her hand on her skirt as if she could wipe away the feel of his touch. "I'll expect the payment in full before you take him."

"I don't carry that kind of cash around, not as often as I get robbed."

Jessica almost laughed at his joke, but caught herself in time. "When can you get it?"

"Tomorrow when the bank opens."

She nodded, slipping out of her seat. "Now I have to see about my brother."

He rose with her. "Arrangements have been made. A coffin's being built. Doc Abbot is taking care of the body." Adam put out a hand to steady her as she swayed on her feet.

Jessica took a deep breath, feeling foolish. Death was a part of life; she knew that. She had grown up with death around her. First Mama, when Jessica was ten, then Papa. Still, Mark's death seemed the hardest to bear. She gazed up at Adam. His hand, touching her arm, made it difficult to think clearly. It was the caress of a man who understood her pain, not that of a murderer's. She stepped away. "I—I'm all right. Just tired. But I want to see Mark."

Adam's dark gaze rested on hers. "Don't you think it would be better if you waited until morning? Why not get some rest. He's in good hands."

"I—"

"Jessica!" The sound of a familiar voice made Jessica turn.

"Kat!" she cried. Before Jessica knew what was happening she was in the older woman's arms. She didn't know if she had run to Kat or Kat to her. All she knew was her new friend's warm, comforting embrace.

"Jessica, you scared the wits out of me ridin' off like that! You're lucky them bandits didn't string you up!" Billy stood just behind his wife, his hands deep in his pockets. "My Billy, fool!" she flung over her shoulder. "He thought you was one of them, but I knew better."

Jessica laughed. "Mr. Sern, here—" To her surprise Adam was nowhere to be seen. He had slipped out undetected in the midst of the reunion. "Mr. Sern, the train detective," Jessica went on, "he thought so too. He brought me back to Loco."

Billy shuffled forward. "We got your stuff if you'd like to come up and get it."

"What stuff? The bandits took my carpetbag. It was all I had."

"There was a hat and your brother's coat. Then them saplings. You want them, don't you?"

Jessica smiled. Her trees! She'd forgotten her trees! "Oh, yes! Thank you for taking them off the train. I do want them."

"Come on up." He wiggled a finger. "We just tucked the young'uns in."

Upstairs, the Wiedenhoeft's room was only a tad larger than Jessica's. All three children lay asleep in one of the two beds, illuminated by an oil lamp.

"Here you go." Kat offered the bundle of apple tree saplings that had been carefully dampened.

Tears came to Jessica's eyes as she fingered the thin saplings through the wet newsprint. "This wasn't supposed to happen this way. Mark and I, we had so many plans . . ."

"There, there, don't fret, sweetheart." Kat wrapped her arm around Jessica's shoulder. "We'll give that brother of yours a Christian funeral and then you can go to Seattle with us. Billy's brother Elsmere's got us a fine house, big enough for all of us."

The thought was tempting ... It would be so much easier for Jessica just to say her good-byes to Mark and get on that train. But what was easy, wasn't always what was right. As long as that Black Bandit roamed the West, there would be more train robberies, more deaths. Besides, the taste of revenge was what she craved.

Jessica looked at Kat. "Thank you for the offer, but, I can't."

"Are you sure, Jessica?" Billy asked. "We'd be willin' to help you in anyway we could."

Jessica wiped her tears with her dusty sleeve. "There is something you can do."

"Name it."

Jessica pushed her saplings into Kat's hand. "I want you to take my trees."

"I couldn't!" Kat protested.

"No." Jessica folded her arms over her chest in determination. "I just want you to take care of them for me until I reach Seattle."

"But you're taking the train with us, aren't you?"

"I'll be along after a while. But there's something I have to do first."

"You're not serious about catching those bandits, are you?" Kat whispered.

Jessica backed her way to the door. "Someone's got to."

"That's a lawman's job," Billy piped in excitedly. "Adam Sern's job."

"I don't want to talk about this anymore tonight. My mind's made up." She rested her hand on the door frame, watching the shadows the oil lamp cast. "Could you go with me to make the funeral arrangements tomorrow, Kat? Mr. Sern has bought my stallion, so I'll have money to do it up right." She laughed. "Brass band if we can find one."

Kat passed the bundle of trees on to Billy and came to the door. She patted Jessica. "Listen to you, you're talking half-crazed. Chasing after the Black Bandit, indeed! What you need is some sleep. Tomorrow the world'll make more sense."

Jessica offered a smile to the only friends she had. "Good night. I'll see you tomorrow." Slowly she walked down the dark hallway to her room. Kat was wrong. She was thinking clearly, more clearly than she ever had in her life. She knew what she was going to do and how she was going to do it. She had a plan. The only thing that could possibly upset her plan . . . was Adam Sern.

Jacob Dorchester slammed his fist on the train depot counter. "What do you mean, sir, that you cannot tell me if she's passed through Ogden? You're employed here, are you not?"

The clerk who worked the night desk rolled his eyes heavenward and then returned his gaze to the newspaper in his lap. He was too busy reading an editorial on the Black Bandit to argue with this silver-haired puss-in-boots. The man was obviously out of his element in his fancy black suit and round bowler hat. "I'm tellin' you, buster. We ain't supposed to give that information out. Besides, it might take days to track down one Miss Jessica whatever-her-name-is."

"She's going by the name of Jessica Landon. Young girl." Jacob brushed his immaculate suit at the shoulder. "Beautiful brown hair to here. An angel. You couldn't miss her."

The clerk chuckled. "Your wife, you say? Sounds more like your daughter!"

Jacob's cheeks colored. Slowly he leaned over the counter, his anger barely in check. "I will pay you," he said, tight-lipped.

The clerk looked up with interest. "I could lose my job."

"I can pay you *well*."

The clerk sighed, folding his newspaper. "Might take me a day or two. Can't do it when anyone else is in the office."

Jacob slid a bill across the wooden counter. "I'll be at the Peachtree Hotel. My name is Mr. Dorchester. Jacob Dorchester, and it is *vital* that I find my wife."

Chapter Four

"Sern, we've been expecting you. Come in." Miles Gordon, a representative from the Union Pacific Railroad, waved a manicured hand.

Adam stepped into the small office. The pinewood walls were bare, the floor sanded smooth and white. Gordon sat behind a polished mahogany desk smoking a cigar, its foul smell masking the sweet aroma of fresh sawdust. His assistant, a string bean of a man, stood directly behind him, lost in Miles's immense shadow.

"Miles." Adam gave a stiff nod. He'd dealt with this plump partridge before. The man was far more concerned with how well he appeared to do his job, than how well he actually did it. Adam didn't trust him as far as he could toss him, which wasn't far. He was a good inch taller than Adam and twice his weight.

"So good to see you, Sern. I miss our poker games."

Liar, Adam thought, eyeing his superior. Miles

was a poor poker player and a worse loser. By Adam's calculations, Miles still owed him a hundred dollars in back debts. "Let's skip the pleasantries and get on with it," Adam said.

"Well, come, come. Come in and shut the door." Miles flapped his hand. "No need to put on that savage face of yours. I'm not here to fire you."

Adam lifted a dark eyebrow. "Or have me arrested?"

"Surely you don't think *I* think you're part of that Black Bandit's gang?"

No, you probably don't think I'm part of the gang, Adam mused, *but you're the one who suggested it as a possibility. You'll do anything to cover your own tail.* Adam glanced across the room at Miles, taking his time in responding. He smiled, his sarcasm palatable. "Of course not, Miles. I know I can always count on you."

"True, true enough."

"So why are you here? What brought you out of that whore house in Ogden?"

Miles crushed out his cigar on the top of the desk and his assistant swept the butt, ashes and all, into his own hand. "I'm here, Adam," Miles explained, "not of my own accord but because I was ordered to come and speak with you."

"Yes, yes, get on with it." Adam shifted his weight from one snakeskin boot to the other.

"I was asked to tell you that this is your final chance, Sern. Although you profess your innocence, all indications lead the board to consider the definite possibility that you *are* part of this gang of outlaws."

"My last chance." Adam's dark eyes met the

50

railroad executive's. "Exactly what does that mean?"

"It means—now mind you, these are their words, not mine. It means that if you do not successfully capture this outlaw and bring him to justice, *you* will be charged as an accomplice."

Adam shook his head. "This is ridiculous, Miles. My record is unblemished. I've been working for you bastards for two years now! I'm the best detective you've got!"

"Sern, you have to look at this from their point of view. You have to agree that someone on the inside has been passing on information concerning our payroll shipments."

"I told you in my telegraph. Your courier, Stevenson, was one of them."

Miles shook his head sympathetically. "I know, Sern. But they say all they have is your word and what's the word of a—"

"A what?" In two long strides Adam was at the mahogany desk. He slammed his fist down on the smooth oiled top. "What's the word of a what?" he demanded. "A *redskin!* A *half-breed!*" He leaned across the desk bringing his face only inches from Miles'. "A *red nigger?*"

The railroad executive's jowls shook. "It's not me that's saying it, Sern. You know that. I have a great deal of respect for you native Americans. We're both on the same side, you and I."

"I was hired as a detective for this railroad because I was capable of the job. White, red, chartreuse! What difference does the color of my skin make?"

"You can't blame folks for being wary. John Marks, on the board, just had a brother killed down in Texas. Kiowa massacred his whole family."

"I am not Kiowa! My mother was Ojibwa. I wouldn't know a Kiowa if I fell over one!" Adam straightened up, his black gaze still fixed on Miles's pale face.

"I—I'm just the messenger. They sent me because they knew we were friends. I stuck my neck out for you, Sern. They're ready to string you up in Salt Lake City!"

Adam took a deep breath, tightening and relaxing his fists that hung at his sides. He hated losing control of his emotions. This red man, white man issue was an endless battle. "All right. So this is my last chance. Does the *board* want the Black Bandit alive?"

"If possible. It would be good publicity for our customers to see that the Union Pacific keeps their trains safe for their passengers."

"I want this legal. I don't want to be accused of murder."

Miles pulled at his starched white collar. There was a thin sheen of perspiration across his forehead. "We can take care of that. And there'll be funds to hire a tracker to aid you."

"I don't need a tracker." Adam relaxed his hands. "All right, Miles, I'll catch the bastard and I'll bring him to you." He shook a finger. "Maybe bring him right into one of those board meetings of yours!"

Miles's assistant gave a squeak.

"I hardly think that's necessary." Miles pushed himself out of his chair. "But we will expect a weekly report on your progress."

Adam gave a wave of disgust as he spun around

and headed out of the room. Just as he reached the door he turned back. "I'll catch this Black Bandit, but then that's it, Miles. You'll have my resignation the following day."

"Then what are you going to do? No other railroad would have a—"

Adam stepped into the afternoon sun and slammed the door before he heard Miles's final words.

Outside, Adam headed down the street. He was half tempted to just ride off and let the Union Pacific deal with the Black Bandit themselves. But there would be nothing to stop his employers from signing a warrant against him. What jury would believe a red man's word against twelve railroad executives?

Adam was trapped. The only way to save face, to save his neck, was to bring the outlaw to justice.

"Mr. Sern." A husky feminine voice invaded Adam's thoughts. "Mr. Sern!"

Adam spun around angrily. "What!"

Jessica Landon stepped back. Her clothes were dusted clean today, her shiny brown hair pulled back beneath a sensible hat. He watched her as she took a deep breath, straightening her spine.

"I—I need the money. Zeus is over at the livery stable."

"I said I'd pay you when I got to the bank, didn't I?" He hadn't meant to holler at her, it just came out. He was so sick to death of the prejudice against him. These days he saw enemies at every turn.

Jessica's jaw jutted out as her green eyes narrowed. "I'll have it today or the deal is off, Mr. Sern!"

Before Adam could speak, before he could bring himself to apologize for his harshness, she had passed him and was hurrying down the street, her leather riding skirt flapping in the hot breeze.

Adam gave a sigh and pivoted, heading in the opposite direction. The Loco Federal Loan and Savings Bank building was just ahead.

In silence, Jessica, Billy, and Kat walked side by side to the lonely cemetery behind the Baptist church. The Wiedenhoeft children followed, with Emily balancing her little brother on her hip. A light mist of rain fell, cooling the late afternoon air. The smell of wet alkaline dirt rose up from the ground filling their nostrils. They gave no mind to the mud that splattered their pants and stockings.

When they arrived, the old Reverend Gaines was already standing amid the neat rows of wooden crosses. Two men stood aside, their hats crushed in their hands in reverence. Grave diggers.

Jessica walked up to the new pine coffin and ran her fingertips along the planed wood. The rain fell on the lid making dark round circles of different sizes. The coffin seemed so small; Mark had seemed so much bigger when he was alive. She looked up at the minister and gave a nod. The sooner this was over with, the better.

Reverend Gaines began his short eulogy. The words meant little to Jessica, but the sound of the old man's voice was comforting. She had loved Mark, just as she had loved her parents and now he was gone. They were all gone.

Jessica felt Kat walk up beside her and take her hand, giving it a squeeze. Jessica squeezed back. Kat and her husband had been good friends, but now they were leaving too. A whistle sounded in the distance as a train huffed its way into Loco. The Wiedenhoefts would be on that train when it pulled out of the station.

The minister finished his final prayer with a solemn "Amen" and then the grave diggers came forward. They used twisted old ropes to lower Mark's coffin into the freshly dug hole.

Jessica scooped up a handful of dirt and tossed it into the hole. The dirt hit the pine boards in silence. "Good-bye, Mark," she whispered. "I hope you get that Winchester." When she raised her head she caught a glimpse of another mourner. It was a man wearing a black, wide-brimmed hat pulled down to shield his face from the rain. Her gaze went to the pistols holstered on his hips. The handles were black.

It was Adam Sern.

Jessica turned and started back up the slope to town. The Wiedenhoefts joined her. They walked to the train depot in silence. There was nothing to say. When they reached the cover of the depot roof, Kat reached out and took Jessica's hand. "Are you all right, honey?"

Jessica nodded. "I'm all right. I'll see you in Seattle in a few months."

"I hate to leave you like this. We could stay a few more days."

Jessica watched Billy loading his two small daughters onto the train. He held the baby in his arms. "You can't stay. You've got the children to think of."

"Then come with us." Kat's blue eyes settled on

her friend's. "You can't really mean to chase down those outlaws yourself. It's crazy talk."

Jessica laughed. "If it was Billy who'd gotten shot on that train, what would you do?"

"I'd let the law do their job."

Jessica looked away. She could feel her throat constricting. "If the law had done its job, Mark wouldn't be dead, would he?"

Kat studied Jessica's face for a moment. "There's no changin' your mind?"

"Nope. So go on with you." Jessica wrapped her arms around Kat, giving her a hug.

"All aboard!" cried the conductor.

"Kat! Come on with you!" Billy called from the window.

Kat wiped at her tears with an embroidered handkerchief. "I just hate to leave you like this, with your brother just buried."

"Look at me." Jessica spread her arms. "I'm fine. You're the one crying." Her voice sounded calm, but inside Jessica could feel her heart pounding. If she could just get Kat on that train!

Billy came down the steps and caught his wife by the arm. "We're gonna miss the train with your blubbering." He offered his hand to Jessica, but she pushed it away and hugged him.

Embarrassed by his own emotion, Billy stepped back onto the train with Kat in tow.

"You take care of my saplings," Jessica warned. "Keep them wet."

Billy waved, then leaned out the window. "You promise you'll come to get them?"

She lifted a hand in oath. "With the Black Bandit's scalp on my belt. I swear it."

The train gave a lurch and began to roll, first backward, then finally forward. The Wiedenhoefts waved vigorously and Jessica waved back until they were finally out of sight.

Then suddenly the train depot was empty. The rain hit the tin roof overhead in a rhythmic patter. Jessica shivered. She was damp and cold . . . and alone. Tears slipped down her cheeks. She hadn't cried all day, not when she saw Mark's body, not even at the funeral, but now, there seemed nothing left to do but cry. Against her will, sobs wracked her tired body. She felt so foolish standing here in the middle of the platform, crying like a baby, but she couldn't help herself. Her strength was sapped.

Then out of nowhere came a low comforting voice, a warm touch. "It's all right, sweetheart," he murmured.

Jessica felt herself being drawn into his arms. He was tall and solid.

"Go ahead, Jess, cry. Get it out. All of that pain has to come out or it will tear you up inside."

Jessica clung to him, to Adam. She knew it was him without having to look up into his face. She could feel his heart beating against hers. She could smell him. He didn't smell like dust and sweat like the rest of the men in Loco. His scent was clean and fresh with a strange hint of pine. Jessica had always loved the smell of a pine forest.

"Let's get you to your room," Adam said when Jessica's sobs had subsided. "You're exhausted."

She allowed him to lead her off the platform and down the street to the Red Moon Saloon. She gave no notice to the curious stares of townspeople or to the rain that still fell in a steady downpour. Nothing existed but the comfort of Adam's embrace.

He led her upstairs and into her room. He pushed her gently onto her cot and shucked off her heavy brown riding boots. Then he removed her hat and the wooden pins that held her hair on top of her head. He brushed it out with his fingers, murmuring softly beneath his breath. When Adam pulled back the patchwork quilt Jessica allowed him to ease her beneath it and then cover her to her chin. His long black hair tickled her cheek as he leaned over her to tuck her in.

Jessica's eyelids fell. She was in a dream state, half awake, half asleep. She ached so badly for Mark, for the life in Tennessee that she'd left behind that her chest actually hurt. Fresh tears slid down her cheeks.

"It's all right, Jess," Adam whispered. She heard a chair scrape the floor as he pulled up beside her bed. "Go to sleep. Life won't look so dark in the morning." He slipped his hand beneath the quilt and took hers.

Adam's touch comforted her and slowly her tears ebbed. Somewhere far in the recesses of her mind she knew she should send him away. She hated him, didn't she? Though at this moment she couldn't quite recall why.

"You don't have to stay," Jessica said softly.

"I won't stay long," Adam answered in a low, reassuring voice. "You just sleep."

Already his voice was fading in the distance. She

snuggled further down in the feather tick and drifted off to sleep, clutching Adam's hand.

Jessica woke to a room filled with bright morning sunshine. She stretched her limbs like a lazy cat. To her surprise she realized she was wearing all of her clothes. Her leather skirt was tangled at her knees, her faded white shirt half unbuttoned. As she swung her feet over the edge of the bed, memories of the previous night flooded her memory. She remembered being so cold, so alone there in the depot and then he'd suddenly appeared, a savior. She half smiled. His touch had been comforting. He had brought her home and tucked her into her bed like a small, lost child. Adam Sern had been there when she needed someone the most.

Jessica went to the tiny cracked mirror that hung on the wall. "So what do you think of that?" she asked herself aloud.

What was there to think? She hadn't asked Adam to do any of that. It didn't change any of the circumstances of Mark's death or what she had to do. Adam Sern was still the enemy.

With that settled, Jessica began to perform her morning ablutions. Mark was buried and it was time for her to put her grief aside and start tracking down the Black Bandit and his gang.

With her hair and teeth brushed with the brushes Kat had given her as a parting gift, and her face washed, Jessica was ready to head downstairs for breakfast. She lifted her hat off the chair. Beneath it was a stack of crisp new bills. She swept them off the chair. It was payment for Zeus and then some.

She shook her head as she folded the bills and slipped them into her bodice. That Adam was a strange man. . . . But she didn't want to think about him, not now. It just made everything too confusing.

Downstairs, the saloon was empty. Pauline brought Jessica a fried egg, a spoon of beans, a biscuit, and a mug of cool milk.

The girl watched Jessica as she began to eat. "Reckon you'll be catchin' the next train out now that your brother's buried."

"Mmmm." Jessica knew that the less she said to anyone about going after the outlaws, the better off she'd be. "You have a newspaper here in town?"

"Sure do! Gus Hawkins, he prints a fine paper a couple times a month." Pauline made herself busy wiping off tables.

"Where's his shop?"

"In the telegraph office, of course. Most people does more than one thing in this town. Mr. Moore, he's thinkin' about startin' up a bathhouse. Pedro, he's the barber, he's got one, but he goes on a drunk so often that he's never open."

Jessica sipped her milk, savoring the cool liquid. It couldn't be long after nine and it was already sweltering. "Well, thank you for the breakfast." She wiped her mouth on the napkin and laid it aside. "I was starved."

"Healthy appetite, that's a good sign. I guess I can tell Mr. Sern you're feeling better."

Jessica pushed out of her chair. "What do you mean? Why would you be saying anything to Adam about me?" The moment his first name slipped out,

60

she was sorry. She didn't want anyone in town thinking she was too familiar with him—or he with her.

Pauline picked up the dirty dishes. "Mr. Sern was just askin' about you. He was up early and gone but he asked me to make sure you got a good breakfast. He said I was to run down and check the train schedule for you if you wanted me to." She took a deep breath. "So did you want me to?"

Jessica adjusted her hat on her head. "That won't be necessary, Pauline. But thank you." She went out of the saloon and started down the plank walk in the direction of the telegraph office. She didn't like the thought of Adam Sern having Pauline look after her. Who did he think he was, her self-appointed guardian or something?

She gave a sigh, hurrying down the street. Hopefully the newspaper office would have some old clipping on the Black Bandit. The sooner she got information on the outlaw, the sooner she'd be rid of this town and Adam Sern.

Chapter Five

"Just what do you think you're doing?"

Jessica stared at Adam's boots, then lifted her gaze to take in his handsome chiseled face. He was looking down at her with hooded heathen eyes. This was the first time she'd seen him since he'd taken her back to her room two nights ago.

"Doing?" She glanced. "I don't know what you mean, Mr. Sern." *It's better to remain on a formal basis,* she thought. This man had a way of getting under a person's skin.

"Don't play sweet and innocent with me, Jess. You know exactly what I mean. First you're bugging Gus for newspaper articles on the Black Bandit, then you're down at the train depot trying to buy information from the employees."

Jessica ground the toe of her boot into the dirt. She was sitting on the step outside the Red Moon Saloon just thinking. There was plenty of information out there on the outlaws; it was only a matter of sifting through it. She stared at Adam's boots wondering what kind of snakes had died to make them. "There was a gang that busted through a little town by the name of Sharpston last night. You know it?"

"Sure I know it; it's between here and Logan."

"It had to be them," Jessica mused aloud. "They have to be holing up nearby."

Adam studied her heart-shaped face. He saw barely a glimmer of the woman who had stood at the depot the other night, sobbing like a lost child. There was nothing but hell and fire in this woman's cat-green eyes. She was going to be harder to get rid of than he'd anticipated. "I said, what do you think you're doing?"

Jessica stood, brushing off the back of her skirt. The alkaline dust of northwestern Utah was everywhere; on her clothes, in her hair, on her face. It was powdery and dry, like sifted flour; there was no escaping it. "I'm going to catch myself an outlaw or two, that's what I'm doing, Mr. Sern."

Adam chuckled. "You? A woman? It's *my* job to catch the Black Bandit and his men."

Her eyes met his in a challenge. "You? An Indian?"

Adam stiffened. He ground his teeth. He'd been up against prejudice since the day he left the Ojibwa. Why did it still hurt? "Women don't chase down outlaws."

"It seems men don't either."

Adam felt his hands tighten into fists.

She poked a finger into his chest. "Why aren't you out there? Why didn't you go after them this morning when word came into town that they had raided Sharpston? Surely I wasn't the first person to hear the news."

"For your information, I'm waiting on a federal marshal. I have to be made a deputy marshal to legally track these men—to kill them if I find it necessary." He knocked off his wide-brimmed hat and wiped his forehead. "Why am I telling you this? I don't have to answer to you." He flexed his hands making an effort to keep a cool head. "Look, Jess, I'll catch the bandit and see that justice is done. Let me get you a ticket. Just get on that train and don't get off until you hit Seattle."

Jessica walked up the two steps, turning to face him. She was Adam's height now and could stare straight into his eyes that were as black as the onyx handles of his pistols. "I don't want justice. I want blood! My brother's dead and that man has my carpetbag!"

"The money in that bag is gone, Jess. It's gone."

"I want my bag. I want my mother's picture. I want my grandmother's sugar cookie recipe. I want my money—theirs will do."

He tugged at the long mane of black hair tied behind his head. He'd never met a woman so damned determined . . . except maybe his mother. "You're being unreasonable. You're not thinking clearly. It's the grief."

"You're wrong, Mr. Sern. I'm thinking very clearly." She gave him a shove. "So don't get in my way!"

He watched her turn and stalk off. "I can have you arrested for obstructing justice."

"I'm not that easily frightened off. I'm not stupid either. You think I don't know the sheriff's got better things to do than to arrest nosy women?" She laughed, her voice warm and throaty. "You're just afraid I'm going to get to them first and ruin that knight-in-shining-armor reputation of yours. Wouldn't that be something? I can see the headlines now."

Adam followed her. He was beginning to wonder if the woman was unstable. "Jessica. This isn't a game. These men kill for the sport of it."

"I'm a good shot," she called over her shoulder. She was headed for the livery stable to check on Hera before she turned in for the night. "They say the Black Bandit's aim is lousy."

Adam ran after her, catching her arm. She spun around angrily. "Let go of me."

"You weren't afraid of my touch the other night," he challenged.

"That was different." She refused to look away and she refused to make apologies. "But I didn't ask for it," she went on hostilely, "and I don't owe you anything in return."

He released her. How could he explain to her how much it had meant to him the other night—to feel her warmth, to feel her need him? Hell, he didn't understand it himself. "I don't want you to get hurt. You can go to Seattle," he reasoned. "Find a nice husband. Grow that apple orchard if you want."

She shook her head. "You don't get it, do you?" Her hands fell to her hips as she looked out at the sun setting behind the rooftops of Loco. It was a brilliant half circle shooting rays of golden light. She looked back at Adam. "Mark was *my* brother and that was *my* carpetbag. The newspapers say you've been chasing that bunch for six months. Now it's my turn."

Adam watched as she flounced off, her stride long and determined. He cursed her beneath his breath. He was going to see that woman on a train bound for Seattle if he had to tie her to the caboose!

Cautiously, Jessica entered the Dead Dog. It was the saloon on the far side of town built next to Loco's whorehouse. The barroom was dim, lit by a few odorous gas lamps. The piano music was loud and poorly played. The moment she stepped inside, she wondered if she shouldn't wait and come back in the daylight. Even through the thick cigar smoke she could see the kind of patrons the saloon catered to.

On the far left two buffalo hunters fought loudly over a hand of cards on the table. The hunter wearing part of a buffalo headdress, horns and all, drew his pistol and his partner obligingly redealt.

There was a tinkle of laughter from a half-dressed saloon girl. "There you go, Robbie. You always get what you want, don't you," she told the hunter with the pistol. She leaned over his shoulder, pressing her ample breasts into his bearded cheek.

Jessica looked away, embarrassed. But everywhere she turned there were more nearly naked women being fondled by drunken patrons. One of the girls leaped atop the piano and several men gathered around, clapping to the familiar tune.

Jessica sidled her way to the bar, dodging a hand that crept out to grasp her skirt. *For Mark,* she told herself. *I have to do this for Mark.* She rested her hands on the wooden bar.

"Even', ma'am." The saloon keeper was a giant of a man with a long mane of blond hair he wore in a braid down his back. Around his neck was a string of shiny rosary beads. "If you're lookin' for a job, it's Miss Lil next door you want."

Jessica chuckled. "It's not a job I want."

"Didn't think you did. Don't look much like a sportin' girl. Their eyes is always dull, like they's already half buried."

Jessica slid a silver coin across the damp bartop. "What I want is some information."

He lifted the coin and bit it. "What kind of information you lookin' for? If it's about that gambler they found in my garbage out back, I already tole that sheriff from Ogden, I don't know nuthin' about him. Never seen him before. Never intend to see him again, God rest his soul." He crossed himself.

"I'm looking for another man, a live one. I understand there's a man called Elmo Shine that used to ride with the Black Bandit."

The saloon keeper threw back his head and laughed. "Yer the second one that's been in here today lookin' for ole Shiner. I told that redskinned lawman that Shiner never rode with anybody. He's even been known to spin a tale of bein' a famous Texas ranger, but he's just talk."

"I'll find that out for myself. Where can I find him?"

The saloon keeper poured himself a shot of whiskey and downed it in a breathless gulp. "He had to move on on account of one of Miss Lil's gals was threatenin' to whack his withered worm if he came within a mile of her. He was always wantin' credit and I guess she just got fed up with him."

Jessica ignored the man's crude remark. "Where'd he go?"

The saloon keeper suddenly ducked and an instant later an empty whiskey bottle shattered on the wall behind his head. She flinched. He ducked beneath the bar. A moment later he appeared with a sawed-off double-barreled shotgun. "You do that again, Scooter," he bellowed "and I'm gonna blast you! Can't you see I'm busy conversin' with a lady?"

Jessica resisted the urge to look over her shoulder at the man called Scooter. She cleared her throat.

"Now where was we?" The saloon keeper slid his weapon back under the bar. "That's right. Shiner." He wiped his hands on his filthy apron and poured himself another whiskey. "Like I was sayin', he's moved on—to Sharpston, I reckon."

Jessica smiled. "You think he'd be willing to talk to me?"

"You buy him a bottle of bourbon and he'd be willin' to talk to the devil himself, God rest his soul." He crossed himself again.

Jessica backed away, stifling a squeal as something large scurried beneath her feet. "I thank you for the information."

"Anytime."

She kept her eyes on the packed dirt floor as she headed for the door, trying to avoid any more rodents. God, she hated a rat! She was concentrating so hard that she didn't notice the buffalo hunter until she walked right into his hairy arms. She stumbled back and looked up at the man wearing the buffalo headdress.

"Where you goin', a pretty little thing like you?"

Her chest tightened in fear. "Step aside," Jessica said loudly.

"How about a little drink before you're on your way?"

She tried to brush past him. "I don't think so."

He caught her arm in an iron grip. "When Robbie invites a lady for a drink, he don't like bein' turned down."

The bile rose in Jessica's throat. The man smelled of rotting buffalo flesh. His beard was long and matted with a river of tobacco juice down the center. She twisted her arm, ignoring her own pain as she tried to free herself. "I said, I don't want a drink! Now let me go!" She raised her booted foot and kicked him hard just below his knee.

The buffalo hunter cried out in pain and there was an echo of laughter from behind.

The moment he released her hand, Jessica dove for the door but he managed to trip her. She fell with a cry of anguish, but came up swinging her fists. She caught him in the mouth as he struggled to pin her arms behind her.

"Slow down there, little lady." He lifted her off the ground and swung her over his shoulder.

Jessica gagged as her face was pressed into the buffalo hide that hung down his back. She kicked and screamed. Great tufts of buffalo fur flew in the air as she struggled to breathe.

"Put her down!" the barkeep ordered.

Robbie laughed, his entire body shaking.

"Since when are you one to get in the way of a man's sport, Little Marvin?" The buffalo hunter swung around so fast that it made Jessica's head spin.

70

"That little lady ain't on the menu, Robbie, and you know it."

The buffalo hunter slid Jessica to the floor but gripped her throat with a wide filthy palm. "That right? Who's gonná stop me?"

Jessica gasped for breath, digging her fingernails into the man's hand. Any moment she knew she was going to lose consciousness.

The saloon keeper leaped onto the bartop, his double-barreled shotgun in hand. The cross of his rosary was clenched in his teeth. One of the hammers made an ominous click as he cocked it back. "Me. That's who, you stinkin' buffalo carcass!"

Robbie's mouth split into a blackened-toothed grin. "Think I could get a little help here, Gates?"

A pistol went off behind Jessica's head and the bartender dove for the floor to avoid the other buffalo hunter's bullet.

Women screamed and glass shattered as the saloon broke into chaos. It seemed the patrons needed little encouragement to start a brawl. Shots were fired and men swung heavy fists. Two whores rolled on the floor ripping each other's hair out to the delight of a circle of men.

Jessica took advantage of the outbreak of confusion and jammed her elbow into her captor's groin. The man released her, grabbing for his injured parts. She slid to the floor and began to crawl across the damp dirt to the door.

The buffalo hunter gave a bellow and lunged after her. "Get back here, you bitch. All I wanted was a little sport, but you're gonna get more than that now!"

He caught her by the foot and Jessica rolled over,

kicking him with her free leg. She managed to grasp his pistol, but he knocked it out of her hand. She screamed as loud as she could, praying the saloon keeper would come to her rescue.

A sudden explosion of gunfire distracted Robbie, and she gave him a hard kick in the chin and yanked her leg free from his grasp. Rolling back onto her hands and knees, she scurried for the door. She found the opening blocked by a pair of snakeskin boots.

Adam reached out and lifted her to her feet.

"Look out!" Jessica cried as the buffalo hunter came straight for them.

Adam raised his Colt and Robbie came to a halt.

"You?" the buffalo hunter asked, wiping his bloody mouth.

Adam grinned. "None other."

Robbie gave a friendly chuckle and spat a stream of tobacco juice onto the dirt floor. "We was just foolin'. I didn't mean to bother your woman, redskin." He laughed again. "Did I, darlin'?"

"Did he hurt you?" Adam demanded, keeping his dark eyes fixed on the buffalo hunter.

"No," Jessica breathed, still panting. Her blouse was torn and her new hat had been lost in the scuffle. Her hands went to her neck, massaging the bruised flesh. "I'm all right." She retrieved her hat and returned to Adam's side.

Adam dropped his arm over her shoulder. "Guess we'll be goin' on our way then, Robbie."

The buffalo hunter took another step back. "Be seein' you, redskin. Right fine sportin' you got there."

Adam backed his way out of the saloon. The instant he was on the wooden walk, he spun Jessica around to face him. "What in God's holy name were you doing in the Dead Dog?" he demanded.

Jessica was still so badly shaken that she could barely respond. "In—investigating."

He took her by the arm propelling her uptown. It was dark out with a pale half-moon hanging low in the cloudless sky. A few lamps swung along the street, illuminating their way.

"Well, you almost got more of an education than you bargained for." He pulled her roughly along.

"Where are you taking me?"

"Back to your room."

"Why thank you, Mr. Sern," she said sarcastically. "I don't believe I could have found it without you."

"You're going to your room, and you're going to stay put until morning. Then I'm taking you down to the depot and putting you on the first God-blessed train that rolls through here."

Jessica opened her mouth to protest, but then clamped it shut. What need was there in arguing with this insufferable man? She had all of the information she needed and she had a few supplies. It was time she moved on anyway. "Does the train go through Sharpston?"

"No, it doesn't." Adam pushed through the swinging doors of the Red Moon. "Why?"

She shrugged. "No reason. Just wondering." The fact that the train didn't pass through Sharpston was a minor inconvenience. She allowed him to escort her through the saloon and up the steps.

"Don't tell me you're coming to your senses?"

She massaged her neck. "That buffalo hunter could have killed me."

"Yeah, and he's friendly." Adam pushed open

her door.

She turned to face him. "I suppose you think you deserve to be thanked again, but I've got news for you. I'd have gotten away on my own."

"Good night," Adam said quietly. "I'll be up to get you in the morning."

Jessica nodded. It was strange, but she was almost going to miss this arrogant man. He was someone to talk to . . . or at least argue with. But then she thought of Mark and she stiffened. "The morning, then. Good night." She closed the door behind her.

The following morning Jessica allowed Adam to escort her to breakfast and then to the train depot. With a canvas saddle bag in her hand and a new black, wide-brimmed hat on her head, she walked complacently at his side.

"You said Hera's already loaded?" Jessica had been talkative all morning; Adam had been sullen.

"Taken care of this morning." Everything was falling into place for him. The federal marshal was coming in on the same train Jessica was going out on. With a little luck, by afternoon, Adam would be on the bandits' trail. So why did he feel so irritable?

"And my ticket?"

"Here." He pulled it out of his back pocket and handed the slip of paper to her.

Jessica walked up the platform steps. The train had already arrived and passengers were disembarking. "Guess I'd better get on so you can meet your marshal."

Adam followed her to the passenger car, suddenly

feeling awkward.

She stepped up into the train and turned to him, feeling as if she ought to say something. She offered her hand and he took it. His touch was more of a caress than a handshake. "I guess this is good-bye."

"You'll like Seattle." He let go of her hand. "You'd better get aboard."

She smiled at the thought of outsmarting this strutting buck. Then on impulse she leaned forward to brush her lips against his clean-shaven cheek. Before she knew what was happening he had turned his head until their lips met. She sucked in her breath as his lips touched hers, hot and damp. His great arms wrapped around her, pulling her into an embrace. Jessica put up her arms to struggle, but the heat, the taste of him, made her thoughts spin. Her hands fell to his broad shoulders. The force of his tongue invading her mouth made her shudder with fear, but she had no control over her own response. It was primal. His presence was overpowering; it was all encompassing. His hand cupped her chin as he withdrew.

Jessica raised her hand to slap him, but he caught it in midair.

The heat of anger rose to color her already flushed cheeks. She opened her mouth to speak.

"Don't say anything, Jess," he murmured huskily. "For once, just shut your pretty mouth. Get on the train."

Jessica swallowed hard, staring into his dark pooled eyes. Then she spun around and hurried aboard.

Adam watched Jessica through the window until

she found a seat at the front of the car. He touched his lower lip with his tongue, savoring her taste. How was it that a woman could be all fire and spite and taste like pure honey?

"Sern!"

The voice startled Adam and he turned around. Across the platform a man approached, wearing a federal marshal's badge.

"Marshal. I've been waiting for you. I'm anxious to get on the trail." Adam pushed thoughts of Jessica Landon and her rosy lips out of his mind. She was gone and he was better for it. With that neatly compartmentalized, he could get on with the task at hand. "I've got an office where we can take care of this."

The marshal lifted a hand. "Lead the way, Sern."

Jessica watched from the train window as Adam and the federal marshal disappeared into the depot office. Her hands trembled. She was so angry with Adam she could spit. But she was angrier with herself. How could she have stood there and let him kiss her? Gathering her wits, she grabbed her bag and leaped out of her seat. Getting out the opposite door she'd entered, she hurried to the car to the rear of the train that transported horses. A boy was just closing the doors.

"Stop right there!"

The tow-headed boy looked up in surprise. "Ma'am?"

"I said hold it. I need my horse."

"These horses is all bound for the next stop, M—Ma'am."

"Not my horse," she snapped impatiently. She

glanced around to be sure no one was paying attention and then lifted the heavy iron latch on the door.

"M—Ma'am, y—you can't go in there." He looked at hard packed ground, then at her, then at the ground again. "I—I could lose my job."

"You didn't see anything." Jessica hitched up her skirts and heaved her way up into the cattle car. "You think you could let down the ramp?"

"I—I'm tellin' you, I ain't s—suppose to let the passengers into th—the c—car."

"Look . . ." She threw her canvas bag over her shoulder. "Now you can slide the ramp down and let me lead her out quietly, or I can just ride her out and cause a commotion."

Before the words were out of her mouth, the boy was hurrying to do her bidding. "Wh—what am I supposed to say if someone asks me who u—unloaded a horse. Th—they're gonna come up one shy next s—stop they make."

Jessica grabbed her saddle and bridle and grasped Hera's halter. "Tell them . . . Tell them it was Mr. Sern. Deputy Marshal Adam Sern." She laughed as she led her horse down the metal ramp and away from the train depot where she could saddle up. She was still laughing when she disappeared from the boy's sight.

Chapter Six

Riding east in the direction of Logan, Jessica headed out of Loco. She'd gotten directions to Sharpston from Pauline. "Take the old wagon trail t'ward Logan and bear left at the fork 'fore you hit it. Sharpston'll be ten miles north—northwesterly," the barmaid had said. Jessica just hoped her directions were reliable. The girl said she'd only been there once in her lifetime, with her ma and a wagonful of ladies and that had been years ago.

Jessica had no trouble picking up the wagon trail Pauline had indicated would be two miles out of town. The sun-bleached bones of horses and cattle lay in piles along the path. The skeletal remains of wagon beds and wheels protruded from the ground. Occasionally she passed a simple cross marking a lonely grave. It was all evidence of the travelers that had made the trek northwest to Oregon before the railroads had come.

The sounds of insects chirping melded with the rhythmic pounding of Hera's hooves and the squeak of saddle leather. Small animals dove for the cover of tufts of grass as Jessica rode down the narrow trail carved into the earth by the wagon wheels and horses' hooves of years past.

Again and again Adam Sern came to mind. No matter how hard Jessica tried not to think about him, he kept popping up. She smelled his haunting scent on the hot wind. She felt his touch through her leather gloves. Even now his kiss burned her lips.

Adam was responsible for Mark's death. She hated him for it. But as much as that was a truth, so was it true that she had wanted him there in the train station, wanted him as she had never wanted any man. She had felt her breasts tingle, her stomach grow warm and queasy. Her response to Adam's touch had been nothing like her response to Jacob Dorchester.

"Jacob," she said aloud and then gave a derisive snort. His name left a bad taste in her mouth. How could her father have been so utterly taken by such a man? How could he have given her to him like that, sold her like some brood mare?

Jessica shivered despite the hot sun. "That part of my life is over," she said aloud. "I don't have to think about Jacob. Not ever again."

Hera's ears twitched at the sound of Jessica's voice and she laughed, patting the mare's neck. "We'll settle matters with this bandit and then we'll head out to Seattle," she told her mount. "I'm sorry you had to lose Zeus, but we all have to make sacrifices, don't we, Hera?"

Morning passed and the hot sun rose high in the sky and began to fall. Jessica rode on and on, marveling at the unfamiliar landscape. She'd seen nothing but dry desolation since before they'd hit Salt Lake City, but still, she found the land intriguing. She was in awe of the wide expanses and the great open sky.

Jessica sipped from her new tin canteen on and off during the day to quench her thirst. As evening approached she began to get nervous about finding water. She hadn't come upon a stream all day, not even a dry bed. God, what she would give for a cool drink and bath. The powdery dust that sifted through her clothing had mixed with sweat making her gritty and tired.

Finally, at dusk, Jessica came upon a slow-moving muddy stream that she surmised must have been running off the mountain range she could see far to the east. Relieved, she followed it half a mile off the wagon trail and hobbled Hera in a patch of green and brown grass. Spreading out the saddle blanket on the ground, she made camp with the few provisions she had brought along. There was a small coffeepot, some coffee, a tin cup, a handful of dried beef and a few biscuits taken from the kitchen of the Red Moon Saloon this morning. Building a small fire, Jessica filled the little pot with water and let it heat. She had meant to bathe, but she was suddenly so tired that she thought she would rest first. A cooling breeze came in with the setting sun and she relaxed, stretching out on the ground and cradling her head on her saddle. Though the beef and biscuits were hard and dry, the coffee was fragrant and soothing.

After she had finished her meal, Jessica lay back on the ground again and stared up at the great dark sky filled with twinkling stars. Oddly, she wasn't frightened by the night sounds of scurrying nocturnal animals, and the occasional cry of a coyote far in the distance. She felt peaceful inside tonight. She had a job to do and she knew she would accomplish it, or die trying. She smiled in the darkness, rolling into her saddle blanket. Her father had always said that was one of her best attributes—her determination. Nothing or no one could stop Jessica Landon from getting what she wanted once she made up her mind.

Adam Sern popped into her head and Jessica gave a groan. "Go away," she said irritably.

Hera's ears pricked at the sound of Jessica's voice. "It's all right, girl," Jessica soothed. "Just chasing away the demons." But the demons didn't go away. They were there everytime she closed her eyes. Again and again her mind replayed the scene at the train. It wasn't so much that he had kissed her, other men had done so before. But she had never enjoyed a man's kiss, not like she had enjoyed Adam's. With a sigh, she curled into a ball and drifted off to sleep with Adam still on her mind.

Jessica never heard a sound. Suddenly her blanket was pulled off and she was wide awake, frozen with terror. The derringer she'd bought a few days before was tucked out of reach in her bag. Her eyes flew open.

For a moment she thought she was still dreaming. It was Adam. He was standing over her, his face dark and stoney, her blanket clenched in his hand. By the position of the moon, she could tell she hadn't been sleeping long.

"Adam?"

He threw her blanket aside. "What the hell are you doing out here? You're lucky you haven't gotten skinned alive!"

She sat up, rubbing the sleep from her eyes. "What are you talking about? There aren't any Indians left out here. I read it in the newspaper."

"You believe everything you read? Not two weeks ago a man and his wife were killed just outside of Logan."

"Horse thieves. I read about it back in Salt Lake City."

"Horse thieves, true, but they're Ute and a bad bunch at that. They've got a Kiowa leader called Crooked Nose."

"The article didn't say it was Indians, just horse thieves," she murmured sleepily.

"I don't suppose the article told you the man and wife were tortured? It didn't tell you how long that poor woman lived before they finally killed her either, did it?"

Tears rose in Jessica's eyes and she blinked them away. "How do you know so much?"

"It doesn't matter." He rested his hands on his hips, staring down at her. "Now tell me what you're doing out here in the middle of nowhere with a beacon fire burning."

She got up and went to her campfire and picked up a stick to toss into it.

Adam jerked the wood from her hand and sent it hurling into the air. "Answer me!" he barked in a low, threatening voice.

"I told you!" She stared at him through the darkness, her jaw set. "I'm going after the outlaws. I'm going to get my carpetbag back and I'm going to kill the man who murdered my brother."

"That doesn't tell me why you're *here*."

Jessica watched him compress his hands into tight fists. "I'm headed for Sharpston, of course. That's where they were last seen. Besides that's where Elmo Shine is. They say he used to ride with them."

Adam broke into a grin. "You're going to Sharpston, *this way?*"

"This is the right way, isn't it?"

"If you're going to circumnavigate the world. Sharpston is *west* of Logan, you're headed north. You'd walk right by it."

Jessica's face grew pale. She swallowed. "Pauline said I could take this trail to Logan and then take the left fork before I hit town."

"That fork leads north of Logan to *Sparkston* and that old town has been abandoned for years. Some fools tried their hand at mining, half of them died of cholera and the other half of whiskey." He paused. "Of course they say that's where the Ute horse thieves hole up. Maybe you could ask Crooked Nose if *he's* seen Shiner."

Jessica looked away, fighting the lump that was rising in her throat. How was she going to kill Mark's murderer if she couldn't find him? She couldn't track and she was unfamiliar with the territory. If she wasn't murdered by horse thieves, she would likely die of thirst.

She stared at the dying fire, ignoring Adam who

84

was pouring himself a cup of her coffee. The thought occurred to her that she should just give up. She should get on a train in Logan and set out for Seattle. She could join the Wiedenhoefts. They were nice enough people. She might enjoy living with them and their children.

But when she thought of Mark lying dead on the train seat, blood staining his chest, she knew she couldn't give up. If she couldn't track the Black Bandit down on her own, she'd get help.

Jessica lifted her eyes to watch Adam settle by the fire. He rested a Jennings repeater rifle across his lap and sipped the coffee from her new tin cup.

"Well?" he said.

"Well what?" She watched the light and dark shadows of the fire dance across his bronze face.

"Well, go ahead and say what you were going to say. I can see your jaw flapping."

She snapped her mouth shut. What made him so arrogant? What made him think he knew everything? He didn't. He didn't know what the bandit looked like, did he? She took a deep breath. "I was thinking, that since you and I are after the same thing we ought to—well, you know, join up."

He broke into a grin. "Join up, madam?"

"Catch the bandit together. They told me down at the depot your job's on the line. They said there was even talk of prosecution. Nobody thinks you're part of the bunch, but they say it won't matter."

Adam scowled, tossing the remainder of his coffee into the dirt. "Me, take you along? You're joking, right? Too long in the hot sun?"

Jessica kicked a tuft of grass and dirt sprayed at

him, dusting his chest. "I don't appreciate your jokes! You think you know everything. Well, you don't! What you don't know is that you need me."

"Need you?" He chuckled. "I need a woman on the trail like a coyote needs pockets."

"Guess I just met the first coyote that needs pockets, because you need me, Adam, like it or not. I can help you catch the Black Bandit."

"How?" He stretched out, tucking his hands behind his head. "Just for the sake of argument."

"Let's say you get into Sharpston and the Black Bandit's there. How do you recognize him? How do you know he's not sitting in the barber's chair next to you? He's avoided being caught because no one recognizes him. No one has ever seen his face in a holdup." She paused a moment before dealing her final card. "No one but me."

Adam sat up. Was she telling the truth? "When did you see his face?"

"When we fell on the floor, after you were hit. I pulled off his bandanna, trying to get up."

"You got a good look?" His eyes narrowed. "You could identify him if you saw him again?"

"In an instant. I'll never forget those eyes."

Adam's gaze fell to the burning campfire. He hadn't counted on this. Why did it have to be Jessica? It could have been anyone on that train. Fate was a funny thing, his mother had always said. Life was in the stars, already mapped out before we were ever born. He looked at Jessica standing there in the darkness watching him. He could feel his heart pounding in his chest. Was Jessica Landon his fate?

"You think you could describe him for a newspaper artist. If we could get a sketch—"

"I could, but I won't."

"You could be fined for withholding information—jailed."

Jessica laid down, rested her head on her saddle, and pulled her blanket over her shoulders. She knew she had him. She had seen the look of defeat in his eyes. "So jail me, Adam. That, or shut up so I can get some sleep."

Jessica woke before dawn to find Adam saddling Zeus. She scrambled up. "Time to move already?"

He ignored her.

Scratching her head sleepily, Jessica began to pack up camp. After refilling her water can, she saddled Hera. By the time she mounted, Adam had been waiting ten minutes on her. The moment she hit the saddle he rode off, backtracking the way she'd come.

All morning Jessica rode beside Adam, keeping up, but just barely. They rode into Sharpston at noon.

"You keep your mouth shut, you understand me?" Adam told her. He was in a black mood, his mouth twisted in a scowl.

"Does this mean we're going to find this man together?"

He rode up to a saloon and dismounted. "There's a general store down the street. Get some provisions. A saddlebag, another canteen, bacon, beans, a good knife." He glanced at her. Her skirt had fallen back to expose all of her calf and a good deal of her shapely thigh. "And some decent clothes," he amended gruffly.

"Decent clothes?" She looked down at her leather riding skirt and cotton blouse thinking she'd dressed quite sensibly.

"You've got to wear something under that skirt besides those damned long legs of yours."

Her cheeks colored as she straightened her skirt as best she could. She'd never discussed her under-clothing with a man and certainly not a man like Adam. "It's too hot for bloomers."

"Just do as I say. It might keep you from a spider bite. Besides you'll need something to wear crossing the rivers."

"Crossing rivers?" She arched a feathery eyebrow. "How far do you think we'll have to go?"

He tied his Appaloosa securely to the hitching post. "Maybe we'll find him right here in town, but probably not. I don't know how far we'll have to go, but my opinion is that you may be in for a long haul, Jessica."

She watched him walk through the saloon doors. "Hell and fire, Hera, that man's irritable!" She directed the mare up the street.

The storekeeper of McCall's General Store and Apothecary was a short man with a handlebar mustache that seemed to reach to his pointy ears. When Jessica entered the store, he popped off a stool and came around the counter offering his hand.

"Afternoon, miss. Can I help you?"

Jessica stared at the snakes in the cages lined up on the counter with the jars of horehound candy. A rattlesnake hissed at her, shaking its tail in a hollow, deathly rattle.

"Oh, don't mind them. That's my boys."

"Your boys?" She swallowed. She had heard of rattlesnakes, but this was the first she'd ever seen.

"My boys. That's Matthew"—he indicated the rattler—"Mark, Luke, and John. Had 'em for years. Make fine pets. Would you care to get a better look? I could take one out." He reached for the latch on Luke's cage.

"No, no." Jessica put up her hands. "I'm kind of in a hurry. If you could just help me make a few purchases."

"Where you headed?"

She eyed the snake cages nervously. "I'm not sure. I'm riding with Adam Sern. We're going after the Black Bandit and his men."

The storekeeper gave a low whistle. "Sern, taking a lady? Damned if I ain't heard it all now. You his wife?"

Jessica laughed. "Not hardly. The Black Bandit killed my brother and I intend to see justice served." She saw no need to tell him *she* intended to dole out the justice.

He twirled one of the handlebars on his mustache studying her intently. "You must be one hell of a lady to ride with that half-breed. They say he ain't got no heart. Say he left it in Ca-na-dy. That's where he's from you know."

"Look, Mr. McCall, Sern's waiting on me, so if you could just sell me a saddlebag and few odds and ends, I'll be on my way."

"That I can do, but the name's not McCall." He rummaged around in a wooden crate near the door.

"The sign out front says McCall. You're not the

owner?'' She glanced about the one-room store. It was poorly stocked and the roof leaked. There were several buckets placed strategically around the room to catch any summer rain.

"I'm the owner, but my name's Nelson. I won this store off'en McCall. Played three nights straight. My full house took his store, his horse, his daughter, and a worthless mine down Ogden way."

"His daughter?" Jessica watched the man cut a hunk of cured bacon.

"Lucretia." He gave nod. "Sweet little thing. She weren't but thirteen, but she made a fine wife. We got three sons, healthy as mules."

"What happened to McCall?"

"Darned if I know. Rode out of here on a burro. That was three years ago and we ain't seen him since." He wrapped the bacon in newspaper. "How 'bout a little cornmeal?"

"Whatever you think we'll need. But I can only take what I can carry in those saddlebags."

The cow bell on the door rang, and Jessica turned to see who was coming into the store. It was Adam. She gave a little smile. "Find anything out?"

"Aren't you done yet?"

Nelson quickly stuffed several paper-wrapped items into the new leather saddlebag. "Just about got her set. Having a sale on provision packs. Nice skinnin' knife, canteen, needle and thread, laudanum, fry pan, you name it and she's got it."

Adam glanced at Jessica. "You get some drawers?"

Her cheeks colored. "Mr. Nelson. Have you got something in the way of ladies' clothing?"

"Not much. Go on through the back curtain and

90

let my wife show you what's back there. We don't get much call for ladies' clothes. The whores are the only ones in town that buys much." The storekeeper looked over his shoulder. "Lucretia," he shouted. "Lucretia!"

A moment later a young girl stepped shyly from behind the curtain in the back doorway. "Wayne?" She spoke slowly, drawling out the sound of each letter.

"Lucretia, honey, take this lady back and see what you can do for her about some drawers."

"Don't know that we got any drawers, Wayne," the girl went on, slowly.

Impatiently, Adam shifted his weight from one leg to the other.

Nelson looked up at Adam's face and waved at his wife. "Just take her on back. These folks got to get goin'!"

Jessica followed the girl into the back room.

"Like I said," Lucretia took a breath as if worn out from talking, "we ain't got much in the way of ladies' clothes."

"Just show me what you have. I need bloomers. I've got cotton drawers." Jessica was embarrassed by the whole situation. She just wanted to get out of the store and hear if Adam had found Elmo Shine.

"Right there, that's all we got," the girl answered.

Jessica picked among the pile. There was an old-fashioned corset with bone insets and faded pink ribbons. She tossed it aside. Next she came to a short wool jacket trimmed in velvet. If it fit, it would help keep her warm on a cold night, even if it would look a little silly. She dropped it near the door. She then

91

discarded two pairs of silk stockings, a yellow poke bonnet—she preferred her new black wide-brimmed hat made much like Adam's. At the bottom of the pile was a pair of purple satin bloomers adorned in green scalloped lace. "This is all you've got?"

Lucretia looked at her sympathetically and pushed back a lock of white blond hair. The young girl was breathtakingly beautiful, but barely more than a child. "One of the girls over to the saloon ordered 'em, then she rode out with a gambler 'fore they come in."

Jessica held up the bloomers. They would fit, but they weren't exactly what she had in mind. With a groan, she stepped into them and hiked them up.

"They look right nice," Lucretia said in her dog-slow manner. "Darn if I shouldn't order me a pair."

"They're whore's bloomers," Jessica complained.

"But they're right purty."

"Jessica!" Adam called from the front room. "Let's move. This isn't a social visit."

Jessica snatched up the jacket and came through the curtain. "I'm ready. I just have to pay Mr. Nelson."

Adam's dark eyes followed her movement. "He's paid. You got something on under that skirt?"

She picked up her saddlebags. "Yeah, now let's go."

"Let me see."

She looked up at Adam in disbelief. Color flooded her cheeks. "What?"

"I said, let me see."

"Adam!"

"You want to ride with me? You come prepared.

Now hitch up your skirt and let me see."

Jessica balked. She was embarrassed and angry that Adam would do this to her in front of the storekeeper and his wife.

"Are you with me or not, Jessica?" Adam's voice was low. It was a dare.

"I'm with you, right to the gates of hell if that's how far we have to go to catch the Black Bandit." With that, she dropped the saddlebags to the floor and caught her soft leather skirt, hiking it to her thighs.

Adam threw back his head and laughed at the sight of the whore's purple and green bloomers beneath her sensible riding skirt. He laughed so hard that his eyes went teary. Furious, Jessica snatched up her saddlebags and hurried out. She could still hear Adam's laughter as she slammed the door behind her.

Chapter Seven

"This here was hers." Pauline pushed open the door to the room Jessica had slept in. "Nobody been in it since. I swear it."

Jacob carried his leather valise into the room and laid it on the faded quilt spread on the cot. He lifted his head, sniffing deeply as he let his eyes drift shut. The scent of Jessica's fresh, young body still lingered in the room. "How long has she been gone?"

"Two days," Pauline told the silver-haired gentleman.

Jacob sat down in the single chair and ran his tapered index finger along the washbowl rim. Surely his Jessica must have rinsed her face in this bowl. "Where did she go?"

"Mr. Sern put her on a train for Seattle." Pauline chewed on her lower lip in indecision. Finally she spoke. "But I ain't so sure that's where she's headed just yet."

Jacob looked up. "What do you mean?" When the girl hesitated, he became insistent. "You must tell me! Jessica is my wife."

Pauline's eyes went wide. "Your wife! She didn't say anything about being married. She said she didn't have any kin with her brother bein' dead now."

He stood and wiped his brow with an embroidered handkerchief. "If she didn't go to Seattle where might she have gone?"

"Sharpston, maybe. I gave her directions as best I could. Though I'm not so sure now that I did her a good turn."

"She didn't take the train?"

Pauline chuckled. "Don't no train go through Sharpston. Logan's probably the closest stop."

Jacob folded his handkerchief on the original fold line and then slipped it into his coat. "You said her brother was dead?" It was an afterthought.

"Got shot during that robbery a few days back. Didn't you hear 'bout it? They say it was all over the wires."

Jacob glanced out the window at the miserable, dirty street below. "Where's the boy buried?"

"Right here in Loco, behind the Baptist church. It's the only burin' place we got. Want to see his grave? I can take you there."

"No, that will be all right. But tell me, are you certain it was Mark Landon?"

"Well, Miss Jessica certainly must have known her own brother! She made the arrangements herself."

Feeling weak, Jacob removed his bowler hat and sat down on the cot. "I believe I'll rest and then take my supper here in my room."

Pauline grimaced. "Guests usually eat downstairs

in the saloon.''

"I'll pay you for your trouble." He stretched out on the cot, feeling light-headed, but took care not to let his boot heels touch the quilt. "Right now I'd like you leave me be. Later I'll have you direct me toward the telegraph office. I'll need to send my lawyer a wire concerning the boy's death.''

Although she knew she'd been dismissed, Pauline hung in the doorway. There was something about the gentleman that didn't quite fit. How could Jessica have married a man like this?

"That will be all," Jacob said sharply.

Pauline bobbed a curtsy and hurried out of the room, closing the door behind her. As she walked down the hall she wished she hadn't offered so much information to Mr. Dorchester. If there was one thing she had learned growing up in a whorehouse, it was which men were dangerous and which weren't. It was instinct, her mother had told her. Well, this man was dangerous. She could smell it on his toilet-water breath.

Jessica was strapping her saddlebags on Hera's back when Adam came out of the general store with a few more items. In silence he packed them on Zeus' back and then gave a nod. "This way.''

"Where are we going?" Jessica slipped the last buckle and hurried after him, her anger over the bloomers forgotten.

"Think before you speak, Jess." Adam tapped his temple with a bronze forefinger. "Why did we come to Sharpston?"

"To see Elmo Shine." She caught up with him, and stretched to match his stride. "You found Shiner?" She broke into a smile. "I *knew* we could do this together!"

"I don't see *we* doing anything. I'm doing the looking while you yap."

Jessica chose to ignore his comment. "Where is he?"

"The saloon keeper said that if it was before three, we could find him at the livery stable."

"He works there?"

"No, he sleeps off his drunks."

Jessica rolled her eyes. "Great. He'll be loads of help."

They came to the livery stable and Adam stepped back, extending a hand. "Ladies first. I thought I'd let you do the talking. It seems to be your talent."

She walked through the archway into the dim stable. The air smelled of hay and must and fresh horse dung. Dust motes floated in the rays of sunshine pouring through the small windows.

A man stepped out in front of Jessica and she stopped short. "Can I help you, little lady?"

She stared at the bearded man. "Um, yes. I'm looking for Elmo Shine. The saloon keeper said we could find him here."

The livery stable owner glanced at Adam, then took a step back. "You got to be Sern. There's only one lawman in these parts that's a redskin."

"Is he here or not?" Adam's voice was cool and forceful.

"Old Shiner, hell yeah, he's here. He in trouble

with the law?''

"Where is he?" Jessica looked around but saw nothing but horses in box stalls and tack hanging from the beams. "We just want to ask him a few questions."

The man stepped back. "The hay pile most likely." He jerked his head toward the rear of the dilapidated stable.

Jessica led the way, picking her way through piles of manure and broken wagon pieces. In a back corner there was a pile of fresh hay stacked nearly to the ceiling. She could make out the shape of a man curled into a ball at the bottom of the stack. Jessica glanced doubtfully over her shoulder, but Adam only offered a sardonic smile.

"Mr. Shine," she called as she approached the sleeping man. "Mr. Shine."

The man gave a groan but made no attempt to lift his head off the hay.

"Mr. Shine, I need to talk to you." Jessica gave him a push with the toe of her boot. He reeked of cheap liquor and human urine. "Mr. Shine?"

Elmo rolled over onto his back and stared up, trying to focus. "Gladys? That you?"

"Mr. Shine, my name is Jessica Landon and I need to speak with you."

He sat up and scratched his armpit. His face was tanned and wrinkled by the sun; his head sported a shock of white hair. "You ain't Gladys, are you?" He seemed disappointed.

"No, sir. Are you well enough to talk?" She crouched down to stare into his bloodshot eyes. His whiskey breath was enough to turn her stomach. "Mr. Shine, I'm told you rode with the Black Bandit."

Elmo looked up with interest. "Darn right I did, but don't nobody believe me. Nobody knew me 'fore I was a drunk. Nobody believes I'm a sharpshooter. That damned Larry, he couldn't shoot the broadside of a whore's bottom."

Adam stooped beside Jessica. "Larry? You mean the Black Bandit?"

Elmo wiped his mouth with his filthy sleeve. "That Black Bandit stuff, the newspapers made up. They called him that 'cause he always wears that darned black bandanna. His name's Larry Caine. 'Course he don't go by that 'lessin' he's feelin' cocky."

Jessica looked at Adam and smiled. "I think we should take Mr. Shine over to the barber, get him a bath and a shave, find some clothes, and fill him with a hot meal."

Adam winked. "Just what I was thinking."

Shaved and wearing a fresh set of clothes, Elmo Shine looked like a new man sitting across the table from Jessica.

"Yup, a Texas Ranger I was. Down on the Rio Grande."

"So what makes a Texas Ranger join with a man like Larry Caine?" Adam watched Shiner shovel beans into his mouth.

"Got restless. Just picked up with the wrong bunch, I guess. I didn't realize what they were doin'

100

'til it was too late to get out. First it was just a little *regulatin'*, then they went to robbin' a bank here and there. When I said I wanted out, Larry carried my wife, Gladys, off and shot me and left me for the buzzards down Kansas way." He sopped up the remainder of the bean drippings with a biscuit, and crammed it into his mouth. "It was just luck a man and his wife come along and picked me up."

Jessica leaned across the table. "I want you to help me, Mr. Shine."

He pushed back his plate. "Call me Shiner. I ain't Mr. to nobody no more."

"All right, Shiner. I need your help." She looked at Adam. "We both need your help. This Larry Caine and his men killed my brother during a train robbery."

Shiner shook his head. "I knew it was Larry the minute I started hearin' 'bout those train robberies. It's just like him to ride the train and let the boys do the work. Larry always did have a lazy streak in him."

"Shiner. Do you know where he might be? Do you know where we could find him?"

Shiner pushed back in his chair and thrust a toothpick between his teeth. "You aim to go after him?"

"I've been sent to bring him back to Salt Lake City to stand trial," Adam answered.

Jessica glanced at Adam, wondering if he realized she had no intentions of letting Larry Caine live long enough to stand trial.

"I got a few ideas where he might be." Shiner reached for his beer. "I could take you."

Jessica shook her head. "That's not necessary,

101

Shiner. Just tell us. There's no need for you to risk your own life."

Shiner slapped his palm on the table. "Missy, that man took my wife, raped her, let the boys have a go at her, then slit her throat. They found her a few days after they found me." Tears rose in his eyes. "Larry took my pride, then my wife, then my dignity. You think my life means anything to me?"

Jessica turned her gaze to Adam and he nodded slightly. He held her in his power for a moment and she remembered his tenderness after Mark's funeral. She looked back at Shiner. "If we get you a horse, can you be ready to ride by morning?"

"Tonight," Adam corrected. "We ride tonight."

Shiner wiped at his tears, feeling foolish. "I can ride tonight. I know two places right off hand. I was through these parts with Larry six, seven, years back."

Adam stood. "I'll take care of the horse, you just see that you don't get drunk before sunset."

Shiner looked up at the half-breed deputy. "I give you my word, as a Texas Ranger."

Jessica slid out of her seat and followed Adam. "You think we can trust Shiner?" she asked at the door.

Adam nodded. "I don't know why I didn't chase him down three months ago when I heard about him. Everyone told me he was a liar, I assumed they were right. But that man"—he shook his finger—"his pain is real. He's telling the truth all right."

She folded her arms over her chest, looking back at the old Texas Ranger. She liked talking like this to Adam . . . as an equal. It was comfortable, like a worn saddle. "I thought the same. I just didn't know if taking him with us was a good idea."

"Directions can be a funny thing out here. If the man's willing to take us, we'd be fools not to accept." Adam's hand fell to his pistol and he absently stroked its onyx handle. "Look, Jess. I thought maybe you could just stay put tonight. No sense in you losing sleep. Even if we're lucky it'll be days before we catch up with them."

Jessica smiled. "Oh, no you don't. I stay here, you take Shiner, and that'll be the last I see of Adam Sern. You think I'm stupid? I'm going with you."

He studied his boots, then lifted his gaze to take in her lovely face. "I'm having second thoughts. Taking a woman—"

She cut him off before he could finish. "Adam, you're not responsible for me. This is my decision. I'm going after Larry Caine with or without your help. If you're so concerned, you'll keep me beside you"—she grinned—"where you can keep an eye on me."

On impulse Adam reached out and caught a lock of her hair that had come loose from the braid she wore down her back. She watched him, wondering if he would try to kiss her again . . . half hoping.

Suddenly, Adam released her hair and spun on his heels. "Be mounted at sunset," he said and then walked out the door.

Adam, Jessica, and Elmo Shine rode out of Sharpston, Utah, at sunset and headed west toward the Wasatch range of mountains. They rode side by side, talking little. Occasionally the two men dismounted and studied "the signs." Jessica couldn't understand how they could possibly gather any information from tracks in the dirt, but she kept silent. The terrain grew steeper and they began to climb, riding old paths cut through the wooded mountains.

Jessica rubbed her neck, shifting in her saddle. The summer night air grew cool and she shrugged on the short wool jacket she'd bought at the general store. The excitement of setting out in search of Larry Caine and his outfit had worn off and now she was just plain tired. Hera's gait was so rhythmic and steady that several times she found herself drifting to sleep. Each time, she shook the cobwebs from her head, mentally chastising herself. If she wanted to ride with Adam she knew she had to stay alert. With Shiner at his side, she wouldn't put it past Adam to leave her behind.

The waning moon rose high in the sky and began to fall, and still they rode on. Shiner's first guess had led to nothing but an empty log cabin so they moved on, riding up through the mountains. Despite the chill, Jessica had to fight hard to stay awake. How far were they riding? The sky was already turning pink in the east. The sun would soon be up.

Suddenly Jessica realized someone was pulling her out of her saddle. Startled, her eyes flew open and she met Adam's gaze. He pressed a finger to his lips and then pointed. In the dim morning light she could make out a column of smoke rising above the trees in the distance.

Adam brought his lips to her ear. "An abandoned

logging camp," he whispered. "Shiner says it's probably them."

She nodded. His warm breath in her ear made her feel dizzy. "So what do we do? Ride in now before it gets light out?"

He smiled, keeping his hand on the small of her back to steady her. "You've been reading too many newspapers. We don't do anything now but wait. We don't know who it is or how many there are."

"Where's Shiner?" she whispered.

Adam's arm fell comfortably on her shoulder as he leaned to speak again. "Gone to take a look. Why don't you lay out your bedroll and get a little sleep. It's going to be a long day."

After a short nap, Jessica sat in the brush, watching the smoke, wondering if Larry Caine was at the bottom of the hill. Again and again she checked her derringer. All day Shiner and Adam took turns sneaking through the woods, down the side of the mountain the three-quarters of a mile to where the logging camp stood. By midmorning Shiner had identified three of the men in the cabin as men who rode with the Black Bandit, but there was still no sign of Larry Caine. Finally Jessica got a chance to go down and have a look with Adam late in the afternoon.

For a long time she crouched in the green foliage beside him, watching in silence. Laughter and an occasional shout came from the cabin. Twice, men wandered out into the yard to walk to the outhouse or simply relieve himself in the grass.

Adam only chuckled. "You stay put and I'll send Shiner down. I think I'll circle around back and give my legs a stretch—see what I can see from that angle."

Jessica impulsively reached out and touched his arm. "Be careful," she warned.

He smiled and nodded. "You just stay where you are and if any shooting starts, you go back to the horses and wait. You know the way back to Sharpston."

She gave a half laugh. "I'm not going anywhere without you."

"I mean if we're killed, Jess," he said softly.

She nodded, trying to hide her fear at the thought of something happening to Adam. "I can find my way back."

He squeezed her hand and then took his rifle and slipped through the brush. A few minutes later, Shiner appeared.

"Seen anything, girl?"

Jessica shook her head. "No sign of him yet."

"Yeah, well, he's a sly dog, that one." Shiner removed a small flask from his coat and took a sip. He offered the bottle to Jessica, but she refused.

"If he's here, why haven't we seen him?" she asked impatiently.

"Maybe he ain't here. Maybe he went into some town to celebrate, to deposit money even. They say he's got accounts in half the banks in these parts. Course maybe"—Shiner returned his flask to his coat pocket—"just maybe the bird ain't got out of the sack yet."

Jessica pushed her hat off her head and wiped her brow. She was hot and tired and her legs were beginning to ache. Carefully she eased herself to a sitting position. "Do you see Adam?"

"No, but he's out there. Them Injuns, they can slip right under your nose and ya never see 'em 'til it's too late."

Jessica smiled. "He's the first one I've ever met, even seen up close. A girl over in Loco said he was just a half-breed, but I don't know."

Suddenly Shiner rose to his feet.

"What? What is it?" She tugged on his coat.

Shiner crooked his finger, breaking into a broken-toothed grin.

Jessica stood and looked down the mountain through the trees. Her breath caught in her throat. It was him! The Black Bandit!

"That's him, isn't it?" she whispered.

"Daggoned if it ain't, the son of a bitch!" Shiner cocked his rifle.

"Wait." Jessica laid her hand on Shiner's barrel. "We have to wait for Adam to come back. We have to have a plan."

"Plan!" Shiner gave a snort. "I thought I'd just save the deputy marshal the trouble of haulin' Mr. Larry Caine all the way back to Salt Lake City. Thought I'd just kill him myself."

Jessica watched her brother's murderer hang a piece of mirror from a tree branch and wet his face with water from a basin. "Not if I can get to him first, Shiner."

The old Texas Ranger glanced at her. "Got a vicious streak in you, don't you, girlie?"

She pulled her pistol from her belt and spun the cylinder to be certain every chamber was loaded. "The man murdered my little brother and took every

107

possession I owned. I can't get Mark back, but I can get my carpetbag."

"Well, if he's still got that bag of yours, you just leave it to Elmo Shine. I'll get her back." He started down the mountain.

"Wait! Where're you going?" she whispered.

"Down to get a closer look-see."

"We should wait for Adam." She watched Caine lather his face with soap and reach for a straight-edged razor.

"I just wanna be sure it's him. My eyes ain't as good as they once was."

Jessica started to go with him, but then crouched in the cover of the trees. Instinct told her to wait for Adam. She watched Shiner make his descent, carefully picking his way down the slippery bank.

Then, all at once, Shiner's feet went out from under him and he went sliding down the side of the mountain.

Larry Caine jumped up and reached for a rifle that leaned against a tree. "Boys!" He ran for the cover of the cabin as men spilled out, rifles aimed.

"Up there!" Larry shouted, his voice echoing in the treetops.

Shiner scrambled to his feet and opened fire. A bare-chested man fell immediately.

"How many?" one of the men shouted.

"Can't tell," another answered, diving for the cover of a rain barrel.

Someone came running up behind Jessica and she whirled around, her pistol aimed. It was Adam.

"What the hell happened?" he demanded, slinging a belt of ammunition over his shoulder.

"I told Shiner to wait, but he wanted to have a look. Caine's down there, I saw him."

"Where? Which one is he?"

Jessica parted some branches. "He's gone. Inside, I guess. He was wearing dark pants and that red shirt of his. Brown hair."

Adam caught Jessica's shoulder. "You stay here. I get into trouble and you ride like thunder out of here, you understand me?"

But Jessica was already running behind him. "I'm not staying out here by myself!"

The moment Adam was in range he began to fire. Caine's men had taken refuge behind a turned-over wagon and a few outbuildings. Shiner fired and reloaded his ancient Henry rifle as fast as he could.

Jessica watched the confusion, no longer flinching with each rifle shot. She held her pistol tightly in her hand, watching the door to the cabin, waiting for the Black Bandit.

Jessica heard Adam's cry before she saw him fall. Before it registered that he had been hit, he was already rolling down the side of the mountain into the line of fire.

"Adam!" she screamed.

"Run, Jess! Run!" he managed and he rolled over and over again leaving a trail of blood in the pine needles.

Jessica scrambled down the mountain after him.

Chapter Eight

When Jessica reached Adam he was laying with his face on the ground, his rifle pinned beneath him. "Adam!" She rolled him over, keeping low in the brush. The outlaws were still firing. Bullets whizzed over her head, ricocheting off the tree trunks. "Adam!" She grabbed his shoulders and shook him. There was so much blood on his shirt that she couldn't tell where he'd been hit.

Shiner kept up the gunfire as he crossed toward Adam and Jessica. "He hit bad?" The Texas Ranger reloaded his rifle rapidly.

"I don't know!" she answered, amazed at how calm she remained. She tucked her pistol into her belt and took Adam's face between her palms. "Adam, can you hear me?" She shook him again. "Adam, for God's sake, answer me!"

His eyelids fluttered. "Jess?"

"Yes, yes, I'm here."

"Damn! I've been shot," he said weakly. "Must be losing my touch." He tried to laugh.

"You've got to get up, Adam. We can't stay here."
She took his hands. "You've got to get to the horses.
We stay here and they'll kill us all."

Adam pulled himself to a seated position. He
pressed his hand to his left shoulder. "It's not that
bad. Just give me a second. I can still shoot." His
speech was slightly slurred as if he'd been drinking.

"You're bleeding like a stuck pig." She let go of his
hands, and steadied him with her knee as she picked
up his rifle. "How're you going to shoot if you can't
walk?" She offered her hand. "Come on, Adam, for
me. On your feet."

Shiner kept up the fire, but the outlaws were
beginning to move closer, realizing there was only
one rifleman in the trees. "You two best git while the
gittin's good," Shiner flung over his shoulder.

"We're not leaving you here," Jessica protested,
helping Adam to stand. "We'll take care of Adam,
then we'll come back in a day or two."

"We won't all get out of here," Shiner answered.
"There's too many of 'em."

"I can't leave you here!"

Adam leaned heavily on her, his arm wrapped
around her shoulder. "He's right, Jess." His breath
was slow and labored. "We won't all make it out. I'll
stay."

"Hell, you will!" Shiner reloaded his Henry.
"Miss Landon, you just get the deputy marshal up to
them horses and ride like hell. I'll take care of this
bunch. Seems I owe 'em one."

"You'll just hold them back until we get mounted,
won't you? You'll be right behind us, won't you?"

The Texas Ranger grinned. "Right behind you,

girlie." Then he took off, with a war whoop, racing straight down the mountain toward the outlaws.

Jessica and Adam stumbled up the side of the steeply overgrown bank. Twice they both fell, and once Jessica dropped Adam's rifle, but somehow they managed to reach the horses. Adam slumped to the ground.

"Oh no, you don't." She grabbed him beneath the armpits and pulled with all her might. "You've got to get on Zeus. I can't lift you."

On the second try Adam mounted the horse. He hung onto the pummel, his head sagging.

Jessica mounted. "Do we go or wait on Shiner?" She rested her hand on Adam's thigh, afraid he was going to fall off his horse.

"He said he'd catch up," Adam answered, trying to sit upright.

The sound of crashing underbrush caught Jessica's attention. "Here he comes!"

Out of the bushes came Shiner. "Run! Run!" he cried.

To Jessica's horror he was soaked in blood, his rifle was gone, but he was still running.

Someone was coming up the mountain after him. The hidden outlaw fired and Shiner went down. The outlaw burst through the underbrush and before Jessica could think, she swung her rifle onto her shoulder and beaded in on the murderer. She recognized him as one of the bandits who had been on the train the day of the robbery.

The outlaw shot, and Zeus shied, racing up the mountain, with Adam clinging to his back. Jessica pulled her trigger and the outlaw stumbled backward under the impact of the bullet.

Jessica wheeled Hera around and rode up beside Shiner. There was no breath left in his body. Up close she could count four wounds. A tear trickled down her cheek.

The sound of gunfire drawing closer warned her of the approaching men. "I hate to leave you here," she whispered.

"Jessica!" Adam cried weakly.

She gazed up to see him fifty yards ahead of her. "He's dead."

"Come on, sweetheart. He didn't mean to make it back."

Jessica glanced down at the Texas Ranger again.

"Damn it!" Adam cried. "Let's move!"

Wiping her tears with the back of her hand, Jessica caught Shiner's horse's reins and rode after Adam.

Jessica rode behind Adam, praying he didn't pass out and fall off his horse. If he fell, she would never get him astride again. They rode as hard as they could through the dense mountain overgrowth. In the time that it took for the outlaws to return to camp and mount their horses, Jessica and Adam had turned off the path and cut north along a ridge, hoping to lose them.

Finally Adam and Jessica slowed their horses to a walk to give them a breather. She rode up beside him, resting her hand on his arm. His handsome bronze face was pallid and drawn, his eyes half closed. There was a sheen of fever-induced perspiration across his forehead.

"Adam?"

His dark eyes met hers. "I'm all right."

"We need to stop and let me get a look at that shoulder."

He tried to moisten his parched lips with the tip of his tongue, but his mouth was too dry. "We move on."

She unscrewed the lid from her canteen and brought the water to his mouth. She watched him drink thirstily. "You're burning up with fever. If your shoulder turns green you'll lose the arm, maybe your life."

"They could still be following us." He wiped his mouth on his sleeve. The simple motion set him off balance and he began to slide off the saddle.

Jessica steadied him. "They're not following us. Too drunk. You said so yourself. We've made ten turns since we left them. How can they know where we are if we don't know where we are?"

Adam closed his eyes, trying to muster some strength. "We keep moving."

"It'll be dark soon. The horses are beat."

Adam sunk his heels into Zeus' flanks and the horse broke into an easy trot. He knew that what Jess said made sense, but he wanted to put as much distance between them and the outlaws as possible. He felt so damned guilty. He should never have brought Jessica along. It could have been her that had been hit, been killed. So what if she could identify Larry Caine? It was Adam's responsibility to catch the outlaw, not some young woman's. He had never needed anyone's help before. What had made him think he needed hers? "I said we move on," he called

115

to her gruffly.

Jessica caught up, riding beside him. She knew a fever could keep a man from thinking straight. "All right, we'll ride a little farther, but let's start looking for a place to camp. I'm tired even if you aren't."

"Don't patronize me!"

She studied him through the fading light of early evening. *What was it in his past that makes him so bitter?* she wondered. She had a sudden urge to reach out to him, to comfort him.

They rode for another hour in silence. Occasionally, Jessica spotted a sight that looked suitable for camping, but Adam just rode on, ignoring her. As the sun was setting behind the mountain they climbed, they rode into a small, grassy clearing.

"How about here? I can hear water."

Adam made no reply.

Jessica reined Hera in and patted the horse's neck. It was a perfect spot. She turned to speak to Adam again, just in time to see him neatly knocked off his horse by a low-lying branch.

"Adam!" She leaped off Hera and ran to his side. She knelt and brushed his shiny dark hair off his cheek. He was burning with fever. "Adam?"

"Just keep moving," he managed. "Keep riding."

She nodded. "Right. You'd leave me behind, wouldn't you?"

He opened his eyes and then closed them again. "I might," he croaked.

"I almost believe you," she answered. "You're right, you know. I should be the one leaving you. What do I care what happens to you? It's your fault Mark's dead." She heard her own words, but she felt different about them than she had a few days ago.

Jessica stood abruptly. She caught Zeus, then Hera and Shiner's mount and tied them on short lead lines to trees. Then she began to unload their bags. She debated whether or not to build a fire, but decided one was necessary if she was going to brew some sort of tea to bring down Adam's fever. She gazed up at the trees that stretched high into the sky. The foliage was so dense here in the mountains that she was certain no one would see the smoke or even the flames from any distance. It was a chance, but she decided to take it.

She built a small, hot fire and then went through the woods in search of the stream she heard bubbling in the distance. She felt at home here in the mountains which were much like the Smokies her grandparents had lived in. The only difference seemed to be the altitude. Jessica still found herself short of breath on occasion, but she was adjusting.

After leading the three horses to the stream to drink, she put her coffeepot of water on to boil. Adam remained unconscious, but she managed to roll him onto his bedroll to get him off the damp ground. Making a small torch to light her way, she picked through the grass and weeds nearby, searching for plants she recognized. What Adam needed was a good strong herbal tea to bring down the fever. With that and a poultice on his gunshot wound, he'd be as good as new in a few days.

Much of the plant life was different from what Jessica was familiar with in Tennessee, but she managed to find several plants that she thought were what she needed or close to it. To her delight she found several sprigs of what her grandmother had always called "sow's tail," a guaranteed remedy for a fever. Returning to the camp, she began to boil the leaves and strips of bark she'd gathered.

When the brew was strong enough, she sat on the ground and lifted Adam's head, cradling it in her lap. "Adam."

He stirred.

"Adam, listen to me. I want you to drink this."

She brought her coffee cup to his lips, but he pushed it away. "No," he mumbled. "Got to get you out of here, Jess. Can't see you hurt. My responsibility . . . my fault, not yours."

She spoke sharply. "Adam! Drink this or I'll pour it down your throat. I haven't got time to be a nursemaid. I've got a man to track!"

Sure enough, her harsh words brought him out of his fugue. "You're pushy," he muttered, taking a sip of the tea. "You're too pushy for a woman and this stuff tastes like piss."

She laughed. "Drink it. All of it and then I need to look at your shoulder. It's bleeding again."

Slowly Adam drained the cup and then laid his head back, closing his eyes again.

"Oh, no you don't. You can't sleep yet." Jessica set down the cup. "I want you to roll onto your side so I can look at the exit wound. You're lucky the shot went straight through."

"I don't feel lucky," he answered drowsily. "I can't believe I got shot. It's my own fault. I should have been thinking about what I was doing instead of thinking about you."

"Oh, so it's my fault." She went to the fire and

118

brought back the poultice she'd concocted and a pan of hot water. "I didn't ask you to look after me. I can take care of myself, take care of you, too, it seems."

He closed his eyes. "Christ, you've got a mouth. Why did I have to join up with a woman with a mouth?"

"Because you need me." She dipped a square of cotton rag into the hot water and pressed it to his shoulder.

"Ouch! That's hot."

"You want to lose your arm? I can amputate, you know. I sawed off a leg when I was sixteen."

"What's a girl from Tennessee doing amputating limbs?"

"Actually it was a goat leg, but my grandma said it's the same principle with a man."

"Terrific. I've got a goat mutilator nursing me."

"You sound better already." She eased him onto his back. "I told you my tea was good for you."

Adam rolled onto his side. He didn't like lying here so vulnerable like this. Jessica's touch felt too good against his skin. "Horses taken care of?"

"Watered and tied. There's plenty to eat, so I didn't give them the oats. Thought I'd save them."

"Wise."

"I'm not entirely stupid, Adam." She wrapped his shoulder carefully with a strip of cloth she'd torn from his spare shirt in his saddlebag.

"No," he murmured, catching a lock of her hair. "I don't suppose you are." He brought the hair to his lips and she paused, her green eyes settling on his face. "Sweet," he murmured. "You smell so sweet."

His voice was a soft caress that made her tremble

inside. "Get some sleep," she whispered. "You'll be stiff, but much better by morning. The bleeding stopped and there's no sign of infection." He released her hair and she stood. She offered him a smile and then walked away, utterly confused by the energy, the tenderness that had just passed between them.

Jessica poured the remainder of the tea into her cup and set it aside for morning. She refilled her coffeepot with water and ate another biscuit and a strip of beef while she waited for her coffee to brew. When it was hot and fragrant, she poured the coffee into Adam's cup and stretched out on her bedroll to relax.

When she had retrieved Adam's cup and shirt she had been tempted to look through his saddlebags. She was interested to know what a man like him carried. It somehow seemed like a reflection of the person to know what they packed when they set off on a journey.

Jessica pulled off her boots and warmed her feet by the fire. Though it was summer, it was cool at night high in the mountains. She curled up, thinking of the items she had packed that night she and Mark had slipped out of Jacob's house, that night she'd fled his bedroom.

She'd taken the money, money that was rightfully hers, from Jacob's safe. That was what she and Mark had intended to buy their farm with. But she'd also taken the tintype of her mother, her father's watch, and the stack of recipes written on scraps of paper in her grandmother's flowery handwriting. Those were the things that were dear to her, and those were the things she wanted back if Larry Caine still carried them.

Jessica took a sip of coffee, then looked at the cup. It seemed rather intimate to her to be drinking from a man's cup . . . from Adam's. She glanced across the fire at him.

He lay sleeping peacefully, his saddle blanket thrown over him. By the light of the fire she could see his chest rising and falling evenly. She could also see his face. The color of his skin still fascinated her. It was beautiful. She remembered the conversation she and Kat had had that day on the train and smiled. God, he was handsome. Not handsome like Jacob Dorchester, not pretty. Adam Sern was striking. He was utterly masculine.

She watched Adam's lips part as he breathed and she wondered what it would feel like to kiss him again, to be kissed.

"Oh, God," she moaned aloud. "What's wrong with me?" *The altitude*, she thought. *It's affecting my brain.* She took another sip of coffee and then lay back, resting her head on her saddle. Adam's rifle was within arm's reach.

She closed her eyes, letting her thoughts drift over the day's events—anything to take her mind off Adam Sern and her obvious, wicked desire for him.

She thought of Elmo Shine. She didn't know if he'd really been a Texas Ranger, but he'd fought like one. She only wished he hadn't had to die. As her mind replayed the scene, as she saw Shiner running toward her, the blood covering his chest, tears rose in her eyes.

She had killed a man today. She'd shot him in the chest and watched him fall back, dead before he hit

121

the ground. That realization made her tremble. It was frightening to think that she had killed a man. He had gunned down Shiner and she would have been next. She'd had no other choice. But would she have done it a few weeks ago, a few days ago? It was hard to believe that her life had changed so drastically in the last few weeks, and all because of men who tried to control her—Papa, Jacob, Larry Caine, even Adam.

Her gaze settled on Adam's sleeping form. She wasn't afraid of Jacob. She wasn't afraid of the Black Bandit. But Adam? Adam frightened her. He frightened her because somewhere deep inside he touched her in a way no one had ever touched her before.

Chapter Nine

Jessica woke to the smell of bacon frying and the sound of it sizzling in the pan. She opened her eyes, surprised to see Adam crouching beside her, turning breakfast with a fork.

She yawned. "Adam?"

He turned to her, a smile on his face. He had his right arm in a sling made from the remainder of his shirt she had torn up the night before to make his bandage. "I thought you'd sleep 'til noon."

"Noon?" She ran her hand through her tangled hair. "It's barely sunup. How long have you been awake?"

"A few hours." He watched her as she brushed the sleep from her eyes. There was something about her that drew him to her . . . something about the way her hair fell gloriously disheveled over her shoulder. "I'm not one to sleep long."

She pushed herself up on her elbows to get a better look at his bandages. "No bleeding in the night? Fever gone?"

"I feel fine. Whatever that slimy potion was you gave me, it killed the fever. I gagged the rest of it down this morning."

"It will keep away the infection, too. It was a recipe of my grandmother's."

"My grandmother, She-who-speaks-softly, used to fill me with rotgut like that when I was a child." He shrugged, a nostalgic smile on his lips. "Funny, I never got sick."

Jessica looked up at him, her hand still resting gently on his bandaged shoulder. He had made no move to back off. He just watched her. A strange, exhilarating charge filled the morning air.

"What do you want of me?" she finally whispered. She could feel his light breath on her cheek. His nearness was intoxicating.

"I don't know, Jess." He traced the line of her jaw with the tip of his finger. "I tell myself I want nothing from you or anyone else, but"—he drew in his breath—"there's a bond between us. You feel it, don't you?"

"I feel it," she answered in a half whisper.

Adam smiled, cupping her chin. Slowly he lowered his mouth to hers, brushing his lips. "No good could come of it."

"We shouldn't," she heard herself respond as she wove her fingers through his sleek shining hair. "I mustn't." But as the words slipped from her mouth she was already pulling him to her. She met his gentle, exploring kiss hesitantly, but as the heat rose in the pit of her stomach she parted her lips. Adam's kiss deepened and she clung to him. He tasted like the mountains, moist and clean, and wild. When his hand touched her breast, she gave an audible sigh. She twisted her tongue, delving deep, wanting more. It had never been like this with Jacob; he had never made her blood race hot and cold through her body. With Jacob she had only felt unclean.

"Adam, please," she whispered against his lips. "I—I can't. Please don't." She laid her hand on his and he lifted his head. His hair, the color of a winter midnight, hung in a curtain about his face. She stroked his stubbled cheek as she let her eyes drift shut, trying to catch her breath. "I don't know how to explain . . ." She looked away, still breathless. How could she have been so brazen? She had no one to blame but herself. She'd asked for this. Any man would have responded the same.

"It's all right, Jess," Adam murmured, kissing the lobe of her ear. His voice was hoarse.

"No, it's not all right." She turned to look back at him. "It isn't all right, Adam," she repeated insistently. "I didn't mean for this to happen again. I don't want it to."

He sat back so that they were no longer touching. So that he could think. Nothing made any sense. What was he doing kissing her, touching her, making himself feel like this inside? Nothing but pain could come of it. That was all he had ever gotten from anyone but his parents and grandparents and they were dead.

"I'm sorry," he said roughly. "I shouldn't have—"

She got up, not wanting to hear his gentle words. "Let's not talk about it, Adam. There's nothing to talk about. It was a mistake." She turned the bacon that was beginning to burn. "Let's just make sure it doesn't happen again."

He nodded. "All right, Jess." He got to his feet. "Let's eat and then head for Sharpston."

"We're not going back to the logging camp?"

He poured her a cup of coffee and then one for himself. "What do you think the chances of them being there are?"

"Not good, hmm?"

"Lousy. Our Black Bandit's not a man to stand and fight when he can run. We need to go back for supplies and I should send a wire to Union Pacific and let them know we're on Larry Caine's trail. They'll want to know his identity, anyway."

"I think we should ride back to the camp."

"I'm in charge of this operation." He bit into a slice of crispy bacon. "I say where we go and when. You don't like it, you can ride alone."

Jessica drained her coffee cup and dropped it into her saddlebag. She saddled Hera, then rolled up her bedding and tied it behind the saddle with her new leather bags.

Adam watched as he sipped his coffee and finished off the rest of the bacon. "What are you doing?"

She removed her coffeepot from the embers and poured the remainder of the dark brew in the grass. Dropping the pot into her saddlebag, she untied her Appaloosa and mounted.

"I said, where are you going?"

"Back to the mining camp."

"You can't go alone." He stomped the coals of the fire, kicking dirt on them to put it out.

"Watch me." Jessica slipped her pistol into the waistband of her skirt and started Hera back down the mountain.

Adam muttered an oath beneath his breath as he watched her disappear into the trees. Disgusted, he packed up his share of the camp. He had a little difficulty mounting Zeus with only one hand, but he finally managed. "I ought to just let her go," he told Zeus as he caught Shiner's horse's lead line and tied it to his saddle. "If I had a lick of sense, I'd just let her go!"

When Jessica and Adam approached the logging camp midmorning, it quickly became apparent that the hideout was abandoned. There were two shallow graves in the soft humus in front of the log cabin.

"It looks like you and Shiner got two," Jessica said, dismounting. She pulled her derringer from her skirt and started for the cabin. "I'll have a look inside."

Adam's first impulse was to go with her, but he forced himself to remain astride. If Jessica was going to travel with him, he had to know what she was made of. He had to know she could stand on her own ground. Besides, he was fairly certain the cabin was empty.

A minute later she stepped back into the sunlight, visibly shaken.

"What is it?" Adam called.

"Nothing. Nothing but this." She held up a sheet of paper taken from her own carpetbag. Scrawled across her grandmother's recipe for shortcake was a note.

"What?" Adam rode up beside her. "A note?"

She nodded. "It says, 'Back off, redskin, or you're a dead man.'"

Adam took the paper from her trembling hands. "The paper's yours?"

"Out of my carpetbag." She took it back when Adam was done with it. "He's still got my bag, I just know it."

Adam rested a hand on his sinewy thigh. "Let's get up the hill. We'll bury old Shiner and then get into town. We'll spend the night, get provisions in the morning, and then ride out."

"Which way?"

"West," Adam answered.

Jessica mounted and then reined in beside Adam. They rode up the hill side by side. "Why west?"

He shrugged. "Just a feeling."

"A feeling?" She gave a laugh. "Not a lot to go on, is it?"

"Got any better ideas?"

She ducked a low branch. "No."

"You don't have to go with me. You could catch a train out of Logan tomorrow or the next day." He glanced down at the ground. "Look, old Shiner's rifle."

She dismounted, retrieving the Henry repeater and remounted. "I'm not giving up. I killed a man yesterday, Adam. It's too late to turn back."

He gave a nod. "All right, but count this as your warning. We get into Idaho, which is my guess where we're headed, you won't be able to just hop on a train."

Jessica rode up to where Shiner lay and dismounted again. She pushed his rifle into her saddlebag, assuming she'd inherited it because Adam already had a rifle. "Consider this conversation closed. Now let's get this man buried and get to town."

Despite the fact that it was nearly midnight when Adam and Jessica rode into Sharpston, the town was still alive with sights and sounds. Piano music and laughter spilled into the street and lamplight flickered, making it seem like daylight. A gray-haired woman with a willow broom ran down the plank sidewalk chasing a pack of barking dogs. Two cowboys argued hotly on the barber's steps. A woman dressed in a pink satin petticoat and boned corset hung out an upstairs window calling to a drunken soldier below.

Jessica looked at Adam, a smirk on her face. "Some interesting towns you've got in these parts. Home in Tennessee we were all in bed by nine."

Adam laughed. "It's a certain kind of man or woman that comes west. They're different than people in the East. Some are looking for freedom from the mores of society, others just want peace and quiet."

"What about you?" She rode beside him. "What were you looking for when you came west? Pauline said you were from Philadelphia."

Adam stared at his horse's twitching ears. "Philadelphia, it seems like a million years ago, a million miles away."

"That's where you were raised?" she probed softly.

"I lived with my parents among the Ojibwa until I

was twelve. When my parents died, I went to Philadelphia to live with my grandparents."

"You liked it there?"

"Once."

They came to a hotel and Jessica dismounted. "So why *did* you come west?"

Adam slid off the saddle, then leaned on it casually, watching her hitch the three horses. "To escape. To find some peace."

She stopped what she was doing and looked up at him. Those were the same reasons she and Mark had left Tennessee in the middle of the night. "Have you found it?"

He pushed her black felt hat playfully off her head. "I don't know," he answered softly. "I didn't think I had but—" He paused, bathing in her green-eyed gaze. Was what he searched for not a place, not a job, but a person. Was Jessica what he'd been searching for since he'd left Philadelphia? "The jury's still out on that, partner. I'll get back to you on it."

Jessica shook her head, watching Adam as he walked passed her and into the hotel. The man wasn't making any sense. But then he never did . . .

Inside Adam ordered two meals and a room. A girl ran into the back to summon the proprietor.

"One room?" Jessica lifted a haughty eyebrow. "Two kisses"—she whispered—"and you think I'm ready to share your cot?"

He grinned. He didn't know why he was in a good mood this evening, but he was. There was something about Jessica that lifted the gloom in his heart. "Are you?"

"Certainly not!"

He gave a sigh. "Too bad. But actually, I ordered one room because I think we need to stay together and stand shifts. Larry Caine knows who I am and he knows I'm looking for him. I wouldn't put it past him to hire someone to kill me. He's a nervous man, and I would imagine I've got him worried."

Jessica's cheeks reddened. Why didn't she think before she spoke? What made her think Adam wanted to bed her? How could she have said such a thing? And why was he grinning at her liked that, like he enjoyed her embarrassment.

The proprietor came through the curtain in the back. "Out," he stated flatly.

"What?" Jessica said.

"I said, out, redskin." He leaned over the wood counter. "This establishment is closed to Negroes and reds." He glanced at Jessica. "And their whores."

Adam shot his hand across the counter and grabbed the proprietor by his starched shirt collar. "What did you say?" he demanded.

The man struggled to catch his breath. "It's my right. My hotel. I said get out or I'll call the sheriff. You can go across the street to Maimie's. My place is respectable. I don't take dirt like the two of you."

Adam drew back his fist in a fury and Jessica caught it. "Adam. Let's go."

He held his fist in midair, glaring at the hotel proprietor.

"Adam! We haven't got time for this. We'll just go across the street."

Slowly he lowered his fist and loosened his grip on the man. "You're lucky I'm in a good mood tonight. You're lucky there's a lady present."

Jessica took Adam's hand. "Come on. Let's go. I'm hungry."

Adam released the proprietor and allowed Jessica to lead him out of the hotel. They said nothing as they crossed the street. Jessica had heard of the prejudice against Indians, but had never been witness to it. Her heart went out to Adam.

"It's just one man," she murmured, entering the lobby of Maimie's.

"Not one man," Adam answered, his anger barely checked. "An entire country. *My* country. Mine before it was theirs."

"You cool down." She let go of his hand. "I'll get the room. We both need sleep and a hot meal. We can ride out in the morning and be free of the likes of him."

Adam rested a hand on his hip. "Christ, Jess, you're such an innocent. I can tell you, there's no escape." His dark angry eyes fell on hers. "I ought to know. I've been running for years."

Jacob Dorchester lay back on a four-poster bed in the hotel room, watching a young sable-haired woman undress. "That's it, Jessica. Take it off. All of it."

"Didn't I tell you once, my name's Lacy, not Jessica. Now let's see your money. I don't come cheap. You want a cheap whore, you can go down the street to the whorehouse and stand in line like the rest of 'em."

Jacob dropped a coin on the table beside the bed. The whore laughed. "You got to be kiddin'. I named my price, now put your coin on the table or I take a walk."

Reluctantly, Jacob replaced the coin with a ten-dollar gold piece.

"That's more like it." Lacy picked up the coin and tucked it into a satin bag. "Now, we can do some business."

Jacob licked his dry lips, watching her strip down until she was nude. "That's it," he whispered. "But, but brush your hair forward. It's not right, Jessica."

She pulled a hand of hair forward. "That better?"

He smiled. "Oh, yes, Jessica. Perfect. Just perfect. Now come to Papa." He put out his arms.

Lacy sat down on the creaky bed, allowing him to embrace her. "Don't you want to get undressed?"

Jacob shook his head. His face was breaking out in pinpoints of perspiration. "Your voice isn't right. Don't talk. Just do what I say."

The whore rolled her eyes. "The richer the stranger," she muttered under her breath.

Jacob pushed her roughly onto her back. "I said, no talking, now shut up!"

Lacy lay back on the satin pillowcase, staring up at the handsome gray-haired gentleman. When her eyes met his, the smile fell from her face. There was something about this seemingly harmless man that frightened her. He twisted his fingers in her hair pulling it taut against her scalp.

"Ouch! That hurts!"

He straddled her, fully clothed. "I said shut up!" He drew back his hand and slapped her hard across the face.

"Oh, no." She tried to push him away. "I don't go

for that, Mister, no matter what you pay. You've got yourself the wrong girl."

Jacob shoved her back and pinned her arms to the bed. "You can't deny me, Jessica. You're mine. You've always been mine. The papers were signed. It's legal."

Lacy trembled with fear. "Let me up or I'm going to scream," she told him, keeping her voice even. "I didn't agree to no rough stuff."

He yanked a white handkerchief out of his pocket and stuffed it into her mouth. Lacy tried to scream, but nothing came up but a muffled groan.

"Oh, Jessica." Jacob shook his head. "Why do you have to make it so hard on yourself. Why are you running from me? I just want to love you."

Lacy stared up at the man, terrified.

He grabbed her hands and pinned them with his knees so that she couldn't move. "You make me very angry when you behave like this. I've come a long way to get you."

Lacy bucked and kicked beneath him, but the weight of his body on hers was too great. She was trapped.

Jacob lowered his head to taste one of her large brown nipples. "Oh, Jessica. So sweet. We could be happy, you and I, if you'd just behave yourself. If you'd just do what I said." He pulled a silver penknife from his vest pocket.

Lacy panicked. She shook her head wildly, calling out, praying someone would hear her muffled cries.

Jacob ignored her protests, turning his attention to the penknife. He flipped down the blade, then twisted it, watching the way the lamplight reflected off its sharpened edge.

Lacy's eyes went wild with terror and she began to fight in earnest again.

He grabbed a thick lock of her hair and leaned forward until his lips nearly touched hers. She froze, squeezing her eyes shut, knowing her life was coming to a bloody end.

With one swift movement Jacob hacked off the strand of hair and immediately slid off the bed, releasing Lacy.

The whore sprang up, yanking the handkerchief from her mouth. "You just get back," she warned. "Get away from that door!" Shaking with fear, she grabbed her dress and stepped into it, forgoing her undergarments. She then slipped into her shoes, grabbed up the pile of underclothing and her purse and started for the door. Jacob had moved to the window, seeming to have forgotten her presence. He stood there toying with the hair he'd cut from her head.

Noiselessly, Lacy slipped from the room.

Jessica stood at the window of the tiny room she and Adam shared. He was asleep, stretched out fully clothed on the single bed. It was her turn to stand watch first.

Adam's easy breathing filled the small, dark chamber. She smiled. All of the hate and anger she'd seen a short time ago was gone, washed away by sleep. He seemed so peaceful.

Annoyed by the feelings he stirred inside her, she glanced out the window at the hotel across the street.

135

How could the proprietor have spoken like that to Adam? How could he have felt such hate for a man because of the color of his skin?

Suddenly Jessica's breath caught in her throat. She yanked aside the curtain and stared across the way. Only a moment before, there had been a man in the window. A man she thought she had recognized, though she knew she couldn't have. She shivered, turning away from the window. "Don't be silly," she said aloud. "I'm just tired. I'm seeing things. It couldn't be Jacob."

Chapter Ten

At Jessica's urging, Adam went to the general store at sunrise. He got Nelson out of bed and bought enough supplies to get them through the several weeks of traveling he anticipated. Rested, with his arm healing nicely, he was anxious to go after the infamous Larry Caine, but Jessica suddenly seemed driven. When he came out of the store she was waiting for him, dressed to ride.

"I thought we'd just go from here," she told him, accepting several items wrapped in brown paper.

"You don't want a hot breakfast first?" He arranged the supplies carefully in his saddlebag. They'd sold Shiner's horse, deciding against taking a pack horse to make better time. "This may be your last chance to get a decent hot breakfast for a while."

She glanced nervously up the deserted main street of town as she stuffed her supplies into her bags. Jacob Dorchester's face had haunted her dreams last night. She *knew* that man in the window couldn't have been him—Jacob was in Tennessee—but she

137

felt uneasy just the same. "No. Let's head west. You said yourself that the sooner we're on their trail, the better chance we'll have of catching up with them."

Adam glanced over the saddle at her. She was pale this morning, her face drawn. "You all right?" The shock of being concerned for Jessica's welfare had passed. It was almost a comfortable feeling now. It had been a long time since he'd cared about anyone but himself.

"I'm fine." She tightened the strap on her saddlebag and shoved Shiner's Henry muzzle down into it so that it was easily accessible. She caught Hera's reins, smoothing the Appaloosa's warm neck.

"Didn't sleep well?"

She shrugged. "I slept fine. I'm just anxious to get out of this town."

Adam swung into his saddle. "A week from now I'll wager you'll be dying for the sight of a town, even one as pitiful as Sharpston."

She wheeled Hera around, headed out of town. *As long as I'm out in the open, away from saloons and hotels, I won't have to be worrying about imagining every gray-haired man I see is Jacob,* she thought.

Adam and Jessica rode north at a steady, grueling pace. "It will be like finding a needle in a haystack, finding Caine and his men," Adam told her as they rode along a mountain range at midmorning.

"You mean we won't find them?" Jessica had relaxed once they were a few miles out of Sharpston and now she was actually enjoying the ride north through the scenic mountains of northern Utah. The pace was slow and the land steep. Several times they had to dismount and lead the Appaloosas.

"No. I just mean it won't be easy. We'll need to keep hitting towns. Our Black Bandit likes cards and he likes his shave and bath. He won't stray too far from civilization . . . too inconvenient. I'm thinking we need to ride west out of the Wasatches. There's a little hole on Blue Creek up on the Idaho line that Shiner mentioned Caine's partial to."

"West it is then," Jessica agreed. She smiled at Adam. It was nice riding with him when they weren't arguing. He had an opinion on just about everything and was anxious to discuss those opinions, whether it was the annexation of a new state or the reason why the South fell some twenty-odd years ago. It was exciting for her to have someone to talk to again. After her father's death there had been no one. Mark was too young to be interested or knowledgeable in anything but guns and fishing and Jacob had considered it below himself to speak of anything of importance with a female.

The afternoon passed, and evening fell upon Jessica and Adam. They camped near a spring at the foothills of the mountains. By dawn they were riding again, back out on the flat, dry plateaus of Utah.

"Mormon land," Adam told her as they slowed to take a rationed sip of their water. "The *Promised Land* they called it." He laughed. "I don't know why the hell they settled here. Nothing but wasteland."

"I don't suppose it is a wasteland to them," Jessica mused. "When we rode the train in through the mountains down into the basin where Salt Lake City is we saw men and women tending crops. There were houses everywhere."

"I suppose Brigham Young figured no one would

bother him and his people out here in the middle of nowhere. Who'd be fool enough to come this far west?"

Jessica wiped her forehead with the bandanna she wore tied around her neck. The sun was so hot that it drew out every drop of moisture in her body. "There's always a fool, isn't there?" she answered.

"You didn't tell me why *you* came."

Jessica shrugged. "Sure I did. Mark and I"—she drew a deep breath—"we were going to start that apple orchard."

"By why so far from Tennessee?"

"No reason to stay," she answered, treading carefully. "Our parents and grandparents were dead. We just thought we'd make a fresh start."

Adam studied her green eyes until she looked away. There was something in the tone of her voice that made Adam think she wasn't giving him the entire story. It was on the tip of his tongue to question her further, but Jessica picked up her reins and sunk her heels into Hera's sides.

"You coming?" she called over her shoulder as she galloped away.

Adam and Jessica reached Blue Creek just before sunset. "Water!" Jessica cried, flinging herself off Hera. She ran down the bank, flopped down, and began to scoop up handfuls of water and drink greedily.

Adam came to stand beside her, his long shadow casting over her shoulder. She looked up. He was pulling off his snakeskin boots.

"I don't think I've ever tasted anything quite so good," she told him as she splashed water on her face

140

letting it run in rivulets down her shirt.

Adam laughed, unbuttoning his shirt. "A woman of simple pleasures; I like that."

Jessica sat up, the smile falling from her face. She had just realized that Adam was undressing. "W— what do you think you're doing?" she stammered.

"Going for a swim. Aren't you?"

She pulled her hat off her head. "That's not what I mean and you know it. You're taking off your clothes." She couldn't take her eyes off him as he shed his faded blue shirt to reveal a hard, muscular, suntanned chest. A narrow trail of inky black hair ran down the center, disappearing below the waistline of his dungarees. Jessica moistened her upper lip. "You can't take your clothes off here."

"What? You bathe in your clothes?" His hands fell to the waist of his pants and he unbuttoned the top button.

Jessica spun around, her hand clamped over her mouth. Adam was standing two feet from her stripping off his clothes!

"You wanted to ride with me, didn't you, Jess? Just one of the boys," he teased.

She could hear him stepping out of the denims. She could feel her sunburned cheeks reddening. Her mouth went dry. Against all reason she turned her head to look back at him.

Adam broke into laughter and leaped off the bank. Jessica caught sight of long bronze legs and bare muscular buttocks before he disappeared over the bank. He was still laughing when he surfaced.

"Christ, you're a fresh breath of air, Jess."

She stood, crossing her arms over her chest. He was

141

laughing at her! "I fail to see the humor here," she answered icily.

"It's just that it's been a long time since I came across a modest woman." He ducked under the water and came up pushing his long black hair behind his head. "I think I kind of like it. Now come on in."

She shook her head. "I'll wait until you're through."

"Don't be silly, Jess. Enjoy the water while you have the chance. We can't sleep here tonight, not safe. Too many people pass by this spot. It's one of the few places on the creek where the water is deep enough to get wet."

Jessica ran a hand over her damp, tangled hair. The water looked so cool and inviting.

"I'm disappointed. I wouldn't think you'd let me keep you from a bath."

After a moment of hesitation, Jessica began to unbutton the back of her skirt. Of course she wasn't going to let him keep her out of the creek! What did she care if he was buck naked! She'd seen naked men before. She stepped out of her skirt and then the single white petticoat that had turned various shades of gray.

Adam burst into another fit of laughter at the sight of her standing on the bank in her camisole and purple and green bloomers.

"I don't suppose I could convince you to take off the rest," he called, floating on his back.

She kept her eyes on the water in front of her, ignoring his obvious male anatomy. "Not hardly."

Adam watched her enter the water. She hadn't waded out far when she lowered herself into a sitting position.

He swam over beside her. "Get away from me!" She splashed water in his face.

"You're getting awfully excited about a little bare flesh, Miss Landon." He couldn't help but notice the transparency of her wet camisole. Through the sheer, wet cotton he could see the outlines of her brown areolas and the nubs of her nipples.

She splashed him again. "I'm *not* excited!"

He laughed, circling her.

She watched him, feeling like his prey. She rubbed sand over her bare arms and legs, scrubbing away the days of dirt.

Adam reached out to touch her hair and she swatted his hand. "Don't touch me."

"It's a stick. You want a stick in your hair?"

She looked up guiltily, holding still so he could remove it. "No. Of course not."

"So quit being so jumpy." He hurled the twig in the air and watched as it fell into the water and sent ripples across the surface.

"How far up the creek is this place Shiner told you about?"

"Day, day and a half ride." Adam watched her bathe, intrigued by her glistening skin and silky wet hair. Her eyes were a clear, unclouded green, not the speckled green so many people had. Despite the fact that she wore her hat when they rode, there was a patch of sunburn across the bridge of her nose and her cheekbones. He reached for her again and she lowered her head.

"What? Another stick?"

"No."

Adam's voice was so soft and startling that she lifted her gaze to meet him. His callused fingers brushed her cheek.

"Adam . . ." She didn't know what to say. Her eyes closed as she fought off the heat rising in the pit of her stomach.

He leaned over her and kissed her gently on the mouth.

"Adam, we said this wouldn't happen again," she said weakly.

"I know." He kissed her again.

"Adam, this would just get in the way. It would make things too confusing."

Hs kissed her, this time touching her lip with the tip of his tongue.

"Adam—" She could feel her resolve waning. "Adam, we've got Larry Caine to worry about. I don't even like you."

"You like me," he murmured in her ear.

"You should have protected my brother."

"I'm so sorry about your brother." His voice was raw with emotion. "I'd have died in his place if I could have." He kissed the length of her neck, sending tremors of pleasure down her spine.

"You're not listening to me," Jessica insisted. She could hear her own voice odd and breathy.

"I'm listening. You just keep talking." He slipped beneath her in the water and pulled her onto his lap.

Jessica's hands fell on his shoulder as she stared eye to eye at him. Up close like this she couldn't think straight. Everything was a jumble. He was kissing her, confusing her.

"Jess, my sweet Jess," he crooned.

"Adam, please."

"Shhhh, just kiss me. You know you want to kiss me as much as I want to kiss you. I wouldn't hurt you, I swear it."

She met his lips. *Just one kiss,* she thought. She could feel her heart pounding as their tongues met.

Adam's hands felt so good on her bare arms, on her face. When he brought his hand up to cup her breast, her eyes flew open. She looked at him, then at her breast straining against the wet, transparent cotton. "Adam," she breathed.

He brought his mouth to the wet material, testing her hardened nipple with the tip of his tongue. Jessica gave a groan. *This's gone too far,* she thought deep in the recesses of her mind. But as his tongue stroked the ripening bud, she arched her back, guiding his head with her hands. "Oh, God, Adam, please don't do this to me," she moaned softly.

"You don't like it?" he asked, teasing her other nipple with his thumb.

"Yes, I like it," she told him breathlessly. "That's why it's wrong." She pressed her lips to his, knowing she was losing the battle within herself. "We said we wouldn't do this."

He caressed the mound of her breast. "You're not making any sense," he whispered. "If you want me to stop, just say so, Jess."

She threw back her head so that he could kiss the base of her throat. She knew she should tell him to stop, but it felt too good. If this was a sin of the flesh, it was a glorious sin. At this moment it didn't matter that she knew she was headed straight to hell for it; it was worth it. All she wanted was Adam and these glorious sensations.

Adam slipped his hand into the waistband of her purple bloomers and she stiffened.

"Relax," he whispered. "Float in my arms. Just feel, don't think. Don't analyze it." His soft, sensuous voice tickled her ear.

Jessica felt her muscles weaken. She was being swept by a tide so strong, she had no way to control it. She could only ride it out.

Adam stroked her inner thighs and Jessica moaned, resting her head on his broad shoulder. The cool water and his warm hand on her flesh was exhilarating. When he lifted her out of the water and carried her to the shore she clung to him, returning his kisses with equal fervor. Right or wrong this was where she wanted to be right now, here in Adam's arms.

He laid her gently on their pile of clothes and began to peel off her wet bloomers and camisole. She lay there like some wanton whore, watching him, reveling in the feel of his eyes on her nakedness. Then Adam stretched out over her, pressing his wet, hard male body against her.

Jessica tried to catch her breath. "No." She shook her head. "I'm not ready to . . . to . . ." Her eyes met his. "I'm a virgin," she murmured, her voice barely audible.

Water ran in rivulets off Adam's ebony hair onto her bare breasts. "I won't do anything you don't want to do, I swear it. I just want to touch you, Jess, that's all." He kissed her softly. "I've got all the time in the world, sweetheart."

"Just touching?" she asked.

146

He kissed her cheek. "I told you. Nothing you don't want to do."

She relaxed beneath him, marveling at the new sensations brought on by his entire body pressing against hers. Surprisingly, despite his size, he wasn't heavy. It felt good to be surrounded by him, by his power.

Adam lowered his face to the valley between her breasts and kissed her. His hot kisses burned a path over her flat belly, down her leg. He stroked her with his hands, caressing every inch of her damp, quaking body.

Jessica took deep ragged breaths. The darkening sky whirled overhead. There was nothing but Adam and the lightning sensations that riveted her body.

Adam stretched out beside her and kissed her again, his hand falling to the apex of her thighs. To Jessica's horror, she rose up instinctively to meet his probing fingers. She rolled her head, fighting the waves of pleasure that were coming rhythmically.

What am I doing? she thought suddenly. *We can't do this! We swore we wouldn't! I can't get involved with Adam. I can't fall in love with him!*

She grasped his hand. "Please," she murmured, stilling his motion. She lifted her lashes to meet his gaze, her green eyes pleading. "Please stop, Adam."

"What is it? What's the matter, sweetheart?" He brushed the wet hair from her cheek and kissed her gently.

"Oh, God, Adam." She squeezed her eyes shut, mortally embarrassed. "What have I done? What did I let you do?"

He pushed up on one elbow and caught her chin,

turning her head so that she was forced to look at him. "It's what men and women have been doing since the creation. Love is what we were meant for."

Love, she thought. Just the word petrified her. "We said no more kissing. We said—"

He pressed his finger to his lips. "I know what we said. I meant it as much as you did that day, but Jess"—he took a deep breath, frightened by the words on the tip of his tongue—"Jess, I'm falling in love with you."

She swallowed hard. "Don't say that!" She pushed him aside and jumped up, snatching her wet bloomers and camisole. "Please don't say that."

Adam sat up, pushing his wet hair off his shoulder. She had turned her back to him and was fumbling with her clothes, trying to redress. His expression turned hard. "It's because I'm a red man, isn't it?"

"Don't be silly, it's because—" she took in a sharp breath. She didn't know why—a thousand reasons. Mark . . . her parents' unhappy union . . . Jacob. Jacob said he loved her, but his love was obsessive; it was twisted. If that was what love was to a man, she wanted no part of it.

"Because why?" Adam demanded. "Where's your courage, Jess? Go ahead and say it." He grasped her shoulders, and spun her around. He was out of control. He was filled with rage. "You'll roll around on a creek bank with a red man, but you could never love one! Is that it?"

Jessica lifted her balled fist and hit him hard on the jaw.

Before Adam could stop himself he felt his palm make contact with her cheek. The moment he did it, he was sorry.

Jessica lifted her hand to her stinging cheek. She opened her mouth to speak and then clamped it shut, feeling tears fill her eyes. Without a word she turned and ran.

Adam stood frozen for a moment, his hands clamped at his sides. He was shocked, horrified by his behavior. He'd never hit a woman in his life. *Dear God, how could I have done such a thing?*

He stared up at the gray sky. The sun had set and darkness was settling in. He had to come to terms with being Ojibwa. His mother had told him that so many years ago. It wasn't how others felt about him, it was how he felt about himself.

"Jessica!" he called after her. She was still running, stumbling along the bank. "Jessica, I'm sorry." His voice cracked. "I didn't mean to hurt you. I'll never do it again. I swear to God!"

She kept running.

He bolted after her.

Then she went down, a scream piercing the air.

"Jessica!" Adam shouted.

"Adam!" she cried. "Help me!"

She was only thirty yards away but it seemed like thirty miles as Adam rushed toward her. "What is it?" he called. "What's wrong?"

"Snake," she answered, her voice so shaky he could barely comprehend her words. "I've been bit."

Chapter Eleven

Adam sprinted the last few feet and went down on his knees beside her. Jessica lay crumpled on the ground holding her calf, her eyes shut.

"Jess?"

"A snake. A snake bit me and now I'm going to die."

"You're not going to die." Adam studied her face carefully, watching for fatal signs. He'd once seen a boy die of a snake bite. The childhood friend had gone into convulsions and was dead within minutes of the bite.

Adam lowered his head, grasping her calf. "Let me see." He squinted. Damn, but it had gotten dark fast. "Where's the bite, Jess? You have to help me."

"Here." She fumbled with her fingers. "Feel it. Two bumps."

His fingertips touched the tiny mounds. "What kind of snake?"

She laid back, suddenly feeling dizzy.

"Jessica! *What kind of snake?*"

She shook her head. "Don't know, but it was a small one. Guess you'll have to cut it and bleed me."

Adam fingered the bite. He knew he had minutes, maybe seconds, to make a decision that would mean Jessica's life. "I don't know, Jess. If you got a low dose of the venom, you'd be better keeping your blood volume up. It'll dilute the poison."

She lay on the grass trying to remain calm. "It hurts, Adam. You sure we shouldn't cut it?"

"My grandmother always took care of the snake bites in our village. If a man made it back to the village, he never died."

"All I know"—she took a deep breath—"is you cut a snake bite and—and, try to suck out the poison, then let it bleed." Her face suddenly felt hot. Her heart was pounding violently. She was sick to her stomach.

Adam lifted her head into his lap and stroked the wet hair plastered to her forehead. "Jess, try to listen to me. The bite's not that bad. If it was . . . If it was you'd already be dead."

Her body started to tremble and she closed her eyes. "C—cold."

He brushed her forehead with his fingertips. She was flushed. He stood and lifted her into his arms. She leaned against his bare chest, looping her arms around his neck.

"I'm sorry I hit you, Jess," he told her, kissing her clammy forehead.

"I hit you first," she answered weakly. "You made me so damned mad. You always think you know what you're talking about, but you don't."

"I don't care if you hit me first, it's no excuse.

There's no excuse for a man to ever hit a woman."

She thought of the blow she'd received from Jacob just before she and Mark had fled. It had been over spilled sugar. "I'm hot," she murmured. "Why am I shivering?"

"It's the fever coming on. We'll get these wet clothes off and wrap you up in front of a fire."

She rested her head in the crook of his neck. He smelled so good. Like the mountains. She remembered the intimacy they had shared only a short time ago. "Thought you said"—she took a deep breath—"we couldn't camp here. Not safe."

"We'll have to take our chances, but you let me worry about that." He eased her to the ground near the hobbled horses and began to peel off her wet undergarments. She lay there like a babe, too weak to move. She was getting sick so fast that Adam wondered if he shouldn't have bled her. But he knew snake venom affected the nervous system and there were no convulsions, no tremors of the limbs. That was a good sign.

When he'd stripped her, he redressed her in his dry shirt and wrapped her in his bedroll blanket. He left her to lay on the bank while he walked upstream a short distance looking for a better place to camp. In the darkness he saw nothing but wide open plateau. "The promised land," he said aloud. He shook his head, returning to Jessica. They would have to stay here and hope no one dangerous came along. He started a fire with dry grass from the bank. There wasn't much to burn—no wood. He scooped up dried horse chips and dropped them onto the fire. It was smoky but it would keep up a decent blaze.

Then Adam filled the coffeepot with water from the creek and set it on the spider to heat. He crouched beside Jessica. "Jess, can you hear me?"

Her teeth chattered. "C—cold. Leg hurts."

He lifted the blanket letting the firelight fall across her calf. He winced. Vicious red streaks ran lengthwise up her leg. It was swelling, the flesh growing shiny and tight. "You're all right," he soothed. "I'm going to put a mud pack on that leg." His grandmother had always said there wasn't a wound a mud pack wouldn't help.

Adam went back to the creek and scraped dirt off the bank with his fingernails and mixed it with water and some grass to hold it together. He carried the handful of mud back to where Jessica lay and packed it on the snake bite.

"Cold," she whimpered. "I'm cold, Adam."

He picked up his rifle and leaned it within reach. Then he lay down and drew Jessica into his arms. "Try not to move," he whispered in her ear. "Let that mud harden. It'll draw out the poison."

She snuggled against him, her whole body quaking with chills. She was hot to the touch. Adam was burning up beneath the bedroll blanket and the saddle blanket he'd added, but he lay there, holding her, trying to comfort her.

The moon rose high in the sky and the stars came twinkling through the blanket of night. Jessica slept while Adam kept vigil, praying . . . thinking.

She had hurt him today. He had told her what he had never told any woman before and she had rebuked him. She'd become angry at the thought of his love. He blinked back the moisture that seeped into his eyes. Was he never meant to have that love between a man and a woman that was so precious? His father and mother had been happy together. Even his grandparents had a bond that had gone unbroken to their death. Adam wanted to love, to be loved like that.

He stared up at the constellations. She said it wasn't because his skin was red, but he knew she'd lied. It was the way all white men felt. Wasn't that why he kept running?

Dawn came and still Adam stayed awake. Jessica had slept fitfully, her fever raging. As the sun rose she grew quiet and he sat up staring at her lovely ashen face. Her breathing had grown faint and for a moment he feared she was dying.

"Jess, don't leave me. I can love you if you'll just let me. I can prove to you that it doesn't matter what color a man's skin is. I'm the same as you inside." He clasped her hand, raising it to his lips. "Jess, can you hear me?"

Her eyelids fluttered.

"Jessica?"

She tried to moisten her lips. "Sorry, so sorry," she croaked.

"Shhh." He smoothed her hair as he crooned softly. "It's all right. Just sleep. I'll be here, Jess."

Adam kept vigil all day, through the night and through the following day. Her fever rose and fell and then rose again. Her leg grew so swollen that it looked to Adam as if it might burst, but he kept applying mud packs and finally the swelling began to subside. At sunset on the third day Jessica stirred, calling out to him.

Adam came running along the bank, a dead rabbit flung over his shoulder. "Jess?"

"Water," she said, her voice barely audible. Her head was pounding and her entire body ached as if she'd been in a brawl. But the pain told her she was alive.

He flung down the rabbit and quickly brought her back a cup of water.

She tried to hold the cup but her hands shook so badly that all she could do was splash water down the shirt she wore. She laughed weakly as he pushed her hands aside.

"Let me help." He knelt and pushed back a corner of the makeshift tarp he'd constructed to keep the sun off her during the day. He brought the cup to her lips and watched her drink. God, he was glad to hear her voice. He'd come so close to losing her that it frightened him to think about it.

When she'd had her fill, she fell back on Hera's saddle. Just lifting her head had exhausted her. She stared up at Adam who watched her anxiously. "I'm all right," she whispered, reaching up to stroke his bearded cheek. "Thank you for taking care of me. I thought I was going to die."

He covered her hand with his. She was warm to the touch but not hot like she'd been. "I didn't do much—pour a little water down you, keep a pack on your leg." He shrugged.

"You could have just left me to let the snake finish me off."

"I wouldn't leave my partner behind." He brought her hand to her lips, kissing her fingers one by one. "I want to tell you how sorry I am that I hit you the other night."

"Stop apologizing. I hit you first."

He shook his head emphatically. "It doesn't matter. It's not the same thing."

Her eyes met his. "To me, it is, Adam. I shouldn't have hit you no matter how mad you made me."

"Let's forget about it, then. I've got a rabbit. I'll boil it and you can have some broth."

She wrinkled her nose. "Broth? I want roasted rabbit. I'm starving."

He laughed. "All right. But let's have a look at that leg first."

She looked up. "Do we have to?"

He pushed back her blanket, taking care not to reveal any more of her leg than necessary. If he had any hope at winning Jessica's heart, he knew he would have to tread carefully. The next time they made love it would have to be on her initiation, not his. "It looks much better."

Jessica looked down, then groaned and turned away. "It looks like it's going to fall off!"

"Just be glad you didn't see it yesterday," Adam teased, touching her calf gently.

She watched him press the streaky red and black flesh in several places and then cover it again with the blanket. "It's hard to believe one little snake could do that. It didn't even hurt when it bit me."

Adam rose to his feet. "You were lucky, damned lucky. Now let's see what we can do with this rabbit."

"I'd help," she offered, resting against her saddle. "But I don't think I'm quite up to it."

"You just rest. After we eat we'll see about getting you on your feet and down to the creek."

"You telling me I could use a bath?"

Adam glanced over at her from where he was assembling the spit. Images of Jessica's naked form in his arms came floating back.

She blushed as she recalled what had happened a few days ago in the creek. But it seemed like that had been years ago . . . almost as if it hadn't happened. But Jessica knew that it *had* happened and she was afraid it might happen again. She couldn't let herself love Adam; she couldn't let him love her. They were out here searching for the Black Bandit and once they found him, once Jessica got her revenge, she would leave Adam and never see him again. That was the way she wanted it.

"Jess . . ." Adam's voice broke through Jessica's thoughts.

"Mmm?" She looked up guiltily.

"You feel all right?"

She nodded. "Just tired."

"Lay back and rest. Take a nap. I'll wake you when the rabbit's done."

"You'd better," she answered as she closed her eyes. She didn't want to look at him, at his shiny black hair. She didn't want to watch the way the bare muscles of his arms and chest flexed as he worked. She wished he'd put on his shirt.

The next thing Jessica knew, Adam was shaking her. "Dinner's on," he murmured in her ear. "Up to it?"

She opened her eyes to find that the sun had set. A fire crackled only a few feet from her and the heavenly smell of roasted rabbit wafted through the air. She took a deep breath. "That smells wonderful."

158

He helped her sit up.

She felt woozy the minute she lifted her head off the saddle she was using for a pillow. Adam caught her arm and steadied her.

"This is ridiculous," she complained.

"Give it time. You're bound to be weak after not eating for a few days."

She smiled at him. "You're a good nurse. I hate sick people."

"Remind me not to get sick while you're around then."

"You'd better not." She accepted the plate he offered her. "I've already put us behind by three days and I can't see me riding tomorrow."

Adam lifted a piece of delicately roasted rabbit off his plate. "It may not matter. Our Mr. Caine may well be sitting in a saloon somewhere celebrating."

"You can go on without me if you want." She chewed on a leg. "I told you I wouldn't hold you back."

"We'll stay here a day or two until you get your strength, then we'll head for the nearest town. You can catch a stagecoach to Promontory Point. There you can get that train to Seattle." Once Adam captured the Black Bandit, he'd head for Seattle and Jessica. It was difficult for him to imagine courting a woman, but the thought had crossed his mind.

Jessica stopped chewing. "Train to Seattle! What are you talking about?"

He stared at her across the campfire. "You certainly don't think you're going on with me. You nearly died!"

She shook her head, attacking the piece of rabbit

again. "I swear, Adam Sern, you've got the thickest head! I set out to catch the Black Bandit who killed my brother and I don't intend to give up. I want my carpetbag."

"I'll bring you your damned carpetbag, if he's still got it."

Jessica's green eyes narrowed dangerously. "He's still got it all right, and I intend to get it back."

Adam took a drink of water from his cup, letting her words spin in his head. Damn, but Jessica was determined. He admired her for it. There'd be few men who would go on after what she'd been through since they left Loco.

"All right," Adam conceded. "We'll just wait until you're up to riding, then we'll find that town, I'll send a wire to the Union Pacific. Then we'll see what information we can pick up."

"No." She pointed at him. "You go tomorrow. I'll stay here and rest. By the time you get back in a day or two, I'll be fit to ride."

"I can't leave you here!"

"I'd leave you here if you were the one who'd been bit."

"Jess"—he tried to speak calmly—"it's not the same thing. Why do you insist upon comparing us? You're a woman for Christ's sake!"

"A *woman* who had to steal what money was rightfully hers, sneak out of a house in the middle of the night with her little brother and come across the country alone! A woman who shot and killed a man on a mountain a week ago!" She set down her plate, no longer hungry. "I'm your partner, Adam. You said so yourself. We're equals. It's the only way we

160

can make this work. If you're not in agreement, you can just ride out now. I'll go on my own when I'm ready."

Adam wanted to take her in his arms. He wanted to kiss away the deep crease that ran the length of her forehead. He wanted to hold her, to ease the pain he heard in her voice. Instead he just sat there, staring at her across the open flames.

When Adam made no response, she lay down and pulled her blanket over her shoulders, leaving him to his own thoughts.

At sunrise Adam helped Jessica down to the creek where she bathed and then dressed in her own clothing. He left her plenty of horse chips for a campfire, fresh rabbit, plus dried foodstuffs from the saddlebags.

"I don't feel right leaving you out in the open like this," he told her as he saddled Zeus.

She rested her back against a rock, soaking her injured calf in the creek. "We don't have any choice. I'll be fine. No one's been through here in days."

"You've got Shiner's rifle?"

"And ammunition. Got my derringer, too." She hobbled to her feet. Her leg throbbed when she stood, but she knew she needed to keep her circulation moving.

Adam swung into his saddle. "You see anyone coming, Jess, and you hide along the riverbank. Don't let anyone see you."

"You don't think someone's going to realize I'm here when they see this camp?" She shifted her weight off her bad leg as best she could.

"Jessica—" He took a deep breath, annoyed by her

flippant attitude. She was such an innocent. She didn't realize what dangers surrounded her. But maybe it was better that way. A man could drive himself crazy imagining all the ways he could die. "Just do what I say. I'll be back as soon as I can."

"Don't forget those herbs I want for my leg."

"I won't." He pushed his black hat onto his head and picked up Zeus' reins.

"Go on," Jessica urged. "The sooner you go the sooner you'll get back." She gave Zeus a slap on his hindquarter and the Appaloosa leaped forward.

Jessica watched Adam ride north, his blue-black hair blowing over his broad shoulders. She smiled, waving. Her chest felt tight, not because Adam was leaving her behind, but because she knew she could never give him what he wanted. The other night he had said he was falling in love with her. She couldn't allow that to happen. He deserved better. She had no intentions of ever loving any man. She sighed, wondering if there had been no Jacob . . . would she have felt differently?

Jessica lowered herself to the ground to give her leg a rest. She couldn't think about Adam now, or about the feelings he stirred inside her. The Black Bandit was her concern. She had to get better so that she could go after him and his men.

The morning passed and Jessica rested on the creek bank, drinking when she was thirsty, napping when she was tired. Sometime late in the afternoon a strange sound woke her. For a moment she lay on the ground, listening, wondering what the rumbling was. It was a strange vibration in the ground. Then, suddenly, she sat up, looking to the east. Hoofbeats!

162

Jessica pushed herself up off the ground and grabbed Shiner's old Henry. She looped a belt of ammunition over her shoulder. She could see the horses now, racing toward her. There were men on horseback. She could hear their voices as they hooted and hollered.

Suddenly her mouth went dry. Indians! She thought of the horse thieves Adam had told her about. The Kiowa, Crooked Nose, and his band of renegade Utes.

They spotted her seconds after she spotted them. A rifle shot echoed across the bare plateau. An arrow whizzed past her head.

Jessica stumbled down the creek bank. She couldn't run and she doubted she had the strength to mount Hera. Of course it was too late for that now. The Indians were headed straight for her.

Jessica threw herself down on the bank and fired. On the second shot a man fell from his horse. Another arrow flew over her head. Bullets whistled through the air. She shot a second man off his horse. The Indians suddenly split into two groups, one taking the herd of horses north, the other group backing just out of her firing range.

Jessica panted as she reloaded. She was petrified. A thousand thoughts raced through her mind. Why had she let Adam go off without her? How could she have been so stupid as to have let a snake bite her, for God's sake! There were at least twenty Indians out there. She didn't have a chance in hell.

Jessica rested her cheek on the bank, parting the grass and reeds. The Indians who had remained, twelve maybe, were talking among themselves. Then they split into groups.

Hera whinnied.

Jessica's eyes darted back and forth trying to watch the Kiowa leader and the three groups all at once. Then she saw her Appaloosa being led away. She fired at the redskinned thief, but missed.

A rustling sound in the grass behind her made her turn her head. She saw no movement, but the hair bristled on the back of her neck. Her hands were trembling so badly that she feared she'd pull the trigger of her rifle unintentionally.

One of them was behind her. She could feel his presence in the still, hot air of late afternoon.

The instant she saw the Indian move in the grass on the far bank, she fired. He bellowed, the force of the bullet pushing him backward. His blood was a brilliant red that stained the brown and green grass. Slowly his rifle slipped from his hands.

Jessica turned back.

The leader of the Indians, who had remained just out of her firing range, barked a command. Slowly the braves who had not gone with the horse herd, made their way back to him. There was more talking. A few disgruntled protests. Then the men squatted, and watched.

Jessica knew she'd hear no more from them until nightfall.

Chapter Twelve

It seemed as if night would never come. Jessica lay on her stomach in the wet grass, her bare feet dangling in the water. Her leg hurt so badly that her mind was playing tricks on her. She kept thinking she heard Adam's soft voice, but he never came.

She stared out at the group of renegade Indians and saw them staring back. They were laughing as they passed around a bottle of bourbon. She could almost feel their hot, liquor breath on her face. She was dying of thirst, yet she was so frightened to take her eyes off them for a moment, that she'd had nothing to drink in hours.

Dusk settled in and Jessica blinked against the exhaustion that threatened to overtake her. She massaged her injured leg, all the while keeping her rifle aimed. Her only chance was to hold them off until Adam made it back. She laughed, her dry lips cracking painfully. How many days did she think she could hold off a pack of Indian horse thieves?

She thought about just jumping up and running

toward them, firing until they fired on her. It would be an easy way to die, probably not too painful. But then she thought of Mark, and of Larry Caine. She couldn't die yet, not as long as the Black Bandit walked this earth.

Jessica squinted through the darkness. She could see the Indians moving. Some of the ones who had taken the horse herd north returned. Others walked north, to take their places, she supposed. Occasionally a brave threw back his head and filled the air with a primal howl.

They're just trying to unnerve me, Jessica told herself. She flexed her stiff fingers. Why didn't they do something! This waiting was agonizing. If they were going to attack her, why didn't they attack and get it over with? She rolled onto her side, trying to take some of the weight off her leg. She could feel her face growing hot as her fever returned. Tears ran down her cheeks.

She wanted Adam. She didn't want to be brave anymore. She was tired and she wanted to sleep; she wanted to sleep in his arms.

When the first Indian made his move, running straight for the creek bank, Jessica beaded in and shot him in midair. The Ute fell and squirmed in pain, crying out to his friends. The braves behind him screeched and someone ran to him. To her surprise, the would-be-savior simply cocked his ancient carbine rifle and shot the wounded man in the head.

Jessica fired and the savior fell flat on his stomach, firing back. Several arrows flew through the air. The Indians hooted and danced in circles, seemingly amused. After a round of gunfire, the man crept back to his friends. Jessica reloaded. She had to be more careful with her ammunition from now on. She was running low.

More time passed. The renegades seemed to give up on her for a while. They lit a small fire and cooked some fish. The smell was heavenly. Jessica's stomach growled. Against her will, she dozed on and off, her rifle clutched in her hands.

The night passed and dawn came. To Jessica's surprise, she was still unharmed. She had half hoped that during the night the Indians would give up and leave her, but the light of morning proved she had no such luck. The Indian renegades were still there and the leader was angry. She could hear it in his short, gruff commands.

Hours passed. Every once in a while an Indian would fire an arrow or a round of ammunition in her direction. She never fired until they got close. She killed two more, wounded one.

By nightfall, Jessica was so tired and her leg ached so badly that she was having a difficult time remaining conscious. Once one of the Indians sneaked up so close that he pelted her and the grass around her with several rocks before she was able to get her rifle onto her shoulder and shoot the cowboy hat off his head. Those of the Indians still remaining burst into merry laughter. This had all become a game and she was the prize.

When the blanket of darkness settled in, Jessica roused herself. She had decided she couldn't stay put any longer or she was going to go mad. She had to find a safer place to hide. If she could just last another day, she knew Adam would be back.

When the renegades lit their campfire and began to play a hand of cards, she wrapped her ammunition belt around her neck and let her body slip noiselessly into the water. She figured she'd just float down stream a ways. If they couldn't find her in the morning, maybe they'd just give up and move on. After all, they had to be bound somewhere with all of those horses. Her only regret was that she would lose Hera. They would take her horse with the rest of the herd.

The cold water was reviving. Jessica drank thirstily and then allowed the slow current to drag her along. She let her bad leg float and it eased the pain the pressure of her weight had put on it. She could still hear the Indian's voices as she floated around a bend.

Then she saw him.

By the time she raised her rifle to her shoulder the leader of the renegades was on her. Jessica slammed the butt of the rifle into his face. Twice it went off. He grabbed a hank of her hair and shoved her face under the surface of the water.

Just when Jessica thought her lungs would burst, he lifted her head above the water. She took in great gulps as she swung her fists wildly. She lost the rifle. She kicked and screamed. She bit him hard enough on the arm to draw a gush of blood. He rammed her head under the water again.

The next time Jessica surfaced, she was barely conscious. In the distance she could hear the other Indians calling out to their leader, laughing, congratulating him.

The leader hauled her out of the water and threw

her down.

Jessica forced her eyes open and stared up at him. Pale moonlight reflected off the Kiowa's face. His long, thin nose had been broken in several places. *Crooked Nose.* This was the man Adam had warned her of, the man who had tortured and killed the husband and wife a few weeks back.

Crooked Nose's lips turned up in a grin. "A woman!" he accused in English. "A woman has held you at bay, my worthless friends."

The others gathered around to stare at her. One reached out and grabbed a fistful of the wet material of her shirt but the leader gave him a vicious kick, knocking him over.

"A brave woman such as this is not fit for dogs like you. She's mine!"

Jessica's green eyes narrowed. "I belong to no one. Kill me!"

The Kiowa laughed, grasping her arm and pulling her to her feet. Jessica stumbled and went down. He jerked her up again and shoved her forward. "We shall see," he warned. "We shall see."

Adam entered a boardinghouse dining room in the small town of Blades on the Idaho border, and took a seat at the end of a long table. Shortly, a young pigtailed woman in a flowered apron approached him.

"Meal's been served, sir. It's on past ten o'clock."

"Any leftovers?"

She nodded. "Reckon there is. Bit of potatoes, a turnip or two, maybe some biscuits. I could heat it up, but I'd have to charge you the same as if you had a sit-down meal."

"It doesn't matter." He waved his hand. "Just get me something to eat. What have you got to drink?"

"Cow went dry. Got water, water, and water."

He grinned. "Water it'll be then. Just scrape up what you can find. I'm in a hurry."

"Late to be leavin' town. You sure you don't want to spend the night? We got good clean rooms, Jasper and I do. Fresh straw mattresses."

His dark eyes settled on her speckled blue ones. "You'd let me sleep beneath your roof?"

"Why?" She arched an eyebrow. "You got some kind of disease?"

"Well, it seems there are a lot of people that don't take to men like me."

Her eyes narrowed. "Your money's just as good as the next man's, Mister. Your manners are better than most. You're certainly welcome here."

The thought was tempting, but he wanted to get back to Jessica. "No. Thank you. Just the meal."

"Be right back, then."

Adam leaned back in his chair, watching the woman disappear behind a chintz curtain. He could hear her banging around in the kitchen. Footsteps sounded on the staircase and he looked up. A gray-haired gentleman came down the steps and sharply turned the corner.

Adam tipped his black hat and nodded politely.

The man lifted his nose into the air with a haughty "hrumph" and headed out the screen door, letting it slam behind him.

Adam's brow creased. *What an odd little man,* he

thought. He obviously was an Easterner and well out of his element. He was dressed more for a Sunday tea than for the sort of entertainment he'd be finding in the saloon up the street.

When the pigtailed woman returned with a chipped plate full of food and a mug of water, Adam asked her about the boarder.

"Oh, he's a funny duck, ain't he?" She leaned against the table, folding and unfolding her dishrag. "The name's Mr. Dorchester. Been here a few days. Says he's lookin' for his wife."

"His wife?" Adam sampled the boiled potatoes and turnips.

"He says she run off. He's tracked her all the way from Tennessee."

An eery feeling crept over Adam. "Tennessee?"

"Yup. He's taking a stagecoach out of here in the mornin'."

"Where's he going this late at night?"

The woman's suntanned cheeks colored. "Where you think he's going? That man, he's got an appetite. We've only got two whores in town and they say he's keepin' both busy. Outbid a cowboy the night before last. Paid ten dollars, I hear."

Adam sipped the cool water. "Sounds like he really misses his wife," he commented sarcastically. He thought of the young whore, Sue Ellen, who he'd just spoken to in a back alley near the saloon. She knew of Larry Caine and had provided him with some excellent leads as to where he might be headed. Adam wondered if it was Sue who'd be servicing the old coot tonight.

"That's just what I thought." She took a swipe at

the table with her dishrag. "Well, I guess I'd best be getting upstairs to pull off Jasper's boots. I'll be back down to check on you in a few minutes."

"Here, let me pay you now." He reached into his pocket for a few coins. "I really am in a hurry, but thanks for the meal. It was good."

She swept the coins off the table and jingled them in her hand. "I used to dream about ridin' out of this town with a man like you," she mused. "Then I married Jasper, we built this boardin' house, had six babes, buried three. Guess I'm content enough, but sometimes . . ." She glanced out the window at the moon hanging bright in the sky. "Oh, I'm just bein' foolish. You have a good night." Her blue eyes met Adam's wishfully one last time. "I hope you get where you're goin' in such a hurry."

Adam thanked her again, then pushed his hat down on his head and strode out of the dining room and through the front door. All he could think of was Jessica and holding her in his arms again.

"Dear God, but I hate a red man," Jacob Dorchester commented, watching through an upstairs window of Johnson's Saloon as Adam rode by. "I don't know why the army doesn't just round them up and shoot them. Drown the babies and save ammunition."

Sue Ellen McCleen looked up from the bed with disinterest. "What do you care long as he ain't marryin' your daughter?"

"Because, don't you see, that's what they're doing?" Jacob crossed to the rickety bed. "They're muddying American blood!"

Sue Ellen drew up her knees to her chin. She was sitting in the middle of the mattress stark naked as the gray-haired man had instructed. "Oh, horseshit! The way I see it, they're more American than we are."

Jacob reached out and struck her hard across the face. "Watch your mouth, young lady. I'll not have you use language like that in my presence. I'm old enough to be your father!"

"Ouch!" She stroked her cheek. "That hurt. You hit me again and I'm liable to clobber you back."

Jacob grabbed her arms and pulled her toward him. "You do as I say, Jessica."

"It's Jessica, I am, huh?" She rolled her eyes. "Well, what is it you want Jessica to do for you besides sit here? I went through that song and dance of lettin' you in the back so nobody'd see you, now let's get on with it. Time is money, buster."

Before Sue Ellen knew what was happening, Jacob pulled out a bandanna and tied it over her mouth. She struggled, trying to pull off the gag and he slapped her hands away.

"I said, I don't like your mouth, Jessica. Maybe that'll keep you quiet."

The whore tried to speak again, but her voice was nothing but a muffled jumble of sounds.

"That's better." Jacob sat down on the bed beside her and stroked her shiny brown hair. "You've always had such pretty hair, Jessica." He twisted a lock around his finger. "I just wish you hadn't run away."

Sue Ellen stared wide-eyed with fright at the gray-haired man. Slowly she slipped her right hand beneath the mattress and pulled out a knife.

Jacob caught the glint of the steel and threw himself onto her, pinning her against the stinking mattress. Sue Ellen fought, kicking and twisting her body. He pried the knife from her hand. The gag he'd tied around her mouth muffled her cries for help. She swiped at him with the knife and nicked his arm. He gave a yelp and snapped her wrist with one violent twist of his hand.

Suddenly he had the knife.

Sue Ellen squeezed her eyes shut against the searing pain in her chest. She felt her body convulse and then there was nothing but soothing, inky blackness.

Jacob lay prostrate on the whore, panting, gasping for breath. The knife protruding from her chest pressed into his shoulder. He got up and slid off the mattress. There was a spot of blood on his black coat so he went to the washstand to dab water on it. He looked back at the dead girl.

"Oh, Jessica, I didn't mean to hurt you, love," he told her shakily. "But you have to learn to do as you're told if you're going to make a good wife." With his coat blotted clean, he walked over to the bed and slipped his penknife from his inside coat pocket. He opened it and carefully cut a lock of hair from Sue Ellen's head.

"You're mine," he murmured as he began to braid the hair in a tiny circle. "You'll always be mine, Jessica."

Adam rode all night without tiring. He could go

days without sleep and not have it affect him. It was one of his funny quirks he had brought back to the white man's world when he'd left the wilds of Canada. He was anxious to get back to Jessica. If she was well enough to ride, they would set out immediately.

The word from Sue Ellen was that Larry Caine had a brother in Seattle. She was sure enough of it—she'd once been married to Toby Caine. Adam also found out in Blades that folks were talking for hundreds of miles about the half-breed Deputy Marshal Sern, and the mysterious woman he rode with. Adam was said to be a red man on the warpath with the Pentagon's blessing. Jessica was supposedly a sharpshooter from Dodge City, avenging her parents' and eight brothers' and sisters' death.

Adam laughed aloud as he urged Zeus into an easy lope. He knew Jessica would enjoy the tall tale. He stared out at the open, desolate land of northern Utah thinking of the sable-haired woman who had touched his heart. There was something about her innocence that excited him, that made him feel good about the world again. He had had that feeling as a child back in Canada when he had lived happily among his mother's people. But then, after his parents' death and his move to Philadelphia to live with his grandparents, he had begun to sour. The more he saw of the "civilized" world, the less he wanted to be a part of it. The filth, the starvation, the poor working conditions in the cities, had been what turned him west in search of something new, something fresh and untamed.

Was Jessica that untamed beauty he sought? He

didn't know. He supposed he'd just have to wait and see . . .

At dawn the following day, Adam approached the bend in Blue Creek where he'd left Jessica. "Jess," he called, not wanting to frighten her, or be shot at. "Jessica, it's me!"

Oddly, he didn't see Hera. "Jessica!" The horse was gone and so was Jessica. He rode right into the camp and slid out of the saddle.

Her coffeepot sat on a flat rock near a cold fire . . . a campfire days old. Her saddlebag lay in the grass along the bank, its contents scattered. Her tin coffee cup rested on the edge of the creek partially filled with sand and water.

Adam kicked the tufts of grass on the bank, searching for more evidence. "Jessica!" He called her again and again, but heard nothing but the sound of his own voice.

Then he saw the arrow sticking out of the far bank. He walked downstream a short distance and crossed the shallows. A sickening feeling rose from his belly, constricting his throat. It was a Ute arrow. And there were empty cartridges everywhere. He waded back across.

A battle. The closer he looked, the more he realized that a battle had been waged on the banks of this creek. As he began to scour the area, he prepared himself for finding Jessica's body. But there was no body. There was dried blood and tracks where bodies had been dragged away, but no Jessica. He picked up the empty cartridges. None of them could have come from Jessica's Henry.

A scrap of color caught his eye and he walked down

the bank again. Tangled in the grass was a small strip of green lace—from her ridiculous bloomers. Upon closer inspection he realized that this was where she had lain and fought the Utes. There were empty cartridges from Shiner's old Henry everywhere. She'd used most of her ammunition from the amount of cartridges he found.

Adam stared out at the empty land that stretched in every direction. Tears welled in his eyes. He had failed again. He hadn't protected Jessica. She had been here, she'd fought a hell of a battle, and now she was gone. He took the handful of empty cartridges, and flung them into the air. "Noooo!" he cried. "Nooo!" The metal cartridges rained down.

The Utes were peaceful, what was left of them. Why would they attack a woman?

Crooked Nose. The thought came to him in an instant. Crooked Nose was said to be traveling with a band of Ute renegades, men no longer accepted by their own tribes. They were horse thieves and murderers.

Adam remounted. He rode in circles studying the tracks in the dry, hard dirt. Though several days old, it was easy to find the renegades' trail. They had approached from the east with a herd of twenty-five or so riderless horses. There had been nearly as many men on horseback. They had to have been headed for the creek for water.

Seething, Adam knew he should have moved Jessica to safer ground. Of course when he left her, she wasn't able to travel.

Adam rode back to Jessica's deserted camp and watched the running creek. *So where are the bodies,* he wondered. There was no sign of buzzards here. Then he remembered the buzzards he'd spotted not more than half an hour back. They'd been circling something to the east.

Adam retraced the creek bank. He rode out to where the buzzards gathered, scaring them off as he galloped into the center of them. There was a mound of rocks piled in a haphazard manner . . . a quick burial. The stench of rotting human flesh made him gag. He had to force himself to dismount. He had to be certain that Jessica's body was not among those left beneath the rock pile.

Gathering his courage, Adam began to shift rocks. Christ! How many had she killed!

Six. He counted six dead Utes, but Jessica wasn't among them. He quickly replaced the rocks.

Pride swelled in Adam's chest as he rode back to the campsite. A flicker of hope burned bright in his heart. Jessica had managed to kill six of the bastards. If her body wasn't here—and it wasn't or the buzzards would have found it—the only conclusion he could draw was that they had carried her off. He studied the tracks again to be certain she hadn't escaped, but there were no lone riders.

Adam thanked God silently that his mother had taught him to track so well. By reading the signs in the dust he figured that eight Utes, one riding double, had left this creek bank. They took one riderless horse—Hera. He was certain those were her hoofprints.

Adam packed up Jessica's belongings and strapped her saddlebag onto Zeus. Then he mounted the Appaloosa and followed the Utes' tracks. The riders rode north, joined with the horse herd and more men, then headed northeast.

Wyoming. He knew Crooked Nose and his men were headed for Wyoming where they could sell their stolen horses. But they wouldn't get far. Adam sank his heels into Zeus' haunches and rode into the wind. "Hang on, Jess," he murmured. "I'm coming."

Chapter Thirteen

Jessica slumped forward in the saddle, trying to avoid physical contact with Crooked Nose, but it was impossible. His thighs and calves touched hers; she could feel his hard maleness pressing against her buttocks as she rode in his lap. She twisted her fingers in his horse's mane to keep from tumbling to the rough ground. With her wrists tied, and the horse beneath her galloping at an unrelenting pace, it was all she could do to remain astride.

The Indians who'd captured her had been riding like this since dawn. Jessica had begged that she be allowed to ride Hera, but the Kiowa leader had flatly refused her, cuffing her on the head. He'd insisted she ride on his horse, in front of him, where he could keep his eyes and hands on her. Once he'd mounted behind her, he'd warned her of attempting to escape. He'd vowed she wouldn't get far. He had whispered of terrible things a man could do to a woman before she died.

Escape. Jessica would have laughed if her throat

hadn't been so parched, her lips so cracked and bloody. Escape to where? She didn't know where she was or where Crooked Nose and his men were headed. They were riding north, in the unbearably hot, pounding sun—that was all she knew. Even if she *did* know where she was, she was smart enough to realize there was no way to escape with fourteen half-crazed savages breathing down her neck.

All morning one Ute brave after another had come forward to speak with Crooked Nose. After the second brave had approached, Jessica had realized that they were trying to buy her from their leader. They spoke partly in English, and partly in their own tongue. Their crude gestures made it quite obvious what they wanted. An Indian with a shaved head had offered a shiny Colt pistol and a cavalry cap in return for her *services*. Another had offered a belt of male and female red-haired scalps. Her captor refused each with a shake of his head and an angry shout. It appeared he meant to keep her. She shuddered with revulsion as she contemplated his intentions.

When Crooked Nose had captured her last night, she'd expected to be raped, by him, by all of them. She'd expected to be tortured and killed. If she could have broken free and run, she would have. She'd have let them shoot her in the back before she'd have let them take her. But her injured leg had been so bad that she'd been unable to walk. The Kiowa had carried her over his shoulder and dumped her near the campfire. He'd bound her wrists and ankles until her circulation was nearly cut off, and then all of the men, except for the watch, had gone to sleep.

In the morning they rose before the sun came over the horizon, broke camp, and joined the renegades guarding the horses upstream. They'd been riding at a cruel pace since then, not stopping for water or to relieve themselves. It was well past noon.

Jessica tried to rest her aching head on the horse's wiry neck, but the jolting of its gait wouldn't allow her to relax. All she could do was hold on and pray Adam was on his way.

She thought of Adam often as the day passed as she drifted in and out of consciousness, suffering from heat exhaustion. She filled her mind with sweet, haunting memories, blocking out the heat of the day and the throbbing pain in her leg. She thought of Adam's glossy black hair, and the masculine scent of his bronze skin. She thought of the way he had touched her that night on the creek bank. She imagined the taste of his lips on hers. She felt the weight of his hard sinewy form pressing against her. He'd awakened her to sensations she'd never experienced, to emotions she'd not realized existed within her.

What *did* she feel deep inside her heart for Adam? It frightened her to even think about it. She remembered what he had said that night. He'd said . . . She squeezed her eyes shut. He had said he thought he was falling in love with her.

Love? She didn't want love from any man. Love from a man was nothing but pain, suffering . . . heartache. Her father had said he loved her mother, Rose, and what had that gotten Rose but unhappiness and an early grave? She'd died in childbirth a short year after Mark had been born. Jacob had said he loved Jessica. What had that gotten her, but fear and resentment? He had valued her only as a prized possession. He had dressed her in silks and lace for appearance' sake, but treated her like a pet. He never consulted her in his dealing with her money. He never asked her opinion when he sold her father's farm after his death. Not even for the funeral did Jacob ask about her wishes. He had made arrangements for Mark to go to boarding school in South Carolina. Jacob insisted on total control of her life from the time she woke until the time she slept. Had Jessica remained in Tennessee, she would have led a lonely life as the wife of a man she detested.

The horse beneath her came to a sudden stop and Jessica roused herself. She squinted in the blinding sunlight of midafternoon. Crooked Nose sprang down from his mount and dragged her after him. Jessica crumpled to the ground.

The Kiowa jerked her to her feet. "Stand, woman. Where is the strength I saw in you yesterday when you fought as a warrior? Where is your fight? I should have let my men have you!" he spat.

Jessica stared at him, her jewel-green eyes filled with hatred. "Give me my rifle and I'll show fight."

"You can't even stand!" He steadied her with one hand.

She jerked up her leather riding skirt to reveal her swollen calf. "I got bit by a snake a few days ago."

Crooked Nose's pitch black eyes narrowed as he studied the wound. "Snake." He nodded. "Your medicine must be strong to fight such evil." He glanced down at her calf streaked red and black. "Tonight when we stop I will make a pack to take out the poison."

She dropped her skirt as the other braves glanced at her curiously. Several had stopped for a short break to stretch their legs. They meandered in circles, talking among themselves in their native tongue and sipping from water skins. The horse herd moved on.

Jessica glanced back at her captor's face. His skin wasn't an even sun-baked hue like Adam's; it was blotchy and miscolored. Crooked Nose was precisely the same height as she was, so her gaze met him full in the eyes. "I'd rather have my leg drop off than have you touch it."

Crooked Nose tipped back his head and gave a bark of laughter as he pulled an army canteen from his saddlebag. "Drink." He raised it to her lips.

Jessica wanted to refuse, but knew it was foolhardy. Crooked Nose didn't care if she drank or not. It would be hours, perhaps days, before she got another chance. She took several gulps to wash away the alkaline dust of Utah from her mouth. Then she pushed the can away.

"Aye." The Kiowa gave a nod as he sipped from the canteen. "You are a wise woman; a finer warrior than these dogs that follow in my pack. Perhaps if you please me well, I will make you one of my wives."

"You'd be better to let me go."

He screwed the cap back on the canteen. "And why is that?" he asked with amusement. He stepped on a small lizard and crushed it.

She took a chance. "Because I belong to Adam Sern."

Crooked Nose jerked up his chin. "Sern?"

She smiled a half smile. Pauline had said Adam had a reputation. "You know him?"

"I know *of* him."

"He's behind us, you know. A day, maybe two. But he can travel faster than you and this herd of horses."

Crooked Nose studied her face, trying to discern if the white woman spoke the truth. Sern was a half-breed lawman from the northern country. A formidable foe. "You say you are his?"

"Yes. We're tracking a man who robbed a train. Larry Caine."

Crooked Nose laughed again. "That woman-child! One of my men once caught him in Kansas. They say he cried for mercy. He gave up his horses and his woman in exchange for his life."

Jessica thought of Shiner and his wife Gladys. Hadn't Shiner said that had happened in Kansas? She wiped the sweat from her forehead. "Well, I suggest you and your men get riding, because when Adam catches up with you, he's going to be damned angry." She sighed staring off at the mountains in the distance. "He hasn't got time to mess with you boys."

Crooked Nose lifted his hand to hit her and she caught his wrist. The Kiowa laughed. "You are bold. I would kill a man if he touched me as you just have."

She released him. "Don't hit me," she threatened. "Kill me if you want." It was already obvious to her that he didn't intend to kill her. He wanted her for his own, as some trophy. "But don't put a mark on my body. Adam won't like it." She tried to speak in terms he would understand. She knew she was taking chances, but she also knew she might well be saving

186

her own life. "He will torture you slowly, before he kills you, if you harm me. Otherwise"—she shrugged—"your death will be honorable."

The smile on the Kiowa's face faded. He grasped her roughly by the waist and heaved her onto his horse. He shouted to his men and they remounted quickly. A moment later Crooked Nose mounted behind her and they rode off.

Near dusk, Jessica heard a commotion among the braves. She lifted her heavy eyelids to see something far on the horizon. Crooked Nose reined in a moment later. Several Utes spoke to him and then rode off in the directon of whatever it was they saw. The brave with the red scalps dangling from his belt led.

Crooked Nose ordered his men to round the horses into a tighter herd and then directed that they move on. Up ahead Jessica could hear shouting and whooping as they neared their prey. Rifle shots sounded on the silent plateau.

"What is it?" Jessica asked. She craned her neck, squinting.

Crooked Nose chuckled. "My men—they need a little fun." He rested a hand on her shoulder. "You are tired. We will stop soon."

She shrugged his hand off her. "I can ride. Were I you, I'd want to put a little more distance before I made camp."

The Kiowa gave a grunt and urged his horse into an easy lope.

As Crooked Nose and the horse herd neared the Indians who had rode ahead, Jessica realized that it was a wagon they had surrounded. The Utes rode in circles whooping and slinging arrows into the wagon bed. Some fired rifles over their heads. Her stomach went sick as she saw a man stand and shoot from the wagon only to be run through with a short lance. A boy raised up off the wagon bed and shot one of the Utes clean off his pony. A moment later the boy, no older than Mark, pitched off the back of the moving wagon, a Ute arrow protruding from his chest.

Jessica buried her face in the horse's mane. If there had been anything in her stomach, she knew she would have been sick. The Utes dismounted and began to fight over the father and son's weapons. They unhooked the horse that drew the wagon and added it to the herd. Then they set fire to the old beat-up wagon, bodies and all. They tossed their dead companion's corpse onto the blaze. Crooked Nose rode by the desecration with disinterest. He barked a command.

Sobs threatened to wrack Jessica's body. It was all she could do to muffle her tears in the horse's mane, but she refused to let her Kiowa captor realize how close she felt to being beaten. It was her strength Crooked Nose admired . . . her strength that was keeping her alive.

Adam dismounted from Zeus and went to have a look at what was left of the burnt wagon. A partial skeleton, the flesh on it burned black and melted, protruded from the rubble.

"Christ!" Adam stared up at the great open sky. He felt so damned helpless. Crooked Nose and his men were headed due north through the mountains and onto the great Snake River Plain. They probably intended on making it to Idaho Falls where they could sell the stolen horses.

He touched a charred piece of wagon seat. Although the embers were no longer burning, the wood was still warm. He figured he was two days behind them.

The thought of Jessica among Crooked Nose's band made him sick. He *knew* what kind of man the renegade Kiowa was. He'd seen what was left of the bodies of the man and wife near Sharpston. What if Crooked Nose had harmed Jessica? What if she lay dead only a mile ahead? Adam knew he would drive himself crazy if he didn't stop thinking of all the possibilities. Jessica had survived that fight on the creek bank. Her desire to live was strong. Besides, Crooked Nose wouldn't have bothered to take her along if he hadn't intended on keeping her alive.

Adam remounted, buried his heels into his Appaloosa's flanks and rode on.

Jessica picked up one foot, set it down, and picked up the other. It was mechanical. All she could do was concentrate on each step.

Once Crooked Nose and his men had reached the mountains, the trek had become more unbearable for her. The band moved slowly, picking their way through the mountains, trying to keep the horses together. Crooked Nose still refused to allow her to ride Hera, so she rode in his lap, or walked.

She actually preferred the walking, though her leg still hurt like hell. At least walking, even on the short lead line Crooked Nose had tied around her neck, she felt some freedom. She hated riding in his lap, his sweaty body pressing against her.

They rode from sunup to sundown, stopping twice a day for water. The pace was grueling. Jessica was so exhausted that she couldn't think. All she could do was step . . . step . . . step.

As the days passed she began to wonder if Adam was truly coming. What if something had happened to him in Blades? What if he'd been shot? Gotten sick? What if he'd gotten information on Larry Caine's whereabouts? What if the Union Pacific Railroad had ordered him to move on? What if this was his way of getting rid of her? He'd told her which direction to ride if he didn't return. Maybe Adam had never planned on returning for her.

Jessica stirred her thoughts round and round in her head until her mind was nothing but a jumble of confusion. Adam wouldn't leave her behind. She knew that. She would never leave him. They were partners, weren't they?

When Crooked Nose and his men rode out of the mountains, Jessica was thankful for the flat terrain. The only thing good about crossing the mountains had been the relief from the unrelenting sun.

At sundown the Utes made camp. Someone had ridden away at sunup and had since returned with bottles of whiskey. The men started a campfire and roasted the hind quarters of a deer they'd shot in the mountains the day before.

Jessica lay on her side, in the shadows of the flames, watching the men as they grew rowdy with drink. She wondered how far a town must be that the

Ute was able to go get whiskey and come back in one day. She wished to God she knew where she was. Idaho maybe. She was so tired, her body so exhausted, that she couldn't think. Geography classes back in Tennessee when she was a girl seemed to have taken place a million years ago.

Out of the corner of her eye, Jessica caught sight of Crooked Nose unfolding a piece of canvas a good twenty yards beyond the circle of light the campfire radiated. She pushed up on one elbow, curious.

The Kiowa leader was erecting a tent. It became obvious very quickly. A tent? Jessica hadn't seen any tent before. Where had it come from and what did Crooked Nose intend to do with it?

A moment later he appeared at her feet. "Tonight we sleep there," he told her. "Get up. You will bathe."

Jessica lifted her lashes to stare up at Crooked Nose. "I don't need a tent. I'm fine here." She patted the saddle blanket she was stretched out on.

"Do as I say, Jess-i-ca. I will walk you to the stream that comes from the mountain. It's not far."

When Jessica made no move to get up, he grasped her arm and pulled her to her feet. "My leg," she protested.

"Your leg is better. I saw no limp today. The swelling is almost gone, the color is good. You have survived your test of the snake."

Jessica trembled. The Kiowa's face was taut and stark. He was not in the mood to be toyed with. "I will not sleep with you in that tent. I told you. I belong to Adam Sern."

Crooked Nose tightened his grip on her arm until

she flinched with pain. "You will do as I say or I will give you to my men. I can promise you they will not be gentle."

Her eyes met his in challenge and she realized this was the time to back off. She walked beside him obediently. The Utes behind them whistled and called out, making obscene noises. She ignored them, refusing to let them penetrate her concentration. There was still time. She wouldn't let Crooked Nose touch her, not after what she and Adam had shared. She'd die first, but the time to die hadn't come yet.

Crooked Nose led her a half mile back to a streambed and stopped. The moonlight filtered down from the sky to reflect off the trickling mountain water. "Take off your clothes," he ordered.

The moonlight illuminated his splotchy face. He waited calmly.

Jessica shook her head. "I won't."

"You will or I will." His hand darted out to catch the sleeve of her soiled shirt. The sound of tearing material filled the night air.

She took a step back. The thought of this man undressing her made her skin crawl. "All right," she said, her voice fierce, but barely a whisper.

She stood in the moonlight, her green eyes riveted to his as she pulled off her boots and her wool socks. She stepped out of her leather riding skirt.

The Kiowa parted his feet, taking an easy stance. He nodded approvingly.

She slipped out of her torn shirt and let it fall to the ground.

Crooked Nose gave a flip of his hand. "The rest."

A shiver ran up her spine. She wore nothing but

her bloomers and a sheer camisole.

He reached out and she shrank back. Tears slipped down her cheeks as she shed the remainder of her clothes.

"Now," Crooked Nose told her, his eyes taking on a glint of lust. "Into the water. I want no woman that stinks."

Backing into the stream, she cupped handfuls of water and let them run down her naked limbs. She kept her eyes on the Kiowa's as she washed away the journey's dust and grit. To her surprise, Crooked Nose made no advance toward her. If he did, she would wait until he touched her and then she would rip his knife from his belt and sink it into his heart.

"Your hair," he commanded from the darkness.

She waded into deeper water and flung her head forward, dipping it into the cold running water. She heard Crooked Nose enter the quiet pool and she lifted her head, the water streaming down her face. Her hand shook at her side as she flexed her fingers, her eyes falling to the knife on his belt.

"That is better. Come. I have brought clean clothes."

"I don't want clean clothes." She followed him, climbing the bank behind him. "I'll wear my own."

He snatched up her dirty riding clothes before she reached them. "You will wear this into the camp, or you will wear nothing."

She took the square of clothing he offered and shook it out. It was a soft leather tunic. She dropped it over her head and pushed her arms through the sleeveless armholes.

They walked back to the camp in silence.

"Let me have my clothes," she said when they reached the light of the fire and picked up her boots.

Crooked Nose laughed and with one heave threw her clothing into the fire. The Utes laughed.

"Now go to the tent and wait for me," the Kiowa told her softly in her ear. "Remember what I said I will do to you if you try to escape."

Jessica tried to take deep even breaths as she made her way to the tent. This wasn't the end. She wasn't ready to give up yet. She thought of Adam and the closeness they'd shared.

That filthy Kiowa wouldn't touch her. He'd lose his life first!

Chapter Fourteen

Adam crept through the shadows, his ebony eyes fixed on the Ute braves that gathered around the campfire. He counted their number and guessed his odds against a fight with them. He thought them fair to middlin'.

He shifted his gaze to the Kiowa leader who stood near the fire sipping from a bottle of whiskey. Crooked Nose. The man who'd kidnapped Jessica . . . A man he had heard tales of since he'd come west, but a man he had never laid eyes on before. The firelight danced off the Kiowa's splotchy face. Even at this distance Adam could see the multiple breaks in his nose that had healed improperly, giving him his name. The Kiowa's mouth was pursed in a tight scowl. It was said Crooked Nose held to no code of honor. In his twisted mind, there was no right, no wrong. He took what he wanted, horses, human lives—it made no difference to him.

Adam crouched, resting his hands on his knees. He surveyed the landscape and calculated the distance to where the herd of stolen horses grazed. He considered his options. The tent was far enough away from the campfire that there was a chance he could just sneak in, take Jessica, and together they could disappear into the night. But a part of Adam wanted to stand and fight Crooked Nose. He wanted to avenge the injustices, the innocent lives the renegade had sacrificed.

Adam dropped onto his hands and knees and crawled across the hard-packed ground to the rear of the tent. This wasn't the time to settle with Crooked Nose. He had to get Jessica to safety. He had to track down Caine who slipped farther and farther from his reach each day. Adam had to save his own honor. A coyote howled mournfully in the distance.

He reached the tent. "Jess . . ."

"A—Adam?" Jessica answered. It was him! She couldn't believe it! He *had* come for her!

"Yes."

"Oh, God, Adam, get me out of here!" She pressed her hand against the canvas of the tent and was rewarded by the warmth of Adam's touch. She couldn't see him, but she could feel him. She held back her tears.

"Just hang on, sweetheart," he murmured. He slipped the daggered point of his knife into the canvas and tore a long slit to the ground. He thrust his hand between the folds and Jessica grasped it.

"Can you see Crooked Nose?"

"Yes," she whispered. "He's looking this way."

"He can't see you. He's standing in the light, you're in the dark. Come on, Jess."

"Adam, he knows something. You'd better back up."

Adam reached through the slit in the canvas and grasped both of her arms. "I'm not going anywhere without you," he told her as he pulled her out of the tent.

Jessica threw her arms around Adam's neck, a sob escaping her lips. "Oh, God, Adam, I thought you weren't coming!" She showered his face with kisses.

Adam pressed his mouth to hers. "Not coming? I thought we were partners." He smoothed her wet hair, reveling in the feel of the soft skin of her cheek.

She looked into his ebony eyes. The moonlight streamed down, bathing his face in golden light. "Adam," was all she could say as tears formed on her lower lashes. It was on the tip of her tongue to tell him she loved him, to tell him that it would be all right for him to love her, but she couldn't. There were still so many doubts. She was still so scared.

He kissed her again, then dropped into a low crouch. "Your leg. Can you run?"

She nodded. "Where's Zeus? Which way are we going?"

"Through the horse herd."

Just then a shout of alarm sounded. Footsteps pounded toward the tent.

Adam grabbed Jessica's hand and they ran straight for the herd. "Keep low," Adam called in a hushed whisper. "They haven't seen us yet. The horses will shield us."

Jessica ran as fast as she could, clutching Adam's hand. She could hear the commotion behind her and she threw a glance over her shoulder. By the faint light of the fire she could see Crooked Nose standing beside the tent looking out into the darkness as the Utes rushed forward.

"Duck," Adam shouted as they reached the edge of the horse herd.

She dove beneath a spotted mare's belly, clutching Adam's broad hand tightly. "Hera, I want Hera."

"What?"

"I want Hera," she repeated. "She's all I have left of my papa."

Adam swore beneath his breath. He pushed horses aside, moving deeper into the herd. The animals were growing restless, shifting on their haunches and swishing their tails. They nickered softly to one another.

"Jess, for Christ's sake! What's more important? Your life or the horse?"

"I want my horse. People have taken from me too long. I want Hera," she insisted stubbornly.

"I'll come back for her once I get you to Zeus."

Jessica pulled her hand from his. "No!" she whispered harshly. "I want my papa's horse!"

"Jessica! Give me your hand!" The herd began moving as the Utes skirted it, shouting directions and diving beneath horses' bellies. Adam flailed his arms in the darkness, trying desperately to find Jessica. "Jess!"

"Which way, Adam? I'll meet you there."

He could hear her voice, but he couldn't see her. He couldn't feel her! They were caught in a sea of moving horses. His chest tightened with panic. He had had her in his arms and now she was gone. "Jess, don't be stupid," he hollered.

"Which way, Adam?" She walked farther from him, running her hands over the horses as they passed by, praying she would recognize Hera in the darkness.

"South, on the ridge. Two miles, maybe," he called desperately. The horses were breaking into a trot now, spooked by the human commotion.

Jessica ran with them, caught up in the wave of movement. It was all she could do to keep their hooves from crushing her bare feet.

Adam raised his head above the horses' backs, hoping he would catch sight of Jessica. A Ute arrow swished over his head and he ducked down again. If he called out to her, he would reveal his position to the Utes. Where the hell was she?

In desperation, Adam grasped the nearest mane and flung himself onto a warm, broad back. Here, above the horses, he hoped to get a better view. He prayed he'd spot Jessica. Several Utes swung onto horses and rode ahead of the herd, trying to pull them back before they broke into a stampede.

Adam ducked another arrow. Damn! They'd spotted him! He hung low on the horse's back, refusing to draw his pistol. If he pulled the trigger, the sound of the shot might well drive the horses into a stampede and then Jessica would be trampled.

Jessica became more frightened as the horses jostled and bumped her in an effort to move forward. She'd lost sight of Adam and the Utes were everywhere. Horses pushed past her. She shoved her shoulder into one of the horse's haunches when it stepped on her foot. If she didn't get astride one of them, she was liable to be crushed. Catching a wiry mane, she leapt onto a horse's back. She lowered herself, burying her face in the animal's neck.

The heady scent of horse flesh was all too familiar. "Hera? Hera, is that you?" She patted the horse's neck. It was Hera! Jessica could tell by her gait. She squinted in the moonlight and made out the rounded spots of the Appaloosa's lineage.

But now that she'd found Hera, where was Adam? The Utes were turning the horse herd back. If Jessica was going to make a break for the mountains in the distance, it would have to be soon. She raised up on Hera's back. There were silhouettes of men on horses everywhere. Then she saw Adam. The Utes were closing in on him.

He spotted her at the same moment. "Go!" he shouted as he drew one of his onyx-handled pistols. "Run!"

He fired as arrows whizzed through the air in response.

Jessica managed to turn Hera from the herd and direct her toward the mountains to the south. She watched over her shoulder as Adam broke from the herd, his horse in a dead run. He fired again and again. The Indians drew their rifles and shot back in rapid succession.

"Adam!" Jessica screamed as his horse veered right. "You're going the wrong way."

"Ride!" Adam shouted as he drew his second pistol. With no reins to control the horse the steed was out of control, barreling across the dark plain.

Out of the corner of her eye she saw his horse stumble. The animal went down on its front legs and rolled, screaming in a high-pitched wail. The Utes had shot the beast. Adam sprang free and ran.

Jessica lost sight of him in the darkness. She clung to Hera's back as her horse raced toward the mountains and freedom. "Adam," she sobbed. "Adam!"

She wanted to turn back, but she didn't. She knew there was a good chance he was already dead. No man could outrun a horse. But what if they'd captured him? Adam had said it was worse for a man to be captured by a band of renegades than to be shot and killed by them. She knew she had to go back, but first she'd find Zeus. Surely Adam's rifle was in his saddlebags.

In the distance Jessica could hear the sharp shouts of braves and the voice of Crooked Nose. It was obvious he was enraged that they'd let her slip away in the commotion. Clouds had drifted across the sky so that the moon was shaded. It was too dark for her to see anything.

Jessica let Hera slow to a walk once she was certain none of the Utes were following her. She rode up the ridge letting Hera lead the way to Zeus. The horses nickered softly to each other. When Jessica reached Zeus, she dismounted. Sure enough, Adam's rifle was strapped to Adam's saddle along with Shiner's old Henry. Adam must have found it on the creek bank.

Jessica reached into the leather bags for ammunition, hoping to also find some clothing to cover her near-nakedness. She had to go back to camp to see what had happened to Adam. She had a gun and ammunition, now all she needed was a plan.

At dawn, Jessica watched Crooked Nose's camp

through a spyglass she'd found in Adam's saddlebag. She studied the horse herd and counted the braves. There was one missing; Adam must have killed one. Immediately, she made out Crooked Nose as he strutted to and fro shaking his fist angrily.

Some twenty yards from the smoldering campfire Jessica saw three Utes standing in a circle looking at something on the ground. She caught Hera's reins and led her forward so that she could get a better look. Zeus followed on a lead line.

The next time Jessica looked through the spyglass she swore softly. It was Adam they were gathered around. He was tied, spread-eagle, to the ground, but she was filled with relief, just knowing he was alive. The Ute with the red-scalp belt tossed something at Adam and Adam flinched.

Jessica crouched on the ground, thinking. If Adam couldn't get into the camp and get her out, there was no way she could succeed in rescuing him. But she couldn't leave him to be tortured, to die in the hot, unrelenting sun.

With a sigh, she mounted. She'd go to Crooked Nose and she'd bargain with him. What else could she do? Adam had risked his life to save her. She owed him the same.

A sound of alarm went up within minutes as Jessica approached the renegade camp. A Ute was sent out. It was the baldheaded brave who wore the cavalry cap. He seemed surprised to see her. She rode past, ignoring him. She headed straight for the camp and for Crooked Nose.

When she entered the circle of braves, she rode straight up to the Kiowa leader. She wanted to run to

202

Adam, but she refused to give in to her emotions. She had to deal with Crooked Nose on his level if there was any chance in hell she was going to get herself and Adam out of here alive.

Crooked Nose watched Jessica dismount, giving special attention to her long, bare legs. She still wore the sleeveless leather sheath he had given her the night before.

He took an easy stance, his hands tucked behind his back. "You return, my warrior. I thought I had lost you."

"I come to bargain." She stepped up to him, letting Hera's reins slip from her fingers.

He lifted a bushy black eyebrow. "Bargain?"

"You know, a deal." She adjusted her black felt hat, thankful for the wide brim that shielded her face from the hot sun. "You give me something. I give you something in return."

"You want Sern?" he asked with amusement. "He must be a stallion. It seems unfair, I've not given you a ride yet. Perhaps you should compare before you choose."

She ignored his gibe. "You stole from him. He's done nothing to you. Why do you hold him?"

He shrugged. "My men, they grew bored."

Jessica caught Hera's reins. "I have two horses here. There're none finer. You give me Sern, I'll give you the horses."

Crooked Nose wandered over and stroked Hera's neck, then Zeus'. "Of course, one of these was mine already."

"You *stole* my horse. I offer her to you honestly. These two Appaloosas are worth more than that entire herd of workhorses and Indian ponies."

Crooked Nose scratched Hera's ear thoughtfully. "You rode into my camp after you were free. Why?"

"For Adam."

"He is your husband?"

"No. My partner. I told you. We're looking for Larry Caine."

The Kiowa lifted his head to study Jessica's sunburned face. "I wish I had a man so loyal, so brave."

Her green eyes searched his for some flicker of humanity. "He would have done the same for me. He did."

Crooked Nose scowled. "Then you are both fools."

"You just said I was brave." She gave him the barest smile. She could tell she had him thinking by the expression on his mottled face.

The Kiowa gave a wave of his hand. "Come, sit. Eat with me and we will bargain."

"I want to see Adam first."

The Ute braves that had stood silently around them shouted in protest.

"What? You think I'm going to cut him free, our horses are going to sprout wings and we're going to fly away?" She directed her comment to Crooked Nose.

He nodded thoughtfully. "It would not surprise me. Yes, you may see him, but only for a moment." He barked a command and the Utes backed off. A brave wearing Adam's hat and boots stood stone-still for a moment, then stepped out of her way.

Jessica grabbed her canteen off Hera's saddle and went to Adam. He was tied to the ground with leather thongs and wooden stakes so that his arms and legs were spread. His feet were bare, his torn clothes splotched with blood. His face had been cut with a whip. There were thin raised welts across both cheeks. She knelt beside him. "Adam," she said softly, refusing to let her voice break.

"Jess?" He opened his eyes, licking his parched lips.

She let some water from her canteen trickle into his mouth. "I don't know what you're doing out here in the sun without your hat," she teased.

He laughed and then flinched.

"What?" She slid her hand gently on his chest glancing over his body. There were no serious wounds, she quickly surmised.

"Ribs. Cracked, I think." He opened his eyes again. "What the hell are you doing here? I thought you got away."

"I did. I came back for you, partner." She gave him another drink. "And I don't mind saying, I'm damned annoyed with you, Mister Deputy Marshal. I've got a man to track. If you keep slowing me down, I'm going to leave you behind."

He laughed at her joke. He knew how desperate their situation was. He knew she knew. "Oh, Christ, Jess," he said finally. "Is this bad luck or what? I feel like we never had a chance, you and I."

"Well, maybe it's time we gave ourselves a chance, huh?" She leaned over him and kissed him softly on the mouth.

Adam stared up into her liquid-green eyes. "I never really apologized for what happened at the creek. I didn't mean to scare you off like that."

"Look, you're not dying yet, so save your confessions." She gave him one last sip of water and then screwed the lid on the canteen. "I got to go now."

"Go where? What's going on?"

"Crooked Nose and I are going to have ourselves a little powwow. See if we can strike a bargain."

"A bargain? You'd be safer bargaining with the devil himself."

"I thought we'd exchange your life for . . . I don't know, those fancy snake-skin boots of yours that I hate so much."

He wiggled his toes. "Where are my boots? I'd hate to lose them. An old man made them for me down on the Mexican border."

"Last time I saw them there was some Ute walking around in them."

He laughed again, then flinched.

"Your ribs. I'm sorry," she whispered.

"I guess it's too late for me to tell you you shouldn't have come back."

She stroked his stubbled cheek. "Mmmhmmm."

One of the Utes standing a few feet from her grunted and waved her away. Crooked Nose was calling her.

"I've got to go," she told him. She brushed her lips against his one last time and then stood, slinging her canteen over her shoulder. "Just be patient."

Jessica walked past the Ute braves, around the campfire, and up the slight bluff to where Crooked Nose's tent still stood. He sat in front of his tent, his arms crossed, waiting for her.

She sat where he indicated—across from him. He handed her a slice of venison off his plate. She gave a nod of thanks and bit into the savory meat, suddenly realizing how hungry she was.

They ate in silence, washing the meal down with water. Finally Crooked Nose spoke. "So it's a bargain you want?"

"Yes. My horses for Adam's life."

He shook his head. "It's not enough."

"Everything in our saddlebags. Just leave us with one rifle."

He picked his teeth with his finger, extracting a piece of meat. "Still not enough." He ate the sliver.

"Adam's got money in the East." She'd heard it, but she didn't know if it was true. At this point she was willing to offer anything.

"A man can only carry so much money."

Jessica pushed back a lock of her sable hair behind her ear. "If you kill him you'll have the law down your back. He's an important man to the Union Pacific railroad."

"I hear they'd like to see him hang for Caine's doin's. Him being a half-breed."

"You said you'd be willing to bargain." She studied the face she'd come to hate. "What is it you want?"

"You . . ."

She looked away, a lump rising in her throat. How much did Adam mean to her? "You mean, I come to you willingly and you let Adam go?"

"You give yourself to me?" the Kiowa questioned softly.

She met his gaze, her lip turning up in disgust. "I don't know if I could bear it."

He laughed and toyed with the hilt of the knife he

207

wore in his belt. "What's say we make a wager?"

"A wager? What do you mean?"

"I told you, my dogs grow restless. They'll soon be fighting among themselves if I don't scrape up some entertainment."

"What are you talking about?" The casual sound in his voice frightened Jessica. There was something razor-edged about it.

"A wager. Sern wins. He gets you. Sern loses. I get you. Sern loses his life."

"What does Adam have to win?"

Crooked Nose stared out over the open plain. "It is an ancient challenge, met by only the bravest, the strongest, the most honorable . . . the most foolish."

"Adam could win. I know he could." She rose up on her knees. "Tell me, what is the challenge?"

His black-eyed gaze fell on hers. On his face was a wicked smile. "It is called"—he inhaled, his grin widening—"Trial by Fire and Beast."

Chapter Fifteen

"Oh, shit!"

Irritated, Jessica knocked her hat off her head. The narrow ribbon caught and it swung down her back. "What?" She stared down at Adam, who was still tied to the ground. "What?"

He took a deep breath. The heat was unbearable. Jessica's naivety, her *stupidity*, was beyond belief. He spoke slowly, emphasizing each word. "Do you know what Trial by Fire and Beast is?"

She dropped a hand on her hip. He was making her angrier by the second. How dare he speak to her in that patronizing tone! She was risking her own life trying to rescue him. She didn't have to come back! She was safe on that mountain ridge! "No. I don't know what Trial by Fire and Beast is, but the options were pretty limited, buster." She looked out across the Snake River Plain that loomed to the north. "I was trying to save your miserable life. The negotiations were pretty one-sided."

"Jessica, no one agrees to something without

knowing what it is! I'd told you there'd be no dealing with a man like Crooked Nose!"

She kicked the stake that secured his left foot to the ground. "I was trying to help! Was I supposed to just let you die?"

He stared up at her, moistening his parched lips. "Why don't you just go ahead and shoot me now?"

"What?"

"Jess, there are easy ways to die and then there are hard ways to die." His black eyes met hers. "Trial by Fire and Beast is the hard way to go."

"So you're not even going to try?" she shouted angrily. "Because if you're not, I think I'll just walk on out of here now. I've got an outlaw to track and then I've got an apple orchard to start. I haven't got time for—" Her voice broke and she turned away, ashamed of her tears. She was so damned angry with Adam. She had tried! This was their only chance!

The Ute wearing Adam's hat and boots brushed past Jessica and leaned over Adam. Adam glared unflinchingly when he whipped out a jagged-bladed knife. The Ute sliced the ties that bound their captive to the ground and walked off without a word.

Jessica dropped to her knees and Adam tried to sit up. "They're freeing you!"

"Not hardly. It's all in preparation for tonight's entertainment." Adam ran a hand through his dusty hair, fighting the dizziness that churned in his head.

"Entertainment?"

He laughed. "Me, honey. I'm the entertainment." He cradled his head in his hands. This was all so ludicrous. If he'd just left Jessica behind in Loco, none of this ever would have happened. He'd have Caine by now. His name would be clear. He wouldn't be in love with an aggravating, irritating, naive woman with lips of honey. He wouldn't be in jeopardy of losing his life for the benefit of a band of renegades' amusement.

"What do you have to do?"

He shook his head. "Listen. There's not a lot of time. I need to prepare myself. I'm going to tell you what I need and then you're to go to Crooked Nose."

"What if he doesn't agree?"

"He'll agree. It's the competitor's right." Adam took her hand. "Then I want you to go, Jess. Ride out. Walk if you have to."

"I'm not going without you," she stalled. She didn't want to tell Adam the terms of the agreement. She didn't want him to know what he meant to her.

"I could meet you in Idaho Falls." He kissed her dusty palm. "Jess, I don't want you here. I don't want you to see me fail." He lifted his chin so that he could stare directly into the green eyes he'd come to love. "I don't want you to see me die. This is a terrible way for a man to die."

She put her other hand over his. "You're not going to die. You can't, Adam. I want you to see my orchard."

"Sweetheart, there's a distinct possibility I'm not going to get to see your orchard. Now for once, hush that tempting mouth of yours and do as I say."

She lowered her head, resting her cheek on his hand she still clasped. "I *can't* leave," she said softly.

He sucked in his breath. The sun was so hot. His

211

mind reeled with the pain of his wounds and the anticipation of what was to come. He hadn't heard her correctly. He couldn't have. "What do you mean you *can't?*"

He'd spoken so softly that she'd had to strain to hear his words. "The bet, Adam. I'm part of it."

He swore softly. "Winner take all?"

She nodded. "You lose, Crooked Nose kills you—"

"If there's anything left of me."

"Then I'm his," she finished. She lifted her head to look into his eyes again. "It was the only way . . . our only chance."

He stood, lifting her with him. "Guess I can't lose then, huh, love?"

Just after dark the Utes began to beat their drums rhythmically. At first it was a soft, gentle beat interspersed with the hollow sound of bone and gourd rattles. They had built two huge campfires, side by side with space enough for a man to walk between them. Just beyond the fires they had dug a deep pit. As the fires, fueled by wood brought down from the mountain ridge, grew higher and hotter, the rhythm of the drum increased. They beat louder and louder until the sound drowned out Jessica's thoughts.

She and Adam sat in the shelter of the Kiowa leader's tent, listening . . . waiting. She trembled with fear. This barbaric rite was far more frightening than she could ever have imagined. She stared across the tent at Adam. He was not the man he had been this morning, yesterday, the day she'd met him.

212

In the hours before dusk he'd transformed himself from a lawman to an Ojibwa warrior. He had bathed in the creek, washing away the dust, and sweat, and dried blood, from his limbs. He had donned a loincloth. He had combed his long, inky black hair with a wooden comb and braided sections of it into intricate patterns, decorating it with colored beads. Then he had walked back to the tent in meditative silence and began the ritual of painting his nearly nude body.

Adam had explained to Jessica the meaning of each color, each symbol, each diagonal line, in a soft haunting voice as he had smoothed the paint on his bronze skin. She stared through the darkness at his handsomely chiseled face. Blue and white symbols of his Ojibwa lineage marked his forehead. Across his cheeks were narrow and wide diagonal lines in blue and red . . . the red symbolizing the blood of his enemy, the blue, his intended victory. Across the wide expanse of his bare chest were more symbols. They told tales of the bravery of his mother's people.

The Utes broke into a deafening chant and Jessica's head snapped up. Her gaze locked on Adam's. His eyes seemed as black as the depths of hell. The silence that separated them was intense, yet drawing. She reached for him, but he crawled out of the tent.

Jessica was filled with overwhelming dread. "Adam," she called as she scrambled out of the tent after him.

She found him stretching his limbs like a wild cat. He flexed his arms and his legs, the sinewy muscles rippling with strength. His bronze skin glistened in the firelight. "It is time," he said formally.

"Oh, God, Adam, I don't want you to do it! Just let me go to him."

He shook his head in a slow, ominous motion. "Too late, love. The challenge has been accepted. I'll do what must be done. As long as I breathe I cannot offer you to Crooked Nose."

His voice made the hair on the back of her neck stand up. It was Adam's voice, low and sensuous, but there was something else lurking beneath the familiar tone, something dangerous, something to be feared.

"A token," he told her softly, offering his open hand.

"What?" She looked up at his empty palm in confusion. The Utes were banging their drums in frenzy. They hooted and hollered and spun in circles, dancing around the campfire.

"A token to take with me on my journey."

She spread her hands. "I have nothing. Crooked Nose burned my clothes. Caine has my carpetbag." Tears slipped down her cheeks. "I have nothing to give you."

He slipped a hand over her shoulder, threading his fingers through her sable-colored hair. "A kiss will be enough."

Nothing seemed real as Adam pressed his warm lips to her trembling ones. The drums, the howl of the renegades, the heat of Adam's touch . . . This couldn't be happening.

She threw her arms around Adam's neck and kissed him deep and hard. It was a kiss of desperation, of

214

unfinished words. "Adam," she moaned.

"Shhh." He caught one of her tears on the tip of his finger and brought it to his lips to taste the saltiness. "I need you to be strong, Jess. Whatever happens . . ."

She stared at him a brief moment, then lifted her chin with resolve. "Whatever happens," she echoed.

Adam turned away and began to walk toward the campfires.

"Wait," she cried. "I *do* have something."

He glanced over his shoulder.

She swiped up a small eating knife from the ground outside the tent and lifted a strand of hair off her shoulder, sawing through the thick lock. "Here." She stretched out her hand and forced a smile. "A token."

Adam accepted the lock of hair, bringing it to his lips. He inhaled deeply and was enveloped by the fresh, clean scent of Jessica. His eyes met hers. "Thank you. If I could give you a piece of my heart in return, I would."

"You already have," she whispered.

He held her mesmerized for a moment, lost in the depths of his ebony eyes. A hush fell on the camp as she and Adam broke through the circle of men and approached Crooked Nose. Two braves followed as guards, weapons drawn. There was no turning back.

The soft sound of a drum, and the crackle of the intense fire was all Jessica could hear. The Kiowa grasped her arm and pulled her against him. He glanced up at Adam. "Are you ready?"

Adam met his gaze, his own bold and aggressive.

"I am."

In an intimate motion, Crooked Nose dropped his hand onto Jessica's shoulder and brushed the rise of her breast with his fingertips. He smiled a smile that dared Adam to flinch. The Ute guards drew closer. Adam watched the Kiowa, tight-lipped, his hands clenched into fists at his sides.

For a moment, Jessica thought Adam would lose control, but he didn't. His chest rose and fell evenly as he stared Crooked Nose down, his dark eyes like daggers in the night.

The grin fell from Crooked Nose's face. He dropped his hand and motioned to Adam to follow him. "Gather, men, and witness!" the Kiowa called.

The Utes broke into a soft, ominous chant as they gathered around their leader and the challenger. There was something primal about their voices uniting as one and rising into the heavens with the embers of the campfires.

Crooked Nose squatted. Adam did the same, an arm's length from him. A Ute approached and offered his leader a long clay pipelike tube and a tiny leather packet. The Kiowa tapped a few puffs of a yellow-green powder from the packet into the end of the pipe.

Adam braced himself as Crooked Nose inserted the tip of the clay pipe into Adam's nostril and blew into the other end. A tiny puff of yellow-green powder rose from the pipe as the drug was administered.

Adam rocked back slightly.

Jessica lunged for him, but Crooked Nose caught her. "Easy, my Jess-i-ca," he whispered in her ear.

216

"There are some men who die of the magic before the trial ever begins."

She twisted, trying to break the Kiowa's grip, but he sunk his fingers into her arm entrapping her. Her eyes fell on Adam, who was still crouched, his eyes half closed.

"Adam," she whispered. "Adam, stand."

Crooked Nose gave her a shake. "Silence! You can give him no aid! The man must meet victory or death alone!" He laughed and the Utes cackled.

Her gaze darted back to Adam. She prayed silently.

Slowly, he began to rise. A drum picked up its beat, another followed.

Adam forced his eyes open. There was a streak of bright light that pierced his brain, confusing him. He saw a woman . . . Jess, then another . . . Jess again. She multiplied again and again before his eyes until he clutched his head and groaned with pain.

"Adam," she called . . . they all called.

He turned his head. The enemy . . . he could hear them, he could smell them. He heard the drumbeat of challenge. The enemy was everywhere, multiplying. Breaking, then dissolving into one again.

Someone grasped his arm and he swung a fist bashing him in the face. There was a ripple of laughter, a few voices, then a thousand. The bright white light was blinding, it was deafening. Then he heard the voice again.

"Adam, it's all right."

He turned to her, to the Jessica, and slowly they melded into one. Beside her stood a man, an evil man. He pointed. Adam turned.

Before him a blaze burned hotter than hell itself. Two blazes, three . . . four. They went on and on in a line that stretched to the limits of his imagination. He was surrounded by fire, a wall of hate and heat.

"Walk!" the evil voice, the voices commanded. "Walk!"

Adam took one staggering step forward. The Jessicas cried out. He blinked again and again, trying to focus, trying to fight the stark, immobilizing fear that threatened his sanity. Even in his drug-induced state he knew what he had to do. He stared up at the great wall of fire. The heat was so intense that his skin burned. He could smell the scent of singed hair . . . his own.

He took another step.

The drums pounded faster, harder. Loud, frenzied voices egged him on. "Walk," they called. "Walk the fire!"

Adam concentrated. He knew he must trust his own instincts, the instincts born to all people of the Ojibwa. He dug deep within his soul and took another step foward. The pain of the blinding light in his head was easing. He could still smell the burning wood, still feel the heat of the blaze on his flesh, but he could feel something drawing him to the right. Someone was calling him in a soft, gentle voice.

Adam lifted his head. A vision appeared, first wavy and without substance, but then slowly taking form. "Jess?" he called softly.

Somewhere in the distance, behind him, he heard a woman sobbing. He threw a glance over his shoulder. It was Jessica, all of the Jessicas, sobbing. *Concentrate, focus,* he told himself. He turned back to the apparition. How could *this* be Jess when there were so many of them behind him?

"Jess?" he whispered again. She was nude, her long pale limbs glistening in white light. Her thick, silky hair was brushed across her back in a cloak of sable-brown. Her green eyes glimmered as if she held some secret she wanted to share. She reached out to him, beckoning him. She called him, yet he heard no voice.

Adam took another step forward. He could feel the power of the drug waning. There was fire all around him. He could smell the heat, yet there was a cool mist, a path, leading through the inferno.

The Jessica surrounded by white light led him through the wall of fire. Each time he thought he would reach her in another step, she floated back. All he wanted was to touch her, to take her into his arms and feel the love she radiated from within.

Just one more step . . .

She smiled. Then slowly she began to fade. Her limbs disappeared, then her torso. The white light seemed to absorb the apparition until there was nothing but a face . . . then only white light.

"Jess!" Adam stumbled forward, out of the fire, reaching for her, grasping the air.

Suddenly the ground gave way. There was a scream, high-pitched and filled with fear. It was Jessica.

He landed at the bottom of the pit in a crouched position, his face protected by his hands. At first he smelled only dirt and smoke, but then he became aware of the heady scent of an animal. Something growled at the far side of the earthen pit.

Adam straightened. The fall seemed to have cleared his head. The drug's illusions had faded. Now he only saw cold reality. The pit had been dug into the ground only waist deep, but three sides had been built up with wood to make him feel as if it was deeper.

A badger. On the far side of the pit he could see it. He nearly smiled at the Kiowa's ingenuity. Adam had expected a wolf, maybe a coyote. But not a badger. A badger could rip a man to shreds with its long yellowed claws and fanged teeth. It was a painful way to die.

The animal was about two feet long. It had silvery grizzled gray-black fur marked with white stripes and patches. Its black beady eyes darted to and fro with fear and pain. Even in the shadows of the pit he could see its long sharp, deadly claws. The Utes had tantalized it before throwing it into the pit, Adam was sure of it.

Above, he heard voices. He glanced up. The Utes began surrounding the pit. A drum still beat rhythmically. Crooked Nose appeared with Jessica in tow. She'd been crying. There was a mark on her cheek where she'd been hit, by the Kiowa's hand no doubt. A trickle of blood oozed from the corner of her mouth. Adam winked at her.

Jessica offered a bittersweet smile. She couldn't believe Adam had made it through the fire! Just when he had been about to walk directly into one of the campfires he had veered right and walked between the two.

"So, you have survived the first stage of the challenge," Crooked Nose said, not bothering to hide his angry disappointment.

Adam returned his gaze to the snarling badger. "So I have."

Crooked Nose gave a nod and one of the Utes lowered a pole into the pit and prodded the animal.

The badger sprang and Adam jerked up his hands to protect himself. He felt the claws dig into his forearms. The smell of his own blood was thick in his nostrils.

The Utes broke into a roar of shouting and laughing.

Adam grasped the badger and flung it. The animal screamed as it hit the dirt wall and scrambled after him again. The moment its long yellow teeth made contact with Adam's bare leg he swept it up by its back legs and threw it again making it somersault before it hit the back wall.

The animal lay stunned for a moment. One of the Utes lowered the pole down and jabbed the beast. The badger came up snarling. The moment it spotted Adam it attacked again. He beat it with his fists, trying to grasp its neck. The badger clawed and snapped its jaws, slashing Adam's arms.

Sweat and blood ran down Adam's face temporarily blinding him. He could feel his heart pounding in his chest. He held the badger at arm's length. He'd be damned if he'd be beaten by a weasel! He drew it to him and threw it as hard as he could.

The animal hit the dirt wall and slid to the ground. It was tiring. The Utes shouted and shook their fists in disappointment. Just as the badger rolled back onto all fours one of the Utes swung the pole and knocked Adam to the ground. The moment he hit the floor the badger pounced on him. It ran over his chest, it claws sinking into his flesh. It snapped its jaws aiming for his neck.

Adam heard himself cry out in surprise . . . in anger. They had cheated. The sons of bitches had cheated!

Ignoring the pain of his wounds, Adam grasped the badger by the head, twisting its neck. He leaped to his feet and swung the animal over his head. But instead of snapping its neck, he released the screaming beast and it flew through the air, out of the pit, hitting one of the Utes in the chest and knocking him to the ground.

The Ute screamed and several braves came to his rescue beating the animal off with clubs and sticks. Adam took the instant of confusion to run to the side of the pit where no wall had been built and to leap up out of the death hole.

Jessica flew into him, throwing her arms around his neck. Adam held her tight, panting. His whole body was on fire from the razor cuts of the badger's claws and teeth.

Crooked Nose came to them.

"I have met the challenge," Adam managed. "We are free."

The Kiowa's blotched face was completely blank for a moment and then he smiled. With a wave of his hand there were Utes all over them, tearing Adam and Jessica apart.

Crooked Nose caught Jessica and yanked her into his arms as the Utes dragged Adam backward toward the blazing campfires.

"I have met the challenge," Adam screamed. "I have earned the right to go free and take my woman!" He fought and twisted like a madman deranged by betrayal.

The Kiowa looked at Jessica, trapped in his arms, and then turned his gaze to Adam. His face twisted in a sneer. "You didn't really think I was gonna give her up, did you?"

Chapter Sixteen

Rage bubbled up in Jessica. After all Adam had endured, Crooked Nose had no intention of letting him live . . . of setting her free. "You son of a bitch!" Jessica muttered under her breath. With one swift movement she rammed her elbow into the soft pit of Crooked Nose's stomach. He gave a grunt of surprise, then just as he drew back his hand to slap her, Adam broke free of the Utes.

He barreled into Crooked Nose and Jessica, knocking them both over. She scrambled to get out of Adam's way as the men swung fist against fist, rolling in the dirt.

Crooked Nose barked a command to his men, but to Jessica's astonishment, none of the Utes moved to aid their leader. The entertainment arena had moved from the pit to the bare ground. It was the Ojibwa against the Kiowa now, rather than the badger.

So his dogs have turned on him, she thought, eyeing the braves carefully. This could be the break she and Adam needed. A stroke of luck. There was no loyalty among this band of renegades. They had tired of following Crooked Nose's commands.

She watched them as she backed up slowly, moving toward the herd of horses. She and Adam would need their horses to escape. The Utes were passing around bottles of whiskey, laughing, shoving each other as they watched their leader and Adam fight in the dirt. The Kiowa shouted to his men again as Adam flopped him over and pinned him to the ground.

The Utes laughed harder. Adam was holding his own, slowly gaining ground. The small Kiowa was wiry and fast, but Adam held the upper hand in brute strength. Again and again Adam's fist connected with Crooked Nose's jaw. Blood poured from his nose and mouth.

Jessica took another step back. She and Adam would need the rifles and saddlebags that were in Crooked Nose's tent. She bumped into a bare chest and swung around. It was the Ute with the red-haired scalps decorating his belt.

He snatched her arm. His smile revealed jagged teeth and red receding gums. His breath reeked of whiskey.

"Let go of me!" She tried to twist from his grasp, but he held tight.

He hit his chest with his hand, then pulled her along.

"No! No!" She shook her head vigorously. "I won't go with you."

He said something in his native tongue, then began to drag her.

Suddenly Jessica realized he was kidnapping

her . . . from Crooked Nose, from Adam. She knocked him in the ear with her fist, but it only bounced off his skull. She dug her heels into the ground, screaming, but no one heard her. The Utes were too busy making a racket. Adam and Crooked Nose still wrestled on the ground beating each other to a pulp.

"Goddamn it, I'm sick to death of men hauling me around!" she shouted, dragging her feet. "I'm not going with you!"

The Ute grasped her by the waist and tried to fling her over his shoulder. "Wife," he said in barely comprehendible English.

"The hell I am!" She lifted her knee just as he swung her over his shoulder, hitting him in the jaw. The Ute stumbled, lost his balance, and tumbled to the ground with Jessica still in his arms. The minute she hit the dirt, she scrambled away, shoving the doeskin dress down over her bare buttocks.

The Ute caught her boot and Jessica screamed, pounding the ground as he pulled her toward him. "Adam!"

Adam jerked his head in the direction of her piercing scream. Crooked Nose rolled free of Adam and gave him a kick in the ribs, rolling him into the pit. Adam crashed through the wooden wall the Utes had built and disappeared into the earth.

Crooked Nose bounded to his feet and sprinted across the camp. He hollered to one of his men, but it was obvious they intended to give him no aid. They were enjoying themselves all too much.

The Ute with the red scalps leaped up and ran for the horse herd, dragging Jessica, who was kicking and screaming. The Kiowa shouted for him to halt.

Jessica glanced over her shoulder to see Crooked Nose headed straight for them and gaining on them. He passed the Ute, holding out a knife clutched in his hand. The Ute ducked, but too late. Crooked Nose buried the knife to the hilt into the brave's back.

Jessica ran. The Ute fell, dead before he hit the ground. Crooked Nose veered right, straight into her path. He grasped her by the waist and whistled. A horse burst through the herd. The Kiowa lifted Jessica, tossing her onto the animal's bare back, and mounted behind her.

"Adam!" Jessica screamed. Was he dead? She twisted, scanning the camp. He was nowhere.

Then she saw him running toward her.

Crooked Nose sank his heels into his horse's flanks. The herd began to move.

Adam mounted the first horse he came to on the fringe of the herd. Without a bridle he had to guide the animal with pressure from his knees, but the horse responded.

Adam gave an ear-rattling whoop and the herd broke into a run. Rapidly he gained on Crooked Nose and Jessica, their horse slowed by carrying two riders.

"Free her!" Adam shouted.

"She's mine!" Crooked Nose bellowed in Jessica's ear.

All she could do was hang onto the horse's mane for dear life. If she fell, she knew she'd be trampled.

Adam rode up beside them and swung a heavy fist, slamming Crooked Nose in the jaw. The brave rocked under the impact, but held tightly to Jessica's waist.

Jessica screamed, her own voice echoing in her ears.

Adam hit Crooked Nose again. The Kiowa swung back, but Adam easily dodged his blow.

"Your hand!" Adam shouted. "Give me your hand!"

Jessica stared at his hand for a moment. Though the horses rode side by side, there was still a good foot and a half between them.

Crooked Nose attempted to turn his horse but he'd lost control in the stampeding herd.

"Your hand!" Adam shouted again.

Jessica reached for Adam. Crooked Nose brought his fist down on her forearm, but he was so off balance, that his blow was weak. She felt Adam's fingers tighten around hers.

"Trust me!" he shouted.

"No! She's mine. Jess-i-ca is mine!" Crooked Nose screamed as Adam lifted her off the horse.

Jessica was petrified as she felt herself being pulled off Crooked Nose's horse. The thunderous sound of the herd's hoofbeats pounded in her ears. She knew she was going to fall. She knew she was going to be trampled.

In desperation, Crooked Nose grasped her legs.

Adam pulled Jessica across the chasm between the two horses, dropping her into his lap.

"He's got my feet!" she cried.

Adam held onto her as tightly as he could, but he could feel her slipping. "I'm losing you!"

Jessica kicked as hard as she could and felt the weight of Crooked Nose fall from her feet. She heard him scream as he toppled from the running horse.

She heard the pounding hooves and the splintering of bones as his body was crushed by the herd of horses he'd stolen.

Adam rode with the herd until they slowed and came to a stop. Then he pulled Jessica up so that she straddled the horse, facing him.

"Adam," she sobbed. "Adam!"

"Shhh." He kissed her mouth, her cheeks, her eyelids. "It's all right, sweetheart. You're all right."

She clung to him. "I was so scared. Oh, God! Why do these things keep happening to me?"

He slid off the horse and pulled her down with him. He stood there in the darkness holding her until her tears were spent. Finally she looked up at him, wiping at her tears. "I'm such a baby," she told him, ashamed of herself. "I've cried more since I met you than I've cried in my whole life."

He laughed, pulling her hard against him. God, she felt good in his arms, flesh against flesh. He could feel her heart beating, his own pulse racing. "I'd say you've earned yourself a good cry," he assured her, stroking her hair.

She sniffed, looking up into his dark eyes. "What about them?" She glanced over her shoulder at the Utes in the distance.

He looked back at the campfire a quarter of a mile in the distance. The drums had ceased. There were silhouettes of men, but no one seemed to be in any great hurry to see what had become of their leader. Adam kissed the top of her head. "I don't think they're going to bother us. If they were, they'd be here by now."

"Here comes one." Jessica watched as the silhouette of a Ute brave approached them. It was the man wearing Adam's boots and hat. She could see the outline of the hat on his head. He stopped halfway to them, crouched to see something on the ground, then came toward them.

Jessica felt Adam stiffen as the Ute walked up to them. She held onto Adam. Her strength was gone. She was sick to death of being brave.

The Ute stopped a few feet from them. There was silence for a moment. Then he removed Adam's hat, then his boots and set them on the ground. He signaled with his hands.

Adam interpreted for Jessica. "We took a vote. You're our new leader, Ojibwa."

"The leader?" Jessica echoed.

Adam glanced up at the moon, full and glorious in its golden splendor. "Your leader?" Adam signed.

The Ute began to signal again.

Adam spoke slowly. "The Kiowa's dead. You fight your own battles. The Kiowa—"

The Ute scowled, adding an obscene gesture for emphasis.

"The Kiowa," Adam went on. "We always fought his battles for him."

Adam released Jessica and picked up one boot at a time, slipping his bare feet into them. He signaled back to the brave, his bloody hands moving quickly. "I thank you for the honor to lead you and your men," he said aloud, picking his words carefully. He didn't want to insult them. He honestly didn't think he had enough strength for another fight and there were still ten or eleven braves. "But I must go and take my woman."

The Ute nodded appreciatively. Then he began to signal again.

Adam said nothing for a moment.

"What? What did he say?" Jessica asked.

"He said," Adam answered, his voice laced with amusement, "I will give two horses, a bottle of whiskey, and a Cavalry pistol for the Jess-i-ca woman." He mimicked her name in the manner Crooked Nose had pronounced it.

"Well, say no!" Jessica snapped.

Adam glanced over his shoulder. "It's tempting," he said as he turned back to the Ute. He began to signal. "She's nothing but trouble, but no." He shook his head for emphasis. "She's mine."

The Ute shrugged as if to say it had been worth a try.

Adam put his hat on his head and motioned for Jessica to follow. Together the three started for the campfires. "I'll take my horses, my bags, my woman, my guns." he signaled, speaking. He looked at the Ute who walked beside him in the darkness. "You will be the leader."

They veered around Crooked Nose's crumpled, lifeless body. Jessica looked away.

The Ute hit his chest with his fist in surprise.

"Yes, you." Adam answered with hand signals.

The Ute grinned, throwing back his shoulders to strut into the camp. The other braves gathered around, flasks of whiskey in their hands. They were laughing, but the tone had changed. Jessica felt no fear this time when she entered their circle.

The Ute Adam had made the leader quickly explained what was happening in his own tongue.

The braves seemed to accept the decision without complaint. One or two men made comments.

The Ute turned to Adam, his hands flashing in the firelight.

Adam interpreted. "They accept. You are welcome to sleep the night in our camp and go on your way in the morning." He glanced at Jessica. "What do you say? We spend the night, get an early start in the morning?"

Jessica laughed as she walked out of the light of the fire toward the tent where her belongings were. "You stay, if you like, Adam Sern. I'm getting the hell out of here."

Adam laughed, and then turned back to the Ute, thanking him for his hospitality, but declining his offer. A few minutes later Adam appeared at the tent with Hera and Zeus saddled and ready to ride. Jessica strapped on the saddlebags and mounted. She pulled her doeskin skirt down over her bare thighs as best she could.

Adam swung astride. "Ready?"

She nodded. "Which way?"

"I thought we'd go back into the mountains for the night. I've got to have some sleep. I can't tell you the last time I closed my eyes. But there's no sense in letting them know which way we're headed. They might sober up by morning and change their minds."

She clicked to Hera and the horse started south. "I don't care which way we go as long as it's out of here."

They circled the camp. Adam waved to the Utes in salute and together he and Jessica rode south.

233

Behind her, she could hear the soft pounding of a drum and singing. She and Adam rode in silence for several minutes. Then suddenly something ran in front of their path. The horses shied.

"What was it?" Jessica patted Hera's neck to calm her.

Adam reined in. A few feet away he could make out the silhouette of an animal. "I'll be damned," Adam muttered.

"What?" Jessica turned in the saddle.

"You see it?"

She nodded as she glanced back to Adam, her eyes meeting his. "The badger," she murmured.

"I was supposed to kill it." He sat back in the saddle, his eyes fixed on its beady ones. They watched it for a moment, then it loped away, disappearing into the darkness.

Jessica felt Adam's hand slip into hers. "Let's get the hell out of here, sweetheart."

At the stream in the foothills of the ridge, they stopped for water. Jessica slid to the ground and followed Adam. "You probably should wash some of that blood off and let me get a look at those bites and scratches. Wounds like that can turn bad fast," she told him as she watched him throw down his hat and pull off his boots.

Her breath caught in her throat as he tossed his loincloth aside and waded into the water. Even bloodied and covered with dirt he was the most beautiful man she had ever seen. The sculptured muscles of his back and biceps rippled as he leaned over and cupped water to splash his face. The moonlight played off the water that ran in rivulets down his chest. Each droplet glistened.

Adam glanced up to see her staring brazenly at his nakedness. Their eyes met and he offered his hand. "Jess . . ."

His voice was a caress to her ears. No man had ever done for her what Adam had done. He'd risked his life for her. He'd been willing to die so that she might live. She pulled off her boots and stepped into the water. It was cold despite the hot night air.

Adam still held his hand outstretched.

She stood a few feet from him. Her heart pounded. Her mouth was dry. Her hands trembled. What was this she felt? Desire . . . lust? Or was it more? The word *love* hovered in her subconscious mind.

She picked up the hem of the doeskin dress and lifted it over her head. She heard Adam inhale sharply.

Her eyes met his again. She thought she would be embarrassed standing in front of a man stark naked. But she wasn't embarrassed, she wasn't ashamed. His gaze made her breasts tingle, her stomach turn in knots. There was a certain excitement to have a man stare boldly at her unclothed form.

Adam came to her. He took her hand with his and brought it to his lips. She let her hand fall to his shoulder. His flesh was cut to ribbons.

"Adam," she whispered. "I'm so sorry." She scooped up a handful of water and let it run through her fingers over his shoulder.

His eyes drifted shut. His flesh burned from the badger's scratches and bites. The cool water soothed him. Her fingertips brushing against him made him shiver with pleasure. Gently she washed him, rinsing away the blood and pain, replacing it with tingles of desire.

He entwined her fingers in his. Their lips met . . . gently at first. Hesitantly. There was so much to say. This wasn't the time or the place to fulfill his fantasies, to finally hold her in his arms and make love to her as he had done only in his dreams.

"Jess," he whispered in her ear. "I've wanted you for so long."

She didn't know what to say. She looked into his ebony eyes, smoothing his brow. She didn't want him to think she was silly. "I never thought I would want this," she whispered. "I never thought I would want a man to touch me." She took his hand, lifting it to her breast. "But I want you, Adam. I want you to touch me . . . love me."

Adam's mouth crushed hers. His arms tightened around her until she thought she would faint for want of air. His hands glided over her damp body, setting her flesh on fire. They were both panting. Their mouths met again and again as she pressed her hips to his, craving the feel of his male hardness against her.

Adam swept her into his arms and carried her to the bank. She threaded her fingers through his wet hair as he knelt and laid her gently in a patch of grass. Moonlight illuminated his chiseled bronze face. She caressed his cheek, murmuring his name.

Adam kissed her bruised lips. He touched her chin with the tip of his tongue, then made his way to the valley between her breasts, leaving a trail of dampness. Jessica held her breath in tingling anticipation, watching, until his lips met the peak of her breast.

She arched her back, crying out with pleasure. Her nipple was already puckered, hard with desire. He stretched over her, covering her pliant body with his own muscle and sinew. He suckled one breast and then the other. She ran her hands over his back, her fingers playing lightly over every inch of him.

When Adam's hand touched the tender flesh of her thighs, she parted them. Her whole body was alive with sensation. She could feel her blood pulsating through her veins. She wanted him. She wanted to be consumed by the sensations.

Adam stroked the nest of curls between her thighs. "So soft," he whispered. "So sweet."

She raised her hips to meet his touch. His strokes made her cry out with pleasure. But they weren't enough. She wanted more. "Adam," she managed. "Please."

He lowered his head over hers, taking in her green eyes, smoky with desire. "Jess, you are my heart," he told her, his voice raspy with longing.

She parted her thighs, accepting his engorged member. She cried out with surprise, with intense sensation. She had expected pain, but there was no pain, only a tightness which soon eased.

Adam took a moment to let her adjust to the feel of him and then he began to rock gently. Jessica cupped his hard muscular buttocks, guiding his rhythm. Waves of pleasure rolled over her as she raised and lowered her hips to meet his thrusts. He lowered his head to her shoulder, murmuring soft words of encouragement. He tried to pace himself, wanting to prolong her pleasure as long as he could.

Jessica rode the tide of sensation, adrift with pleasure, wanting it to go on forever. Their bodies rose and fell as one until finally, half sobbing, she grasped his shoulders, crying out with intense fulfillment as her body convulsed again and again.

The sound of Jessica's voice brought Adam over the crest. He groaned and gave a final thrust, spilling into her.

For a moment neither could do anything but gasp for breath. Finally Adam rolled onto his side, relieving her of the pressure of his body. Jessica sighed as he slipped from her.

She lifted her heavy eyelids, smiling up at him. "That was . . ." She didn't know what to say. No words could describe what she had felt, but not just physically. This man, Adam, had touched her heart.

He kissed her damp forehead, smiling down at her. "Yeah. It was, wasn't it?"

She laughed, laying her head back on his arm. Above, the dark sky hung like a canopy with pinpricks of white light shining through. The moon was half covered by a drifting dark cloud. As her body relaxed, conscious thought began to return. She thought of Caine, of Jacob, of Mark . . . "We've really complicated things here, haven't we, partner?"

Adam raised up on his elbow and stared into her eyes. "No. I told you, I've fallen in love with you."

She sighed, closing her eyes. "I don't know if I love you. I want you, even now. Again." She laughed at her own brazenness. "I need you. But love?" She raised her lashes. "I don't know if I can love you . . . if I'm capable."

He kissed her softly. "Tell me, Jessica, tell me why you're running. Tell me why you're afraid. Tell me who hurt you."

She shook her head. How did he know she was running? "I can't."

He nodded. "I could help." He thought of the man at the boardinghouse who was looking for his wife. It was an awfully strange coincidence that the man would be from Tennessee. Adam wondered if he'd just made love to someone's wife. He wondered if he cared. He kissed her again, covering her body with his leg and arm, as if he could protect her from whatever or whoever was out there that she feared. "It's all right, then," he whispered. "For now I've got enough love for both of us."

Chapter Seventeen

After a few hours of rest in the foothills, Adam and Jessica rode northeast. Wanting to make up for lost time, they rode hard, putting mile after mile between them and the Utes. It was well after dark when they finally came into the town of Pocatello on the Portneuf River.

"This is still part of the Oregon territory," Adam told her, "but it won't be long before Idaho's a state. I give it ten years. People are settling here fast. The railroad's coming in. Miners making their fortunes."

Jessica nodded. She was worn to the bone. Adam's voice was comforting. He knew so much; she could listen to him by the hour.

"There's a place with rooms to rent." She pointed. Ahead was a huge new frame house with a lantern hanging by the door. The light from the lamp illuminated a scrolled sign advertising rooms and meals.

Adam rode up to a hitching post and dismounted. "I'll go in and see about a room. Then we'll find a livery stable. Hera and Zeus could both use a good rubdown and some grain.''

Jessica slid out of her saddle and came around to Adam. She was so tired she could barely walk. Now that her ordeal with the Indians was over, she was beginning to realize the hell they'd put her through. She laid her hand gently on his arm. "I have a better idea. Let me get us a place to sleep. You find the stable and put up the horses.''

Adam bristled. "I can get a room.''

"I just thought we'd avoid any confrontations. Neither of us has the energy for it tonight. Once the room's rented they won't put you out, not with you carrying that badge.''

He scowled. She was right. He knew she was right. But it hurt. He wanted to feel like he could care for her. What good was he if he couldn't rent a damned room for the night without getting into a brawl?

She stroked his forearm. "Please. I just want to sleep in your arms.''

He glanced over her. "And what makes you think anyone's going to rent you a room? You look like a savage yourself,'' he said testily.

She ran a hand over her doeskin dress. It was all she had. She knew she looked a sight wearing her riding boots and wide-brimmed black hat and squaw's dress that fell to her midthighs, but it couldn't be helped.

Self-consciously she combed her fingers through her wild, tangled hair. "I'll manage." She took a saddlebag off Hera's back and flung it over her shoulder. She watched Adam lead the horses away and then looked up at the sign that swung overhead.

BARTON'S HOTEL. The building was brand spanking new; she could smell the fresh-cut lumber and the fumes of just dried paint. The hotel was of modern architecture with multilined roofs, walls of windows, and a front porch that stretched the length of the building and wrapped around the side. Even in the darkness she could make out the subtle pink and white exterior paint.

Jessica pushed open the door with the oval glass window. The moment she stepped inside the hotel and her dusty boots hit the thick carpet at the entryway, she wished she'd let Adam get the room himself. A lady and a gentleman enjoying evening tea at a table in a parlor to the left looked up at her. The woman gave a gasp and brought an embroidered handkerchief to her mouth. The man's handlebar mustache began to twitch.

Jessica looked down at the scrolled pink carpet. Her boots had left dusty footprints. She was tempted to turn and run. She'd be lucky if the proprietor didn't toss her out on her ear, looking like she did. But she was tired and she didn't want to look for another hotel or boardinghouse. What right did someone have to give or deny rooms on the basis of how she or anyone looked? If she had the hard cash, she had a right to the room. Spotting a small desk, she marched up and hit the brass bell. It dinged. When she got no immediate response she whacked it again.

A flowered pink and lavender chintz curtain parted in the doorway behind the desk and a well-dressed, red-haired man with a great red beard appeared. He blinked, obviously startled. "Good Lord, woman, do you need help?" He stared at her doeskin dress and tangled hair. A white woman in Indian clothing! The poor woman had obviously been captured by savages. What a miracle that she was still alive!

"I need a room. I have money."

The woman was obviously out of her head. Only God knew how she'd been tortured! "Did Indians do this to you, ma'am?"

She rolled her eyes heavenward. "You think I'm voluntarily walking around half-naked down the street?" She leaned on the desk, with both hands. "Yes, Indians did this to me; now give me a blasted room!"

The redhead stood frozen for a moment and then broke into a smile. He pulled his registry book from a drawer and began to flip through the pages. "Guess the Indians didn't make out too well."

"Guess they didn't."

He picked up a quill and dipped it into an inkwell. "Name?"

"There'll be two of us. Deputy Marshal Adam Sern will be paying."

The redhead's mouth dropped open. He stared in disbelief. "Sern? You're traveling with Sern?" He slapped his knee. "I'll be damned. I thought it was all gossip! A good week ago somebody came through here telling some tall tale about a half-breed deputy marshal and a gun-toting female tracking the Black Bandit." His eyes fell to the Smith & Wesson six-shot revolving pistol she'd traded her derringer in on. It had been a gift to Adam from the Utes, but since he already had his onyx-handled Bisleys he'd given it to her.

Jessica pushed back a lock of her hair and glared

back. "Could I just have the room?"

He slapped the counter. "It's yours—free of charge."

Just then the front door opened and Adam walked in. He had saddlebags thrown over his shoulder and both rifles in one hand. He glanced up at the crystal chandelier, alight with dozens of candles, that hung above his head. He raised a dark eyebrow.

Jessica couldn't resist a smile. Adam wore dungarees, a blue shirt, and the snakeskin boots she hated, but she remembered him in his loincloth. Her cheeks went hot. She couldn't help thinking about what they'd shared last night.

"Is there trouble?" Adam asked. His voice was low and rumbly. It sounded odd to Jessica enclosed by the walls of a wallpapered room. His voice was one meant for the open land.

"Problem? Good Lord, a'mighty, no!" The redhead hustled around the desk and clasped Adam's hand, pumping it, "Pleased to meet you, Deputy Marshal. I was just telling the lady here that the room's on the house. Got a honeymoon suite. You're welcome to stay as long as you want. Honored I'd be to have a famous lawman like yourself in my humble establishment."

Adam glanced down at the hand that was still jerking his.

The redhead let go. "The name's Barton, Goliath Barton."

"That's kind of you, Mr. Barton." Adam brushed past him and took Jessica's arm. "Now if you wouldn't mind showing us to our room . . . The lady and I could use some rest."

245

Barton flew around the desk, swiped a key off a hook, and raced for the winding, polished staircase. "Right this way, Deputy Marshal."

"The lady will need a bath." Adam purposely didn't use her name. If Jessica was running, and after what she'd said last night, he was convinced she was, he didn't want to reveal anything she didn't want to reveal. He'd figured he'd get to the bottom of it, but all in due time.

"You're in luck, Deputy Marshal, because Barton's Hotel sports the first running water in Pocatello. We've two windmills pumping water into some of our suites. Hot and cold for the lady's pleasure."

Jessica's feet sank into the floraled carpet that ran down the center of the staircase. "I think I could get used to this, Deputy Marshal," she teased, taking in the surroundings. The walls were papered in more vines and flowers in multicolored pastels. Another chandelier hung from the ceiling at the top of the staircase. "The deputy marshal will want something to eat, Mr. Barton." She looked at Adam and smirked. He pushed an elbow into her side.

"Of course, of course," the redhead agreed as he led them down a corridor. "I'll fetch the cook and have something brought up momentarily." He slipped a key into a polished brass lock and turned the doorknob. Then, taking a lamp off the wall, he entered the room, and it filled with light. Jessica and Adam followed.

The suite was even more elaborately decorated than the front hall and parlor. The room was done in lavender and blue pastels with pink roses everywhere. A giant four-poster bed, rose petals carved on the headboard, dominated the room.

"This is the bathroom, ma'am. I'm sure you'll find it to your liking. Just turn the handles and you've got water at your fingertips. Flush pot, too." Barton pushed open a door off the bedroom.

Jessica dropped her saddlebag onto a horsehair chair and a puff of dust rose and filtered into the air. Adam set his and Jessica's rifles by the door and walked to the window to close the heavy brocaded pink drapes. "Looks like a damned whore house," he muttered.

Barton scurried to and fro, lighting lamps. "We've just opened. With the railroad expanding, there'll be more need than ever for good clean living arrangements."

Adam walked Barton to the door while Jessica explored the bathroom. "You'll send up that meal?"

Barton hesitated, obviously disappointed that he wasn't going to be invited to stay and chat. "Right away. Isn't there anything else I can do? Turn back the bedsheets? Start a fire?"

"I don't think a fire will be necessary. It still must be eighty degrees out." Adam walked him into the hall. "Mr. Barton, I'd appreciate it if you wouldn't tell anyone we're here. I don't want to attract attention, if you understand what I mean."

"I do, I do, you being on the trail of the Black Bandit and redskins being after you." His brown eyes went wide. "I know just what you mean."

Adam nodded, knowing there wasn't a chance in hell the proprietor was going to keep his mouth shut. "Well, I thank you." He stepped into the suite and closed the door, leaving Barton still standing in

247

the hall.

Jessica was sprawled on the immense bed, surrounded by pink, ruffled, chiffon bedcovers. She giggled. "Wait until you see the running water!"

Adam shook his head. He'd been tired, exhausted, but the sight of Jessica's creamy thighs, that impish grin on her face . . . His fingers found the buttons of his shirt and he began to undo them.

She lifted a feathery eyebrow. "We're going to take a bath, eat, and then sleep, *right?*"

His eyes were cloudy with rising desire. "Right."

"Can you believe Barton? You're famous!" She sat up, removed her boots and woolen stockings, tossing them to the floor.

He threw aside his shirt and sat down to shuck off his boots. *"We're* famous, you mean."

Her smile fell. "We're not staying long, are we?"

He shook his head as he skinned off his tight-fitting dungarees. "Not long. A day or two. Just enough time to scan the newspapers, check in with the railroad. Once we see if there's any word on Caine, we'll decide where to go from there."

She nodded, watching him as he strode across the plush lavender carpet toward her. "Is this really what a whorehouse looks like? I've never been in one."

"I wouldn't think you had, little Miss Innocent from Tennessee."

She leaned back on the bed, tucking an arm behind her head. "Actually, I'm not from Tennessee. It's just where my father settled after the war."

He reached the end of the bed. "Where are you from?"

She grinned. "You'll never guess."

He grasped her bare feet and Jessica squealed. "Where?"

"Philadelphia." The instant it came out of her mouth she scrambled to get away, but he was too quick for her.

"Philadelphia!" He grasped one of her ankles and dragged her slowly toward him. "That explains why you don't have a southern accent." His eyes narrowed. "You mean to tell me we were walking the same streets?"

"I was a skinny, freckle-faced girl with skinned knees." She clawed the bedclothes, trying to hold on, but the filmy material slipped through her hands. "You wouldn't have noticed me."

"I'd have noticed you." He held her firmly with one hand while he caressed her thigh with his other.

"Let go of me, Adam, I'm dirty." She kicked at him.

"I like you dirty."

She laughed and rolled over onto her stomach, trying to crawl away. "That doesn't sound very romantic."

He flopped onto the bed. "Romance is for dime novels. It's not real." He grasped her by the waist and flipped her onto her back, straddling her. "This is real." He brought his mouth to hers.

Jessica ran her hands over his shoulders, bringing him closer. Her laughter died away as his kiss set her lips on fire.

None of this made any sense. She needed Adam like she needed air to breathe, food to eat. All day they had ridden and talked. All day she had thought of what it would be like to be in his arms again, naked, flesh against flesh. They had fallen so easily into the relationship of lovers. In one day, it seemed as if they had been together a lifetime. She still didn't know if she loved him; she knew she didn't want to. She also knew their relationship couldn't last. There were Mark and Jacob to keep them apart. But for now, for today, tomorrow, maybe the next day, she would enjoy every touch, every word Adam offered. She would worry about the rest of her life later.

"How about a bath?" Adam whispered in her ear.

"Together?"

"Don't look so shocked." He kissed the tip of her nose. "You bathe with me in the creeks. That was quite a bath last night."

Her cheeks reddened. It sounded strange to hear Adam speak of their lovemaking so openly, so comfortably. "I don't know."

He slid off the bed, encircling her wrist and hauling her after him. "Come on, sweetheart. Where's your sense of adventure?"

"Adventure!" She stopped short. "I've had more than enough adventure with you to last me a lifetime, *Mr. Deputy Marshal!*"

"All this was your idea." He waggled a finger at her. "You're the one who insisted on going after the Black Bandit."

She grabbed his finger and bit down lightly on it. "All right. A bath." She shrugged. "What's a bath with a man after you've fought off a band of renegades!"

"There's the spirit!" Adam caught her hand again and led her into the bathroom, whispering into her ear. "It'll be an adventure, I promise."

Jessica laughed and closed the door behind them, shutting out the world if only for a little while.

The following morning Adam was gone when Jessica woke. Beside her bed was a breakfast tray and a note. She rubbed her sleepy eyes.

My heart,
Gone to telegraph office, then newspaper.
Stay put. Will bring you clothes.

A

She smiled, bringing the note to her chest. What was wrong with her? Why was she afraid to love him? The man was wonderful! As good as their love-making had been the other night, last night was better. Last night they had taken the time to get to know each other's bodies. She had touched Adam and been amazed by the pleasure she felt in giving him pleasure. The bath water had been warm and softly scented with honeysuckle, his touch had been . . . She sighed. It made her mouth dry and her heart pound just thinking about it.

She pushed out of bed and put on a silky pink robe she found last night in the bathroom. Then she opened the brocade drapes, letting the sun pour in. Heavens! It was nearly noon. She went back to the bed to sit cross-legged and eat her breakfast. She lifted a linen napkin to find little potato pancakes, a bowl of baked apple slices, spiced with cinnamon, muffins, jam, and a whole pot of fragrant tea.

She was just finishing her meal when a key slipped

into the door and Adam walked in carrying a brown paper package. "You're awake."

She smiled. He was dressed in a new red shirt and a pair of soft navy pants, his gun holster slung low on his hips. His boots had been shined. His thick black hair was pulled back and tied behind his head with a strip of rawhide. His rugged handsomeness was breathtaking.

"You shouldn't have let me sleep. I'm going to get soft with running water and a feather bed."

He crossed the room and sat on the edge of the bed. "You were exhausted. You needed the sleep. I don't think there's much chance of you getting soft, not a famous sharpshooter like you."

She laughed, giving him a push. "What's in the package? Something for me?"

He brought up his hand to brush her cheek with his knuckles. What was it about this woman that made him so happy, that filled him with such a desire to care for her, to protect her? "Yes, it's for you, but the price is a kiss."

"A kiss? You got plenty last night, and not all on your face if I recall," she dared sassily.

He shrugged, trying to push away thoughts of their lovemaking, else they'd never get anything else done today. "Nonetheless, the price is a kiss."

She leaned and kissed him chastely on his smooth-shaven cheek.

"Nope. That won't do. I could get a kiss like that from my sister, if I had one."

She tried to pull the package from his hands. "Come on, let me see."

"It's just a dress. Pink," he told her.

"Oh, God, you didn't. I'm suffocating in pink!"

He pushed the package into her hands and got up.

Jessica's fingers flew over the string, untying it, and pushing back the brown paper. "Oh, Adam, it's beautiful." She pulled out a gown of soft blue cotton sprigged with tiny green leaves. The neckline was high, but could be buttoned down. The waist was clipped and shapely, but the skirt was full for riding.

"It's nothing fancy. They had laces and bows at the mercantile, but I didn't figure that was what you wanted."

"It's perfect." She picked up several items of underclothing. "And underwear, too!"

"I tried to find a pair of purple and green bloomers but they were fresh out."

She went to reply, but spotted a tiny brown packet at the bottom of the pile of undergarments. She looked up. "What's this?"

He paced uncomfortably. "Open and see."

She tore open the packet and a silver locket on a chain slid into her hand. "Adam," she breathed. It was shaped in a heart with tiny vined flowers carved on its face. Seeing the hinge, she opened it. Inside was a lock of ebony hair. Tears clouded her eyes as she looked up at him.

Adam hooked his thumbs in his pockets, shifting his weight from one boot to the other. His chest tightened. He knew what he wanted to say, but it was hard. She said she couldn't love him. He was taking a big chance, maybe making a fool out of himself. "To my mother's people, the Ojibwa, a lock of hair is an ultimate gift. In giving a lock of hair you give a piece of yourself, of your heart, forever." He paused,

253

frightened by the tears that loomed behind his eyelids. "You pledge your love."

Jessica jumped off the bed and ran to him, flinging herself into his arms. What could she say to him? If she didn't understand herself what she was feeling, how could she explain it to him. For a long time they just held each other and finally Adam kissed her forehead and backed away.

"Put it on for me." She held the precious locket out to him, her cheeks still wet from her tears. "And tell me what you found out. Has there been any sign of our Black Bandit, Caine?"

Adam fastened the delicate gold chain around her neck and touched it where it hung between her bare breasts. "I've got somebody at the newspaper reading through articles that have involved trouble in the area in the last two weeks. But Caine's been here. I just know it. I can feel it in my bones." He clenched his fist, turning away. "I've got to catch him, Jess. The Union Pacific's not pleased with my progress."

She rested her hand on his shoulder. "We'll find him, partner. I promise you."

Chapter Eighteen

"You sure you'll be all right?" Adam leaned in the doorway watching Jessica brush out her long brown hair. In the sunlight he could see the golden highlights that made her hair shine like a halo.

She grimaced. "Don't be silly. I can certainly find my way to the mercantile and back. I got along two weeks without you."

"But that was under the *protection* of Crooked Nose," he answered sarcastically.

She waved her hand. "Don't mention his name. I don't want to talk about him, not ever again. It's over, I'm safe, and we've got a job to do." She pulled back her hair and began to braid it in a thick plait down her back.

"Well, you just behave yourself and no snooping around. I don't want to catch you in any saloons."

"I'm going to buy some soap and tea," she said innocently. "How could I possibly get into any trouble?"

He turned to go, then spied her holster and pistol

hung over a chair next to the door. "Just the same, you'd better carry this."

She tied a ribbon in her hair and set the brush aside. "Over my new dress?" She came across the lavender carpeted room. "You're not serious?"

"Completely." Adam reached around her narrow waist and strapped the holster on, letting it slide to her hips. "You're in this deep, you might as well take the final plunge."

She looked down at the leather holster and pistol. She had to admit that the weight of the weapon felt good. It made her feel safe. "I sure hope I don't get into any gunfights on the street. I'd never be able to get the blasted thing out of the holster."

His laughter mingled with hers as he kissed her on her mouth. "I'll meet you back here in a few hours, hopefully with some good news."

She kissed him a second time, and then let him out the door. A few minutes later, Jessica locked the door and went downstairs. The minute she appeared on the carved staircase, the redheaded Barton came rushing toward her. He took the steps two at a time, meeting her halfway down the landing.

"So glad to see you, ma'am. You're looking lovely this morning!" He glanced at the pistol in her holster excitedly, and then took her arm.

"Good to see you, Mr. Barton."

"And how is the suite? Everything to your liking, ma'am? I told Louise to be certain you had plenty of fresh towels."

"The room is fine. The running water is heavenly."

"I have someone I want you to meet, if you don't

mind." He began to lead her past the front desk and into the parlor.

"Actually, Mr. Barton, I have some errands to run," she answered uneasily. She didn't know why the proprietor was making such a fuss over her. It made her uncomfortable.

"Mr. Lansing?" Barton waved to a tall, slender, blond gentleman. "This is her. This is the woman tracking the Black Bandit." He looked back at Jessica. "I didn't catch your name, ma'am."

Several people seated in the parlor turned to stare. Jessica glanced at Barton uneasily. "I really should go."

But Lansing had already bounced out of his seat and was taking her hand. He kissed the back of it. "Theodore Lansing. Pleased to meet you, ma'am."

She nodded.

"Sit, please."

"I really shouldn't."

"Just for a moment," Lansing assured her. "Barton. Tea and some of those cakes." He waggled a finger at a table beside them laden with confections.

Jessica watched Barton hurry from the room. She glanced back at Lansing and smiled hesitantly.

"They say you're traveling with the half-breed, Deputy Marshal Sern."

"I am." She looked out into the parlor at the people still staring, then turned her gaze back to Lansing. The man had a hawk-beak of a nose.

"They say you're avenging your family's murder."

"My brother's. The Black Bandit killed my brother on the Union Pacific route from Salt Lake City to Ogden. My brother and I were on our way from

Tennessee. We intended on settling near Seattle."

"I see. But they say the deputy marshal was already on the Black Bandit's trail. They say he needed your expert tracking abilities. They say the Union Pacific brought you in on the job."

Jessica laughed. "What *they say* is incorrect, Mr. Lansing. I'm with the deputy marshal, he's not with me." Her eyes met his. "And who is *they* anyway?"

"The newspapers, of course. The story just hit back east. The readers are dying for the latest word."

Jessica scowled, realizing that Mr. Lansing was busy taking notes, scribbling fast and furiously. "Mr. Lansing, what is that you're writing?"

"Notes, of course. I'm a novelist. You'll make a perfect heroine for my book."

She laughed at the absurdity of it. "You write dime novels? You want to write one about me?"

"I was sent from my newspaper in Chicago to find your true identity, but I think it's better if you don't give me your name." He waved his hand with a flourish. "More mysterious that way, don't you think?" He began writing again. "My work will, of course, be one of fiction, but dedicated to you, a true woman of the West."

Jessica pushed up out of her seat with a groan. "I want no part of your novel, Mr. Lansing."

He bobbed out of his seat. "Where are you going? I have so many more questions. Mr. Barton hasn't served tea yet," he finished with a squeal.

"Good day, Mr. Lansing." Jessica started out of the parlor, ignoring the nosy stares.

"They say you were captured by the Sioux, a band of red men guilty of General Custer's demise. They say you suffered horrendous, humiliating ordeals before you managed to escape."

Jessica burst into laughter. "Even *I* know, Mr. Lansing, that there are no Sioux in these parts." She swung open the front door.

Lansing followed in her wake. "The people back east don't know that. You must admit it does make a fine story!" He caught her sleeve. "Ma'am, you must help me. This is my chance to get out from under bylines and follow my life's dream of becoming a novelist!"

She yanked her sleeve from his grasp. *"Good day, Mr. Lansing."*

He followed her off the porch and onto the wooden sidewalk. "Can I come to you with questions?"

"No! Leave me be."

"Ma'am, you must understand, this is my chance to make my fortune, to see my name on my first novel."

Jessica spun around. "Mr. Lansing! That is enough. I will not answer any more questions and I do not authorize you to use anything about me in your dime novel."

"But, ma'am—"

Jessica lowered her hand to the Smith & Wesson in her holster and Lansing's jaw snapped shut.

His eyes widened in terror as he looked from the gun to her face and back at the gun again. "G—Good day to you then. I won't trouble you anymore." He turned around, hurrying back toward the hotel. "Good day."

Jessica had to snicker as she watched the dapper man run from her, his spindly legs shaking in fright as he made his retreat.

Still chuckling to herself, she walked up the street and into the first mercantile she came to. She spent a good hour inside, sucking on horehound candy and picking out a few necessities. She hadn't wanted to take Adam's money, but he'd insisted. He swore he would make her pay him back when they retrieved her carpetbag.

Secretly, Jessica was beginning to have her doubts. They'd lost two weeks' time. Caine could be any-where. But Adam swore the murderer had been in Pocatello, if he wasn't still there. Adam also told her about what the whore had told him in Blades, concerning Caine's brother in Seattle. Adam seemed confident they were still on the Black Bandit's trail; she only prayed he was right.

Out in the sunlight, Jessica swung her brown-packaged bundle as she walked along the sidewalk. There was no need to hurry, Adam had said he might be a few hours. The street was busy with carts and wagons and an occasional carriage. There were a multitude of pedestrians ranging from bonneted women to soldiers in uniform. A group of young boys ran down the sidewalk chasing a hoop with a stick. She saw miners everywhere.

The sound of gunshots jerked Jessica out of her reverie. Right in front of her a saloon door swung open and a man burst through the doorway.

"Stop him!" someone shouted from inside. "Stop that murderer!"

Before Jessica could think, she dropped her package and her hand found her pistol. She whipped it out of her holster and went down on one knee as

Adam had instructed. "Stop or I'll shoot," she hollered, cocking the hammer.

The fleeing man turned right and started down the sidewalk.

"I said halt! Drop to the ground or I'll blow you off your feet!" She fired above his head and the man pitched himself facing down on the planks. He threw up his hands in surrender.

Patrons of the saloon poured out of the door. Everyone was talking at once. Jessica walked up to the accused, lying prostrate on the sidewalk. Miners followed in her footsteps. "Throw down your weapon," she ordered.

"Here comes the sheriff," someone shouted. "Make way for the sheriff!"

The captured man slid his pistol across the sidewalk and Jessica signaled one of the miners to pick it up.

The sheriff burst through the crowd. "All right, all right. Back up, men, give me some room. Joe, tell me what the hell's going on here!"

A man in a white apron whom Jessica presumed was a bartender, stepped up. The miners from the saloon and other passersby formed a circle around Jessica, the captured man, the sheriff, and the bartender.

"That slimy bugger kilt Leroy, Sheriff. Said Leroy was cheatin' at five stud, only I know Leroy weren't cheatin', cause the cayuse was the one with the ace in his hatband." Joe pointed an accusing finger at the man still lying on the dusty sidewalk.

"So where's she come in?" The sheriff gave a nod in Jessica's direction.

"She caught 'im!"

There was a round of applause. Someone behind Jessica offered to buy her a drink. Another miner's offer was cruder.

The sheriff walked up and laid his hand on the warm barrel of Jessica's pistol. "Well, well, missy. Where'd you learn to sling a six-shooter like that?"

One of the sheriff's deputies grabbed the perpetrator by the collar of his filthy shirt and lifted him off the ground. "Dag gone," the murderer complained. "Ain't never been in a town where they use ladies for lawmen." The deputy escorted him toward the jailhouse.

The sheriff turned back to Jessica as she shakily returned her Smith & Wesson to her holster. "What's your name, missy, I'll need it for the record."

A man in a blue felt hat shyly offered her the package she'd dropped. "I won't be detained, will I? I didn't shoot him, I just slowed him down."

The sheriff, who was a handsome, middle-aged man, gave a wry grin. "Don't see any need to keep you, if you provide the necessary information. You've done no wrong, though I have to admit, the deputies and I are usually the ones to catch the criminals and like."

Jessica glanced at the body of the man being carried out of the saloon. His head was slung back unnaturally and his chest was covered in blood. "Yes, sir, whatever you need to know."

"First things, first," the sheriff answered. "Name and what your business is here in Pocatello."

"My name's Jessica Landon. I'm traveling with Deputy Marshal Adam Sern."

Excitement rippled through the crowd. Jessica looked up to see the dime novelist, Mr. Lansing, lick his pencil and begin to scribble frantically on his pad of paper. She turned back to the sheriff, lowering her voice. "We're tracking the Black Bandit, sir."

The sheriff gave a low whistle. "I'll be damned—'scuse my language, ma'am—but I thought that was all a bunch of buffalo chips, a man like Sern traveling with a woman. Of course I guess you aren't just any woman, are you?"

"Sheriff, I did what any citizen would do. Someone yelled to stop that man, so I stopped him."

He shook his head. "Damned if you didn't."

Just then Adam pushed through the crowd. Jessica looked up in relief. "What's goin' on here? You all right, Jess?"

"What's going on?" Lansing cried. "Miss Landon here's just caught herself a murderer, of course. Who knows how many he'd have mowed down before he moved onto the next town!"

Adam's gaze fell on Jessica. "No trouble, huh? Just buying a soap?"

She glanced at the sheriff. "Can I go now?"

"I reckon you can. Just check in with me before you leave town."

She nodded and started down the walk. The crowd parted to make way for her and Adam, who walked at her side.

"So much for remaining inconspicuous," he remarked.

She groaned. "It all happened so fast."

"*What* happened so fast?"

"I was just on my way back from the mercantile. I

263

heard a gunshot from the saloon and this man came barreling out. Someone hollered from inside to stop him." She lowered her voice dismally. "So I stopped him."

"Kill him, Miss Sharpshooter?"

She looked up at Adam, scowling. "Of course not. I just told him to drop to the ground or I was going to . . ." She moaned. "Why do these things keep happening to me?"

He laughed, dropping his arm onto her shoulder. "Just the wrong place at the wrong time, I suppose."

"Lot of help you are. My name'll be plastered across every paper this side of the Mississippi by noon tomorrow."

Adam noted the desperate tone in her voice. "Well, we won't be here much longer. I have an idea you and I might well be taking a train ride."

"What do you mean?"

He pulled out a roll of papers that he'd had tucked in his back pocket. "I mean I've got all of the names of the passengers who left Pocatello in the last three weeks."

"Larry Caine's name is there?" She looked up hopefully.

"No, but then he wouldn't use his real name. He knows we're onto him. He's been running since we met with him up there in the mountain at that abandoned camp."

"There must be hundreds of names on that list. How will we ever know if he's one of the passengers?"

"Because, Jess, criminals follow certain patterns. When they use aliases, the names usually resemble their own. A little luck"—he touched his temple with his forefinger—"a little thought, and we should have our man by suppertime." They reached the Barton Hotel and Adam swung open the door for her. "After you. I don't want to get in your way when you've got that pistol slung on your hips."

She jabbed him in the stomach as she passed. "Very funny. Now come on, Mr. Deputy Marshal, let's find Larry Caine."

Jacob Dorchester sat alone at a corner table at the Double Aces Dance Hall on the edge of Pocatello. He watched a scantily clad dancer strut across a platform stage, swinging her hips to the tinny music of a piano.

He lifted his glass to his lips and sipped his bourbon. "Ah, Jessica, what are you doing here half-naked in front of all of these men?" He murmured to himself. "Why can't you be a good girl?"

"Excuse me, sir. Mind if I have a seat?"

Jacob looked up to see a thin, blond-haired man offering his hand.

"The name's Lansing. Theodore Lansing. Do you mind?" He tossed his bowler hat on the small round table.

"Actually, sir—"

Lansing was already taking a seat across from Jacob, and blocking his view of the dancer with the sable-brown hair. "You look lonely. There's nothing like being alone in a strange town." He waved to a painted girl who immediately brought him a drink. "So what's your business, Mr. . . . ?"

Jacob eyed the intruder. "Dorchester. Jacob Dorchester."

"Where from?"

Jacob shifted his chair slightly so that he could see the girl again. She'd been joined on the stage by a uniformed soldier who was twirling her in circles. The two laughed uproariously. Jacob glanced back at Lansing. "Tennessee."

"My God!" He slapped a palm on the damp wooden table. "Then you'll have to get together with Miss Landon."

Jacob flinched. "What did you say?"

Lansing looked up with alarm. He didn't like the tone of the stranger's voice. "I . . . I said you'll have to meet Miss Landon, the female sharpshooter in town. She says *she's* from Tennessee." He laughed uncomfortably. "Small world, isn't it?"

Jacob glanced up at the stage and then back at Lansing. His hand tightened on his glass until the novelist thought it might shatter.

Lansing pushed out of his chair. "Well, guess I ought to be on my way," he said uneasily. He swiped his bowler hat off the table.

Jacob ignored him.

Lansing tipped his hat and then hurried away.

For a long time Jacob just sat there. His Jessica. She was looking for him. But he'd already found her. There she was . . . on the stage, dancing, laughing, her pert breasts bouncing in the soldier's face. Jacob scowled. He signaled to the painted woman serving the drinks. "That girl," he said, pointing to the stage.

"Polly?"

"That girl, with the brown hair, I want to buy

her a drink." He slipped a coin to the barmaid.

"I'll send her right over."

"Anything yet?" Jessica lay across the bed reading over the list of names Adam had brought from the railway station. She'd been studying them so long that her eyes were beginning to blur.

Adam sat on the floor, bare chested, sheets of paper spread out around him. "Nothing under Caine, nothing like Caine. Botwell, Buckworth, Cadwell, Casper."

She sighed. "This isn't going to work."

"Just keep looking."

She rolled onto her back. "Let's get something to eat. Maybe get some fresh air. I'm feeling fenced in."

"I thought you liked the running water."

"I can't see the stars. I can't breathe for all these pink ruffles!" She lifted the bedcovers and let them drift to the bed.

"I'll be damned," Adam breathed.

Jessica rolled over. "What?"

"I'll be goddamned!"

"What is it?" She crawled off the bed and went to kneel beside Adam. He tapped a name in a long list of names.

"Lawrence . . ."

"What? Move your finger. I can't see. Lawrence? Toby Lawrence?"

"Don't you get it, Jess?" His black eyes met hers. "Lawrence—Larry."

"So where does Toby come from?"

Adam smiled. "There's the trick of it. Toby Caine

267

is Larry's long lost brother, residing in Seattle."

Jessica let out a squeal and threw her arms around Adam. "You did it!"

"It says right here. Toby Lawrence took a train two weeks ago. Destination—"

"Seattle!" she shouted.

"Smart girl."

Jessica pushed aside the papers and dropped into his lap. "You're the one who figured it out. Guess I picked the right partner, didn't I?"

Chapter Nineteen

The moment Jessica stepped out into the hallway the following morning, she heard the commotion downstairs in the hotel lobby. She could hear men and women in heated discussion, but she couldn't make out what they were saying. She had half a mind to look for a back way out of the hotel. After what had happened yesterday, she had no use for crowds.

Adam came out of the suite and locked the door behind him. "What the hell's going on down there?"

She dropped her hands to her hips, giving a shrug. "I don't know, but we haven't got time for it if we're going to make a train out of here today."

"I can hear that writer friend of yours from here. Sure you wouldn't like to give an interview before we head for Seattle?" He grinned.

"No interviews," she snapped.

"What's the matter? Fame not what you thought it would be?"

"I didn't ask for fame. I'd have let the murderer get away if I'd known people were going to be banging on our door in the middle of the night asking for autographs!"

Adam dropped a kiss on the top of her head, inhaling the fresh, clean scent of her hair. "Come on then, Miss Sharpshooter. Let's see what the fuss is and then we'll be off on our business."

Reluctantly, Jessica followed Adam down the grand staircase and into the lobby. "What's this all about?" he demanded. The room was filled with citizens dressed in their Sunday-best, arguing and snapping at each other. They spilled out of the lobby and into the plush parlor where midmorning tea was being served.

Barton came from behind his polished desk, puffing up with self-importance. "Haven't you heard, Deputy Marshal? Gads, you folks sleep hard! There's been a horrendous murder right here in our fair city of Pocatello!"

"Murder? Who?"

"One of the dance hall girls," Barton answered. "It happened not three blocks from here."

"Atrocious murder." Lansing stepped from the crowd, pad and pencil in hand. "Grizzly murder. I'd like to hear your comments, Deputy Marshal. Yours as well, Miss Landon." He poised his pencil.

Adam swore beneath his breath. There was so much noise, he could barely think. "My comments!" He gave a humorless chuckle. "I don't have any comments because I don't know anything about the crime."

"She was nothing but a whore," a gentleman in a brown plaid coat commented dryly. "It's gals like that that keep the church pews empty on Sunday

270

mornings. Good riddance, I say."

A large bosomed woman pushed her way up to the gentleman in the plaid coat. "You just shut your mouth, Henry Watkins. It's a whore today, your precious buck-toothed daughter tomorrow! I say none of us is safe as long as that killer stalks the fine streets of Pocatello!"

"Stabbed her," Lansing went on, turning his attention back to Adam. He scribbled on his pad of paper and flipped a page. "Multiple stab wounds. Crime of passion, I'd say. Wouldn't you, Miss Landon?"

Jessica glanced up at Adam, then back at Lansing. She'd lost patience with this man. "I wouldn't know, Mr. Lansing. I'm not involved in the investigation and I don't intend to get involved."

Lansing wrote as fast as Jessica spoke.

"These people are here because they want something done." Barton injected. "They don't want a deranged murderer stalking their streets. Pocatello's a decent city."

"Damned right, we want something done," a cattleman near the doorway hollered.

Adam shifted his weight from one boot to the other. "I'm sure your sheriff is quite competent."

"Competent, hell," the cattleman went on. "Pardon me, ladies." He looked back to Adam. "He's too busy doing paperwork to even hear us out."

"They want to hire a decent lawman," Barton explained. "They'll pay—in gold, of course."

Adam put up his hands in defense. "You've got the wrong man. I work for the Union Pacific. I'm not for hire."

Barton glanced at Adam sheepishly. "No offense meant, Deputy Marshal, but these folks were thinking more on the lines of hiring Miss Landon."

Jessica gasped.

Adam couldn't resist a chuckle. "I don't know about that. You'd have to ask her. Of course I don't know that I could spare her. This is an awful tough man I'm tracking. Up to this point, she's been invaluable in my investigation."

Jessica flashed Adam an angry glance. "Good God, no. I'm not for hire. I'm not a lawman."

"You captured that murderer single-handed just yesterday, didn't you?" Lansing asked, pencil waving.

"Yes, well no, well . . ." She exhaled in frustration, looking to Adam for help.

Lansing licked his pencil point and wrote rapidly.

Jessica reached out and snatched the pencil from the dime-novelist's hand. "Will you stop writing!"

"Just trying to get the facts, ma'am. It's my job," Lansing argued defensively.

Jessica slammed the pencil down on his pad of paper. "Then get these facts, Mr. Lansing. I am not a lawman, I'm not a sharpshooter, and I do not intend to hire myself out to investigate some poor girl's murder."

"She was young, looked just like you." Lansing paused, pencil in midair. "Remarkable likeness, come to think of it. My God! Don't you care?"

A shiver of unexplained fear rose up Jessica's spine. *Looked just like me . . . remarkable likeness . . .* An image of Jacob flashed through her mind and she pushed it aside. What was wrong with her?

She was being overly suspicious. Jacob had gotten a little rough with her on occasion, but he certainly wasn't capable of murder! And he wasn't in town! "Of course I care! But this case should be left to those with experience. The sheriff will get to the bottom of it."

"Right!" a slim man standing in the doorway to the parlor commented sarcastically. "Just like they got to the bottom of it in Blades."

"Blades?" Adam's eyes met the gentleman's across the room. He'd been in Blades only a few short weeks ago speaking with Sue Ellen. "What are you talking about?"

"Somebody stabbed and killed some poor chippy in Blades a few weeks back. We're all beginnin' to wonder if it weren't the same man. In both cases nobody saw nobody come or go. They just found her dead in the morning."

"Let's go," Jessica said to Adam. "We've got to get to the station and check the schedule. I don't want to miss our train."

Adam looped his arm through hers protectively. "All right," he said so that only she could hear. "But I want to go down to the sheriff's office and talk to him."

"You're leaving?" Barton hurried after Adam and Jessica as the crowd parted to let them through the lobby. "You're going to abandon us in our time of need, Miss Landon?"

Lansing followed in their footsteps. "Choosing to abandon justice for personal vendettas, Miss Landon?"

Jessica whipped around. "Personal vendetta, Mr.

Lansing!" She laid her hand on his chest and gave him a hard shove. Barton caught him before he fell. His paper and pencil went flying.

"My fourteen-year-old brother had a hole the size of my fist blown through his chest." Her eyes narrowed dangerously as Lansing stared back at her looking as if he might cry. "Personal vendetta, Mr. Lansing? You're damned straight!"

"Whew!" Adam shook his head as he hurried Jessica out the door. "Remind me not to ever make you angry."

"Adam, this isn't funny."

He took her arm, patting her hand. "I know it isn't, sweetheart. I understand how you feel about your brother, about your privacy, but it's either laugh or cry sometimes, isn't it?"

"I just want to get out of this town. We can go today, can't we?" She hurried along the plank sidewalk, wanting to put as much distance between herself and the dime novelist as possible.

"If there's a train heading north leaving Pocatello today, we'll be on it. There are some advantages to working for the railroad."

She offered him a half smile. "I can go back to the newspaper and see if that man found anything on Caine, if you'll go to the train depot."

"You don't just want to tag along with me?"

She frowned. "Adam Sern, I can take care of myself."

"All right. You go to the newspaper office two blocks down on Thorton Avenue while I'll get two train tickets. How about if I meet you up the street at that fancy clothing store on the right." He pointed.

"Fancy clothes? What in heaven's name do you need with a suit?"

"I just thought we might travel in style."

"What are you talking about? You already bought me a dress, and I'm going to pay you back for it."

He stopped on the sidewalk and kissed her. He wished he could kiss away the frown lines on her face, the fear lurking behind her eyelids. There was something Jessica wasn't telling him, about this town, about the murder of the girl . . . about something. "Just go on. I'll meet you in half an hour."

With a nod, Jessica set off in the opposite direction. The morning sun was hot on her face. The slight breeze was like the air rushing out of an oven, but it smelled pure and clean. It felt good to her to be outside, away from the thick carpets, bed ruffles, and toilet water odors of the hotel. The first night the bed had felt good beneath her, and the running water had been fun, but she was anxious to move on.

She turned the corner and crossed the street in front of a mule team pulling a wagonload of manure. She wrinkled her nose. From the smell in the air, the man was a pig farmer. She stepped aside a rain barrel and continued up the street. The reflection of a Winchester rifle in a window caught her attention and she stopped.

She touched the glass of the store window wistfully, thinking of Mark. Then she saw him. *God, I'm imagining things now*, she thought wildly. *Not Jacob . . . not here! It was impossible!* For a moment she was so paralyzed with fear that she couldn't move. She wanted to turn around, to prove to herself that it wasn't Jacob, that it was just a man who looked like him, but she couldn't. She *knew* it was him. Somehow, deep in the recesses of her subconscious, she had known all along that he was here in Pocatello.

As Jessica's initial shock and fear eased, they were replaced by anger. She watched Jacob in the reflection of the glass as he spoke to a man across the street. He was asking for directions.

How dare you! Jessica raged inside. *How dare you follow me across the country! How dare you try to interfere with the one good thing that has come from Mark's death!* She thought of Adam and the love they had shared in the last few days. This was what love was supposed to be—trust, independence, freedom to come and go as she pleased. Adam's love wasn't stifling like Jacob's had been. It wasn't cruel or manipulative.

Jessica was tempted to march across the street and confront Jacob Dorchester. Never in her life had she despised him as much as she despised him right now. She wanted to shout at him, to tell him to go away and never let her set eyes on him again. She wanted to tell him that she had never wanted to marry him, it had all been her father and his warped sense of responsibility. She wanted to tell Jacob that she wasn't a naughty girl who had run away as she had run away from him as a child. She wanted to tell him that she loved Adam Sern and that she wanted to marry *him*.

Jessica caught her lower lip between her teeth and bit down so hard that she tasted blood. What was she thinking! Marry Adam! Adam had never said anything about marriage! Of course she couldn't marry

276

Adam. He had his job with the railroad. She had her saplings to retrieve and that orchard to get started.

She watched the startlingly handsome gray-haired Jacob tip his bowler hat to the man he had spoken to and then continue on his way. She watched him until he disappeared around the corner past a saloon and then she hurried in the direction of the newspaper office.

She wouldn't confront Jacob! She wouldn't give him the pleasure of trying to belittle her. She'd just take that train to Seattle. He'd never find her. He'd give up and go home to Tennessee and his fancy house and servants and she'd never hear from him again.

In less than an hour's time Jessica and Adam were inside Mrs. Colin's Clothier, laughing as Jessica modeled a stylish green and white flowered shirt-waist and forest green skirt. For the moment Jacob Dorchester was forgotten.

"It's beautiful," Adam told her. He sat on a rosewood settee, smoking a cigar.

Jessica waved at the smoke in the air. "I look silly and you stink! Where on earth did you get that cigar?" She stood in front of an oval floor-length mirror while Mrs. Colin fussed with the skirt's bustle. They were the only customers in the store.

"I got it from the sheriff and I think you're a picture of loveliness, don't you agree, Mrs. Colin?"

The dyed redhead flapped her hands wildly. "Saints alive, I don't believe I've ever seen a woman take to clothing so well."

Jessica turned sideways to study her reflection. "I look malformed. What did the sheriff have to say about the girl who was murdered?"

"I'll talk to you about it later. As for the womanly fluff, I believe the word is *fashionable.*"

"Fashionable or not, some of these undergarments have got to go. I'll roast on the train!"

Mrs. Colin's mouth dropped open and she looked to Adam for support.

He took a puff of the smelly green cigar. "Don't look at me. If the lady says there's too much underclothing, there's too much."

"W—what do you propose we remove?" the shopkeeper stammered in shock.

Adam just laughed. "Ask the lady. And while you two settle this, I'll try on that mess you've got hanging in the changing room."

A few minutes later Adam returned.

Jessica brought her hand to her mouth. Adam looked so silly, yet so handsome at the same time. He had shed his dungarees, his cattleman's shirt, even his snakeskin boots. He was now wearing a finely cut, black serge, single-breasted suit. The coat was so well tailored that it made his broad chest look even broader. Under his arm he had tucked a black wool hat with a black ribbon band. He was as fashionable as Jacob Dorchester would ever be.

"And what may I ask are you laughing about, madam?" He popped his hat onto his head, tilting it at a cocky angle.

Jessica couldn't help herself. She bubbled with laughter. Was this truly the man who only a week before had worn nothing but a loincloth and face paint? God, she loved him.

Loved him. She smiled and opened her arms. Seeing Jacob Dorchester there on the street had made her realize that she *did* love Adam; she loved him more than life itself. But what she was going to do about it, she didn't know.

Adam came to her and swung her into his arms.

"We look silly," Jessica protested. It felt so good to be in his strong embrace.

"We make a damned fine couple, don't we Mrs. Colin?" Adam asked dropping a kiss on Jessica's slender neck.

Mrs. Colin clasped her hands together. "A fine couple, indeed." She began to gather several dresses, skirts, and blouses Jessica had tried on. "So what will it be, Miss Landon?"

"All of it," Adam said with a sweep of his hand.

Jessica laughed. "We can't take it all. Remember, I don't have any m—"

Before she could finish what she was saying, he clamped his mouth down on hers. "You heard me, Mrs. Colin. We want all of it. And throw in some ribbons and whatever else it is women like. But we need it delivered to the train station within the hour. Miss Landon and I have a train to catch."

The shopkeeper gave a squeal of delight. She would make more in this sale than she'd made all summer. "It won't be easy, but it can be done, Mr. Sern."

"See that it is. We'll wear what we've got on." He steered Jessica toward the door. "But we want our old clothes. If you don't get my boots to me, we don't take any of it. I'll leave you half of the payment now, half at the station." He laid bills on a counter near the door.

"Thank you, Deputy Marshal, thank you," was all the redhead could say.

Adam tipped his hat and escorted Jessica in all of her finery out the door. "Shall we go, Miss Landon, I believe we have a train to catch."

All Jessica could do was laugh as the striking half-breed led her out of the shop and down the sidewalk.

Jacob caught sight of Lansing across the smoke-filled Double Aces dance hall and signaled him to approach.

Lansing hesitated, an uneasy feeling coming over him. He waved back, offering a stiff smile. A journalist like him couldn't turn anyone away. If the man said he had a story, he was worth listening to.

"Mr. Lansing." Jacob gave a nod. "So glad you could join me. A drink?"

Lansing shook his head, pulling up a stool to the table. He spoke quickly, as he always did. "Terrible thing, that young girl's murder," he said making polite conversation as he pulled out his pad of paper.

Jacob's face contorted oddly. "Murder? There's been a girl murdered? What girl?"

"Didn't you hear?" Lansing leaned across the table, a genuine smile lighting up his face. Heaven but he loved to be the first to tell a tale! "It was a grizzly thing! She worked right here in this dance hall. They say there were pools of blood on the floor. I didn't see it myself, but my sources are dependable. A serial murder the newspapers are calling it. She's the second girl, you know."

"The second in Pocatello?"

"No, of course not, the first was in a little town southwest of here called Blades. The girl's name was Sue Ellen Caine but that's confidential."

Jacob shook his head. "What's the world coming to? What kind of madmen stalk our innocent girls?"

Lansing chuckled nervously. "Well, I would hardly say she was an innocent. She was a whore, you know."

"Poor child."

"They say he cut a lock of her hair."

Jacob gasped.

"There's more on the hair but I couldn't get the information, not for love nor money, and believe me, I tried the money." Lansing licked the lead of his pencil. "So you sent word to my hotel that you had a story for me. What have you got?"

Jacob swished the bourbon in his glass, watching the brown liquid swirl round and round. "I'm looking for my wife, Mr. Lansing."

"Missing person. Good, good." He scribbled a note. "Always a good story."

"You said you spoke to her."

Lansing looked up. "Spoke to her? Who?"

"My wife."

"Well, who is your wife, sir?"

Jacob sipped his bourbon, taking his time in responding. "My wife is Jessica, Jessica Dorchester. She is apparently traveling under her maiden name, Jessica Landon."

Lansing dropped his pencil. "My God!" was all he could manage.

"You *have* spoken to her, here in Pocatello, have you not?"

"She's your wife?" Lansing scrambled to find his pencil, afraid he would miss a word.

"She is. I want to take her home. You must tell me where she is."

"W—well, I— Your wife?" Lansing shook his head in disbelief. "She's traveling with a man, you know. A half-breed deputy marshal."

Jacob's face froze in anguish for a moment, but the expression vanished as quickly as it had appeared. "I don't care. I just want my wife." He leaned forward and struck his fist on the table. "It is imperative that I find her. We have some legal matters to deal with. My lawyers are getting anxious."

"Why did she leave you, if I might ask?"

"She's an ill woman. She needs my care."

Lansing's eyes narrowed. "She seemed well enough when I talked to her. We nearly slugged it out over a difference of opinion. She's quite a woman."

Jacob was losing patience. His face was growing red; his manicured hands were beginning to tremble. *"Where is she, Mr. Lansing?"*

The dime novelist scratched his chin. "Well, sir, I . . . I believe she's on her way to the train station."

"The train station!" Jacob leaped out of his seat and hurried for the door.

"Mr. Dorchester, wait," Lansing cried, running in pursuit. "I have more questions for you! Is your wife in legal trouble? Exactly what type of illness does she have?"

Jacob pushed out the saloon door and ran across

the potholed street, heading straight for the train depot.

In the distance was the sound of a steam locomotive heating its engines. The train gave a high-pitched whistle.

"Wait!" Jacob shouted, turning the corner. He could see the station ahead. He could see the train moving slowly, car after car passing the platform as the train picked up speed. "Stop that train! I must get aboard!" he cried in desperation.

The train moved faster, the whistle sounded again in a final screeching whine as it pulled out of the station.

By the time Jacob reached the depot platform, the caboose was five hundred feet down the track. "Please! Stop the train!" he called to a uniformed man.

"Stop the train?" The attendant gave a laugh. "Ain't nobody stoppin' that train. You'll have to catch tomorrow's."

Jacob swept off his hat and wiped his brow with a handkerchief, clearly winded. "Where's the train bound?" he called as the uniformed man walked away.

"Washington territory," was the response. "That train's headed for Seattle, mister."

Chapter Twenty

Jessica sat in a velvet upholstered chair, her feet propped on a cushioned footstool. She and Adam were riding in a private Pullman car decorated in gilt and furnished with expensive velvet chairs and drapes. The floor was covered with a Turkish carpet, floral in design and color-coordinated with the drapes and furnishings. "The entire car all to ourselves? You're kidding!"

Adam sat across from her watching the scenery pass. They had just pulled out of Pocatello and were westward bound. It felt good to be aboard the Union Pacific again. It had become a home of sorts to Adam in the last two years. "I told you there were advantages to working for the railroad. I thought we'd just sleep here. The berthing cars are a nightmare."

Jessica rolled her eyes. "Mark and I hated them. Every time the train went around the corner one of us would fall out of our bed. There was no privacy even with the curtains. We gave up after the third night and started sleeping in the day coach. Some of the cars had hinged upper berths that folded down out of the ceiling above the seat. That wasn't too bad."

Adam's gaze settled on her. "I can't believe you came all the way across the country alone like that."

"I wasn't alone." She stroked the red velvet arm of the chair. "I had Mark."

"You know what I mean."

Solemnly, her eyes met his. "If you have a good enough reason, you'll do just about anything."

"What was your reason?" he asked softly, leaning forward in his chair. "Tell me why you ran, Jess."

"I don't want to talk about this."

"Can't you trust me? Whatever you've done, I don't care. If you're in trouble, I'll help you."

She got up out of her chair and walked to a small table where there was a pitcher of cold lemonade. She poured herself a glass. "I didn't do anything wrong." Her voice sounded foreign in her ears.

Why *couldn't* she tell Adam? He said he loved her; he said he didn't care about her past. But Jessica cared. She took a sip of the icy lemonade, letting it slide down her throat. She felt so utterly foolish being taken in by Jacob, being manipulated by him and her father. It had all happened so quickly; Papa's illness, the engagement, Papa moving all of his accounts into Jacob's name. Then Papa had died and Jacob had become insistent that she marry him immediately. But he was going to send Mark away. That's when she'd stolen the money from the sale of her father's farm and she and Mark had run away.

Jessica looked up to see Adam standing an arm's length from her. He was watching her with those big, dark, hooded eyes of his. "You don't have to tell me."

"Good, because I wasn't going to," she said, covering her pain with sarcasm.

"You don't have to tell me *now*." He took the glass from her hand and sipped it. "But later, tonight, tomorrow, two weeks from now, you have to tell me. I have to know what I'm dealing with if you and I are going to spend the rest of our lives together."

It was on the tip of her tongue to ask him who had said anything about spending the rest of their lives together, but she didn't. She was so confused inside, confused about Jacob, about Adam and the part he'd played in Mark's death, about her love for Adam. How could she love a man whose job it had been to protect her brother? But she *did* love Adam. Did that mean she loved Mark less?

Adam handed her the glass of lemonade. "Come and sit down and I'll play you a game of backgammon."

She looked up at him sullenly. "I don't know how to play backgammon."

"Then I guess I'll have to teach you." He slid a small table across the carpet and wedged it between the two high-backed velvet chairs.

"You said you talked to the sheriff?" She took her seat, relieved he wasn't going to pressure her into talking about anything she didn't want to talk about.

"I did, but he didn't have much to tell me. At least three girls have been murdered by this man."

"Three? No one said anything about three murders."

"They're trying to keep it quiet until the evidence has been studied. The third murder actually took place between the murder in Blades and the one in Pocatello. The sheriff wouldn't say where."

"That's scary. How does the sheriff know it's the same man?"

Adam opened the leather-bound backgammon case and began to set up the marble pieces. "Apparently the girls look very much alike. Young, dark brown hair, pretty, and all three were whores. All of the murders took place in the girls' rooms. No one ever saw a man come or go." He paused a moment. "I knew one of the girls, Jess. It was Sue Ellen Caine, Toby's wife. I apparently talked to her the night she was murdered."

"I don't want to talk about this anymore." Jessica rubbed her forearms, feeling goosebumps beneath her fingertips. "Just teach me how to play so I can beat you."

Adam looked up. "You certainly are particular today about what we talk about."

"Let's just play." She creased her brow. "Are you sure Hera and Zeus are all right?"

"Safe and sound. I saw to their loading myself while you were at the hotel picking up our things. Now roll to see who goes first and I'll play you through a game."

Jessica picked up the ivory dice and shook them in her hand. "Get ready to lose, Mr. Deputy Marshal!"

The two played backgammon for hours. At first, Adam won, game after game, but then as Jessica caught on and formed her own strategy, she began to beat him. They laughed and talked as they played, discussing their childhoods and the happiness they had known.

Finally when the shadows began to lengthen and Jessica had to get up to light several gas lamps in their private car, Adam packed away the backgammon board. "I don't know about you, but I'm starving. Shall we retire to the first-class dining car to sample a little boiled salmon? Perhaps some baked red snapper in piquant sauce? Or we could just call the porter and have him bring a meal in."

"Snapping turtle?" She wrinkled her nose. "My grandma loved turtle, but I don't care for it."

Adam laughed. "Red snapper, it's a kind of fish, sweetheart."

Jessica dropped her hand to her hip. "Well, how am I supposed to know?" she said, refusing to be embarrassed. "I'm not as worldly as you are! I've never been in a fancy restaurant, or a first-class dining car!"

"Then by all means, let's dine in style." He offered her his arm.

She accepted, and together they walked through another first-class car and into the dining car, meant only for first-class passengers.

The car was as elaborately decorated in velvets and rosewood as their own car had been. Polished wooden tables were laid out with fine linen and china. Crystal glasses caught the lamplight and shone brilliantly in the faces of the exquisitely dressed passengers.

Adam led Jessica to an empty table set for the evening meal. He slid onto one bench; she sat across from him. "How much money does it cost to travel across the country like this?"

"Don't ask." He pulled his linen napkin from a crystal water goblet and spread it across his lap.

"Good God, Chester, it's a redskin!" Jessica heard from across the aisle.

She looked up in surprise to see a middle-aged woman with blue-white hair seated at the table across from them.

Jessica looked at Adam. She knew he couldn't have helped but hear. The entire car had heard the rude woman.

"What do you think you're doing here eating with decent people?" the woman demanded, addressing Adam.

Her little husband reached across the table with a wrinkled hand. "Now, Katrina, love, don't get yourself in a fury."

"Waiter! Waiter!" the woman cried, waving her napkin.

Jessica could see Adam's handsome face growing taut with anger. "We can go," she whispered. "I don't really want to eat here, anyway. Supper in our car would be better."

"Waiter!"

A tall Pullman waiter dressed in a black coat and white shirt came running up the aisle, a tray balanced on one hand. "Yes, ma'am?"

"Waiter, I want that heathen removed from this dining car immediately!"

The waiter turned to look at Adam. He raised a mocking eyebrow. "You have a ticket, sir?" he said haughtily.

"I do. I'm a detective for the Union Pacific."

"I'm quite certain you are, sir, but I must see your ticket," he said, obviously not believing that Adam could possibly be holding a first-class ticket.

"Ticket or no, he should be in the third-class cars with the other filth!" the woman went on.

"Now, Katrina . . ."

"Your ticket, sir," the waiter spat.

Adam whipped out two folded pieces of paper and the waiter examined them thoroughly. Then, without a word to Adam he turned his back on him. "My apologies, ma'am, but it appears this man holds a ticket the same as yours. He has a right to be seated in this dining car."

"A right!" The woman screeched. "He has no right, the red nigger! How dare he think he can come and go among decent society? I demand that you toss him out."

"I wish I could ma'am, but I cannot. It's railroad business."

"He ought to be riding with the cattle!"

"My apologies, ma'am, but I must repeat, there's nothing I can do," the waiter said.

The woman threw down her napkin and got out of her seat, dragging a fur stole. "Well, if *he's* not leaving, I am! God knows I wouldn't take supper with a redskin!" She flounced down the aisle. "Baxter!"

The little man leaped out of his seat and hurried after his wife. "Coming, Katrina! Coming, dear!"

"I'll have my meal served in the parlor car," Jessica could hear the woman telling the waiter as she disappeared into the next car.

Slowly Jessica turned her gaze to Adam. His face

was red with anger, his napkin bunched in one fist. She didn't know what to say. "Adam—"

"Why don't we just order," he said, his rage barely in check.

Jessica opened her mouth to say something, then closed it. What could she say that would comfort him? Nothing. He'd told her he'd lived his entire adult life battling prejudice. He'd said it was a fact of life he had to learn to accept. He had told her it would never go away, at least not in his lifetime.

She picked up the menu. "What shall we have? Roasted partridge, goose and applesauce?" She looked over the handwritten menu at him, trying to be cheery. "I don't know what to choose. I've never tasted any of this! You order for me and surprise me!"

"All right. Now what about wine, will you drink some if I order a bottle?"

"Sure."

Adam scanned the wine list. "I'll be damned!"

"What?"

"They've got a Chateau-du-pape!"

"A what?" She laughed, glad to see that his anger was subsiding.

"A Chateau-du-pape. It's wonderful wine, created by a pope in the seventeenth century. Actually he was a retired pope."

"Retired?" She laid her hand on his. "I don't know much about the Catholic religion, but I thought you were the pope until you died."

"Well, I know plenty about the Catholics. My grandmother had me baptized Catholic when I was thirteen. She was petrified I was going to die and burn in hell before she could get it done." He laughed, shaking his head, thinking of his dear grandmother. Though she hadn't always said or done the right things for him, her heart had always been in the right place. "Anyway," he went on, "this particular pope retired and started a vineyard. It was the first time a wine was made with seventeen different kinds of grapes. Even after all of these years, Chateau-du-pape is still one of the most renowned wines in the world."

Jessica turned his hand in hers, studying his bronze, callused palm. "How do you know so much about wine, Mr. Deputy Marshal?"

"My grandfather was a collector. He had a wonderful cellar in Philadelphia. In his younger days he apparently traveled all over the world collecting rare wines."

"He sounds like he was a wonderful man," she said softly. She liked the shine she saw in Adam's eyes when he spoke of his family. What a tragedy they were dead now. She smiled bittersweetly. They were both orphans now, weren't they?

Adam kissed her palm. "Where is that waiter? He's passed us three times."

"He just must be busy."

When the waiter passed again, Adam touched his sleeve. It was the same waiter who had escorted the rude woman from the dining car earlier.

"Sir?" he said in an arrogant voice.

"You seemed to have missed us," Adam said, trying to remain polite. "Would you mind taking our order?"

"Just a moment or two more. I have other guests you know." The waiter strutted away.

Adam looked at Jessica, twisting his mouth in indecision. He didn't want to make a fuss, not in front of Jessica, not when this was her first fancy dinner. He decided to bide his time.

The two talked for another twenty minutes, and still the waiter didn't return for their order. Tables that had arrived after them were being served their main courses.

Adam leaned across the table. "Are we being ignored here, or is this just my imagination?"

Jessica squirmed in her seat. "Let's just go. I'm really not hungry."

He caught a soft curl that had escaped from her coiffure. "No. I told you we'd have supper in the first-class dining car, and supper we'll have."

When the waiter passed by again, Adam grabbed his arm. "My order."

The waiter lifted his nose. "Your order?"

"I want you to take my order." Adam's dark eyes narrowed dangerously. "That is what you do here, isn't it?"

The waiter sighed, adjusting a white linen towel draped over his arm. "What will it be then?" he snapped.

Adam picked up the menu and glanced at it. "We'll have the boiled California salmon with the French peas, the chicory and lobster salad—"

"Out of the salmon," the waiter interrupted.

Adam took a deep breath. "Then we'll have the capon with egg sauce—"

"No egg sauce."

"How about the duck with currant sauce?"

The waiter kept his gaze fixed on the oil lamp

swinging over the table. "Fresh out of duck."

Adam slammed his fist on the table and several passengers turned to stare. "I just saw you walk by with a plate of duck!"

"That must have been the last serving."

"Adam, let's just go," Jessica murmured.

Adam held up a finger. "Just what do you have?"

The waiter paused. "Oxtail, maybe a few sweet-breads."

Adam slammed down the menu. "Just bring us something. Now for wine, we would like a chilled bottle of Chateau-du-pape."

"I'm sorry. We served our last bottle not an hour ago."

Adam let out a string of curses. "Then bring me a damned bottle of your Chateau Margaux!"

The waiter smiled, his gray-eyed gaze falling on Adam's bronze face. "I'm sorry," he said with exaggerated politeness. "The wine list is incorrect. We have no Chateau Margaux."

Before Jessica knew what was happening, Adam had leaped from his seat and grasped the waiter by the lapel of his black coat. "You son of a bitch," he shouted, enraged. "How dare you treat me like this in front of my guest!"

The waiter gave a yelp as Adam lifted him off his feet and slammed him on the table across the aisle.

The two women seated at the table screamed as crystal and china shattered and food was knocked into their laps and onto the floor.

The dining car broke into pandemonium. Women screamed and men scrambled to get a better view of the commotion.

Jessica jumped up and rushed for Adam. "Adam,

don't hurt him!" she shouted, pulling at his broad shoulders. "He's not worth it!"

Adam pulled back his fist, blinded by fury. How the hell could a woman ever love him, ever be a part of his life when he couldn't get a damned waiter to serve him supper! God but he hated the color of his skin!

"Adam!" he heard in his ear again. The sound of Jessica's voice, her sweet, strong voice made him lower his fist.

The waiter cried like a baby as Adam raised him off the table and brought the man's contorted face within inches of his own. "The lady and I are retiring to our private car. We'll expect the salmon, the lobster salad and the Chateau-du-pape within the hour. I don't care if you have to catch the fish yourself, if my request is not honored, I'll—" Adam leaned forward and whispered into the waiter's ear.

The waiter's face went pale. "Y—yes, sir. Right away, sir."

"Adam," Jessica said calmly, her fingers sinking into his forearm. She could feel the iron strength of his muscles clenched in bitter anger. "Let go of him."

Adam released the waiter's coat, smoothed the lapel of his own black dinner jacket, and followed Jessica down the aisle of the dining car.

When back in their private car, Jessica turned to face him. What did you whisper to that waiter?

"It's not something I care to repeat to a lady."

"Why do you get so angry with people like that? They don't matter to us."

"I have a right to be served in that dining car like anyone else!"

"I know you do, but you don't have a right to kill that man."

Adam stomped across the carpeted floor, taking a swipe at a glass Jessica had left on a table. It shattered as it hit the papered wall.

She flinched. She hadn't realized how much rage lurked beneath the surface of his calm, cool exterior. She hadn't realized just how hard it was for him to have skin a different color from hers.

"Adam—"

"Don't say anything," he said through clenched teeth, his back to her. "Don't say a word! Nothing can change the way the world looks on me. I can't blame you, Jess, for not wanting to love me. Who would give up their life to be with a man who would always subject her to this!"

Jessica could hear the tears in his voice. She could see his broad shoulders quivering. Her heart ached so badly for him that she could feel her own eyes tearing over. She went to him and put her arms around his waist, resting her cheek on his broad back. She smelled the scent of the dye in his new coat. She could smell that familiar, masculine, woodsy scent that clung to him, that reminded her of his bare bronze skin. She thought of the taste of his flesh on the tip of her tongue.

"Adam."

He made no response.

"Adam." Slowly she came around him until she was looking into his black eyes. "Adam, I *do* love you," she whispered. "I didn't want to. Honestly, I still don't want to, but I love you, more than I've ever loved anyone." She wiped a tear from his cheek with her fingertips.

Adam squeezed his eyes shut. He couldn't remember having ever cried in his adult life and here he was bawling in front of the woman he wanted to make his wife. "I've made a fool of myself," he said. "I embarrassed you."

"No." She lifted onto her tiptoes and kissed his mouth. "You didn't."

"I shouldn't have lost control."

"You shouldn't have, but you did." She kissed him again, her tongue darting out to touch his lower lip. "So what! You're only human. You didn't break any bones, only a few dishes."

He wrapped his arms around her, pulling her against him. "Christ, I love you," he whispered.

This time when she kissed him, he opened his mouth, letting her slip her tongue in to sample the taste of him. Their kiss was long and demanding, driven by his anger and her compassion.

When she finally pulled back, gasping for breath, her fingers were already seeking the buttons of his coat. She slipped his arms from it and tossed it to the floor. Then came his starched white shirt. She wanted to brush the tip of her tongue over his hard nipples. She wanted to slip her hand into the waistband of his pants and feel him hot and throbbing, in her hand.

"Jess," Adam crooned as she shed his shirt and brought her mouth to his chest. "Jess, what do I do?"

"Shh," she murmured. "Do? For tonight you just let me love you. You were there when I needed you.

298

Need me, please, just for tonight. Let me be the strong one. Let me drown your pain.''

He threaded his fingers through her thick hair, pulling out the hairpins one by one. She kissed his neck; she sucked one nipple and then the other.

Adam groaned. His fingers found the opening at the back of her shirtwaist. When he couldn't slip the tiny shell buttons through the buttonholes, he ripped them off with one impatient jerk.

Jessica laughed deep in her throat as his mouth found the soft flesh between her breasts. He yanked her corset cover over her head and pulled at the laces of her corset until her breasts were free beneath the sheer chemise.

Jessica's hands flew over the buttons of her skirt and she stepped out of it. Adam helped her with the ruffled petticoat. They kissed as they fondled. He brought his mouth to her breast and left a round, damp spot on her whisper-thin chemise. She threw back her head in ecstasy, combing her fingers through his hair until she had released it from the single black ribbon that held it back.

Adam slipped the lacy chemise over her head and then took her in his arms and knelt, laying her on the carpet. Jessica pulled his head down to her breasts, writhing as his hands covered every inch of her pale skin. Each time he kissed her, on her neck, her belly, between her thighs, his hair fell to tickle her awakening flesh.

She was alive with sensation. She wanted no gentle wooing. She wanted to be loved, to love, hard and fast. She wanted to feel with every inch of her being. She wanted to rid herself and Adam of the pain of life, if only for a little while.

She caught Adam's hands and rolled him off her and onto his back. She straddled him and worked the buttons of his tailored trousers. He groaned as her fingertips grasped his burgeoning rod. She stroked him, glorying in the sound of his raspy, ardent voice.

She flattened herself over him, grinding her hips against his, her breath matching his in pace. "You want to change places?" she whispered, nipping the lobe of his ear with her teeth.

"No," he answered. "Stay here, where I can see you."

She giggled. "I couldn't."

"You could." He caught her hands and entwined their fingers. "Just go easy. We've got a whole lifetime ahead of us, *Ki-ti-hi*."

The unfamiliar word buzzed in her head as she closed her eyes, savoring the feel of Adam hard and throbbing between her legs. Taking a deep breath she lifted up and took him inside, crying out with pleasure at the unfamiliar sensation. For a moment she sat still, savoring his warmth and then she began to rock. He held her hands, calling her, moaning.

Jessica became acutely aware of the steady rhythm of the train as it rumbled north. She heard her own breath mingled with Adam's. She smelled that hot, pungent odor of lovemaking. She felt Adam's hands, strong and masculine in hers. Her entire body was alive with utter pleasure. She wanted it to go on forever. But that need deep within her to move faster was overpowering. Adam released her hands to cup her buttocks in encouragement. She heard him gasp and the sound of his voice in her ears made her climax with sudden intensity. She cried out in rapture as the waves of fulfillment came again and again. Finally she collapsed on Adam, laughing, crying.

He took her in his arms and kissed her damp brow. He pulled a coverlet off the back of a chair and threw it over them, tucking it over her shoulders. "Thank you," he murmured in her ear.

She kissed him, stroking his jaw. "For what?"

"I don't know, just for being here, I guess." He kissed her softly on the mouth and she closed her eyes with a smile.

"Could we sleep here?" She snuggled in his arms, suddenly so tired she couldn't keep her eyes open.

"Anywhere you want," he answered. "Anywhere on the face of this earth . . ."

…her, with sudden sureness. She … 9 out … to
winter as he had finished her … and …
"You're lovely," she gasped in gratitude, "and so
kind."

It was so intimate that he asked anything …
He looked … over and … beaver hat, and he
thought from her tone of self-abnegation … …
you, he almost begged her to …

She faced him frankly, his new … a-bother?
"I had I know what to go on the … hire," she said.
She had her different from … sublime face … that … as
within a shroud.

I asked … "I go? Is you" I … of a … tall
sudden to … the … through … an amount of …
Anywhere you would … he answered, watching
on the face of this … sun.

Chapter Twenty-One

For the next few days, Adam and Jessica remained in their private Pullman car. They had their meals brought in by a porter and slept, sprawled on pillows, on the plush carpet. They played backgammon and poker. They laughed and talked, and laughed some more. They talked about meaningless things; they talked about things closest to their hearts. Their conversations ranged from how to skin a rabbit properly, to the politics behind the War Between the States. But they carefully skirted the subject of the future, of *their* future. They seemed to be feeling each other out, wrestling with their own doubts and dreams.

Late one afternoon Jessica sat cross-legged in a chair, cradling a bone china cup of chamomile tea. She wore a wool shawl over her chemise to ward off the chill of the September air. She stared out the window at the glorious mountains as the train chugged its way through the Wenatchees. Their journey was drawing to an end. By this evening they'd reach Seattle. Adam anticipated that within the week they would have Caine. A part of her was excited at the thought of finally reeking her revenge. Again and again she had dreamed of pulling the trigger on her pistol. But a part of her was frightened at the thought that decisions would then have to be made concerning her and Adam's future.

She loved Adam, she knew that, but if he asked her to give up her orchard to go back to Utah with him, what would she say? The dream of her orchard was too important to her to cast aside, even for Adam. She and Mark had left Tennessee to buy land and grow apples in Washington territory. She owed it to Mark, to herself. But she couldn't very well ask Adam to give up his job with the Union Pacific . . .

She sighed, glancing up at him stretched out on the floor, a book propped in his hand. Of course when he found out she intended to kill Caine, perhaps all of her worries would be moot. Adam was determined to bring the man to *justice*. But justice wasn't enough for Jessica; she wanted blood. She had decided she wouldn't discuss it with Adam; she saw no need. If he thought she had given up the idea of avenging Mark's death, that was his problem. She didn't want to spoil what might be the last few days she would ever spend with him over a difference of opinion. She wasn't going to change her mind and he wasn't going to change his.

Adam looked up, catching her watching him. He smiled. "What?"

She shook her head. "Nothing. I was just thinking what a good time I've had. How special you've made these last few days."

"It has been fun, hasn't it?" He laid aside his book and propped himself up on one elbow. He'd shed his fancy suit for an old pair of clean dungarees, a flannel shirt, and red wool socks. His snakeskin boots stood near the door. He had tied his thick mane of glossy black hair back with a red satin ribbon he'd borrowed from her. To Jessica he never looked as handsome as he looked at this moment. His bronze face was ruggedly masculine, yet there was a light in his black eyes that spoke of tenderness and love.

The thought that she might lose Adam, that she probably would, made her want to cry, to scream, to shout. The world was so unfair. If only there'd been no Jacob Dorchester, wouldn't her life have been different? Mark wouldn't be dead. But then she'd never have traveled west. She'd never have met Adam. She'd never have known what it was to love. It was so painfully ironic . . . the loss of Mark's life had brought her this love. Adam's inability to save Mark had given her the chance to experience what she knew she would never experience again.

Jessica's eyes clouded with tears and she looked away, unable to stand the scrutiny of Adam's gaze. He rose and came to her.

"Tell me."

She lifted her chin. Her eyes met his and she shook her head.

Adam sighed and reached down, taking her in his arms. He sat in her chair, with her on his lap. "You're a stubborn woman, Jessica Landon."

She rested her head on his broad chest, stroking his muscular arm through the soft, worn flannel. "It's all going to end, isn't it?"

305

"It doesn't have to end," he whispered. His breath was warm on her cheek.

"There're too many complications," she argued. Her tears were making a wet spot on his shirt. "You don't know the half of it."

"Jess—" Adam started to speak, then held his tongue. He'd sworn to himself that he'd be patient. If he wanted this woman, if he wanted all of her, heart and soul, he *had* to bide his time. If he tried to force her to tell him why she was running, he would lose her. He imagined her disappearing into the darkness never to be seen again. No. He had to let her offer the pieces to the puzzle. Perhaps, once Larry Caine was safely in jail, she would be able to forgive Adam for the part she felt he played in Mark's death. Perhaps then she would tell him why she had fled Tennessee. Once there were no secrets, she would have no reason not to marry him. He thought of the daughter he had always wanted and he smiled.

Jessica brushed Adam's cheek with her hand and pressed a kiss to his lips. "We should be getting our gear together," she told him.

"We should." He returned her kiss, then brought his lips down the soft curve of her neck to the hollow at her shoulders. He pushed aside the wool shawl and ran his tongue along the lace of the neckline of her chemise.

"But maybe," she went on. "Maybe we should make love one last time here in our traveling hotel room." Her voice was husky with rising desire, warm with humor.

Adam reached behind his head, caught the red tasseled window shade, and drew it down, leaving them in semidarkness. "Maybe," he whispered in her ear as he brought his hand up to cup her breast. "Maybe you're right . . ."

When the train screeched into the station in Seattle, Jessica and Adam disembarked and he went to see about having Zeus and Hera unloaded. Adam had suggested that Jessica wait in their car for him, but she was restless. The train had been wonderful, but she'd had her fill of first-class service. She needed to stretch her legs and breathe the fresh, crisp night air.

Jessica wandered along the train depot platform watching families reunite. She thought of the Wiedenhoefts and her apple tree saplings and wondered if they had reached their destination. Were they somewhere right here in Seattle having their supper? She hoped so. She knew it would be possible for her to purchase saplings, new saplings if necessary, but she wanted the ones she and Mark had brought from Tennessee. Somehow, as long as those trees lived, a part of Mark would live.

Jessica sat on the platform step and swept off her fashionable straw bonnet. She ran her hand through her curled hair. It was fun, dressing like a lady, wearing ribbons and lace, but a part of her yearned to slip into her soft leather riding boots, a split skirt, and her wide-brimmed black hat and ride like the wind. She wasn't a woman meant to be cooped up in parlors. Champagne was delightful, but so was a cool sip from a canteen on a hot afternoon.

"I found you at last."

Jessica blinked. Who had said that? She whipped around, stumbling to her feet. She knew the voice, but prayed she was wrong. Her breath caught in her throat as her eyes met his gray ones. "Jacob," she said softly.

"Jessica, love, finally I've found you!" The gray-haired man looked genuinely relieved. He came down the platform steps. "Jessica, you must come home with me at once." He laid his hand on her sleeve and she jerked back as if she'd been burnt.

"Home with you?" Her laugh was bitter. His words had snapped her out of her stupor. "My home isn't with you! You sold my home out from under me!"

"There's no need to quarrel here in public, my darling." He glanced uneasily at the people who milled around. "Let's find a hotel room and get you into bed. You must be exhausted from the long train ride. I know I am. We can talk tomorrow."

She could feel her hands trembling. She was tempted to turn and run. She owed this man no explanation! But she remembered how hard it had been for her to leave him, how intimidated she had once felt beneath his gaze. She'd been a girl, a frightened girl, that night when she'd fled his home, but now she was a woman. The fear was gone. There was nothing left but anger.

She dropped a hand on her hip. "*Jacob!* You didn't hear what I said. You've never heard what I said. I'm not going with you. I want you to go away and I don't ever want to see you again!"

"Jessica!" He lowered his voice, speaking through clenched teeth. "Your behavior has been inexcusable. I have had to take all of this time off work to come and fetch you. Now get your bags and come along." He looked around. "Where's that worthless brother of yours? I suppose he shall have to come as well."

"He's dead."

His face was oddly blank. "Dead?"

"Killed in a train robbery weeks ago."

Jacob adjusted his bowler hat. "I'm sorry, dear."

"No you're not. You're not sorry. You never liked Mark."

"He was an ill-behaved child."

"You were going to send him away."

"A boy like that needs a good military school."

"Jacob! He was my only living relative!"

He reached for her arm again. "It's pointless to have this conversation on the street. Now get your bag and come before I truly grow angry with you."

She took a step back, wrapping her arms around her waist. "I said I'm not coming."

"You have to come," he snapped. "I need those papers."

She grimaced. "What papers?"

"You know very well what papers! The stock certificates, of course!"

Jessica was utterly bewildered. She stared at Jacob's handsome face in the bright lamplight. There was something strange and unnerving about the way he looked at her. "All I took was the cash from the sale of Papa's farm. I don't have any of your stock certificates!"

"We'll speak of this later. Now come along."

Jessica stepped sideways. "You're crazy. You're out of your mind . . ."

Jacob grabbed for her and she darted right. She ducked under a hitching rail and ran for the steps on the far side of the train platform, her skirts bunched in her hands.

"Come back here!" Jacob cried, trying to follow her. "Come back this minute!" He bumped into a brute of a man, and the man gave an angry bellow. "Excuse me! Excuse me," Jacob apologized. "But that's my wife! That's my wife getting away."

"I'm not your wife!" Jessica shouted as she passed above him on the platform. Her feet pounded on the wooden planks as she ran. Her hat flew off her head, but she didn't care. All she wanted to do was get away from Jacob. She stole a glance over her shoulder. He had gotten tangled in the crowd. She was losing him!

She ran to the far end of the platform, ducked under the rail, and jumped four feet to the ground below. She raced as fast as she could toward the end railway cars. She bumped into men leading horses and cows. "Sorry!" she cried. She could feel her heart pounding. "Adam! Adam!" She dodged a woman herding a dozen bleating sheep.

She passed one car and then the next. There was livestock everywhere. "Adam!"

"Jessica!"

She spotted Adam's tall imposing figure in the dim lamplight. "Adam!" She ran to him.

He turned around. "Jessica, what's wrong?"

She flew into his arms and leaned against him, panting. She couldn't tell Adam about Jacob! The man was crazy. She hadn't stolen any silly stock certificates. What was he trying to do, blackmail her into coming with him by accusing her of theft?

Adam grasped her shoulders and gave her a shake. "Jess, what's wrong?"

She swallowed, trying to calm herself. "A thief," she lied. "He . . . he tried to steal my purse!" She shook the black velvet drawstring purse she wore looped over her wrist.

Adam looked skeptical. "A thief?"

"He tried to pull my purse off my arm, but I wouldn't give it up."

He looked over her head. There were patches of light and darkness. There *could* have been a thief lurking near the station. "Where did this thief go?"

She took a step back. "I . . . I don't know. I ran."

"I've made arrangements for Hera and Zeus to be stabled. Our bags are on the way to our hotel." He took her arm and began to lead her toward the depot. "I think we should speak to a law officer."

"No." She shook her head, pulling away from him. "Let's just go on to the hotel. I'm sure he's long gone and . . . and I didn't get a look at his face. It was too dark."

Adam hesitated. Jessica wasn't a good liar. Someone had scared the living daylights out of her back there, but it wasn't a thief. He turned in the opposite direction. "I'm losing patience here, Jessica. A man can only take so much. I don't know what you're keeping from me, but you sure as hell had better make up your mind to tell me!" Adam thought of the man he'd seen in Blades, the man looking for his wife. Could that wife be Jessica? If she was, what would he do? He couldn't give her up. He wouldn't.

He'd kill her husband first.

Jessica rode up to a pretty gingerbread-style house on the edge of town and dismounted. She tied Hera's reins to the hitching post and then wiped her damp palms on her skirt. Adam had had no trouble locating the gunsmith, Elsmere Wiedenhoeft, and Elsmere, a jolly red-faced man had given directions on how to reach his brother Billy's place. Elsmere had heard the tale of Jessica and had been delighted to meet her. He'd thrown his big beefy arms around her and hugged her as if she was some long lost sister. He'd been able to tell her that the Wiedenhoefts had faired well, but didn't know if her apple saplings had survived the trip. Jessica knew there was only one way to find out, so here she was.

She walked up the painted white steps and across the porch. Every window in the house was framed in filmy white curtains, and the sound of children's laughter could be heard faintly from inside. She took a deep breath and rapped on the door. It swung open immediately and there was Kat, grinning, her arms opened wide.

Jessica accepted Kat's embrace, hugging her tightly. It was so good to see her freshly scrubbed face, those bright laughing blue eyes and thick yellow plaits of hair. "Oh, Kat . . ." was all Jessica could say.

"We didn't know if we'd ever see you again," Kat told her. "Now step back and let me get a look at you."

Jessica took a step back, touching her cheeks. "I'm sunburned and covered with freckles. I know I look awful."

Kat stood with her hands shoved in her skirt pockets. "You look healthy is what you look." She wrinkled her nose playfully. "And just a tad thin."

Jessica removed her wide-brimmed black hat and hung it on a peg on the wall. She wanted to ask Kat about her saplings, but she was almost afraid to. After all it wouldn't be Kat's fault if they'd died. Even as badly as Jessica wanted the saplings alive and healthy, her friendship with the Wiedenhoefts was more important. She ran her hand over the smooth whitewashed wall of the entryway. "It seems like it's been an eternity since I last saw you, and Billy, and the kids get on that train."

"Seems like just yesterday to me." Kat looped her arms through Jessica's. "Now come on into the kitchen and say hello to the girls while I finish up my biscuits. Billy'll be home directly and you know how a man is if his supper's not on the table when he steps foot in the house."

"Oh, I'm sorry. I didn't mean to intrude on your meal. I can come back tomorrow."

"Has the sun dried up your head, girl? You're staying for supper. I killed an extra rooster, you've got to stay." Kat started leading her down the hall toward the kitchen. "So just close your tater-trap and come on."

Just then Jessica heard a squeal and the pounding of footsteps on the stairs. She looked up to see Emily bounding down the staircase, with little Holly in hot pursuit.

"Girls! Girls!" Kat scolded.

Emily and Holly froze on the steps and stared

down through the spindles at their mother.

"If you two wake your brother, I know two little girls that are going to have their tails burned! Now slow down and walk like the young ladies you are!"

The two girls came down the remaining steps at a walk, turned the corner at the banister, and then screamed with delight and raced into Jessica's outstretched arms. They hit her so hard that they knocked her from a squatting position over onto the polished floor.

"Girls!"

Jessica laughed, tickling first Holly, then Emily. "Oh, it's all right, Kat, we're just glad to see each other, aren't we?"

"Yea!" they shouted in unison.

Jessica put out her arms. "All right now, heave ho, and get me up off the floor before I get my tail burned for waking the baby."

The girls giggled with delight as they each grasped one of Jessica's hands and helped her to her feet. Then they all went into the kitchen.

The room was filled with the heavenly aroma of frying chicken. The sound of it sizzling in the pan was tantalizing to Jessica's senses. "It smells wonderful, Kat."

"Well, have a seat and tell me how you've been. I'll just finish up these biscuits." She pushed up her sleeves and reached for the ball of dough lying in the center of the pine table.

Jessica took one of the four chairs. "Not much to tell. We're still on the Black Bandit's trail. But we're close, Kat, real close."

Kat dipped her hands into flour and began to

knead the biscuit dough. "We, is it? You and that fine-looking Mr. Sern."

Jessica couldn't resist a smile. "Yes. Adam and me."

"Newspapers say you and *Adam* have had quite the time. Captured by Mexican bandits, thrown from a moving train?" Kat lifted an eyebrow.

Jessica laughed. "Mexican bandits, were they? Funny, because they thought they were Utes."

Kat's jaw dropped. "You really were kidnapped?"

"Calm down." Jessica gave a wave. "I'm fine. They didn't hurt me. The snake bite, now *that* hurt."

All Kat could do was stare with those wide blue eyes of hers. "Snake bite?"

"A rattler got you did it? Sssssss . . ." Emily took the tie of her crisp, starched apron and snaked it across the table. Kat caught the tie with a floured hand and threw it off the table. "Emily Rose!"

"Yes, Mama."

Holly came around the table to stare at Jessica with eyes identical to Kat's. "A snake bited you? Where?"

Jessica lifted her skirt and pulled down her wool stocking. "Right there." She touched a purple bruise. But it's all better now. I feel just fine."

"So"—Kat began to roll the biscuit dough with a rolling pin—"this fine-looking Mr. Sern ask you to marry him?"

"Kat!"

Kat flipped the flattened dough over and began to roll again. "What? You're telling me you don't want to marry him? What's the matter with him? He have seizures? Coughing fits? Are his teeth bad?"

"Kat . . ."

"Well, if he doesn't ask you, you're just going to have to ask him! If I'd have waited for Billy Wiedenhoeft to ask me to marry him, I'd still be waitin'!" She winked. "Of course I'd still have these three fine young'ens." She reached for a glass and began to cut out her biscuits. "Nope, a woman's got to take matters such as this into her own hands."

Just then the front door banged open. Holly and Emily gave a squeal and raced down the hall. "Papa! Papa!"

A minute later Billy Wiedenhoeft appeared in the kitchen doorway, a daughter propped in each shoulder, the ruffles of their dresses and aprons nearly covering his face.

"Billy."

"Jessica!" He grinned. "I was so glad to hear Elsmere had talked to you. Sorry I wasn't there when you came by the shop." He lowered both girls to the floor and went to give Kat a kiss on the back of her neck. "Looks like our sharpshooter friend is just fine, Kat. I told you she would be."

"Oh, get out of here." Kat gave him a push with a floured hand. "You help the girls set the table. By the time the bunch of you've got it right, supper ought to be set."

Supper was a pleasant meal with fried chicken, mountains of boiled potatoes and butter, fresh peas, and Kat's buttermilk biscuits. Kat and Billy and Jessica talked and laughed through the entire meal. It was as if they had been friends all of their lives. Billy and Kat told about the remainder of their train

316

journey. Jessica told about her and Adam's hunt for the Black Bandit. She was careful not to say anything about the relationship she and Adam had, and they were kind enough not to ask.

Finally, after a huge slice of apple pie, Kat slid out of her seat and began to pick up the dirty dishes. The girls had been excused an hour ago and were in the parlor busy playing blocks with the baby, Paul.

Jessica stood up and reached for her plate, but Kat took it from her hand. "Oh, no you don't. You're the guest. Guests don't wash dishes in my house."

"Neither do wives," Billy teased, taking the dirty dishes from Kat. He glanced at Jessica. "Dishes are always my job and always have been so don't let her fool you into thinking she slaves over a pan of dishwater." He picked up several more dishes and carried them to the sink. "You two go on into the parlor and I'll be in shortly."

"First we've got something else to do." Kat took Jessica's hand and led her out the back of the kitchen, grabbing a lit lantern that hung near the door. In the lean-to off the kitchen, Kat handed Jessica one of Billy's work coats. She slipped a shawl over her own shoulders.

"Where are we going?" Jessica asked.

"I can't believe you haven't said a single word about them."

"About what?"

Kat took Jessica's hand and led her outside into the crisp night air. The dark sky was filled with bright twinkling stars. The three-quarter moon hung low on the horizon, just beginning to make its ascent.

"About your apple trees, goose!"

"My saplings? You still have them?"

"Of course I have them. You asked us to take care of them until you made it here, didn't you? What kind of a friend would I be if I couldn't do such a simple thing?" Kat came to a halt and lifted her lantern.

Jessica took a deep breath, her lungs expanding with relief, with excitement. By the light of the lantern she could see her saplings planted one next to the other.

"With winter coming, Billy thought we'd best get them planted. We figured they'd be safe from the wind here near the barn. Come spring we'll just dig them up and plant them on your land."

"Oh, Kat." Jessica reached out to finger a leafless branch. It was soft and flexible, alive and well. She brought her fingertips to her nose and smelled the sweet aroma of the bark. "How can I ever thank you?"

Kat dropped her hand on her friend's shoulder. "We don't want any thanks, Jess. We just want you to be happy." She smiled and then reached out to brush away the single tear that slid down her friend's cheek.

Chapter Twenty-Two

"You understand the plan?" Adam repeated.

Jessica spun the cylinder of her Smith & Wesson and watch the way the lamplight gleamed off the six bullets as they went round and round. "I understand."

Adam watched her from across the room. She was dressed sensibly in a brown wool skirt and a beige striped shirtwaist. She wore no bustle or other women's trappings. Soft doeskin gloves covered her hands. Her hair was tied back, a black wool hat pushed down over her forehead. She looked like a female version of Adam and he didn't like it.

Since they'd arrived in Seattle nearly two weeks ago, she'd been irritable and jumpy. She continually looked over her shoulder. She refused any intimacy or tenderness. Once she located the Wiedenhoefts and found her saplings safe, she wanted to talk of nothing but the plan to capture Caine.

Adam had eventually located Caine's brother, Toby, in a rundown shack near the wharfs. Adam and Jessica had watched the house four nights running. Last night Adam had finally been rewarded with his first glimpse of Larry Caine, the infamous Black Bandit.

Caine was nothing like Adam had pictured. He was small and unimposing. He had a shock of feminine blond hair and wore a gaudy red hat. Obviously he thought himself safe, or he would have been more cautious. He wouldn't have been walking down the center of the street with a whore on each arm and the three of them singing "Dixie."

"What are you staring at?" Jessica asked, her tone short and accusing.

Adam blinked. "What?"

"I said what are you staring at me for? Are we going or aren't we?"

Adam eyed the pistol in her hand. She'd spent the entire afternoon cleaning it. She'd methodically disassembled it, polished every piece, and then reassembled it. She seemed obsessed.

He tried to make eye contact with her, but she looked away. "You know you don't have to go," he said. "I'd just as soon go alone."

She rammed her pistol into her holster and jumped up from her chair, her eyes flashing with anger. "I've come six hundred miles from Utah. I've been mauled by buffalo hunters, bit by a poisonous snake, and captured by renegade Indians!" She took a deep breath. Her voice was threatening and low. "If you think I'm going to sit here and drink tea while you stroll in and take my brother's murderer, you're wrong! I have to be there. You can't stop me from going. If it hadn't been for me, you'd still be riding through dust in Utah. You owe me!"

Adam put up his hands in protest. "Whoa! Whoa! Wait a minute! I didn't say you couldn't go, I just said you didn't have to. I could do it alone. It's my job, Jess."

She flung open the door and walked out without a reply. With an exasperated sigh, Adam followed, a rifle in hand.

They were in their positions by nine o'clock. Then there was nothing to do but wait. Jessica was hidden behind a parked wagon just past the door of Toby's shack. Adam waited directly across the street where he could see Caine as he came around the corner.

Because they were separated, Adam couldn't talk to Jessica, he could only watch and wait. Everything had been going so well between them when they'd been on the train. After the incident the first night in the dining car they had had no more trouble. The trip had been delightful. The last night Adam had nearly gotten up the courage to ask her to marry him, secrets be damned, but then at the last minute he decided to wait until he had Caine safely behind bars. Once his name was cleared with the Union Pacific, he would give them notice. He'd be free to concentrate wholeheartedly on Jessica and whatever it was about her past that clouded her future.

Adam checked his pocket watch. Almost midnight. He looked over at Jessica. She sat perfectly still, but she wasn't asleep. Keep a sharp lookout, he had warned, and that was precisely what she was doing. Adam sighed, shifting his weight to keep his legs from going to sleep on him. Damned if the Union Pacific couldn't use some detectives like

Jessica. She'd be the best of the lot. He couldn't resist a smile as he stared through the darkness at her. Prettiest, too.

When Adam saw Jessica's head snap around, he immediately turned to face the hill where the road turned around the bend and came down in front of Toby's house. Sure enough, here came the Caine brothers, arm in arm, drunk by the looks of their meandering walk.

Adam had hoped Larry would be alone, but had realized there was the possibility he wouldn't be. With Toby along, things might get sticky. The trick was to take Larry unharmed, without having to shoot Toby.

Adam concentrated on the two men coming down the steep, muddy hill. He could hear their voices now. They were laughing and talking about a hand of poker. One of them had been cheating for the other, but their voices were so similar that Adam couldn't tell who was speaking when.

Adam cocked the hammer on his rifle. He could feel the weight of his onyx-handled Bisleys strapped on his hips. He knew he was armed well enough to protect himself and Jessica. He just hoped she had the sense to stay hidden until he had Caine. That was the plan and she'd agreed to it.

That thought no sooner crossed Adam's mind when movement to his left caught his eyes. It was Jessica creeping forward of the wagon.

Adam gave a wave, but couldn't call out. His eyes frantically darted from Jessica to the Caine boys and back to Jessica again. What the hell did she think she was doing! If he called out to her, he'd give away his

322

own position as well as hers. Damned if he wasn't going to have her hide when this was over!

The Caine boys approached the door to Toby's shack.

Adam watched, muscles taut, ready to spring, as he waited to see what Jessica intended to do. Of course, he already knew what she intended. That was to catch Larry Caine herself. The only question was how.

Just as Toby put his hand on the doorknob, Jessica leaped out of the shadows. "Hands up!" she ordered in a gruff, masculine voice, as she waved her pistol.

The two men threw up their hands in surprise.

Then Adam heard Toby, the shorter of the two, let out a string of curses. "Son of a bitch, it's a gal, Larry!"

Adam fought the urge to run to Jessica's side. If this was what it would take to put Mark's death aside, he'd let it run its course as long as she remained unharmed. Just to be safe, Adam lifted his rifle to his shoulder and beaded in on the brothers.

Larry gave a chuckle. "I'll be."

"Remember me, don't you?" Jessica asked, taking another step closer. "The train out of Ogden, Utah?"

Larry glanced uneasily at Toby.

Come on, Jess, Adam thought. *Make 'em drop to the ground. You can talk later. You have to take 'em and take 'em fast, before they have time to think!* He kept his rifle level on his shoulder.

"Train? What train, little lady?" Larry asked, planting a silly smile on his face. "I don't ride trains . . . least not far!" He looked at Toby.

With that, Toby burst into laughter.

"You killed my brother," Jessica accused.

"You must have me mixed up with some other fine-lookin' fellow. I live here in Seattle with my brother, ain't that right, Toby?"

The brother gave another snicker and slowly began to lower his hands.

Jessica moved her pistol a few inches. "You get out of the way," she ordered Toby. "I've got no bones with you." He paused and she flexed her trigger finger.

Toby licked his lips, suddenly realizing this was no game, this woman meant business.

"G—guess I'll just be goin' inside then, if you don't mind."

"You go in and you stay in," Jessica snapped. "Else I've got six bullets—enough for both of you."

"No, no. That's all right ma'am. I'll just leave the two of you to talk it out." He swung open the shack door and began to back in.

No! Adam thought. *You don't let him go inside! You keep him in plain sight!* Slowly Adam began to rise. This had gone far enough; it was time he stepped in.

The moment the door of the shack slammed shut, Jessica took a step toward Caine. "Go ahead, tell me again. You don't remember me, you don't remember my brother."

Caine tried to lower his hands.

"Keep them up!" Jessica snarled.

Caine stretched his hands toward the dark sky. "I'm telling you, I don't remember you. I don't remember any boy."

"You mean to tell me that you kill so many

fourteen-year-olds that you can't keep track?" She took another step.

Adam came out of the darkness. "All right, Jess, I take over from here." He held his rifle on Caine.

"This here's the duputy marshal sent to track you. He's supposed to take you to jail until you can stand trial." She took another step closer. "You want to stand trial?"

"Jess, I said that's enough!"

Larry Caine began to tremble. "I . . . I told you, I wasn't on any train from Ogden. Never been to Utah. I don't want to stand trial."

"Good, because I don't want you to stand trial either."

It suddenly occurred to Adam what Jessica was going to do. She hadn't crossed three states to see this man brought to justice! She meant to be jury and judge right here on the street! She meant to kill the man!

"Jessica! Don't do it," Adam shouted.

"You stay out of this! Mark was my brother and now he's dead!"

Larry waved his hands, beginning to walk backward step by step. "You don't want to kill me, lady. She's crazy," he called to Adam. "Get her off me! She's crazy. I didn't kill nobody!"

Jessica held out her hands and took aim.

"I ought to let her kill you," Adam called as he slowly began to cross the street.

The minute Adam stepped out of the shadow of the building, Caine recognized him. His face went pale.

"You got the wrong man, Sern, it's my brother you want," he protested, backing up under the window of

325

his brother's house.

"Wrong man, hah!" Jessica shouted waving her pistol. "I've got the right man and now the right man's going to die."

"Jess! This isn't the way!" Adam was slowly making his way to her, but afraid to run for fear of scaring her and making her shoot Caine.

Suddenly the window of the shack shattered and Toby Caine came flying through the splintering glass brandishing a pistol. Jessica went down on one knee to shield herself from the flying shards. Larry cried out as Toby knocked him to the ground.

Before Adam reached their side of the street the Caine boys were up and running. Toby handed a carpetbag to Larry and began to fire on Adam and Jessica.

"Get down!" Adam ordered as he spun and fired.

The men raced up the hill with Toby still firing at them. Larry was ahead, while Toby fell back to cover his brother.

"My carpetbag!" Jessica shouted as she leaped up and ran after them.

"Come back!" Adam screamed. "Damn it, Jessica you're going to get killed!"

"I want my carpetbag! I want my grandma's recipes!"

Adam took off after her. The Caine brothers turned the corner. Adam had his choice. He could stop Jessica, or stop the Caine boys. If Jessica reached them, Toby'd surely kill her.

Adam ran up the center of the street. "Jessica! Stop!"

"They're getting away. He's got my bag!"

Toby appeared from around the corner and fired his rifle. A ricochet sounded only inches from her feet.

Adam threw himself forward, catching her around the knees and knocking her into the muddy, rutted street. Her pistol flew from her hand. She screamed as she went down, and then twisted, pounding Adam with her fists.

"You're letting them get away!" she moaned. "They've got my bag and they're getting away!"

Adam ducked, shoving her face into the dirt as Toby fired again, fifty yards from them now. For a long minute Adam lay still, his body flattened over Jessica's. When he heard no more shots, he looked up. The Caine brothers were gone.

Adam pushed up off the ground and grasped Jessica by the back of her torn shirtwaist. He lifted her to her feet and let go for fear he would hit her. "Now you get your ass back to the hotel, do you understand me?"

Jessica wiped at the mud that covered her face. It stung. She knew she'd been cut by the flying glass. She looked down at her bloody forearm and picked out a triangular sliver. She'd made a terrible mistake—not in trying to kill Larry Caine—but in hesitating. Not only was he not dead now, but he was free again and Adam was furious. She wanted to crawl into the rut in the street and die. She looked up at Adam miserably.

"Did you hear what I said?" he bellowed. "I said get back to the hotel and stay there!"

"W—where are you going?"

He grabbed her pistol from the dirt and shoved it

into the wasitband of his filthy pants. "Where the hell do you think I'm going?" Then he ran off.

Tears ran down Jessica's face as she started up the muddy hill. If she had any sense she'd get back on that train tonight and ride, ride anywhere, anywhere to get away from the men who had wreaked havoc on her life—Jacob, Caine, Adam, what was the difference?

She turned the corner at the top of the hill and headed for the hotel. The difference was that she loved Adam . . .

Back at the hotel, Jessica woke a maid and had water brought up to the room she shared with Adam. The room was nothing like the elaborate one at Barton's in Pocatello, but it was clean and neat and adequately furnished.

Once the copper tub was filled with steamy water, Jessica dismissed the maid and began to shuck off her mud-encrusted clothes. She was disgusted with herself. She'd had Larry Caine right in front of her! Why didn't she kill him?

And what was she going to do now that Adam knew she intended to kill Caine, not see him brought to trial? If Adam didn't catch him tonight, he would go on tracking him, but he certainly wouldn't let Jessica go along. She'd be on her own again.

Jessica let the last of her muddy clothes flop to the floor and then she eased into the hot bath water. She cupped the water in her hands and splashed it on her face. She'd been nicked several times by the glass, but there didn't seem to be any embedded in her flesh. She washed her forearm where she pulled the piece out when she'd still been on the street. Then she lay back and let the water seep up over her breasts and cover everything but her shoulders and head. She was tired and she ached all over. Her head pounded.

She fingered Adam's locket she wore around her neck. What was she going to say to Adam when he got here? Worse yet, what if he didn't come back? What if he was killed? What if he went after Caine and didn't bother to come back, not even to say good-bye?

Jessica heard the door ease open. She knew it couldn't be Adam already; it had to be the maid. "I said that will be all," she called not bothering to open her eyes. "You can empty the tub in the morning." The hot water felt so good that she thought she might just stay in the tub until it turned cold.

When she heard a floorboard squeak near her head, her eyes flew open. Before she could turn, someone dropped a piece of stinking cloth around her head and yanked it tight around her mouth. Jessica screamed, but the gag kept any sound from coming out. She struggled to get out of the tub, splashing water onto the floor.

Wide-eyed with fear, her eyes met her captor's.

He was a big burly man with a patch over his left eye. It was no man she had ever seen before. Her assailant reached for her and she leaped up and out of the tub, going for the door. He caught her arm and wrenched her backward, slipping a sack over her head and letting it fall over her body. Jessica fought as hard as she could, but from inside the burlap bag, her blows made no impact.

Inside the bag it was dark and stifling. The old damp burlap smelled of oats and mildew. *Adam!* she cried silently. *Adam, dear God, help me!*

Suddenly she felt herself being grabbed around the waist and thrown into the air. She fell over her kidnapper's shoulder and a groan escaped her lips as her head banged against his broad, humped back. The next thing she knew, the man was running. Instead of turning right to go down the steps and into the lobby, he went left.

For a fleeting moment Jessica thought the man might just be taking her into another room, but then she felt a whoosh of cold night air. She was brought down off the kidnapper's shoulders and being handed through the window! She gave a violent kick to the accomplice, hoping he would drop her. But all she got was a kick in the head and then there was nothing but blackness.

Chapter Twenty-Three

Slowly, Adam took the steps that led to the second floor of the hotel, leaving muddy footprints behind. He'd lost the Caine brothers somewhere on the dark streets down near the wharf. He'd had Larry Caine within grasp and now he was gone. Adam would be lucky if the Union Pacific didn't have a marshal pick him up by morning. The railroad had threatened to charge Adam as an accomplice if he didn't catch the Black Bandit in due time. Adam imagined "due time" was about up.

His only chance was to find Larry Caine in the next few days. On a hunch, he had left word with the three steamships docked at the wharf to let him know if any men resembling the Caine brothers booked passage or were caught trying to stow away. He'd also sent a messenger to the train station.

Damn Jessica and her revenge! It was her fault Caine was still free. Adam blamed himself for not seeing it coming. He was as angry with himself as he was with her. She'd been so preoccupied with her pistol in the last few days. Why hadn't he realized she intended to use it?

Adam had half a mind to turn right around and head for the nearest saloon. A stiff drink might do him some good. He didn't want to talk to Jessica. He was too damned angry with her! Who was she to think she had a right to kill a man? Yes, Larry Caine deserved to die. But Jessica didn't have the right to kill him, no one did. Only the justice system had that right.

Adam knew it was the practice in the West for towns to be jury, judge, and executioner, but he believed it was wrong. A man accused of a crime in the United States had a right to stand trial and be judged by a jury of his peers. If he was found guilty, only then should he die, and at the hand of a government-appointed executioner, not by an angry crowd or a vengeful woman.

Adam reached the door to their room. It was slightly ajar. "Jessica!" he called in a none-too-pleasant tone. He pushed open the door and rested his rifle against the wall.

She wasn't here.

Adam swore. He kicked the door shut with a muddy boot. She'd come up to their room, taken a bath, and fled, rather than face him. He shrugged off his overcoat and yanked his hat off his head, letting it sail across the room.

She hadn't even had the decency to clean up her dirty clothes. They lay in a heap on the floor, making a muddy pool with all the water that she'd splashed on the hardwood floor.

Water . . . There was a hell of a lot of water on the

floor. Adam picked up her muddy shirt and let it fall to the floor. Her boots lay by the bed. If she'd fled, what clothes had she worn? He went to the trunk of clothes they'd purchased and jerked open the lid. Everything was folded neatly, nothing missing. He was sure of it because he'd bought her every stitch of clothing she owned. Her spare pair of shoes, black kid leather slippers, were at the bottom of the trunk.

No clothes . . . no shoes? Adam let the lid of the trunk slam shut.

Jessica would never have walked out of a hotel stark naked! Someone had kidnapped her! Adam grabbed his rifle and ran out of the room and down the steps into the front lobby. There was no one to be seen. He went back up. *Think,* he told himself. *Think,* Jessica's life could depend on it. He thrust his hand into her bath water. It was still warm. She hadn't been gone long.

He looked down at the water puddling under his muddy boots. There were bare footprints and two pairs of male footprints. Adam immediately recognized his own. But the other set led out the door. The barefooted ones ended abruptly inside the doorway. Jessica had been carried away . . . Adam went down on his hands and knees and followed the man's wet footprints on the wooden planked floor.

She'd been taken left, not right, down the hall. Adam scrambled along the floor. The water stains reached the end of the hallway and then ended—at the window. He threw it open and climbed through. The roof was icy, making it difficult to walk along the cedar shingles without slipping. The cold wind whipped through Adam's shirt and he shivered. He could only imagine how cold Jessica must be . . . wet, with no clothes to protect her against the biting wind. Adam slipped back through the window and ran to retrieve his overcoat and hat.

Back out on the roof, Adam crouched for a moment, staring out at the rooflines of the city that stretched out before him. Which way did the kidnapper go? Adam felt so helpless. Jessica could be anywhere by now. All he could do was dig deep into himself and use his intuition, as he had done when he had conquered the Trial by Fire and Beast. It was how the Ojibwa had lived for a thousand years. With a silent prayer, Adam straightened up and ran along the roof, using his rifle for balance. He leaped to a lower level a few feet below. If he wanted to catch Jessica's captor, he would have to think like him. Which way would *he* go, if he was trying to escape with a woman thrown over his shoulder? After only a moment's hesitation, Adam ran, following some unknown path etched in his mind.

Jessica regained consciousness within minutes. Her head pounded and she was acutely aware of the sensation of swinging like a pendulum, draped over her kidnapper's shoulder. She was so cold that her entire body shook violently. She could hear her captor's labored breathing as he loped along in an awkward gait.

Jessica's first instinct was to struggle but she thought better of it. *It's best to let him think I'm still unconscious,* she thought. *Better to have a plan.* But it was hard to think upside down with all of her blood rushing to her head. She was so dizzy that her stomach heaved.

Carefully, she began to rub her chin against her bare shoulder, trying to push aside the gag. She wondered vaguely if the accomplice who had helped her kidnapper get her out the window was there. She couldn't hear his footsteps.

Slowly the gag began to move. Jessica tried to concentrate. She could hear laughter somewhere far in the distance. It was men, singing, laughing— drunken men. She figured she was in an alley. She could feel damp brick walls very close, although her body made no contact with them. A small dog suddenly began to bark and her captor let out a gruff grunt. He changed gaits, giving a swift kick and the little dog howled with pain. It was all Jessica could do to remain silent. The gag was nearly off. But she knew she only had one chance. She had to wait until they were near someone who could help her. She only prayed they didn't reach their destination before that time came.

When Jessica became aware of the faint sound of creaking wagon wheels, she stiffened. The wagon was growing closer. She was sure of it! They were somewhere near the wharf. She could smell the salt air that she had smelled back at Toby Caine's shack. She could hear the reserve steam engines chugging on a ship.

Her captor slowed to a walk. Jessica knew he must be out in the open where he could be seen. It was colder. She couldn't feel the walls around her and the sounds of the street life weren't as muffled. The kidnapper had to be very close to his destination. She heard a woman's lewd laughter, but the voice was too far away. Besides, the kind of woman who was out this time of night was probably someone who minded her own business. The wagon wheels squeaked closer . . .

Jessica took a deep breath and then, just as the wagon began to pass, she let out a horrendous screech. "Help! Help me!" she cried.

Her captor gave a grunt of protest and began to run.

"Hey, you!" a voice called from the wagon. "What you got in there?"

"Help me!" Jessica screamed. "He's kidnapping me!"

She heard the man in the wagon jump to the ground, the wagon still rolling. He was running! Running after her!

"Help!" Jessica kicked and squirmed, pounding her captor's back. Then she felt him heave her over his shoulder. She hit the ground hard, tumbling head over heels.

"Are you all right?" the man from the wagon asked, down on his hands and knees beside her.

Jessica lay in a daze for a moment. She felt like she'd broken every bone in her body when she fell.

"Ma'am?"

She groaned, trying to clear her head. She was so cold . . . "P—please help me o—out of here."

He fumbled at the tie at her feet that held the feed sack closed. "Who did this to you, ma'am?"

"I . . . I d—don't know." *Liar*, she thought. *You know who. It was Jacob. Your beloved betrothed had you kidnapped to take you back to Tennessee!* Still, it was hard to believe. She'd never have guessed Jacob to be capable of such a thing.

"Hang on just a minute. I can't get her untied, I'll have to get a knife from my wagon." The man laid a hand on the feed bag, touching her thigh. "I'll be right back."

"P—please h—hurry. I'm s—so c—cold!"

"Be right back. Right back!"

Jessica lay trembling with cold on the side of the road. Sure enough, a moment later her savior was back. He sawed at the end of the bag with a knife and suddenly more cold air rushed into the bag and Jessica was free.

The man immediately began to cut open the burlap feed sack. First he uncovered a pair of bare feet, then bare knees. When he got to her bare thighs he exhaled sharply. "Jimminny jackrabbits, ma'am. You ain't got no clothes on!"

"I know I . . . I d—don't have any c—clothes. I . . . I was k—kidnapped out of m—my b—bathtub. P—please j—just help m—me o—out of here." Her teeth chattered so hard that it hurt her jaw.

"Out of your tub! Golly!" The young man paused for a moment and then began to cut away the feed sack again. "I got my eyes closed, ma'am, so you don't have to worry."

A moment later, Jessica was free of the stinking wet material. There kneeling beside her on the filthy street was a young man of not more than eighteen years, his eyes squeezed shut.

She took in great gulps of the cold night air. "C—could I h—have y—your c—coat?"

The boy scrambled to his feet, mortified that he'd

not thought of that himself. He held out the long corduroy coat, his eyes still closed.

Jessica stumbled to her feet and slipped into the coat. "T—thank you," she said, trying to make her teeth stop chattering. "Y—you c—can open y—your eyes n—now."

Her savior's eyes flew open to stare at the woman wearing his coat. She had long dark hair that was wet and plastered to her head. And she had the biggest green eyes he thought he'd ever seen. "Rusty Barker, ma'am." He offered his hand, yanking his knit cap off his head.

Jessica took it and gave it a squeeze before pulling her hand back into the warmth of his coat. "I c—can't thank y—you enough f—for s—saving me, R—Rusty. What on e—earth are you d—doing out this t—time of n—night?"

"My papa's a baker, ma'am."

"It's J—Jessica."

"Papa's got the croup so I was making his bread deliveries for him." He shook his head, replacing his cap. "Papa said I'd see many a strange thing this time of the morning, but he's never gonna believe this!"

Jessica placed one of her bare feet over the other. "L—listen, R—Rusty. D—do you think y—you c—could take m—me back to m—my h—hotel? I—I have t—to get w—warm or I'm g—going t—to have pneumonia."

"Oh! Oh, I'm sorry!" He turned and hurried for his wagon that had come to a stop at the corner. "Right this way. The bread wagon's warm. We keep hot bricks in the back to keep the bread warm." He flung a nod over his shoulder.

Jessica stumbled after him. She'd never been so cold in her life. When she reached the bread wagon, Rusty helped her onto the seat. Though only the back where the bread was stored was covered, the driver's seat was boxed in out of the wind. Jessica leaned back against the seat and felt the warmth from the hot bricks in the back seep through the wall and into her back. The heavenly smell of fresh-baked bread wafted through the cold night air.

Rusty jumped up beside her. "Just tell me where to go, Miss Jessica. I'll have you there before you can say "hot cross buns!"

Jessica huddled under the young man's coat, tucking her feet up under her. She gave the boy quick directions and then pulled the coat up over her face so that only her eyes peered out. She felt as if she'd never get warm again.

They turned the corner and headed into a better section of town. Rusty rattled on about his bread deliveries and the shops he still had to visit. Jessica's eyes kept drifting shut. Rusty's voice and the warmth of the bread wagon coupled with her exhaustion made it hard to stay awake.

The wagon rumbled past several closed shops. Out of the corner of Jessica's eye, she saw a man running down the street. A man in a black hat and overcoat, carrying a rifle. "Stop!" she shouted at Rusty, laying her hand on his.

"Adam!" she cried, leaning out of the wagon. "Adam!"

He stopped and spun around, not knowing where the voice had come from. "Jess?"

"Adam, here!" She waved a hand.

Adam came running across the street. "Jessica! What the hell are you doing in a bread wagon?" His gaze leaped to Rusty. "What have you done, boy?"

"Done!" Rusty swallowed hard, petrified by the huge man with the red skin. "I didn't do nothin' to her! I saw some man running down the street with a bag heaved over his shoulder. Miss Jessica, she was inside the bag stark darned naked." His eyes went round when he realized what he'd said.

Adam grasped Jessica's shoulders. She was barely coherent. "That true, Jess?"

She nodded. She couldn't stay awake much longer.

Adam leaped into the wagon, pulling Jessica onto his lap. Her entire body was shuddering with cold. "Take us to Bailey's Hotel, boy, and fast." He cradled Jessica in his arms, wrapping her inside his own coat. He set his rifle between him and Rusty. "You'll be paid for your efforts, boy. I thank you."

"Pay. I don't need no pay. I'm just glad I could help the lady."

"You get a look at the kidnapper?"

"Not really, sir. It all happened so fast. I was just worried about the lady." He glanced at Adam and then back at the road again. "She was screamin' and hollerin' something fierce."

Adam looked down at Jessica, wrapped in his arms, her wet hair stuck to her pale face. He'd be willing to bet his onyx-handled Bisleys that she knew who'd kidnapped her and why. He brushed back a lock of hair. Well, this was it. His patience had come to an end. If she was married to that fellow back in Blades, it was damned well time she told him. Once he knew the facts, then Adam would decide how to deal with them.

It was nearly noon the following day when Adam was finally forced to wake Jessica. He opened the heavy curtains and let the sunshine pour in, then stoked up the little coal stove in the corner of the room. The weather had turned and snow was lightly falling outside.

"Jess," he called softly. He stroked her cheek, leaning to kiss her softly. "Jess, you've got to wake up."

Her eyes fluttered open and her body went tense as she tried to figure out where she was, who was talking. In her dreams it had been Jacob, Jacob chasing her, Jacob holding her prisoner in a dark, dank room. "Adam?"

"Shhh," he soothed. "It's all right."

She relaxed against the goosedown pillow. Those had only been dreams. She was here with Adam, safe, at least for the time being.

"Listen to me." He took her hand, rubbing it. "I've got to meet a ship. I just didn't want you to wake up and find me gone."

"A ship? Why a ship?"

"A stroke of luck, Jess. The Caine brothers bought tickets this morning to board the steamship *Marissa*. You'll never guess where they think they're headed."

"Where?"

"Alaska."

"Alaska!" She laughed. "Larry Caine is going to Alaska?"

"He's booked first-class cabins to a place called

341

Harrisburg."

"You're kidding. How'd you know?"

"Last night when I lost them by the wharf I left word for the ships to be on the lookout for two brothers, traveling by any name. They didn't even bother to use different names!"

"You've got him!"

Adam stood and walked over to pick up his coat. "I've got him. Now listen to me. You stay in this room while I go down to the shipyard."

Jessica pushed aside the covers and swung her feet over the side of the bed. "I'll go with you."

"What, so you can gun him down before I get a chance to take him prisoner? Forget it."

"Please, Adam, don't leave me here." She wrapped her arms around her waist, cold despite the heavy flannel nightgown she wore. "I'm scared."

Adam's eyes went steely. "Of what, Jess? Of who?"

She ran to the trunk and began to pull out clothes—a chemise, a pair of bloomers, a wool skirt. "I'll tell you! I swear I will." She shucked off her nightgown and dressed quickly. "Just let me go with you." She fumbled with the button of her skirt. "Please, Adam."

He frowned with indecision. He didn't want to take her with him, but he sure as hell didn't like the idea of leaving her here in the room after what had happened last night.

She pulled a shirtwaist over her head and stuffed the hem into the waistline of her skirt. "Please?"

He exhaled slowly. "Your husband? Is he your husband?"

She nearly gasped at how close he'd come to the

truth. "I don't have a husband, I swear it!" She pulled on one muddy boot, hopping on her other foot. "I've never loved any man but you."

Adam handed her a hairbrush and a wide, blue ribbon that matched the flowered shirtwaist. "No husband, hmmm?"

"You've got to believe me, Adam. I can explain everything." She took the brush and ran it through her tangled hair.

"I'm sure you can." He waited until she'd tied back her hair and then held out her new overcoat he'd bought her only days ago. "I just wonder if it will be the truth."

"It will be. But let's take care of Caine. Let me get my carpetbag and what's left of my money. Then we'll talk."

"The money's probably gone. So's the carpetbag."

"He had it last night," she insisted, pulling on her coat.

"He might just be using the bag. Your things are probably gone."

"They're not. I know they're not. Larry Caine's still carrying my grandma's recipes and my mama's tintype."

Adam held open the door. "All right, let's go."

She stopped at the doorway, looking at him. "I don't suppose you'd be willing to hand over my gun?"

Adam laughed as he pushed her out into the hall and locked the door behind him. "Not a chance! Now come on. We'll have to hurry!

*　　*　　*

Adam and Jessica made it to the dock as the *Marissa* was loading its passengers. He left her in a hired carriage and went down to the dock to lay in wait for Larry Caine.

An hour passed and Jessica watched from the carriage as the final passengers boarded. The snow had turned to rain, and an icy wind blew in off the water. She saw no sign of the Caine brothers. Another ten minutes slipped by. The mooring lines were being lifted and the steamship was making preparation to get underway.

She watched Adam hurry down the gangplank and enter a small office near the dock. Moments later he came running out of the office. He jumped into the carriage and ordered the driver to return immediately to the hotel.

"What happened?"

Adam shook his head angrily. "The sneaky bastards! They bought tickets for the *Marissa* in their name all right, but an hour later they traded them for tickets on the *Lady Yukon*."

"The *Lady Yukon*? When does it leave?" Jessica held onto the seat as the carriage whipped around the corner at a high rate of speed.

"You mean when *did* it leave?" Adam sat back against the leather seat. "It left at dawn for Harrisburg." He slapped his knee. "So it looks like I'm on my way to Alaska."

"*We're* on our way," she added firmly.

Adam glanced sideways at her. "I had a feeling you would say that. That's why I asked the harbor master to hold the ship an hour while we get back to the hotel to get our things and I send a telegraph to the

Union Pacific. I'll send a message for Billy Wieden-hoeft to see to Hera and Zeus. I don't figure he'll mind.''

Jessica leaned forward excitedly. Alaska! She'd always wanted to see the Alaska territory. And now she was going to get her chance. Of course she'd also have another chance at Larry Caine.

Chapter Twenty-Four

"Gone? Gone where?" Lansing leaned over the front desk at Bailey's Hotel. "They can't be gone! I haven't finished my story!"

The man behind the desk with muttonchop sideburns gave a shrug and returned his attention to his newspaper. "Well, gone they are. Hated to see 'em leave, too. Good customers. Didn't make a mess and tipped us all when they left. Made no difference to me if he was redskin or not. The color of money is all I care about. The man could have been green for all I cared." Mr. Bailey looked up. "Say, what'd you say your name was?"

"Lansing. Theodore Lansing of Chicago," he answered proudly, drawing himself up to his full height of five foot six.

Mr. Bailey peered over his spectacles. "You the newspaper man that wrote this story about Miss Landon actually bein' the wife of some rich banker from Tennessee?"

Lansing clasped his thin hands with delight. "You

read my article?"

"Right here in the *Daily*." Bailey folded back the newspaper and pointed to an article on the second page.

Lansing leaned over the wooden counter, glancing at the article excitedly. "Well, yes, sir, that's mine all right! I sent the piece back to my editor in Chicago." He looked up anxiously. "I wonder how many other papers across the country have picked it up."

"I can't tell you that." Bailey turned the page. "But I can tell you you ought to be glad that deputy marshal's gone because I could guess he wouldn't be too pleased if he read this article of yours. My guess is he don't know she's a married woman. The truth is, I thought the deputy marshal and the woman was newly married to each other the way they acted. They certainly didn't tell me any different."

Lansing whipped out a pad of paper and a lead pencil. "So you say she's gone again." He scribbled. "Gone where?"

Bailey chuckled. "Alaska!"

"Alaska," Lansing breathed. "Quite a woman! Quite a woman!"

"She and the deputy marshal cleared out of here not more than a few hours ago and in a hurry. He left several messages for different people in town and then was headed for the telegraph office on his way to the dock. I heard him telling the woman he had to send word to his employer."

"The Union Pacific?"

Bailey nodded. "So he said." He watched Lansing write for a moment. "Say, you going to use my name in what you're writing?"

"Would you like me to?"

Bailey grinned and smoothed his long sideburns. "Would be something to have my name in the paper. My brother, Lester, once had his name in the *Daily* on account of his pigs settin' fire to his barn."

"Well, sir, I can guarantee you that this will be hotter news than your brother's swine. Now if I could just get your name and place of residence . . ."

He stood and laid aside the newspaper. "Joseph Bailey. I live right here, of course. Bailey's hotel. Clean rooms, good meals, church on Sunday in the parlor." He waggled a finger. "There's many a folk that like havin' services right here. Convenient they say."

Lansing went on writing. "Well, Mr. Bailey, if you could just give directions to the *Daily*'s office, I'll be on my way."

"Um, I don't suppose you've got a room here in Seattle, have you, Mr. Lansing?"

Lansing looked up. "No, sir, as a matter of fact, I don't. Just got off the noon train. My bag's there by the door."

"I'd be willing to cut the nightly rate if you'd be interested."

Lansing offered his hand. "Done! You'll of course throw in two meals a day."

"I—"

"—Considering the free advertising you'd be getting from an article such as the one I'm prepared to write."

Bailey gave a nod. "Guess two meals a day would be fair."

"Glad we could do business." Lansing tucked

away his paper and pencil. "Now if you could tell me how to get to the newspaper office. I'm certain they'll want this latest exclusive information for the next day's edition."

"I can do better than give you directions." Bailey grabbed his overcoat off a peg on the wall. "I can take you there myself. Martha!" he called, poking his head through a curtained doorway. "Martha, you'll have to come here at once. I'll need you to mind the front desk. I have important business to attend to."

A moment later Martha appeared in the doorway with a baby on her hip, and Bailey and Lansing were on their way.

"So, you've stalled long enough. Out with it." Adam sat across from Jessica on a narrow bunk in a tiny cabin on the steamship, *Marissa*. The room was dark and chilly, but at least it was private. It had been meant for four passengers, but Adam had convinced the ship's captain to find other quarters for the goldminers who'd occupied the cabin only an hour ago.

Jessica sat on her own upper bunk intent on swinging her feet. She refused to meet Adam's gaze. "I told you way back in Loco that I meant to see the Black Bandit dead."

"Jess, that's not what I want to hear about this minute. Though I do intend to discuss it. You could have been killed last night on that street! We could have both been killed!" He let out a long sigh. "The husband. I want to hear about the husband."

"Jacob is not my husband," she said very quietly.

He braced himself. The thought of Jessica with another man made him burn hot with anger inside . . . a man with a name now. Jacob. The man he had seen in Blades. He didn't know why, but he'd just assumed Jessica was a virgin that night he'd taken her by the creek. "Jacob?"

"Jacob Dorchester." She paused. There was so much to tell Adam now that the time had finally come. She wasn't certain where to start. "Jacob was a banker in the town near my papa's farm. I've known him since we moved to Tennessee from Philadelphia. He . . . uh . . . advised my father on money matters. He made several bad investments for my papa, but Papa always trusted him. Jacob, he . . . he always liked me, even before his wife died."

"He *liked* you."

Her voice was barely a whisper. "When I was younger, he was always trying to get me alone. Once he tried to touch me, but I screamed and Mark came into the room."

"You never told your father?" Adam demanded.

She shook her head, fighting the tears behind her eyelids. "I figured it was my fault somehow. I was too embarrassed." She looked up at Adam, her eyes pleading that he understand. "Jacob was a very important man in town. Who would have believed a thirteen-year-old girl?" She paused and then went on. "Besides, he never actually *did* anything. He just made me feel funny. He scared me."

"Get on to the husband part."

"When Papa became ill, there got to be problems with cash before the fall harvest. Jacob managed to get him a loan through the bank."

"At a healthy rate of interest, no doubt," Adam offered sarcastically.

"I don't know about that. Papa refused to let me know anything about his finances. He said it wasn't a woman's worry. So anyway. There was a blight, the crops were poor, and Papa needed more money, only Jacob said the bank wouldn't want to lend anymore without a cosigner on the paper."

"The husband part, Jess. . . ."

"I'm getting to it," she said impatiently. "You see Jacob had asked Papa to let him marry me several times, starting before his wife was actually dead. Then when this business with the loan came up, Jacob offered to cosign if Papa would agree to the engagement. He didn't actually say it, but that's what it came down to."

"He used you as collateral on a loan?"

She jumped down off the bunk and began to pace, wishing the cabin wasn't so tiny. Adam seemed to be bearing down on her, making it hard for her to think. "No, I wasn't *collateral.* You see! This is why I didn't tell you. I knew you wouldn't understand."

"I understand perfectly," Adam ranted. "Your father sold you."

"No, it wasn't like that. Papa loved me." She took three steps, turned, and took three more. "He wanted me to marry Jacob anyway. He knew he was dying and he thought Jacob would be a good provider. That's what fathers think of, you know."

"Just out of curiosity, how old is this Jacob?"

"I don't know! Probably fifty by now."

"I thought so, the perverted louse."

Jessica stopped her pacing in front of Adam.

"Papa was worried about how Mark and I would get along after he died. Papa thought he was doing the right thing in seeing that I was cared for."

"So you married Jacob?"

"No!" Her eyes held his. "You have to say you believe me, Adam, or there's no need to go on."

"I believe you," he answered sincerely. "Go on with your story."

"Well, Papa announced the engagement. The bank gave him the loan, and everything was fine for a while. Jacob escorted me to a picnic, a party or two. He never did any more than give me a few sloppy kisses. But he was insanely jealous and I hated the way he was so possessive of me. I told him I wouldn't marry him, but he didn't seem to hear me. Then Papa died and everything happened so fast. Just the sale of the horse herd was enough to pay back the bank loans, but Jacob insisted on selling the farm. He moved Mark and me in with him and set a wedding date before I had a chance to think. He was going to send Mark to a military boarding school."

"So you ran away instead of marrying him?"

She walked to the door and leaned her back against it, closing her eyes to shut out the memories. "Jacob got strange after Papa died. He didn't treat me the same. One night he told me being engaged was the same as already being wed. He came to my bedroom and he tried to—" She wiped her eyes with the back of her hand. "I told him I'd cut it off if he touched me!"

Adam gave a laugh. "Good for you, sweetheart."

"So, anyway, he stomped out of the room, but he'd said he'd come back and the next time I'd keep quiet and do as he said or he'd make me. I was so scared, I

353

woke Mark. We stole the cash from the sale of Papa's farm out of Jacob's safe." She looked up. "It hadn't been deposited yet. I took a few things Jacob had let me bring from the house, we took the Appaloosas, and then we left."

"For Washington territory?"

"Yes. We saw a travel brochure in the train station. We figured he'd never look for us there and the climate was right for apple trees."

Adam got up off the bunk and went to Jessica, taking her unresponsive form into his arms. "Christ, Jess, why didn't you tell me? You had me thinking you had a husband out there."

She sniffed. "I felt stupid."

"Why?"

"I don't know why! Because I shouldn't have let him sell the farm. I should never have let him move me into his house. I should never have let Papa agree I'd marry him."

"Your father was wrong. It wasn't your fault."

She lifted her arms and wrapped them around Adam's neck. "Papa loved me. He thought he was doing the right thing. It wasn't his fault."

"It *was* his fault." Adam lifted her chin so that he could stare into her teary eyes. "Jess, just because the man made some stupid mistakes doesn't mean you can't still love him. You wouldn't believe the things my grandparents did for my sake that hurt me. That still hurt me."

"Oh, Adam." She hugged him tight. "What am I going to do? Jacob . . . he's following me. He sent that horrible man to kidnap me. He says I have stocks of his. I don't know what he's talking about. I didn't

354

steal any stock certificates!"

"You *spoke* to him?"

"At the train station the night we arrived."

"Thieves, hmmm?"

"I'm sorry. I didn't want to lie to you."

"You didn't want to tell the truth either."

When Jessica made no reply, he led her back to one of the lower bunks and sat down, pulling her onto his lap. He smoothed her hair, brushing his lips across her cheek. He was so relieved she wasn't married. He felt as if a weight had been lifted off his shoulders.

"Come on now, no more tears," he said in a low, soothing voice. "Mr. Dorchester is sure as hell not following you to Alaska. We'll take care of Caine and then we'll go back to Seattle. If Dorchester is still there, I'll have a talk with him. I'm sure I can convince him to take the next train back to Tennessee."

Jessica wiped her tears on Adam's shirtsleeve, relieved that she had finally been able to tell Adam about Jacob. "You're not going to hurt him, are you?"

Adam caught her chin with his hand and brought his lips down to hers. "Only if I have to sweetheart. Only if I have to."

"It's all over the papers, Jessica," Jacob chided, reading Theodore Lansing's article on the female sharpshooter published in the Seattle *Daily Times*. "Everyone's going to know you were a naughty, disrespectful, unappreciative girl."

"I told you, the name's Gloria, not Jessica," Gloria

Riley said with a bored yawn as she flipped through the pages of a magazine. She was stretched out on her iron bed, dressed in black stockings and a red corset. Around her neck, she wore a lavender silk scarf. "Your hour's nearly up. I told you, I take the cash whether you take the services or not."

Jacob glanced over the newspaper at the whore's painted face. He didn't like it when his Jessica wore all of that red rouge on her cheeks and lips. He liked her fresh and clean, the way she used to look when she'd been riding her father's horses in the open fields. He glanced out the window. He missed home. It was too cold here. Why didn't his Jessica just come home? Once they were married properly, once he had the stock certificates, everything would be fine. He wouldn't be angry with her anymore. The money he would make off the stock certificates, now that the South African diamond mine had started producing, would make him a millionaire. He'd take Jessica on a tour of Europe.

The wind howled unmercifully outside, rattling the windows of the cheap tenement house. Jacob looked back at the whore lying unclothed on the bed. "Will you marry me?"

Gloria laughed. "Not on your life. Not even if your breath don't stink. Me, I'm a girl that likes her independence."

Jacob folded the newspaper in the proper creases and laid it on his coat so that he would be certain to take it when he left. "Jessica, Jessica, why do you fight me so? I only want what's best for you. It's all your father and I ever wanted. What would a girl like you do with all of that money?" He sat down on the corner of the bed and the mattress sagged.

"Listen, mister. Your time's almost up. You want to do the dirty deed or not?" She tossed aside her magazine with exasperation. It was cold in the room and she wondered if he would tip her. The extra money might buy more coal. It was going to be a cold night. She and her little boy, Manny, who stayed downstairs with Mrs. Caraway when Gloria was *entertaining* would need all of the coal she could buy them.

Jacob reached for Gloria's dark brown hair and brushed it back off her face. Gloria lay back and spread her legs. "Five minutes," she said, glancing at the small clock on the table next to her bed. "Best enjoy it while you can, buster."

He stretched out over her, fully clothed and pushed down her corset. He took her nipple into his mouth and sucked. "Oh, Jess, I've dreamed of this." He fumbled with the buttons on his pants, not bothering to pull them down.

Gloria glanced at her clock. "Four minutes."

Jacob released his engorged member from the confines of his pressed pants and pushed into her with a grunt.

Gloria stared at the water-stained ceiling as the gray-haired gentleman pumped up and down for thirty seconds and then spilled his seed into her with a satisfied groan. He collapsed on top of her, resting his smooth-shaven cheek on her breast. "Time's up," she declared, trying to push him off her. She wanted to get cleaned up in time to take her little Manny for a decent supper at one of the saloons before the place got too rowdy.

When Jacob made no move to get off her, she pushed him harder. "I said, time's up, buster. Pay for another half hour or get your rump out of my bed!"

Jacob lifted his face from her breast. Sweat beaded above his upper lip. "It's a husbandly right, Jessica." His face was oddly contorted.

Gloria tried to slide out from under him. The man hadn't made a lick of sense since he'd spoken to her down on the street, but he'd seemed harmless. He'd been clean and he'd agreed to pay her ahead of time, so she'd brought him up to her room. He'd insisted on using a back door, to be certain no one saw him. Gloria assumed he had a wife. Didn't they all?

"I said get off me, or I scream for help," she threatened.

Jacob grabbed a handful of her hair and at the same moment caught the scarf around her neck and jerked it tight. "Don't talk to me like that. I don't like it when you talk like that, Jessica."

Gloria clawed at the silk scarf that was blocking her airway. She tried to kick or push the man off her, but he was an amazingly strong man, despite his age. She made a wheezing sound. She knew the man was killing her. All she could think of was her little Manny. Would he get his supper tonight if she died?

"Do you hear what I say?" Jacob twisted the scarf around his hand, drawing it even tighter. His Jessica's eyes were fluttering. Her face was turning bluish. But she had a strong constitution. She didn't give in easily. He had to be sure she'd learned her lesson. He wanted her to tell him where the stock certificates were. He wanted her to agree to marry him immediately.

Gloria ceased to struggle. Her body convulsed beneath Jacob's once, then a second time, and then she went limp. He lowered his head to her breast for a long moment. Her chest was no longer rising and falling. Slowly he loosened his grip on her scarf. "Oh, Jessica, my little Jessica . . . I've done it again, haven't I, my love?"

With a sigh, Jacob climbed off the bed. He buttoned his pants and ran his hands down the legs to smooth the rumpled material. When his clothes were properly straightened he went to his coat and removed his silver pocket knife. He returned to the bed, knelt, and cut a lock from the dead girl's hair. He sat on the corner of the sagging mattress and carefully braided the sable brown lock until it formed a small ring. Tucking away a few stray hairs, he leaned over the bed and took the girl's hand.

"You see, we really are married," he murmured as he slipped it onto her finger. "The fact that we haven't got a silly piece of paper is of little importance. *You* are my wife, my dearest." He held her hand for a moment, then sighed. It was no use. He got up to put on his hat and coat.

Jacob *knew* deep in his heart that this wasn't his Jessica, not really, none of them had been his real Jessica. But his real Jessica was out there somewhere and he knew he would find her. He picked up the copy of the *Daily Times* and tucked it under his arm as he went out the door and headed down the back hallway. Theodore Lansing, that was the man he needed to see; he would know where his wife had gone.

Chapter Twenty-Five

Harrisburg, Alaska Territory
October 1882

Jessica stood on the dock, shuddering with cold as she waited for Adam. The wind was howling and snow was blowing in spirals, making it difficult for her to see. Still, it felt good to be on solid land again. Though Jessica had been lucky in that she hadn't been seasick aboard the steamer, she had grown tired of the ceaseless rocking, sometimes tossing, of the boat.

She turned away from the inlet and squinted, staring through the white curtain of snow. Harrisburg didn't seem to be much of a town. The dock was rickety. There were no streets or order to the few buildings that were strung out between the water and the mountains beyond. There was no sign of life in the town. Even the few passengers that had disembarked from the *Marissa* had disappeared.

Adam came up behind Jessica and laid his hand on

her shoulder. She jumped, startled. "Did you find out about a place for us to stay?" she asked.

"What? I can't hear you!" He cupped his hand to his ear. There was a piece of tin roofing that had come loose off the nearest building and it was buckling back and forth, making a horrendous noise.

"I said," Jessica shouted, "did you find us a place to stay?"

He kept his hand on her shoulder, maneuvering her forward, their two bags in his other hand. "There's no hotel! Harrisburg's only been here a year or two. A man by the name of Richard Harris and his partner Joe Juneau apparently hit gold nearby. The captain recommended I talk to Clyde at the General Store." He pointed to a frame house with a partial porch.

A wooden sign hanging from one of the rafters swung so violently that Jessica couldn't read what it said. Exasperated, she hurried ahead, anxious to get out of the elements and find a cup of hot tea. She pushed open the door to the General Store and walked in. To her surprise she found herself in someone's house. There was a kitchen table, a chest of drawers, closet, and an iron bed.

Two men sitting around a coal stove glanced up from their checkerboard.

"Excuse me," Jessica said, flustered. "I didn't mean to walk in on you. Someone told us this was a store." She started to back out, but the older man, a man with a ring of white hair around his balding head, gave a wave.

"You got the right place, miss. I'm Clyde. What

you need?"

Adam came in the door and closed it behind him. He whipped off his hat and banged it on his knee to knock off the snow. "Good afternoon, gentlemen." He looked around. "Is one of you Clyde?"

The white-haired man gave a chuckle and slapped his knee. "I was just tellin' the lady. This is the place if you're lookin' for supplies." His eyes narrowed. "What in great heavens of mercy are you two doin' here this time of year?"

Adam set down his bags and approached the two men. "The name's Adam Sern. I'm a deputy marshal and I'm tracking a man." He shook Clyde's hand and then offered it to the younger man.

The young one bobbed up. "Johnny Sutterbomb, with Sutterbomb Shipping. Pleased to meet you, Deputy Marshal."

Clyde motioned to Jessica. "Well, don't just stand there like a maiden on her wedding night! Come over and get warm. Me and Johnny, we don't bite, least not this time of year."

Johnny's laugh echoed Clyde's.

Jessica approached the stove slowly, unsure of what to make of the two men. She put out her hands to warm them as she looked around. She supposed the place *could* be a store, of course it could have been a messy one-room cabin too. There were things piled everywhere, in crates on the floor, on the bed, on the table. A wild assortment hung from pegs on the walls. She saw snowshoes, and long underwear, and pots and pans and strings of mittens, even a cured ham.

Adam accepted the flask the men offered and he

took a sip, grimacing. "Damn, that's awful. Which one of you made it?"

Johnny laughed. "Clyde says I'd best run it through the distiller again, else it's liable to kill the whole town in one dose."

Clyde took back the flask and screwed on the cap. "So you're lookin' for a man, are you? What he'd do?"

"He murdered my brother," Jessica offered.

Clyde gave a nod. "So what makes you think he's in Harrisburg?"

"He was on the *Lady Yukon* that came in last week. We'd have been here sooner, but we hit one bad storm after another on the *Marissa*."

Clyde gave a nod. "This killer got a name?"

"Larry Caine," Jessica answered with distaste. "He's traveling with his brother, Toby. They're brown-haired, with one taller than the other. One would be carrying a blue and gold carpetbag."

Clyde gave a nod. "Nobody came in here by that description off the *Lady Yukon*. Course there was several men that got off intending to head north before we got socked in for the winter. Fools." He shook his head. "Lookin' for gold. Hell, there ain't any more than a spit or two of gold in this territory. I told Rick Harris the other day, he's gonna kill himself mining in that quartz."

Adam shrugged off his wet overcoat and hung it over a chair. "Caine might well have gone off with those miners," he told Jessica. He glanced back at Clyde. "Listen, we're going to be needing a place to stay."

Johnny got up off his stool and poured some water

364

into a kettle and put it on the stove to heat. "From the looks of this weather, you're going to be here all winter, like it or not."

"Any suggestions?" He looked at the single room doubtfully. There certainly was no room for them here.

"Well . . ." Clyde propped his feet on Johnny's stool. "That's a hard one. I'd offer you a place on the floor here, but I already got Johnny bunkin' with me. He had a right nice place. Upstairs and down till it burnt to the ground last month while we were celebratin' his birthday."

Johnny shrugged. "Can't rebuild 'til spring when my pop ships the lumber. He wasn't too pleased to hear we'd burnt the house and the office. He's the one that actually owns the shipping line. I'm just running this end."

"The captain said there was no hotel, but surely there must be somewhere we could stay." Jessica pushed back a lock of dirty hair that had fallen forward. She was dying for a bath.

Clyde shook his head. "The only place I can think of that would suit would be Miss Melba's."

Johnny laughed. "Good old Melba. Now there's a woman who can show a man a good time!"

Adam glanced at Jessica. "Shall we try Melba's?"

She sighed. "What choice have we got?" Jessica knew the woman was a whore. She could see it on the men's faces. But was she above staying at a whorehouse? Certainly not. At this point, if the room was clean and the mattress was free of bugs, she'd take anything.

"You could just wait here," Adam suggested,

putting his wet greatcoat back on. "Smells like coffee brewing."

"No, that's all right. I thank you men for your hospitality." She gave a nod.

"Third place on the left past the dog pens," Clyde told them as he moved his black checker. "Can't miss it."

Jessica and Adam trudged through the swirling snow, down the street. It had grown dark while they were inside, though it was barely suppertime. Jessica huddled against Adam's warm back as they made their way to the door of Miss Melba's.

"You wishing you'd stayed in Seattle?" Adam asked as he knocked on the door.

"Of course not," Jessica answered. "Just wishing it had been spring instead of fall when we left."

The door swung open and a pretty woman in her early thirties appeared. "Well, come in, handsome. Don't just stand there and let the whole mountain blow in." She didn't look like a whore to Jessica with her natural honey blond hair, heart-shaped face, and pale blue eyes, but she certainly talked like one.

Adam stepped inside and Jessica followed. "Clyde said you might be interested in renting me a room," Adam said.

Melba broke into a wide smile. "Rent, hell, I'll share my bed, with you, sweetness. A girl can get cold when the wind blows out of the north."

Jessica stepped past Adam and came into Melba's view. "We're looking for a room for the both of us," she said tartly, amazed by the jealousy that burned inside her. "Have you a room for two?"

Never missing a beat, Melba swung out her hand

in genuine friendship. Jessica hesitated a second, then gave it a firm shake. "Pardon me. Didn't know he was taken. You his wife?"

"Not yet," Adam interrupted. "But I'm working on her."

Melba reached for their coats. "Lucky woman you are, then. Well, come on with you. Come in and get warm. I'm alone; business is slow with this weather. I was busy readin' my papers that come in on the *Marissa*."

"This mean you have a room to rent us?" Adam asked, taking an immediate liking to Melba.

"You got cash?"

"I do."

"Do you overindulge in hard liquor?"

"No."

"Sold! I can use the cash to tide me through until the miners and trappers hit here in the spring." She led them down the carpeted hall and into a nicely decorated parlor. "What brings you this way, this time of year?"

"We're tracking the man who killed my brother," Jessica answered, picking up a pretty porcelain figurine off a rosewood table. "My name's Jessica Landon. He's Deputy Marshal Adam Sern."

Adam plucked off his hat and Melba gave a low whistle. "God, if you don't beat all! You not from around here, are you?"

Adam glanced at Jessica, embarrassed. "From Philadelphia originally."

"That's no Philadelphia suntan, Mr. Adam Sern. Don't tell me you're one of those redskins!"

Adam laughed, taking no offense. Somehow the

words didn't seem the same coming out of this young woman's mouth. It was obvious she didn't want to be judged, nor did she judge. "My mother was Ojibwa. I was born in Canada."

Melba gave a nod. "Fine-looking sons you and Jessica are going to be making."

It was Jessica's turn to be embarrassed. She picked up another figurine, wondering if she could live all winter with this straight-talking woman.

"Well, listen," Adam said. "I need to get back down to the dock and get our trunk."

"No need. I'll send Benny."

"Benny?"

"He lives here with me. One of the Indians from up north. He's a mute. Some trapper cut out his tongue years ago when Benny was still a boy. He helps me out. In the summer I try to get a couple of girls in from Seattle so the house gets pretty busy."

"Sounds like you've got quite a business going. I wouldn't have thought there'd be that many men coming through here."

She smiled slyly. "You'd be surprised how far a man will walk for a whore when he's spent the winter in an eight by eight cabin with twelve dogs." She gave a laugh and signaled for them to follow. "Come on. Benny's got supper ready. It's just moose stew, but he makes a fine sourdough bread to go with it."

Adam glanced at Jessica, a smile on his lips. It was infectious. She smiled too and took the hand he offered. Together the two followed Melba down the hall and into a cozy kitchen. There was a man standing at the stove, tending the fire. He turned when they entered the room, and glanced uncertainly at Melba.

"It's all right, sweet," Melba chided, laying her hand on Benny's arm. "They're friends. They're going to be staying with us for a while. This is Adam and Jessica."

Benny gave a nod. He was a short, stocky young man of eighteen or twenty with a broad, flat face. Although Melba called him an Indian, his skin color was nothing like Adam's. His skin was a yellow, muddy brown where Adam's was a rich copper.

Jessica smiled.

Adam gave a nod. "Nice to meet you, Benny."

"Set two more plates, Benny," Melba said, taking her seat at the table. "And let's eat."

Benny gave a nod and hurried to do her bidding. It was obvious he was as fond of her as she was of him.

Later when the meal was over, Melba and Adam talked while Jessica sat in her chair near the door, drifting in and out of sleep. It felt so good to be warm and comfortable again. The boat had been so damp that she had thought she'd never be warm again.

Adam laid his hand on her shoulder. "Hey, sleepyhead, let's go to bed. You're going to fall off that chair in another minute."

Jessica stood, covering a yawn with her hand. "I'm sorry I haven't been much company," she apologized to Melba.

"Pshaw! Don't be silly. I know that boat ride was hell. I had Benny take you up some water for a bath. Soak in the tub and then climb into bed with that handsome man of yours. You'll be fit as new by morning."

Adam draped his hand over Jessica's shoulder and they followed Melba down the hall and up the steps. Her home was small, but comfortable. Rugs scattered the plank floor and delicate flowered wallpaper covered the walls.

Melba led them down the hallway that was lighted by wall sconces everywhere and pushed open a door at the far end. "We call this the green room. Hope you like it. My grandma had a green bedroom. I always wanted one like it."

The room was pretty with green and white vined-leaf wallpaper. It was sparsely, but adequately furnished with a bed, and bed table, a closet, chest of drawers, and a large copper tub. "Oh, we're not taking your room are we?" Jessica asked.

"Nope, you're not. I sleep in the red room. Benny sleeps in the kitchen, except when he's sleeping with me." She gave Jessica a wink. "Well, your trunk's there under the window. Anything you need, just give a holler. Tomorrow I'll introduce you to the folks in town, Adam. Maybe you can get some information about that killer of yours."

"I'd appreciate it, Melba. Jessica and I've come a long way. We don't want to lose Caine now."

"Well, good night to you." She flashed them a smile and closed the door behind her.

Jessica looked at Adam with round eyes. "She's really something, isn't she?"

"She is. But I like her." He came up behind her and began to unbutton her shirtwaist. "She says what she thinks."

"Do you really think Benny *sleeps* with her?"

Adam laughed, brushing aside the material of her shirtwaist to kiss the bare skin of her shoulder. His fingers found the delicate gold locket she wore around her neck. "I don't know about sleeping, but it sounds like he visits, doesn't it?"

Jessica closed her eyes as Adam slipped off her shirt and cupped her breasts with his rough hands, pressing his chest against her back. He kissed her neck and she sighed. "Oh, I've met so many strange, wonderful people, Adam. People I didn't know existed!"

He continued to undress her, kissing her here and there as he cast her clothes aside. "Wonderful people? I guess I never looked at it that way," he mused.

She turned and looped her hands around his neck, fully unclothed now. "Since I left Tennessee, I've seen so much good and bad. But it makes me feel more alive than I've ever felt before. Do you know what I mean?" She gazed up into Adam's dark eyes.

He brushed at a wisp of her dark hair, taking in her heavenly green eyes. "I think I *do* know what you mean. But it's not the world that's done it to me, Jess, it's you."

She laughed and lifted up on her toes to kiss him. "My bath water's getting cold. Want to join me?"

His hands went to the buttons of his flannel shirt. "Best invitation I've gotten all day!"

"What do you mean no one is sailing?" Jacob demanded of the ticket clerk. "I must make my way north to Harrisburg!"

371

The spectacled clerk rolled his eyes in exasperation. "I'm telling you, sir, no steamers are going north in this weather."

"That's what you've been telling me for three blasted weeks!"

"Look, mister, I don't have any control over the weather. All I'm telling you is that this company is not shipping in weather like this. Might not be another boat till spring."

"I can't wait that long!"

"Unless you want to swim, you may have to. Now if you'll excuse me," he slid off his stool, taking with him a bundle of papers, "I have work to be done."

Jacob leaned against the wall of the ticket office, letting his eyes drift shut in frustration.

Lansing watched from the door. "I told you, Jake old fellow, not for love nor money could I get passage for us north."

Jacob's face soured. "Well, we'll just have to keep trying, won't we, Mr. Lansing!"

"Look, I'm as anxious to get to this Harrisburg place as you are. My novel is nearly complete."

Jacob stuffed his hands into the pockets of his finely tailored black greatcoat. "I don't care about your blasted novel, all I care about is my wife!"

"Now, you agreed, I help you find your wife. I bring her to you and I get exclusive rights to the story."

"I know! I know!" Jacob waved. "But you can't bring her to me if we can't get off the dock!" He brushed past Lansing. "Well, we might as well go back to the hotel where it's warm and wait for this storm to pass."

"It's all we can do, Jake." Lansing followed him out of the ticket office and into the freezing rain.

"Gone? How can he be gone?" Jessica asked. She was seated in the parlor with Melba. Adam had just come in after talking with several townspeople.

"He just disappeared." Adam rested his hand on the doorframe. "He most likely went with those miners, but there's no way I can get over those mountains now."

"Damn straight you can't!" Melba looked up from one of Benny's socks she was darning. "You walk out of here and start for those mountains and you'll not come back alive."

"So what do we do?" Jessica asked.

He shrugged. "We wait."

"All winter!"

"You got any better ideas?" he asked impatiently.

"No." She rubbed her temple. "I'm sorry. I was just hoping we could get this over with and start living our lives."

"I know." Adam squeezed her shoulder. "But we've got no choice."

"Oh, come on! It won't be such a bad winter," Melba said, returning her attention to the sock. "We'll play cards, drink a little peach brandy. Think of all of the long dark afternoons you two can spend rollin' on that fine bed upstairs." She grinned.

Adam looked down at Jessica. After a moment she reached for his hand. "All right, so we stay the winter and come spring we go over the mountains after our Black Bandit."

373

"*I* go after our Black Bandit. You sit tight," he corrected, "and think about wedding plans. It'll be the best way to take care of your Mr. Dorchester."

Jessica looked away. She hadn't thought of Jacob in days. When would her life ever be less complicated? As much as she loved Adam, she wasn't willing to give up the thought of seeing Caine dead by her own hand. She didn't know how she was going to manage, all she knew was that come spring, when Adam crossed that mountain range, she was going to be with him . . .

Chapter Twenty-Six

Jessica leaned against the back of a wooden chair, laughing at one of Clyde's inane jokes. The months had slipped by so quickly. Melba, Clyde, Johnny, and the others in Harrisburg had made her and Adam so welcome. In the winter months she had become one of them, and Jessica had found happiness and contentment. Thoughts of Jacob Dorchester and Larry Caine had faded in her mind until they were just bad memories.

Melba stood in the doorway, tears of laughter running down her porcelain cheeks. "If you don't beat all, you dirty old man!" she teased Clyde, who was well over twice her age. She slipped into her fur-lined overcoat. "Now you be sure and come see me soon!"

"Oh, get out of here. You'd give me a heart attack and there I'd be in Johnny's shed frozen stiff till spring thaw when you could bury me!"

Jessica's eyes went wide. "Johnny's shed! What on earth do you mean?"

Clyde poured himself a cup of coffee from the pot on the stove. "You don't think there'd be any burying this time a year do you? March or no, you couldn't get a pick through the first inch of that permafrost. There's no digging graves in the winter, girl!"

She grimaced. "So you put the bodies in sheds?"

Clyde shrugged. "You want 'em in Melba's parlor all winter? I just heard of a man killed in a gunfight in a town over the mountains where they got a body in the General Store's food locker. They shove aside the poor bloke and slice off a hunk of frozen beef."

"God, Clyde, you are the biggest liar I ever laid eyes on!" Melba pulled her red stockingcap over her head.

"I am not. Truth, swear to God on my sister's grave!"

"You said you were an only child!" she shot back.

Clyde snickered. "Be that as it may, I'm telling you, a man was shot in a card game over to Marbleton and they put the body in Jim Carradine's food locker. It was either there or in the shithouse."

Jessica glanced up at Clyde. Sudden images of Larry Caine popped into her head. She thought of Mark and his lifeless, blood-spattered body. All of the hate she thought had subsided over the winter suddenly came tumbling back. The hatred had never left her, only dulled with time, and now it burned in her chest like hot coals. "Killed in a card game, you say?"

"So I was told."

"Poor fool." Melba shook her head. "Well, Jessica, I'd say it's time we get home. That man of yours will be thinking the wolves carried us off. You coming?"

"I'm coming." Jessica put on her greatcoat and fur hat and waved good-bye to Clyde. Outside, she'd not taken two steps when she called to Melba just ahead of her. "I forgot to ask Clyde something, Melba. You go on ahead without me."

"You sure?"

Jessica nodded, her hand already on the doorknob. "I'll be right behind you!"

Inside Clyde's, Jessica walked to the stove where Clyde sat, his feet propped on a wooden crate.

"Fast trip," Clyde commented, lighting his pipe.

"That man killed in a card game, Clyde . . ."

"Yeah, what about him?"

"Do you know who did it?"

He drew on his pipe with a sucking sound. "Buckle McGinnis said it was some newcomer. Guess there was an argument over cards. One man accused the other of cheatin'. The man accused didn't actually do the shootin'. Buckle said it was the brother."

"He wasn't arrested?"

"The dead man pulled his gun first." Clyde blew a series of smoke rings into the air. "Got what he deserved, most folks'd say."

Jessica stared at the bright flames that flickered in the cracks of Clyde's stove. It was the Caine brothers! She was sure of it! Larry Caine had survived the trek over the mountain pass and had lived through the harsh winter to kill again. He was somewhere out there with her carpetbag. She knew the money was probably gone, but her tintypes and her grandmother's recipes . . . she had to get them back!

Jessica cleared her throat. "You said a man by the

377

name of Buckle told you about the murder."

"Buckle McGinnis. Fine trapper. Used to work for the Hudson Bay Company, but now he's on his own."

"Is he still here? In Harrisburg, I mean."

"Reckon he is." Clyde looked, his pipe clenched in his yellowed teeth. "Why do you ask?"

"Where can I find him?"

"Now don't be going off half-cocked, girl. I see that look in your eye."

Jessica set her jaw with resolve. "Where is he, Clyde?"

"Adam ought to beat you, that's what he ought to do," he said cantankerously. "That's how we handled women like you in my day."

"Clyde . . ."

"Down to Lester's. Having a drink and playing a hand of cards I expect."

"Thank you!" Jessica ran for the door.

"Jessica," the old man called.

She flipped the latch and turned the doorknob before she looked back. "Yeah?"

"Hate's a mean thing. It eats you from the inside out. By the time you see it, it's too late. Hate can kill you faster than a whiteout on a January day."

Jessica's eyes met the man's clouded ones and for a minute she thought she might go home to Adam and tell him what she'd heard. But then images of Mark's coffin being lowered into the ground flashed through her mind. She thought of the Winchester rifle the boy had never gotten. It was Larry Caine's fault Mark would never have a Winchester, and he was going to pay . . .

378

Minutes later Jessica walked into Lester's saloon. There was no one inside but the blond-haired Lester and a stranger. The stranger was a mountain of a man with a thick red beard and a head of long hair.

"Are you Buckle McGinnis?" Jessica asked from the doorway. She pulled off her fur hat and let her hair tumble to her shoulders.

The huge man looked up at her from the table where he played cards with Lester. "Depends on who's askin'," he rumbled in a deep voice.

"The name's Jessica. Jessica Landon." She glanced at Lester. "Could you excuse us for a minute? I'd like to speak to Mr. McGinnis in private."

Lester sat frozen for a moment. No one had ever asked him to excuse them in his life. He wasn't quite sure what to do! He popped out of his chair, knocking it over as he went. "C—Certainly, Miss Jessica. I'll just go right in the back. Got . . . got glasses to wash and such."

Jessica waited until the flustered saloon keeper was gone and then she went around the table, set his chair upright, and sat down. Her fingers went to the heavy coat and she unbuttoned it. "I understand you know something about a murder that took place in Marbleton."

Buckle's eyes narrowed. His beard was so overgrown that it covered his entire face except for the tip of his nose and the slits where his eyes were. "I didn't kill him, if that's what you're asking."

She laid her hat on the table. "I'm not interested in the murder. Just the murderers. I hear they were two brothers."

Buckle gave a slight nod. "Jim and Joe Lawrence."

379

Jessica smiled slyly. Could the infamous Black Bandit have come up with a more original name than that? She had him! She had the bastard! "Blond-haired fellows. One this tall"—she lifted a hand—"the other a little shorter?"

Buckle nodded. "One of 'em a runaway husband?"

She thought she detected a smirk beneath the mounds of red beard. "Not hardly. Will you take me to him?" She shrugged off her coat.

"Might. For a price."

"What do you want?"

He leaned across the table. "You?"

"Not on your life," she shot back. "You touch me and I'll blow your face off. I've killed more men in the last year than I can count on two hands."

Buckle sat back in his chair. "Fair enough. Can't blame a man for tryin'." He sighed and poured himself a glass of whiskey. "Guess it'll have to be money," he finally said, obviously disappointed.

"Name your price." When he did, she nodded. She knew she would have to take money from Adam's cache, but she'd pay him back, just like she was going to pay him back all the money she owed him. "When do we leave?"

"Daybreak. Dress warm. Carry light."

"I'll meet you here." She got up and put on her coat. "Just don't tell anybody, all right? This is personal."

He nodded. "No skin off my back. I'd rather not know what you're up to. But you be here at daybreak or I go without you. With this weather break I want to get through them mountains. We're bound for another storm before the thaw comes."

"Good enough." Jessica got up from her seat and picked up her hat. "See you at daybreak, then."

Buckle gave a nod and went back to his whiskey.

That night Jessica lay in Adam's arms listening to his even breathing. She had wanted to tell him about Caine, but she just couldn't bring herself to do it. He didn't understand. He wouldn't have let her go. He didn't know what it was to lose an innocent loved one to violence. She rolled onto her side and looked at his sleeping face. *God* she loved him. She wanted to marry him. She wanted to be a part of the rest of his life wherever that took her, but first this had to be completed. She had left Loco so many months ago bound to catch Mark's killer and now she was going to do it.

Pressing a kiss to Adam's lips, she slid out of bed and began to dress. It would be daylight soon. Her pack was ready and waiting for her, hidden on the back porch. All she had to do was dress warmly and get to Lester's without being seen. Finally, wearing as many layers as she could put on and still walk, she took a last look at Adam and slipped from the room.

Adam slammed his hand on the checkerboard and black and red checkers scattered, flying through the air and raining on the sanded plank floor. "Why the hell didn't you tell me, Clyde?"

The old man ignored Adam's tirade and went on sipping his morning coffee. "Weren't none of my business, besides, I didn't know she was going to take off with Buckle."

"Who is this Buckle McGinnis? How the hell do I know she'll be safe with him?"

Clyde slurped his coffee loudly. "You don't, but my guess is, she's as safe with Buckle as Buckle is with her. That woman of yours"—he shook his head—"she's got a mean streak in her."

"She took a pistol and a rifle. If these two brothers are the Caines, she means to kill the one who murdered her brother."

"Sounds fair enough to me."

Adam glared. "It's not up to Jessica to be judge and executioner! It's my job to bring Caine to justice in a court of law!"

"You mad because she aims to kill the dirty bastard, or because she's going to best you and get to him first?"

Adam turned away, swearing foully.

Clyde chuckled. "Get her harnessed and she'll make a hell of a partner for life, Adam."

Adam stuffed his hands into his pockets, seething. He couldn't think about marrying her now, all he could think of was throttling her when he got a hold of her. Adam turned back. "How do I get there?"

"Where?"

"You know damned well where! Marbleton!"

"Marbleton." Clyde slurped his coffee. "Don't nobody in their right mind get to Marbleton this time of year."

"What do you mean, nobody gets there? You just said yourself Buckle McGinnis came across those mountains and turned around and went right back, taking Jessica with him!"

"I *said* nobody in their right mind. Nobody ever said Buckle McGinnis was sane."

Adam exhaled with impatient anger. "Clyde, who can take me over the mountains? *Today*. I can't let Jessica kill Caine. She'll regret it the rest of her life."

Clyde glanced at the checkers all over the floor. "You spilled my checkers."

"I'll pick up the damned checkers, just tell me who'll get me over those blasted mountains!"

The old man belched and then sighed with pleasure. "The only person I can think of is Benny."

Adam grabbed his coat and ran for the door. "Thanks, Clyde!"

"What about my checkers, boy?"

Adam's only response was a slam of the door.

"What do you mean he'll take me, but he won't take me today," Adam demanded of Melba.

Melba looked at Benny seated at her kitchen table, dressed in a white pressed shirt, reading his Bible. "I mean, he won't go until tomorrow. Monday. Today's Sunday, the Lord's day, according to Benny."

"I can't wait until tomorrow. Tell Benny I can't wait! Jessica left hours ago. I have to catch up with her!"

Melba turned to Benny who shook his head emphatically, never lifting his gaze from his Bible. "I'm telling you, Adam," Melba said. "You're not going to budge him. Ever since that missionary man came through here, Benny's been hell-bent on the Lord. That Bible of his tells him to keep the Lord's day holy and he's going to do it if it kills him. You know how he is; you've been here all winter. Sunday comes he won't cook, he won't haul wood." She dropped her hands to her slender hips. "Adam, he won't even screw. You certainly don't think he's going to haul you through the mountains!"

Adam threw up his hands in disgust. "Lunatics! I'm surrounded by lunatics!" He paused. "Well, guess I'll have to go alone."

"Don't be a fool! You'll die before you reach the first ridge. You won't do that woman of yours any good as wolf bait."

He ran a hand over his face. Melba was right; he knew she was right. But damn Jessica! If she died in those mountains, if Caine killed her . . . He tightened his balled fists. He'd looked all his life for Jessica. He didn't want to lose her now!

"All right," he finally said, heading out of the kitchen. "Fine. Tell Benny tomorrow, but first thing and I mean first thing," he called over his shoulder. "He'll have to say his damned morning prayers walking on his feet instead of kneeling on his knees."

Jessica lifted one leaden foot and planted it forward, followed by the other foot. The wind blew so hard that she was blinded by whirling snow. She was beyond being cold. She no longer felt the weight of her small bag and her rifle strapped on her back. Her face and feet were numb. She'd lost all feeling in her fingers hours ago.

Jessica felt something bump into her. She turned her head slowly to see Buckle's iced-over red beard. She smiled beneath the woolen scarf that covered her entire face except for her eyes. Buckle took her arm and helped her over the snowdrift. It was too cold to talk, but the intensity of his eyes told her to keep moving or she would die.

As she trudged forward she thanked him mentally for the hundredth time for having the forethought to bring along a pair of snowshoes for her. Without them she would never have made it through the mountains.

Hanging onto Buckle's arm, she forced one foot in front of the other, glancing up into the sky. It was amazing that the snow could blow and the sun could still shine. Of course the sun had been up five hours and already it was beginning to set. Buckle had promised they would make Marbleton by sundown. They had to be close.

As if reading her mind, Buckle lifted his mittened hand and pointed. Jessica squinted, pulling down her scarf. The wind had eased and the snow wasn't blowing so hard that it stung her face. In the distance she could see lamplight twinkling.

"Marbleton?" she asked in disbelief.

Buckle nodded.

They came over a crest and started down the last hill. *Marbleton?* Jessica thought. Why it was no more than a huddle of eight or ten ramshackle cabins! How many people could possibly live here in the winter? Even Harrisburg sported a winter population of thirty-six, thirty-eight, counting Jessica and Adam.

"Fine place, don't you think?" Buckle released her arm and forged ahead. "That's my cabin. The big one on the end." He pointed to a log cabin that looked to be twelve feet by fifteen.

She followed him the last quarter of a mile and entered his cabin just behind him. Buckle shed his thick seal-fur mittens and struck a sulfur match to the wood in the iron stove left in anticipation of his return.

Within minutes the airtight cabin began to warm and Jessica began to shed her layers of clothing. She sat in a chair near the fire and loaded her pistol while Buckle hurried about the cabin making coffee and biscuits.

In the three days it had taken them to cross the mountains between Harrisburg and Marbleton, Jessica and Buckle had become good friends. She had no trouble with him making any more indecent propositions. Once she had told him she wasn't interested, he had never mentioned it again. She found that his initial gruffness was only a front to conceal his genuine good-heartedness. When Jessica had explained to Buckle why she was looking for Caine, he had offered quite enthusiastically to kill him himself. But she had insisted she had to do it herself if she was ever going to put Mark's death behind her.

When the biscuits were ready, Jessica and Buckle sat down to eat them, washing the sourdough bread down with cups of black coffee. After the meal, Jessica put on her coat, tucked her pistol into the waistband of Adam's pants she wore, and pulled on her fur hat.

Buckle followed her to the door, carrying her rifle. "You certain you don't want me to go along, just in case one of them boys gets out of line?"

She took her rifle, offering her new friend a quick

smile of determination. "I've got to do it myself, Buckle. But thanks."

He nodded and pushed open the door. "Third cabin down. It belongs to Billy Glick but with Billy gone for the winter, the Caines took it over."

Taking a deep breath, Jessica stepped out into the frigid night air and hurried for the cabin. "I've got you," she whispered over and over again. "I've got you, you bastard!"

When Jessica reached the door, she listened for voices, but heard none. Maybe Larry and Toby were asleep. She knew they were there. Lamplight burned in the window. Taking a deep breath, she hit the door with her fist. To her surprise, it swung open.

Pulling back the hammer in her Henry rifle, she peeked around the corner, but saw no one. The smell of rotting food immediately assailed her nostrils. Cautiously, she stepped inside. It was almost as cold in the cabin as out.

The place was a pigsty of filth. Tin cans and spats of sticky brown tobacco littered the floor. Half-eaten cans of beans sat open on the pine table in the center of the room. The fire in the crude fireplace was nothing but a pile of dying embers.

On the far wall Jessica spotted a platform bed. Beneath the covers she could make out the form of a body. She laid her hand on the trigger. "Caine!"

The body didn't move.

"Caine, is that you? You'd better say something before I blow you off that bed."

She heard a groan and then the covers began to move. She sighted in, just in case this was some trick.

"Wh—who is it?" cried a pitiful voice. He pushed

387

aside the wool blanket and Jessica caught sight of Larry Caine. His hair was dirty and matted, and he had a full beard that covered his face. His eyes were hollowed out with illness, but it was Larry. She'd recognize those weasel eyes anywhere.

"Where's your brother?"

He wiped his mouth. "Carradine's food locker, I expect."

"Dead?"

Larry lifted his head, then let it fall on the pillowless bed. "If he wasn't, he's dead now, ain't he?" He gave a strange little chuckle. "Either the cold or that bullet I put through his head killed him, I'd expect."

Jessica stared at the man lying in the bed. This wasn't how this was supposed to go. She was supposed to take the Black Bandit on man to man and kill him as he begged for mercy. Shooting this pathetic little man seemed like it would be so anticlimactic. "Where's my bag?" Jessica demanded.

Larry's eyes opened. "Your bag?"

"My carpetbag. You stole it from me on the train. The one you robbed north of Ogden."

Larry tried to focus on her standing across the room. "You came all the way here from Ogden to get a bag?"

"No. You killed my brother so I came to kill you . . ." she said not feeling the same anger and hate she'd felt only minutes before. "Only . . . only first I want my carpetbag."

He raised a shaky finger and pointed.

Jessica glanced at the shelf above the cold cookstove. Her carpetbag! Her grandma's carpetbag!

388

She ran to the wall, dragging a chair behind her. Still keeping one eye on Caine, she hopped up and pulled her bag down.

When she opened it, a smile lit up her face. It was all still there! Her grandma's recipes! The old tintype of Rose Landon and her father's pocket watch! Even the pressed violets her father had tucked into the tiny leather Bible so many years ago. And money! There was more money in the bag than she'd put in it months ago in Tennessee.

"You want my money? You can have it," Caine said. "Never brought me no good anyhow."

Jessica dragged the chair over to Caine's bed and sat down, the carpetbag on her lap.

"So you going to kill me or what?" he asked in a pathetic whine.

"In a minute," Jessica said absentmindedly.

She set down her rifle and opened the bag again. There were so many happy memories in this bag! She lifted her mother's faded tintype and studied the prim, proper figure. The young woman held her body stiff and was without a smile. Jessica smiled for her. It was good to see her mother's face again, if only in a picture. Next she pulled out her grandmother's recipes. They were simple recipes copied onto scraps of paper in floraled handwriting. She pulled them against her chest as the tears slipped down her cheeks.

One by one she took the mementos from the old carpetbag and held them in her lap. Hours passed and finally she drifted off to sleep with the Black Bandit asleep in the bed beside her.

Chapter Twenty-Seven

Jessica woke to the sound of the cabin door banging open. Immediately, she grabbed for her rifle and before her eyes were open, she was aiming for the door.

"Jessica!" Adam shouted, halting just inside the door.

She blinked away the sleep in her eyes. "Adam?" He was covered from head to foot in snow. Benny loomed behind him in the doorway.

Adam's voice was stark. "Jessica, put down the rifle."

She jumped to her feet, keeping the Henry pointed at Adam. "He deserves to die." She glanced at Caine who was just beginning to wake, then looked back at Adam.

"Yes, he deserves to die, but not this way. You'll be no better than him if you do it."

"Thank God you came," Caine told Adam weakly. "This crazy woman says she's going to shoot me. I'm awful sick. She's going to murder a defenseless man."

"Shut up!" she snapped. "My brother was defenseless, but that didn't stop you, did it?"

"I told you it wasn't me." Caine tried to raise up out of the bed, but fell back. "It must have been my brother, Toby. He was the bad one."

"We're not interested in your lies, Caine. I know you're guilty. I saw you pull the trigger when you wounded me," Adam said from the door.

'So take me back to Utah. Let me stand a fair trial once I'm better. I need a doctor, Sern. I need one bad." He gave a hacking cough and covered his face with his arm.

Adam looked at Benny standing behind him in the doorway. "It's all right, Benny. You go back to Buckle's cabin."

The native gave a nod and closed the cabin door, leaving Adam, Jessica, and Caine alone.

Adam rested his rifle against the door and began to take off his hat and coat. "You shouldn't have come here without me, Jess."

She could feel her palms growing sweaty. God, she wished she'd killed Caine last night. She didn't want to have to do it with Adam standing here watching with accusing eyes. "You don't understand!"

He watched her cautiously as he walked to the fireplace and threw in a stick of wood. "I *do* understand. I understand you hurt inside. I understand that you miss your brother. But killing that pathetic excuse for a man"—he pointed—"isn't going to bring Mark back. *Nothing* you can do, *anyone* can do, will bring him back."

"Caine doesn't deserve to live," she argued.

"Of course he doesn't. But you can't decide that.

Only a court of law can."

Tears began to run down her cheeks. None of this was coming out right. Adam was making too much sense. But she'd come too far to give into him now! "He could escape. The jury could find him innocent. There's a million ways he could get out of it."

Adam stared at the rifle Jessica still held on him. "So—what? You're going to shoot me, so you can shoot him, so they can hang you?"

The moment he took a step toward her, she cocked the hammer. "Just stand back, Adam. I don't want to hurt you. You know I don't. I want to hurt him." She threw a nod over her shoulder.

Adam's gaze fell to the carpetbag at her feet. "You found your bag?"

She nodded, solemnly. "Everything's there, even the money. More money than he took from me. Other people's money. I don't know how I'll return it."

"I told her she could have it," Caine declared miserably. "Won't do me any good now. I'll die before I ever make it out of here. And I thought hell was hot! It's not. It's cold, it's bitter cold." He shuddered and drew his blanket up to his chin.

Adam looked back to Jessica. "So you've got your things back. Give it up, Jess. Let me have him extradited to Utah where he'll stand trial. They'll hang him for sure."

"They can't hang a dead man." Caine offered in the midst of a coughing fit.

Jessica shook her head, her green eyes meeting Adam's dark ones. "It's not good enough, Adam. He should die by my hand. I owe it to Mark."

Adam turned toward the fireplace and stared into

the flames, his fists balled tightly at his sides. There was just no getting through to her! She was determined. He spun around angrily. "All right! Kill him!"

"Oh, my God," Caine cried.

"What?" she whispered.

"You heard me," Adam shouted. "Kill him. If it's revenge you want. If that's what it will take for you to get back to your life, then go ahead and kill him! I'll turn my back; I never saw a thing," he finished bitterly.

"Please . . . please," Caine begged. "You're a man of the law. You can't let a crazy woman murder me!"

Tears blinded Jessica's vision as she slowly turned to face Caine. She lifted her rifle to her shoulder. At point-blank range the man would never know what happened. Justice would be served.

For a long moment the only sound that could be heard was Caine's pitiful sobbing and the howl of the wind outside.

"I can't do it," Jessica finally murmured.

Adam stood stock still. "What?"

"It's no good." Her hands shook. "I can't kill him, Adam. I can hate him, I can wish him dead, but I can't kill him. I just can't . . ."

"Oh, thank you, thank you," Caine cried.

Adam ran and grabbed the rifle from her hands. "It's all right, love," he soothed as he gathered her in his arms.

Jessica clung to Adam as the tears poured down her cheeks. She cried for Mark, for her loss. She cried for Adam and the love she had found in him. All these months she had tracked Larry Caine thinking

394

she wanted to see him dead. Somewhere along the way she'd lost that need for revenge. Was it Adam and his love that had made her change her mind? She didn't know. All she knew was that she never wanted to see or hear of the Black Bandit again.

Slowly her tears subsided. Adam kissed her wet cheeks, the tip of her nose, her soft pouting mouth. "I love you," he whispered.

"I love you," she echoed, brushing back his long black hair. "I've loved you since the first day I saw you on the train."

"Will you marry me, Jess? Marry me and together we'll plant those apple trees?"

She looked up at him, in confusion. "But what about your job with the Union Pacific? You can't just give it up."

"Of course I can. You didn't think I was going to stay with the bastards after they accused me of being this man's accomplice, did you?"

She laughed. "Guess I didn't really think about it."

He hugged her tight. "I'll have the Black Bandit extradited as soon as he's well enough to travel. We'll go to Seattle and we'll be married."

"No." She stood on her tiptoes to kiss him. "Let's do it in Harrisburg, so Melba, and Johnny, and Clyde can be there. I don't want to wait until we make it back to Seattle. We've already waited too long."

"A lifetime."

She wiped at the damp spots on her cheeks, her face growing serious. "Would you have let me do it, Adam? Kill him, I mean?"

He held her in his gaze for a long moment. "I don't

know, love," he finally said. "I guess we won't ever know."

"We're getting married," Jessica said, throwing herself into Melba's arms the moment she was in her door.

It had been over two weeks since she left Harrisburg. She and Adam had stayed in Marbleton until Caine's fever had passed and then they had hired several natives to carry the criminal over the mountains on a stretcher. He was now being held in the new jailhouse built the previous fall to confine town drunkards.

"Married! I'm just glad to see the two of you alive and kicking. That was a hell of a storm that passed through here while you two were trekking over those mountains." Melba released Jessica and put her arms out to Adam. "Come on, you big brute. The bride-to-be won't mind!"

Adam grabbed the petite Melba, lifting her off the floor in a bear hug. "You'd make a fine wife yourself for some lucky man."

"Pshaw!" She laughed as he set her down. "I've got no time for a man! If this town grows the way I expect it to, I'll be a wealthy woman in a few years. I'd guess miners are going to be pouring in here by the hundreds with Harris and Juneau's latest strike. I've got two new girls coming in the first steamer that pulls into port. Expecting them within the month."

Jessica looped her arm through Adam's. "We want to get married here," she told Melba proudly. "Is there anyone who can do it?"

"Not yet, but Clyde heard there was a preacher coming in on the same steamer as my girls. Seems he intends to reform us all of our ill ways." She slapped the banister. "Let's just hope he hasn't reformed my girls on the trip over!"

Jessica looked at Adam and burst into laughter. Nothing Melba said or did shocked her anymore. Months ago she had accepted Melba for what she was, an intelligent, good-hearted woman who would do anything in the world for a friend. The fact that she made her living having sex with other men was of little consequence.

Adam dropped a kiss on the top of Jessica's head. "Let's get upstairs and change into some clean clothes. Then maybe Melba can scare up something for us to eat. I've chewed enough dried jerky in the last two weeks to last me a lifetime."

"You're in luck," Melba said, heading for the kitchen. "Got a rabbit frying this very minute. I had a feeling you two would pop up soon as the weather broke."

Arm in arm, Jessica and Adam went up the stairs and into the bedroom they'd shared all winter. Once inside, Jessica began to shed her layers of clothes. After wearing Adam's pants and heavy shirts for the last two weeks, she wanted to put on one of her own dresses. She wanted to feel like a woman again instead of a sharpshooter.

Adam walked to the window and parted the chintz curtains. Below, the street had turned to a mire of mud and water. Far in the distance he could hear the great rumble and roar of the ice breaking up in the harbor. He'd been listening to the haunting sound for days. It was a sound he would never forget as long as he lived. Spring was just around the corner.

For a long minute, he contemplated what he wanted to say to Jessica, what he'd wanted to say for nearly two weeks. Finally he found his nerve and turned to her. "Jess . . ."

"Mmmm?"

"Jess, I want to tell you . . ." He paused. This was so hard. "I wanted to tell you that it's not too late to back out of this marriage."

She turned around, wearing only a fresh chemise and stockings. "Back out? Adam, I love you!"

"I know you do. But . . ."

"But what?" Her eyes searched his striking bronze face for understanding.

"Jess, just because two people love each other, that doesn't always mean they can live together."

"I don't understand what you're talking about. I love you. I want to marry you and have your children. It's that simple."

He glanced back out the window, searching for the strength to get what he had to get out. "It's not that simple. No matter where we go, there's going to be problems. People are going to judge me—judge you because of the color of my skin. There are going to be people who won't want to deal with you because of me."

"Adam—"

He held up his palm. "Let me finish. I want you to think long and hard about this. It won't be just you and I who are affected. It will be our children too." He looked up at her standing there in the bright afternoon sun with her long dark hair tumbling onto her shoulders. "I'll understand if you just can't go through with it."

She crossed the distance between them in a heartbeat and went down on one knee, taking his broad, rough hands in her smaller ones. "Listen to me, Adam. I love you." She kissed his knuckles. "And I want to be your wife. I don't care what other people say or think. Who knows, maybe we can even change some minds."

Adam pulled her into his arms with a groan of relief. Not since he was a boy in Canada had he felt this loved. There was something about Jessica that gave him confidence, that made him see good in the world again. "Just promise me you'll think about it," he said softly in her ear.

She pressed her mouth to his and whispered, "Promise." Then she was kissing him, gently at first, but then with more insistence. Already she could feel a heat in her loins spreading as her tongue darted out to meet his. He caressed her bare shoulder, pushing down the lacy strap of her chemise.

"Jessica," he murmured. "It's going to be a good life, isn't it?"

She laughed, lifting her chin as he kissed her neck and moved lower to her breasts.

She found the buttons of his shirt and soon she was running her fingertips over his bare chest, exploring his flat, hard muscles and sensitive nipples. When she cupped the bulge in his wool pants, he groaned, urging her in a husky voice.

Her laughter filled the airy room and she unlaced his pants and released his burgeoning shaft.

"Jess," he murmured as her lips brushed his

responsive flesh.

As she teased him with the tip of her tongue, she could feel her own body growing hot and moist with want of him.

Finally, when Adam could stand the sweet torture no longer, he slid to the floor beside her and laid her out so that the bright sun flooding through the window fell on her lithe nude form. He swept his hands over her, touching here and there, making her cry out with her own pleasure.

When his mouth found the sweet bed of curls at the apex of her thighs, she half sat up, threading her fingers through his hair. "Adam," she called again and again as she turned her head this way and that in utter ecstasy. "Adam!"

With a smile on his lips, Adam stretched his body over hers and took her with one deep thrust.

She raised her hips to meet him in desperate need. "Adam . . . Adam, I love you . . ."

"I love you," he whispered in her ear as his movement quickened.

They rose up and down in the ancient rhythm of love until he spilled into her and they called out in unison as they reached final fulfillment.

Jessica dropped her hands to the floor and lay absolutely still, savoring the feel of Adam's hardness inside her. She sighed when he withdrew and came to rest beside her, cradling her in his arms.

"Look at us," she murmured, her voice still raspy with passion. "Midday with dinner waiting on the table and we're rolling around naked on the floor!"

He stared up into the sunshine at the dust motes floating through the air. "Going to be a fine life," he teased. "A mighty fine life . . ."

A month later, Jessica hurried down the new plank sidewalk of Harrisburg. Because of the impossible mud since the spring thaw, the citizens of the town had been forced to donate money and lumber and build the sidewalk or be swallowed in the mire.

"Good morning to you, Miss Jessica." A miner tipped his hat as he passed.

"Good to see you, Charlie."

"Good to see you, ma'am. Fine day, isn't it?"

"Fine day," she echoed. She had just been to the jailhouse to take Adam his midday meal. He'd been spending much of his time there these days, guarding Caine. The Black Bandit's health had improved so greatly that Adam intended to have him transported on the next steamer out. One of the men from the town had already been hired to escort the handcuffed criminal to Seattle where he would be met by federal marshals and extradited to Utah to stand trial.

In the meantime, Jessica kept herself busy making plans for her and Adam's wedding and the land they would purchase when they returned to Seattle. Her dream of an apple orchard was finally going to become a reality.

For some silly reason Adam had insisted on moving out of Melba's once a wedding date was set. He said it wasn't right for the bride and groom to live together before marrying, *bad medicine*, he had teased. So, he was bunking with Clyde and spending his spare time helping Johnny put up a new house and office.

Up ahead Jessica could see the steam exhaust of a steamship that had pulled into port this morning. She hurried, hoping the wedding gown she'd ordered from a catalog Clyde had given her was on this ship, otherwise, she'd have to make do with what was available in town. The wedding was only two days away!

On the dock, she encountered Mrs. Merriweather, the only other woman in town excluding Melba and her "girls."

"Jessica, how good to see you. You're certainly looking rosy-cheeked today."

Jessica grinned. "I was hoping my wedding dress had come with Clyde's latest shipment."

"Oh, dear!" the middle-aged woman cried. "They just hauled Clyde's things off in the wagon."

"Oh, well." Jessica shrugged. "I'll just walk up to Clyde's. I can help him unpack his merchandise. I haven't got anything to do anyway."

Mrs. Merriweather picked up a handful of her black taffeta skirts and looped her arm through Jessica's. "Guess I'll just have to escort you up there, now, won't I?" The woman turned and headed back into town. "I've heard so much about this dress, I wouldn't miss it for the world!"

Just as Jessica and Mrs. Merriweather started up the incline to the street above, Jacob Dorchester and Theodore Lansing disembarked from the steamer. Lansing lagged behind carrying an armful of bags while Jacob pushed on, pounding his silver-tipped cane on the plank dock as he went.

"Never have I experienced such a dreadful trip," Jacob huffed. "And then to find that there's no lodgings in this godforsaken village!"

"Now, now, Jake old boy," Lansing said, hurrying to catch up. "That fine fellow Clark on board said we were welcome to stay in his house here by the docks. With that awful croup he's got, he says he's heading right back to Seattle where he can find a decent physician." He went on faster than before. "He said the place is stocked with wood and food. No one need know we're here. He said considering the circumstances, he'd be utterly discreet!"

Jacob gave a snort. "He'd better be for what I paid him! I told you, Lansing, I haven't time to dally. This steamer intends to leave the dock in two days. I want to be on it . . . with my wife."

"I understand. I understand perfectly. All I'm to do is find her."

"Find her and then I'll come up with a plan for you to bring her to me. You're not to approach her until I say so."

"Yes, yes, but what about these papers she has with her? How am I to get her to bring those?"

"No need to worry about them. Just get me my wife!" *Once we're married in the eyes of the law,* Jacob thought, *they'll be mine. Even if I can't produce them, I can prove ownership once we're back in Tennessee.*

"There's the house there," Lansing said, pointing to a small frame building. "The first thing I'm going to do is stretch out and take a nap. I'm simply exhausted."

"The blast you are, Lansing. You're going to look for my wife."

"C—couldn't that wait until tomorrow?" He

403

shifted the bags he carried, taking care not to drop any into the mud.

Jacob slipped the key Clark had given him into the keyhole. "You want your story for your silly little dime novel?"

"I . . . I do," Lansing added frantically. "That I do. This story is going to make me famous!"

Jacob turned in the doorway and began to relieve Lansing of the bags he carried. "Then I suggest you begin your investigation, Mr. Lansing . . . immediately!"

Chapter Twenty-Eight

"Ohhh," Melba sighed. "You're beautiful!"

Jessica swept back the train of her white satin Merveilleux wedding gown. "Not very practical though, is it? I'd have been better to spend my hundred dollars on land than on a dress."

"A bride is only a bride once." Melba led Jessica to the freestanding oval mirror and smoothed the white brocaded velvet of her fitted bodice. "There'll be plenty of time for sensibilities after the wedding."

Jessica smiled at her own reflection in the wavy glass. She was so happy she thought she would burst. It was hard to believe that only a few months ago her life had been in such utter turmoil. "I suppose you're right," she finally answered.

"Well, I hate to hurry you, but you're running late." Melba pointed to the white filmy veil on the bed. "And you've still got that trapping to put on."

Jessica smoothed her unruly hair. "I haven't decided whether to wear it up or down." She turned and took Melba's hands. "Could you go down to

Johnny's house and tell Adam I'll be a few minutes late?" At Johnny's insistence, the wedding ceremony would take place in the empty front office of the new house he'd been building since the spring thaw.

Melba squeezed Jessica's damp hands and reached for her reticule. She was dressed fashionably in a black taffeta gown with an enormous bustle. "You don't want me to help?"

Jessica was already running a brush through her hair. "No. I'll be fine." She halted the brush in midair and looked at Melba through the reflection in the mirror. "Actually, I'd like to be alone for a few minutes. This is a big day, a big decision."

"That it is." Melba patted her friend on the shoulder. "Well, I'll get down to Johnny's and be sure the men don't get into the food and drink until *after* the ceremony."

Jessica laughed and gave a wave as Melba went out the door. "Give me half an hour and I'll be there."

"You'd better, or I'm liable to marry the big brute of a man myself!"

Jessica watched Melba disappear down the hall. Then she turned back to the mirror and began the task of piling all of her shiny clean hair onto her head in some fashionable manner.

It was sad to think that neither her mother, nor her father, nor Mark would be here today to witness her happiness. But the friends she had made in Harrisburg were *like* family, and Adam said they must be content with that.

The thought of the bridegroom made Jessica shiver. Adam Sern was going to marry her today! She was going to be his wife! Together they were going to

406

build a future of bright promise. At this very moment her life was perfect and she wanted to savor it.

Tucking the last lock of hair up into the simple coiffure, Jessica reached for her bridal veil. Placing it over the crown of her head, she smiled at her reflection. This Jessica in the mirror was certainly a change from the one who had crossed several states with a pistol strapped to her hip. She turned away with a chuckle. Time was slipping by and she didn't want to make Adam wait.

As Jessica came down the steps she heard a banging at the front door. Gathering her white satin skirting in both hands, she hurried to see who was knocking. She couldn't imagine who it could be; practically everyone in the town was at Johnny's waiting for her!

When she swung open the door, her eyes went wide with shock. "Mr. Lansing!" She dropped the skirts, her ire rising. "What the hell are you doing here?"

"Well . . ." Lansing clasped his hands staring at her attire. "Well, I . . ."

"Didn't I tell you I didn't ever want to see you again! Didn't I tell you I wasn't interested in your silly novel?" She couldn't believe he had traveled all the way to Alaska to get a blasted story!

His Adam's apple bobbed up and down. "Well, yes, yes, you did. B—but that's not why I'm here."

"Why *are* you here then? Why are you following me?"

"It's your husband, ma'am."

"Adam?"

Lansing screwed up his mouth in confusion. "Well, no. Actually, it's Mr. Dorchester."

407

She paled. "Jacob?"

"Yes, yes, and he wants to see you."

She gripped the doorframe until her knuckles went white. "Jacob's here?"

"He is and you must come with me immediately."

She shook her head in disbelief. Would she never rid herself of that man! Her eyes narrowed with anger as she turned her attention back to Lansing. "You can tell Mr. Dorchester that I do not wish to see him. I'm about to be married, married to Adam Sern."

"Married?" Lansing blinked. "Well, you can't be married to the deputy marshal if you're already married to Mr. Dorchester."

"Jacob told you we were married?"

"W—well, yes, of course he did."

"I'm not married to Jacob!" she shouted. "Now let me be!" With that, she slammed the door in the journalist's face.

A second later he knocked again.

Jessica's hands trembled. She rested her cheek on the door. What should she do? Run out the back? Would Jacob ruin her wedding day?

The knocking became more insistent. "Miss Jessica. Miss Jessica. You must listen to me. Your h— Mr. Dorchester is very ill," Lansing lied. "He's dying, ma'am."

Jessica hesitated for a moment and then swung open the door again. "Dying?"

"A coughing disease. He came all the way here from Seattle to see you before he met his maker." Lansing went on faster as he repeated the story he and Jacob had fabricated to lure her down to the docks. "It was a miracle he made the voyage. Miss Jessica, he's on his deathbed. I fear he won't live out the day."

Jessica's face hardened. She wouldn't do it! He wouldn't ruin her wedding day. "Mr. Lansing, I can't. I'm about to be wed. I'm late already."

Lansing looked over the elaborate wedding dress, realizing the girl really was as ill as her husband had said. He could see now that he was going to have to change a few facts if his story was to be publishable. After all, who wanted a madwoman for a heroine? "Miss Jessica, please. It will only take a moment."

"No, Mr. Lansing. I don't ever want to see Jacob Dorchester again. He's a horrible man."

"Y—you won't have to. He'll be dead by sunset. Please, ma'am."

Jessica chewed on her lower lip. It was hard to believe Jacob was dying . . . She knew it would be unchristian not to go see the man. But she had to hurry! Adam was waiting. "Tomorrow."

He shook his head. "Too late," he squeaked. "The man is on his last breath."

Jessica pushed past him. "Then he'll have to take it without me, Mr. Lansing."

"Where's your compassion?" He followed her. He had no time to waste. This was his chance. The steamer was due to leave this evening and Jacob insisted on being on it. If he wanted to get Jessica's exclusive story, he had to get her to her husband! "For the love of God! You would deny a man's dying wish after all he did for you and your family?"

Jessica stopped and spun around. *"Did for me?"* She was so angry that her voice shook.

Lansing lowered his eyes to the plank sidewalk. "Whatever ill feelings you may harbor toward this man, do you think it right to hold it against him on his deathbed?''

Jessica toyed with a seed-pearl sewn on the cuff of her sleeve. What harm could it do if she went to Jacob? If the man was dying, he was no longer a threat to her and Adam's happiness. Where *was* her compassion? "All right," she said softly. "I'll go with you, but I have to tell Adam where I'm going.''

"No, no, no, you don't understand! There isn't time!" He grasped her arm firmly and led her toward the dock and away. "I tell you, it will only be a moment. A final glance at your lovely face before he enters the kingdom of God. That's all he asks.''

She looked over her shoulder, but saw no one to tell where she was going. They were all waiting at Johnny's. Adam would be angry. But at least she could tell him that the matter of Jacob Dorchester was settled. That would more than make up for her tardiness.

"Where is she?" Adam paced the bare floorboards. He was dressed in the suit he had worn on the train trip from Idaho to Washington. "Where is she, Melba?" He could feel panic rising in his chest.

"She'll be here any minute." Melba glanced out the curtainless window. Though the outside walls of Johnny's house and connecting offices were up, no interior walls had been constructed yet. There was just one big empty room with a few skeletal frames where walls would soon be. Sun poured in through the windows filling the room with warmth and bright light. It was a perfect place for a wedding.

"She isn't coming," he said starkly.

"She's coming, Adam. She's just late."

"She isn't coming. She changed her mind."

"She didn't change her mind. She's just fussing with her hair."

Adam came to stand by Melba and look out the window. "She's an hour late. It doesn't take any woman an hour to do her hair."

"She already said she'd be a half hour late, that only makes her half an hour late."

He shook his head sadly. "I knew it was too good to be true." As happy as Adam had been in the past weeks, there had been a small part of him that nagged at his subconscious telling him it just wouldn't come to be.

"Don't be getting all melancholy on me. I'll just go and get her. I'm sure there's a logical explanation." She headed for the door, pointing at the wedding guests milling around. "You just keep that bunch out of the food. They'll have it all eaten before the bride ever gets here."

Adam watched Melba through the window as she hustled down the street toward her house. Not five minutes later she came hurrying back—without Jessica.

Adam yanked off his suit coat as she came in the door. "Not there, is she?"

Melba's pink cheeks were pale. "No. I don't know where she could have gone."

"I'll tell you where she went." He threw his coat in fury. "Gone down to the dock to book passage back to Seattle, that's where she's gone."

"Don't be ridiculous!" Melba signaled for Johnny

411

and the young man hurried over.

"You didn't find her, Melba?"

"No. My girls were both asleep. They didn't hear or see anything. Johnny, I want you to go up and down the street looking for her. Knock on doors if you have to. Just find her."

Adam yanked open the stiff white collar of his starched shirt. "Damn it, why did I let her do this to me! Why did I let her make me love her?"

"Adam, there's something wrong here." Melba's eyes met his. "She wouldn't just not show up."

"You said yourself that she asked you to leave."

"Well, yes. But she just wanted to be alone. A girl has a right to a little privacy before her wedding. It's a big step for an independent woman like Jessica."

"Too big a step, maybe?" Adam ran a hand over his head. "Christ, don't you see, Melba? She changed her mind at the last minute and didn't have the nerve to tell me herself."

Melba took one of Adam's big hands in hers. "You've got it all wrong. I'm telling you, there's something going on here. If Jessica had changed her mind, she'd have told you face-to-face. If there's one thing Jessica Landon isn't, it's a coward. She's in some kind of danger, I just know it."

He gave a humorless laugh, snatching his hand from Melba's. "She sure as hell will be in danger if I get hold of her! She's made a fool of me in front of everyone."

Melba dropped her hands to her hips. "What's wrong with you?" she asked angrily. "You're not thinking right. Jessica loves you. You know that! She'd never leave you, not of her own free will."

"She loves me?" He leaned on the roughly cut windowsill. He could feel the loose sawdust beneath his fingertips. "I suppose maybe she did, but she didn't love me enough to spend the rest of her life with me . . . with a half-breed."

Melba drew herself up in anger. "So that's it, is it? That's why she'd leave you? Because you're a redskin?"

He turned to her, crossing his arms over his broad chest. "Why else? She didn't want to put up with the crap. She wanted to be served when she ordered a meal. She wanted a hotel room without having to sneak me up the back staircase. You can't blame a person for that."

Melba laughed. "Don't flatter yourself. If she was going to leave you, that would be the last reason! If she was going to leave you it would be because you were opinionated, because you were a perfectionist, because you were too damned stupid to see the truth when it's staring you in the face! Not because of the color of your skin."

He turned away, feeling his chest tighten and his eyes grow moist. "So she did leave me," he said softly.

"No," Melba answered. She came up behind him and laid her hand on his shoulder. "She didn't. Because if she was going to, she'd have done it a long time ago. I'm telling you, Adam Sern, that woman loves you more than I've ever known any woman to love a man. And if you think differently, then you're a fool! You're a fool and you don't deserve her!"

For a long moment Adam was silent. He could hear the wedding guests behind him talking quietly. Talking about *him* and the woman who had stood

413

him up at his own wedding. Some were leaving, others were helping themselves to the wedding feast. He could hear their hushed voices as they made their guesses as to what had happened to Miss Jessica. Adam could hear his own strained breathing as he struggled to remain in control.

Adam *wanted* to believe Melba. He *wanted* to believe that his Jessica wouldn't leave him, not after all they'd been through together. But he'd lived his whole life with prejudice. It seemed to be something the white race were born with. Logic couldn't conquer it, maybe love couldn't either.

"Adam Sern?" a deep voice called.

Adam turned in confusion to face the stranger standing in the doorway. He was a tall man with a beard and mustache.

"Yes, I'm Adam Sern. Who are you?"

The man's face was without expression. "I'm Federal Marshal Lionel James and you're under arrest, Mr. Sern. You can come quietly, or you can be chained and carried out of here."

A hush fell over the sunny room. The wedding guests all turned in surprise.

Adam inhaled sharply. His head was buzzing. He felt dizzy. "There must be a mistake. I'm Deputy Marshal Sern. It's the man Lawrence Caine you're looking for. He's the murderer."

The federal marshal spread his legs in an easy stance. His hand fell to his pistol. "There's been no mistake, Sern. There's plenty of evidence. Plenty of documentation. The Union Pacific Railroad has provided us with copies of the telegraph records. We know where you were and when you were there." He paused. "I'll take your badge now. You are no longer recognized in these United States or any of its territories as a deputy marshal."

Adam glanced at Melba. "What's going on here? This some kind of sick joke?"

"It's no joke, sir. Now come along." He reached for Adam's arm.

Adam jerked back. "I have a right to know what I'm being charged with, don't I!"

"That you do." The marshal gave a nod. "Mr. Sern, you're being charged with four counts of murder, one count of rape, with further charges pending."

"Murder! Rape!" Adam exploded. "That's absurd! The murder of who?"

The marshal pulled a piece of paper from inside his coat. "The names of the victims are: Miss Sue Ellen McCleen, also known as Sue Ellen Caine, Miss Becky Larger, Miss Polly Mulvaney, and Miss Gloria Riley." He folded the piece of paper. "All whores, Mr. Sern. All dead. Now come along."

Chapter Twenty-Nine

Jessica's hands were tied behind her back. She twisted until it felt as though the hemp rope would saw through her wrists, but the knots refused to loosen. The rough fibers rubbed her tender flesh at her wrists and ankles until they were raw.

She glanced up at Jacob; he was watching her with a contorted, wild-eyed expression. Jessica drew in a ragged breath. This wasn't the Jacob she had known in Tennessee. That man was gone; he'd been replaced by a madman. She looked away and strained at the knots again as fear thickened in her throat and sent chills down her arms.

She blamed herself for being so gullible. After all Jacob had done; after he'd chased her across the entire country, why hadn't it occurred to her that he would try to trick her into coming to him. Jacob dying, hah! The little worm, Lansing, had lied to her. He was part of the scheme. He'd led her to this vacant house near the docks to see Jacob.

Once inside the dark house, Jacob had grabbed

her. She had fought like a wildcat, scratching and biting . . . anything to get away. She had punched Jacob so hard that she had split his upper lip. But the two men had overpowered her.

Nothing she could say would convince Lansing that she wasn't Jacob's runaway wife. Once Jacob had her tied and gagged, he'd asked that Lansing leave him alone with his *wife,* so that he might calm her. Lansing had backed out of the house and Jessica hadn't seen him since.

Jessica watched Jacob, wondering how she could get through to him. She had to make him untie her. She tried to speak to him again, but the silk handkerchief he'd tied around her mouth prevented any coherent words from escaping her lips. All she could do was make a low, gravelly sound at the base of her throat. She looked at him, her green eyes pleading.

Please, Jacob, she cried silently. *Don't do this to me. Not on my wedding day.*

She wondered what Adam had done when she hadn't showed up at Johnny's. She wondered why he hadn't come for her. Wasn't he looking? She prayed he would run into Lansing on the street. Adam would know to start his questioning there.

Jessica's gaze followed Jacob's movement. He leaned against a crude wooden table, staring at her. He was without his customary black coat, and his white shirt was wrinkled and stained. His silver-white hair was uncombed; one tuft stood up on end. His face was unshaven and bore two days' worth of silvery growth. His lips were twisted into an odd little grin.

"Oh, Jessica, you came to me at last, and in your wedding gown." He clasped hands, tears of joy in his eyes. "You're even more beautiful than I had imagined you would be!"

She grunted against the gag, and struggled, rocking the ladder-back chair she was tied to.

"Now, now, love. Don't be angry with me." He came toward her and reached a hand out to caress her cheek.

Shuddering at his loathesome touch, Jessica squeezed her eyes shut. *Where, dear God, is Adam*, she thought. The feel of Jacob's cold fingers against her skin made her stomach heave.

Jacob continued to stroke her cheek, just above the silk gag. "I would take it off, but you might scream." He spoke to her as if she were a naughty child.

She shook her head violently. "Wouldn't," she mumbled against the cloth. "Just want to talk to you, Jacob." But her voice came out as nothing but a garble of sounds.

Jacob pulled at the creases of his pants and then squatted in front of her. "But you wouldn't scream, would you, love? Now that you've had your little fit and embarrassed yourself in front of Mr. Lansing, you're all done, aren't you?"

She nodded, trying to calm the fires she knew must be blazing in her eyes. She was dealing with a man who was mentally off balance. She had to remember that. She had to ignore her fear and think rationally. If he wanted her to be meek and apologetic, she had to be that . . . anything to save her own life.

"Please, Jacob," she mumbled against the silk handkerchief. "Please," she pleaded, round-eyed

419

with feigned regret. "I won't scream."

Jacob rested a hand on her knee, obviously considering removing the gag. He stroked the slippery white satin of her wedding gown. It was all Jessica could do to keep from flinching. "You promise?"

She nodded.

"Because you know," he said, reaching around to the knot under her bridal veil, "no one could hear you anyway. The sound of that steam engine would more than cover a little peep out of you. And then if you did scream, you'd have to be punished." He stopped, the gag half off. "You don't want me to punish you, do you?"

She shook her head, afraid to tear her gaze from his eyes. As crazy as Crooked Nose had been, she knew Jacob was crazier, and she knew she was more frightened than she had ever been when she faced death at the hands of the renegades.

Jacob pulled away the silk handkerchief and Jessica heaved a sigh. Her tongue darted out to moisten her lips, only her tongue was too dry. "Water," she murmured. "Could I have some water, Jacob?"

He smiled. "Of course, love. Anything else?"

"Y—you could untie me."

"You know I can't do that." He poured water from a battered pitcher on the table. "You'd just run from me."

"No, I wouldn't, I swear it!" she lied. She watched him come toward her with the tin cup of water. "Jacob, the ropes hurt."

He lifted the cup to her lips and she took a small

sip, then turned her head away. "Jacob, you have to tell me why you're doing this to me."

"You shouldn't have run away. You made me the laughingstock of town." He set down the cup and pulled a chair to sit across from her. "I had to leave behind my business to come looking for you."

"I didn't want to be your wife."

He smiled. "But now you've changed your mind, haven't you? Seen your ill ways." He touched the white satin of the wedding dress she had worn for Adam.

She nodded ever so slightly. "But I could never marry a man who keeps me tied up."

He shook his finger. "Aren't you clever. You were always too clever for your own good. I told your father that. He was too free with you. No, I'm not going to untie you. Not yet. I know what kind of temper you have; you might try something foolish and hurt yourself. Once we're on board ship. Once it's left the dock, then maybe, just maybe I could be persuaded to let you go."

"On board the ship! Jacob! You can't take me against my will. You have no right!"

"You're my wife," he replied calmly. "Under the law, I have every right."

"Jacob, if this is about those stock certificates," she said taking a different tact, "I still don't know what you're talking about. I didn't take any certificates. What would you want with them anyway?"

"I know you have them. As your legal husband I'll have a right to them. They're going to make us very rich, Jessica."

"I don't understand. I don't understand what

you're talking about."

"I know, sweetheart, business can be so confusing for women." He leaned on his knees, speaking slowly. "Let me explain it this way. Those stock certificates in the South Africa diamond mine that your papa bought from me years ago are now worth a great deal of money. They found diamonds in that mine just before you left."

"That's why you moved up the wedding date?"

"Of course not! I moved our wedding date because it wouldn't have been right for you to have remained under my roof and not been married to me."

"So you admit we're not married!"

"A technicality, love. In my eyes, we've been married since your papa signed that betrothal agreement." He looked away. "As for your indiscretion with that redskin—"

"Indiscretion!" She ground her teeth with mounting anger. "I love Adam! I'm going to marry him."

Jacob whipped around in a sudden fury. "Fornication is nothing to scoff at, my dear child. You could be ousted from the church!"

Jessica let her eyes close for a moment. *Adam, where are you?* she called silently. *Adam, I need you. Help me!* She opened her eyes. "Didn't you hear me?" she shouted. "That *redskin* as you call him is going to be my husband. This dress is for him, not for you." Her eyes narrowed vindictively. "Never for you, Jacob!"

He reached out and smacked her so quickly that she never saw his hand move. The sound of the slap startled her more than the pain of his palm across her cheekbone. Her eyes teared up as she lifted her chin to look him straight in the eye. "Either let me go, or kill me, Jacob, because I'm not going with you. I'm not going to be your wife, and I'm never ever going to let you touch me. I belong to Adam, all of me."

"I'll kill you before I let you go back to him," he threatened, jumping up out of the chair.

"You haven't the nerve!"

Jacob whipped a long-bladed knife off the table. His eyes glimmered with a strange light as he thought of the other girls . . . the other Jessicas. He'd taught them a lesson, hadn't he? His eyes met hers. "Don't have the nerve, do I?"

Jessica screamed as the knife sliced through the air . . .

Lansing sat on the step, watching the town of Harrisburg's activity with little interest. The plot for his dime novel was not coming along well. It had seemed like such a good idea to begin with, to use Miss Landon . . . Mrs. Dorchester as a basis for his heroine, but now, it just didn't seem right. The poor woman, she had been through so much. It was a wonder she wasn't stark raving mad.

Still, despite her behavior, Lansing hadn't liked it one bit when Jake had pushed her around like that. He didn't care what the man's legal rights were, no man should lift a hand to a woman!

A commotion down the street made Lansing stand and stretch on his tiptoes to see what all of the hullabaloo was about. A good reporter always kept his eyes and ears open. That was how a man found a good story.

Half a block up the street Lansing could see a man leading another man in shackles. A crowd of miners and a petite woman, dressed in black taffeta, hurried behind them. "My God!" Lansing muttered aloud. "It's the deputy marshal!"

He stumbled forward, searching wildly for the pencil and pad of paper he always carried with him. "What's happened? What's happened?" he called, running toward them.

The tall man leading the deputy marshal held up a hand. "Stand back," he ordered. "Make room for the prisoner to pass."

"The prisoner!" Lansing squeaked. He flipped a page and began to write. "What's the deputy marshal done?" he asked, joining the crowd.

"Done? He's not done a thing!" Clyde snapped. "There's been a mistake! I wish the United States Government would leave us the hell alone up here. Why do they think we come? To get away from this bureaucracy!"

Lansing turned to another man. "What's the deputy marshal been accused of?"

"Rape. Murder. You name it," a fellow with the blond handlebar mustache answered. "I don't know if he done it. I just come into town."

Lansing gasped. "Rape and murder? Here in Harrisburg?"

"Noo! Of course not! Bunch of whores down in the lower territories. Idaho, Washington, Utah. A whole bunch of them."

"I—Idaho?" Lansing came to a halt. "One of those girls couldn't possibly have been Polly Mulvaney of Pocatello, Idaho?"

"Polly? Hmmm? I believe there was a Polly. Ask that man up there. Johnny. He knows Sern personally."

The crowd had come to a halt at a small wooden building with a squared-off false front. Across the top were written the words, HARRISBURG JAIL. Lansing pushed and dodged, trying to make it to the front before the deputy marshal was led inside, but he didn't manage it.

Lansing turned to the pretty young woman dressed in fashionable black taffeta. "You a friend of Deputy Marshal Sern's?"

She frowned. "Who the hell are you? I know every man in this town and I don't know you."

He swept off his bowler hat to make a formal introduction. "Theodore Lansing, ma'am, of Chicago, but as of late, a traveling man. I'm a writer. I know the Deputy Marshal Sern. Know him well." He popped his hat back on his head and poised his pencil. "Would you care to make a comment concerning the charges?"

Melba raised a tiny fist beneath Lansing's pointed chin. "If you don't step out of my way, I'm going to knock your teeth out!"

Lansing stepped aside and the woman passed. She strutted up the steps past two burly guards and walked into the jailhouse. Lansing followed, but the guards dropped their rifles, barring the doorway.

"Back up, buster," one of the men barked. "The federal marshal don't want anyone inside until the prisoner is safely locked up."

"You think I could get in to see him?" Lansing asked excitedly. "He's a friend. A dear old friend.

Known him for years."

The guard shrugged. "Just have to wait and see, won't you?"

Lansing smiled. "Wait? Wait I can do!" With that, he plopped himself down on the step in front of the crowd and began to scribble furiously. He could already see the headlines streaking across the nation—DEPUTY MARSHAL GONE BERSERK! KILLS 22 INNOCENT GIRLS, by Theodore Lansing, Jr. "My God!" he whispered.

Inside Melba waited until Adam was escorted to the only cell in the new jail house. Caine stood as the federal marshal opened the door. "What's going on here?" Caine asked.

Adam looked up, his dark eyes fierce and menacing. "You say one word, Caine, and I swear to God I'll rip your head off!"

Caine gave a gulp and retreated to the far side of the wooden jail cell where his mattress lay on the floor.

The federal marshal laid a hand on Adam's shoulder. "I let you out of the shackles you going to behave yourself, Sern?"

Adam looked away. "Sure. Why not? It would be stupid to run. Where the hell am I going to run *to*?"

Melba waited until the federal marshal slammed the door shut and then she ran to the bars. "Adam, what's this about? Do you know anything about these women who were killed?"

He exhaled slowly. "Of course I do. I knew Sue Ellen McCleen."

"Sue Ellen?" Caine asked. "Toby's Sue Ellen?"

Adam shot him such a furious glance that Caine clamped his mouth shut.

"You knew one of the girls?" Melba shook her head. "What about being in the same town at the times that each of the murders took place?"

"It's true." He shrugged. "It's all true, only I didn't kill any whores! I was with Jessica." He squeezed his eyes shut against the memories. The smell of her damp skin after they'd made love . . . The feel of the weight of her breast cupped in his hand . . . The sight of her lithe, nude body. Adam shook his head in fury. She had betrayed him and yet still all he could think of was her . . . his Jessica.

"I know you didn't kill any whores, but the marshal says they've got evidence."

"Where is she, Melba?" Adam whispered, tormented by despair. Without Jessica he didn't care about the murder charges. Without Jessica, he didn't care if they did hang him.

"I don't know, Adam. I don't know where Jessica is. I just know she didn't run out on you." Melba gripped the wooden bars, searching his dark eyes. "You know it, too, don't you?"

"What could have happened? She doesn't know anyone here that you don't know."

Melba pulled off her black taffeta bonnet. "Say, what about that new fellow in town? Standing outside. Says he knows you."

"Someone knows me?"

"Said you were good friends. Short, skinny little man. Says he's a writer?"

Adam sunk his fist into his palm. "A writer? I don't know any writer. Get him in here!"

A moment later, Melba returned with Lansing in tow.

"Adam Sern, if this isn't a sad day!"

"Lansing?" Adam scowled. "What the hell are you doing here?"

"Oh, me, I'm not important!" He whipped out his pad of paper. "What's important is you and these horrendous charges. You didn't rape and kill all of those women, of course."

"Of course not!"

"But someone outside said there was evidence. Hard evidence. They say officials from the Union Pacific are going to be willing to appear in court against you."

"Look, I was there. I was in Pocatello, but so were a hundred other men. So were you! That doesn't mean *you* killed the whore, does it?"

"Me?" Lansing gave a nervous giggle. "Certainly not! I'm not the murdering type!"

"And I am?" Adam swung away. "Hell, why am I talking to you? Just get out of here!"

"B—but maybe I could help," Lansing said, grabbing at straws. He didn't know if the half-breed was guilty or innocent, but he did know a good story when he saw one. "I could help prove your innocence."

"I don't care about that. They couldn't possibly convict me." Adam grasped the rough wooden bars. "What I care about is Jessica. Have you seen her?"

Lansing blinked nervously.

"You have seen her!" Adam shoved his hand through the wooden bars and caught the reporter by the lapel of his coat. "Tell me where she is!"

Lansing froze, paralyzed with fear. "M—Miss Jessica?"

"We were supposed to be married today. She never

428

showed up."

"There's a law against polygamy in this country, Mr. Sern!"

"Polygamy! What are you talking about?"

"H—her husband, of course! Mr. Sern, if you don't unhand me, I shall have to call the federal marshal in here."

Adam pulled Lansing toward him until the man's hawk nose was pressed between the bars. "Who says she has a husband?"

"W—well, her husband of course. Mr. Jacob Dorchester of Tennessee." His pencil and pad of paper slipped to the floor.

"What do you know of Dorchester?"

"O—only th—that he's been looking for her for months. Followed her across the country."

"He's not her husband."

"W—well, certainly he is!"

"You have proof?" Adam demanded.

"O—of course not. Just the gentleman's word."

"Well, the gentleman lies. He had her kidnapped in Seattle. The man's sick."

"S—sick?"

Adam stared into Lansing's pale face. "Wait a minute . . ." Slowly he released his hold on the reporter. "You said he told you he's followed her across the country?"

"Town to town. Met him in Pocatello myself."

"He was in Pocatello the night the girl was murdered?"

Lansing's mouth gaped open. "I met him in the very same dance hall where the poor woman worked."

"Son of a bitch!" Adam's eyes met Lansing's. "Where's Dorchester?" But before the man responded, Adam knew the answer.

Lansing trembled with sudden fear.

"I said, where's Dorchester?" Adam bellowed. "Is he here? Is he here in Harrisburg? Has he got Jessica?"

Lansing nodded ever so slightly. "My God, I've made a terrible mistake! Jake seemed like such a nice man. He said she was his wife. He said he loved her. He said he just wanted to take her home."

Melba spun around. "Marshal! Marshal! I think you'd better get in here!"

Chapter Thirty

Jessica's own shrill scream filled her head. She snapped her eyes shut as Jacob sliced through the air with the knife.

But instead of bringing the cold blade across her throat, he grabbed a hank of her hair and sliced it off.

Her eyes flew open in surprise.

He smiled, holding up the thick lock of hair. "I didn't frighten you, did I, love?"

The uncontrollable rage she had seen in Jacob's face only a moment ago was gone. He seemed calm again, even rational. "I'm sorry, I didn't mean to frighten you."

She stared at the lock of sable brown hair in his hand. "You cut my hair," she accused.

"I always cut their hair." He sat back on his chair and laid the knife on his crossed knee as he fiddled with her shorn lock.

"Their hair?" She shivered ominously. "Whose hair?"

He divided the strand into three delicate threads

431

and began to braid them. "Sometimes young girls like you need to be taught a lesson. They need to be punished. Flaunting their bodies in front of men like that."

The tone of Jacob's voice made the hair on the back of Jessica's neck bristle. Lansing's words came tumbling back. *They all looked like you. Remarkably like you* . . . She lifted her gaze to study Jacob's face. "How long have you been following me?" she asked, her voice barely above a whisper.

"I almost caught up to you in the little place called Loco, Utah."

"Were you in Blades?" she asked, beginning to work at the ropes that held her hands tied securely behind her. A girl named Sue Ellen McCleen had been killed, Adam had said. Toby's wife.

"Just for a few days. But you weren't there."

She thought of the dance hall girl slain in her own bed. "Pocatello?"

Jacob frowned. "I ran after the train, but they wouldn't stop it! I had to ride all the way to Seattle to find you. Then you got away again."

Jessica hung her head, letting her hands go limp behind her. It was no use! She'd never free herself! Where was Adam? Why hadn't he come for her? If he truly loved her, he would have come for her! She lifted her head. She had to ask . . . "Did you murder those poor women?"

His fingers relaxed in his lap. His gaze fell to the knife resting on his knee. "I'd never hurt anyone on purpose. You know that, Jessica." He looked up at her. "I'd never hurt you because I love you." His gaze fell to the floor. "I loved them all, I suppose."

432

"Did you hurt them, Jacob? Did you hurt them *accidentally?*" She twisted her hands behind her, suddenly realizing that the ropes were loosening.

He picked up the braid of hair and began to form it into a ring, a wedding ring for his Jessica, just as he'd given them all a ring. "We're going to be married, you and I. I thought we'd take a tour of Europe once this business with the stock certificates is settled. Would you like that?"

"I'd like you to untie me." She wiggled her fingers grasping a piece of the rope. She was almost free!

"I told you. I can't do that until we're aboard the steamer."

"You can't get me on a boat tied up like this!"

"I have help coming. A nice sailor said he would help me smuggle you on. No questions asked."

"It won't work. You can't keep me tied up the rest of my life!" As her last words tumbled from her lips, the ropes gave way, thus loosening the bindings at her feet as well.

He sighed. "No. I don't guess I can. Once we're married . . . once the stock certificates are mine, some decisions will have to be made."

"Decisions?"

He held up the ring he'd formed from her hair. "You can live with me and be my wife, or you can't live at all."

Jessica kept her hands behind her back to give the appearance of still being tied up. Her gaze went to the door.

He looked at the door. "No one's coming, Jessica. No one's coming for you. From now on you'll have to depend on me, on your *husband.*"

Her lower lip trembled. Jacob had the knife. Would he use it if she ran for the door? Did she have a choice?

Jessica waited until he lowered his gaze to the ring he held in his hand, and then she leaped from the chair. It went clattering to the floor and Jacob jumped up, dropping the hair ring but catching the knife.

Jessica ran as hard as she could, but the white satin skirting of her wedding gown got tangled in her feet.

"Come back!" Jacob shouted, grabbing her wedding veil pinned to her hair.

Jessica's head snapped back. She screamed as she went down with Jacob on her back.

"You're mine!" he cried hysterically.

"Never!" She rolled onto her back and pummeled his chest with her fists. *He's going to kill me,* she thought wildly. *I'm never going to see Adam again!*

Jessica saw the knife flash through the air and she threw herself backward, filling the air with a piercing scream. Her head hit hard against the floor just as she felt the cold blade rip her flesh.

Adam burst through the door in a rage. There lying on the floor was his Jessica, the bodice of her white wedding dress stained red with blood.

Adam gave a warwhoop flying into Jacob. The older man fell back under Adam's impact and the knife went clattering to the floor.

"I'll kill you, you son of a bitch," Adam yelled as his hands found the gray-haired man's throat. "I'll kill you myself!"

The federal marshal and his guards grabbed Adam and wrestled him off the frightened, sobbing Jacob.

434

Adam tore from the guards' arms and fell to his knees beside Jessica's limp body. Melba was already there, pressing her fingers to Jessica's throat.

"Is she alive? Please tell me she's alive," Adam pleaded.

Melba held her breath, waiting for the feel of Jessica's pulse against her fingers. "Yes!" she cried. "Oh, God, yes! She's alive!"

Adam lifted Jessica into his arms, smoothing the hair away from her face. He held her against him, rocking her. "Jess? Jess? Can you hear me?"

Her eyes fluttered open. "Adam?" she whispered.

He hugged her tight. "Yes, sweetheart. It's me. I'm right here."

"Adam, I'm sorry I'm so late." She looked down at her wedding gown, torn and bloodied. "I've ruined my gown."

Adam carefully lifted the torn white satin, almost afraid to see the wound beneath. "Does it hurt?"

"No. But my head sure does!" She rubbed it as Adam took a close look at her wound.

"Just a little cut," he said with relief. "You're not hurt."

"I told you I wasn't hurt. Where's Jacob?"

Adam looked over to see Jacob Dorchester surrounded by the federal marshal and his guards. Jacob had wrapped himself into a ball on the floor and was rocking to and fro. "I didn't mean to kill them," he sobbed. "I only wanted to love them. I only wanted them to love me."

Adam returned his attention to Jessica. "It's all right, sweetheart. The federal marshal will take over from here."

435

"He killed those women, Adam. He thought they were me!"

"I know. They thought I did it. The marshal was here to arrest me." Adam laughed, releasing the tension built up in his chest. "It looked for a while like I was going to be bunking with our friend the Black Bandit."

"They arrested you?" She laid her hands on his shoulders and sat up, still feeling a little dizzy.

"I was in every town at the time that one of the women was murdered."

"Because I was in the town, because *Jacob* was in the town," she breathed.

"Exactly. Except Blades, of course. I'd left you by the creek after you were bit by the snake."

"But Jacob passed by there looking for me."

"On his way to Pocatello," Adam finished.

Jessica hung her head. "I never thought he was capable of hurting anyone. He kept babbling something about stock certificates to a diamond mine."

Adam got to his feet and leaned over to pick up Jessica. "I don't know anything about stock certificates, but I do know someone needs to take a look at that flesh wound across your ribs."

Jessica looped her arms around Adam's neck. "What about the wedding?" She stared into his dark eyes. "We were supposed to be married today."

"It can wait," he soothed.

"It can't wait! Adam Sern put me down."

"Sweetheart—"

Jessica swung her legs over, forcing him to set her down. She felt better already, though her head ached

436

a little and the cut stung. "Are you saying you don't want to marry me?" she demanded.

"Of course not. But we can get married tomorrow, the next. When you feel better."

Jessica turned to Melba who was standing in the doorway grinning. "Does it sound to you like this man is trying to get out of marrying me?"

Melba shook her head in feigned sadness. "Appears that way, doesn't it?" She shrugged. "Guess we'll just have to find you another husband. Plenty available in a town like Harrisburg. Men just dying to find a good woman."

"All right! All right!" Adam said, lifting his hands in surrender. "You want to get married looking like this, we'll get married!"

Jessica flew into his arms. "I love you, Adam Sern," she declared.

Just then Theodore Lansing popped his head in the door. "My God! All safe and clear?" He whipped out his pencil and licked the tip. "If so, I'm ready to take any comments . . ."

Jessica whirled around. "You!" With one swift movement she drew back her fist and slammed the reporter square in the jaw. Lansing went flying backward, out the door.

Jessica shook her fist. "Ouch! That hurt."

Adam looked at Lansing lying prone in the doorway, then back at Jessica and burst into laughter. "I had the exact same intentions, but I guess you beat me to it!"

With a chuckle, Jessica reached for Adam's arm. "Shall we go, love?"

"Most certainly, my love."

Melba was still laughing as the two stepped over the unconscious Lansing and walked up the street.

Late that night Jessica and Adam lay sprawled on the bed in their bedroom at Melba's finishing up a picnic supper . . . their first supper as man and wife. Flickering candlelight glimmered from the bedside tables and the windowsills, casting a soft glow over the room.

Jessica sat, resting against the headboard. Adam lay with his head in her lap, toying with the pale green ribbons on her dressing gown. "Well, Jess," he sighed, "you think our grandchildren will ever believe us when we tell them about our wedding day?"

She took a sip of wine and set the glass aside. *"No one* in their right mind would believe such an outrageous tale." She laughed, leaning to kiss him full on the mouth.

Adam's tongue darted out to taste the sweet wine on her lips. "Mmmm, a feast fit for a king or at least an Ojibwa chief!"

Jessica leaned back, resting her head and letting her eyes drift shut as she ran her fingers through Adam's midnight black hair. "I still can't believe it! Jacob a murderer! What do you think will happen to him?"

"Do you care?" He ran his fingers lightly over the bandages beneath her gown. "After what he did to you? You could have been killed."

"Funny, but I do care. He's sick, Adam. I can't hate him the way I hate Larry Caine."

"Well, I suppose what happens to him will depend

438

on whether they decide to try him or not. If he's found guilty, which he certainly will be, he'll hang."

"You mean there's a chance he won't stand trial?"

He took her hand, threading his fingers through hers. "If he was found to be incompetent . . . insane, he might not have to."

She lifted her head, staring into his dark eyes. "What would they do with him? He certainly can't be let loose to kill again."

"No, no, of course not," Adam soothed, stroking her cheek. "But he could be put into a home for the mentally ill. There he'd live out his life."

She covered his hand with hers. His touch felt so good. "Is there something we could do? To keep him from going to trial, I mean."

"I suppose. If that's what you really want."

"I think we should try."

"In that case I can speak to the federal marshal in the morning before he boards the steamer with Jacob and Caine. They're holding over until tomorrow, then they'll set out for Seattle. Once we're back in Seattle, I'll see what I can do."

She smiled at him. "Thank you."

He kissed her knuckles one at a time. "You're welcome, wife."

"You know, Jacob was still talking about those stock certificates when he had me tied up. He was sure I had them."

"He thought you stole them from him?"

"No, well, not exactly." She ran her fingers lightly over his bare chest. "He said they were my father's. They were stocks in a South African diamond mine that he himself had sold to my father years ago."

"Do you remember any such thing?"

"Actually, I do. Papa was furious. They were worthless."

"So why did Jacob want them?" He rolled onto his side, his head still resting on her lap.

"He said they were going to make him rich." She shrugged. "But he said so many other strange things. Who knows what he meant."

Adam stroked his chin thoughtfully. "He said you had them?"

"He said I took them the night Mark and I left. I didn't take any papers. Just the money from the sale of Papa's farm and a few mementos."

"Where's your carpetbag?"

"What?"

"Where's your carpetbag? Maybe they're in the lining or something."

She laughed. "That's absurd!"

"Come on! Where's that sense of adventure of yours." He got up on his knees, taking her hands. "Just get me the bag and we'll settle it once and for all."

"Adam, I've been through that bag a hundred times in the last six weeks. I know what's in there."

"Afraid you might be wrong?" he dared.

With a groan she climbed off the bed and went to a cedar chest where she kept her clothes. Lifting the lid, she pulled out the worn carpetbag and tossed it to him.

Adam caught it and sat down on the bed, cross-legged. "Come on, sit with me." He patted the bed.

"Adam, this is silly. There are no stock certificates. You said yourself Jacob was crazy."

"Humor me. On our wedding night." He patted the coverlet.

With a disgusted sigh she crossed the room and perched on the end of the bed beside him. "See, I told you," she said as he pulled out the tintype of her mother, the pressed flowers, the worn Bible. "There's nothing in there but silly childhood memories."

"I told you before. No memories are silly." He pulled out the stack of her grandmother's recipes. "What's this?"

She smiled. "Grandmama's recipes. Wait until we get our own kitchen. I'll make you the best tea biscuits you ever put in your mouth."

Adam studied the floral handwriting. On impulse, he flipped one of the recipes over. "Jess . . ."

"Hmmm?"

"What are these written on?"

She glanced at the recipes in his hand. "Written on? Paper, I guess."

"Who wrote these?"

"Grandmama. When she was sick she sent me into Papa's office for paper. She thought she was dying, which she wasn't, but just in case, she wanted me to have the recipes. They've been in the family for a hundred years."

He turned to look at her, a wide grin on his face. "Look at this."

She squinted. "What?"

"The back of the tea biscuit recipe. See the writing?"

At first she didn't, but then, she did make out faint print. "Oh, God," she breathed.

"Stock certificates." He slapped the stack. "A

441

whole pile of them, with Grandmama's recipes written on the back no less."

"I don't believe it," she breathed, taking the delicate papers from his hands. "I just don't believe it."

"My guess would be that on closer inspection we'll find that those are the stock certificates to that diamond mine Jacob was talking about."

"I really did take them, years ago . . ." She looked at him in wide-eyed shock. "I just didn't know it!"

"What do you want to bet those certificates are worth a great deal of money?"

"You don't suppose!"

"How many hundred acres did you want for that orchard and horse farm?"

"Oh, Adam!" She threw her arms around him. "I'm in shock. Do you really think Papa's certificates paid off?"

"Looks like I may have married a rich woman," Adam teased.

Jessica lifted her dark lashes to take in his loving gaze. "Looks like maybe you did, Mr. Deputy Marshal. Looks like maybe you did."

Epilogue

September 1907

Jessica pushed through the screen door and walked out onto the front porch, drying her hands on her apron. "Adam, supper's ready. Could you call the boys? They're in one of the horse barns."

Adam, seated on the top porch step, turned to look at her and grinned.

She dropped her hands to her hips. "What are you gawking at?" she chastised, smiling back.

"You."

"Me? What are you looking at me for? I swear, Deputy Marshal, the sun's addled your brain. You've been looking at me for twenty-six years. Now call your children for supper before it gets cold."

Adam reached for her hand and pressed it to his lips. "You're as beautiful as you were that first day I saw you on the train."

Her laughter filled the cool early evening air as she brushed back a lock of graying hair. "Beautiful! I've given birth to seven children! I'm nearly fifty years old!"

He rose off the step and draped a muscular arm over her shoulder. "What's a wrinkle or two?" He brushed her cheek with his fingertips. "You're beautiful to me."

Her eyes met his and she lifted her chin to meet his lips in a tender kiss. "Know where your bread's buttered, don't you?"

He kissed her again and then, still holding her in his arm, he turned to face the apple orchards that stretched on acre after acre beyond the farmhouse. "What a life!" he breathed. "I never thought I could be this proud of anything . . . this happy."

She leaned her head against his chest staring out at the endless rows of healthy green trees speckled with ripe red and green apples. "We've been lucky, haven't we?"

He took her hand, leading her down the steps. "That we have."

"Healthy children." Jessica pushed aside an apple branch as they entered the grassy orchard.

"Mark graduating with honors."

"Kelsey's married to Paul Wiedenhoeft, with a babe on the way."

Adam plucked a shiny red apple and offered it to Jessica. "And all because you stole a carpetbag of money and ran off."

"You know damned well I didn't steal it! It was mine! Mine and Mark's."

He kissed the top of her head and took a bite of the apple in her hand. "What a mouth you've got, woman! I should have taken old Clyde's advice years ago and beaten the fire out of you."

"Beat me! If you think—"

"Mama! Papa!" a young voice interrupted.

Jessica rolled her eyes heavenward. "Is there ever any peace?" She turned toward the farmhouse, her view blocked by the apple trees. "Out here, Rosy!"

"It's Mark, he's here!" Fourteen-year-old Rose came bursting through the trees, dragging her eldest brother behind her.

"Mark!" Jessica threw out her arms.

"Mama!" Mark, a handsome man of six foot two with his father's coal black hair and his mother's green eyes, swept her into his arms.

Jessica laughed, hugging him. "You weren't supposed to be here until tomorrow!"

Mark plunked her down. "So I made it early." He turned to his father and his hands fell to his sides.

Adam stood for a moment, inanimated, lost in a time long ago. Mark looked so much like he had at twenty-four that it was eery. "So, son, you graduated," he said softly.

"Harvard Law," Mark answered. He knew how important this was to Adam Sern. It felt good to fulfill his father's dreams.

Adam thrust out his arms and hugged his son tight. It seemed as if only yesterday Mark had been a toddler on his knee and they had been planting apple tree saplings. Now suddenly Mark was a man and the trees were bearing fruit. Where had the time gone? Adam took Mark's shoulder's. "I'm proud of you."

Mark looked up into his father's bronze face. "I've already got a job. Marker, Shuwitz, and Porter have hired me in Seattle."

"Seattle!" Jessica cried. "That's wonderful. We've missed you so much. All of us."

Rose grasped her brother's arm. "So what did you bring us?"

He yanked her pigtail. "It's all in my case on the porch."

Rose turned to run, but Jessica caught her arm. "Oh, no young lady. That can wait until after supper. Go set your brother a plate at the table."

"Mama, it's Beatty's turn to set the table."

"Then tell Beatty to do it. But the presents still wait."

Mark reached into his broadcloth suit jacket. "Does that mean you have to wait, too, Mama?"

"Of course not! I'm the mother. I deserve all of the presents my children can give me!" She grinned.

"I found this in a relic bookstore in Boston. It's an old dime novel from the 1880s." He offered the bound book. "Have you ever seen it?"

"When did I ever have time to read?" she asked as her eyes fell on the printed title. "Jessica Brandon," she read aloud. "The tale of a female sharpshooter, by Theodore Lansing . . ." Her mouth dropped open. Her eyes met Adam's.

"I'll be damned," Adam breathed.

"You *did* know this man. I knew it had to be you. I've heard Papa's stories. How many sharpshooting Jessicas could there be?" He flipped open the cover, leaning over her shoulder. "Read the

446

dedication, Mama."

Jessica took a deep breath and read the faded print. "For Jessica, sharpshooter, lawman, and brave pioneer."

Adam burst into laughter as he wrapped his arms around Jessica's waist. "One hell of a woman!"

ROMANCE REIGNS
WITH ZEBRA BOOKS!

SILVER ROSE   (2275, $3.95)
by Penelope Neri

Fleeing her lecherous boss, Silver Dupres disguised herself as a boy and joined an expedition to chart the wild Colorado River. But with one glance at Jesse Wilder, the explorers' rugged, towering scout, Silver knew she'd have to abandon her protective masquerade or else be consumed by her raging unfulfilled desire!

STARLIT ECSTASY   (2134, $3.95)
by Phoebe Conn

Cold-hearted heiress Alicia Caldwell swore that Rafael Ramirez, San Francisco's most successful attorney, would never win her money . . . or her love. But before she could refuse him, she was shamelessly clasped against Rafael's muscular chest and hungrily matching his relentless ardor!

LOVING LIES   (2034, $3.95)
by Penelope Neri

When she agreed to wed Joel McCaleb, Seraphina wanted nothing more than to gain her best friend's inheritance. But then she saw the virile stranger . . . and the green-eyed beauty knew she'd never be able to escape the rapture of his kiss and the sweet agony of his caress.

EMERALD FIRE   (3193, $4.50)
by Phoebe Conn

When his brother died for loving gorgeous Bianca Antonelli, Evan Sinclair swore to find the killer by seducing the tempress who lured him to his death. But once the blond witch willingly surrendered all he sought, Evan's lust for revenge gave way to the desire for unrestrained rapture.

SEA JEWEL   (3013, $4.50)
by Penelope Neri

Hot-tempered Alaric had long planned the humiliation of Freya, the daughter of the most hated foe. He'd make the wench from across the ocean his lowly bedchamber slave — but he never suspected she would become the mistress of his heart, his treasured SEA JEWEL.

Available wherever paperbacks are sold, or order direct from the Publisher. Send cover price plus 50¢ per copy for mailing and handling to Zebra Books, Dept. 3313, 475 Park Avenue South, New York, N.Y. 10016. Residents of New York, New Jersey and Pennsylvania must include sales tax. DO NOT SEND CASH.